MIDNIGHT SECRET

by

SERENITY WOODS

Copyright © 2025 Serenity Woods

All Rights Reserved

This book is a work of fiction. The names, characters, places, and incidents are products of the writer's imagination or have been used fictitiously. Any resemblance to persons, living or dead, actual events, locales or organizations is coincidental.

ISBN: 9798263051785

CONTENTS

Chapter One 1
Chapter Two 10
Chapter Three 21
Chapter Four 31
Chapter Five 42
Chapter Six 50
Chapter Seven 59
Chapter Eight 70
Chapter Nine 81
Chapter Ten 92
Chapter Eleven 101
Chapter Twelve 112
Chapter Thirteen 120
Chapter Fourteen 131
Chapter Fifteen 141
Chapter Sixteen 150
Chapter Seventeen 160
Chapter Eighteen 170
Chapter Nineteen 180
Chapter Twenty 189
Chapter Twenty-One 198
Chapter Twenty-Two 208
Chapter Twenty-Three 217
Chapter Twenty-Four 228
Chapter Twenty-Five 237
Chapter Twenty-Six 246
Chapter Twenty-Seven 251
Chapter Twenty-Eight 261
Newsletter 266
About the Author 267

Chapter One

Marama

"*E tuahine!*" It's Māori for "Hey, sis!" so when I turn, I'm not surprised to see my little brother, Kingi. Actually, 'little' is a bit of a misnomer—he's six-four and huge, with a big shaggy beard and long wavy hair, and could easily double for Jason Momoa. But he is younger than me. Today is his twenty-eighth birthday, and I turn thirty next month.

I'm sitting at a table by the poolside in the gardens of the Midnight Club on Waiheke Island off the coast of Auckland, New Zealand, where he decided to hold his birthday party. As he walks up, the clock in the club strikes midnight, and a huge cheer rises as balloons and glitter are released from the ceiling onto the people on the dance floor inside. Outside, our family and friends who haven't yet retired for the evening clink glasses and toast the new day.

I hold my half-full champagne glass up, and Kingi taps his whiskey glass against it, then takes a seat.

"It's not your birthday anymore." I gesture at the badge on his T-shirt that says 'Birthday Boy.'

"True." He laughs, unclips it, and tosses it on the table. Then he has a mouthful of whiskey, observing me with his warm amber eyes, which are a shade darker than mine. "You okay?" he asks.

I smile. "I'm fine. Why?"

"You look tired."

"It's midnight. I'm normally in bed by ten. It's only you weirdos who stay up into the small hours." Part of the reason the Midnight

Club is so named is because the group of businessmen and women who run it often work late into the night.

He grins. Then he leans forward on the table. "I've got something to tell you."

"Oh?"

"I put your idea forward, about holding an exhibition of your work here, and they've given it the green light."

My mouth forms an O, and I inhale with pleasure. I've recently completed a series of paintings inspired by my travels around Europe, and I'd been hoping they'd display them here. "That's amazing, thank you!"

"Can't do the lobby, though," he says, "that space is fully booked for several months, so they've suggested the Morepork Room."

My excitement is like a feather blown up into the air that now drifts slowly back to the ground. The lobby would have been the perfect place, in full sight of rich guests checking into the resort who would have money to burn, and facing all the billionaires and millionaires heading for the Midnight Club. The Morepork is just a boardroom, and it's not even off the lobby—it's along a corridor to a function room, and it hardly gets any passing traffic. I'd hoped for much more, especially considering my brother and father are both members of the Midnight Circle consortium that runs the place.

But Kingi's expression is eager and happy—he's pleased that he's been able to arrange this for me. I don't want to spoil his birthday by being ungrateful.

"Thank you," I say as graciously as I can manage. "I really appreciate you doing that for me."

"No worries at all. Glad I could help." He finishes off his whiskey and gestures at my glass. "You want another?"

"No, I think I'm done. I might head off home soon."

"Lightweight." He laughs, gets up, and kisses the top of my head. *"Aroha ki a koe, e tuahine."* I love you, sis.

"Arohanui, Kingi." It means big love, Kingi, and I add a warm smile.

My smile fades as he walks away. Don't be so unappreciative, I scold myself. All publicity is good publicity. But it's impossible to stop frustration and resentment rising inside me.

"Hey you." Helen, a good friend of mine, drops into the chair that Kingi has just vacated. She's heavily pregnant, and she lifts her feet onto the chair opposite to rest her legs. "I was just eavesdropping," she confesses. "So they're going to exhibit your work in the Morepork? I'm not surprised you're pissed." She's obviously seen my dissatisfied expression.

I have a mouthful of champagne. "The lobby was already booked, so I do understand."

She purses her lips. Then she says, "Do you know whose work they're showing there through April and May?"

"No..."

"Jason Ridgeway."

My eyebrows lift in surprise. Jason is younger than me and far less established as an artist. It's going to be huge exposure for him.

"What a shock," she says, her voice dripping with sarcasm. "I'm sure it has nothing to do with him being a white male."

I take a deep breath and blow it out slowly. She may be right... but I don't want to appear bitter. "Jason's a great artist. And they'd already given him the space—I can't expect them to pass him over for me. That wouldn't be fair."

She blows a raspberry. "They wouldn't bat an eyelid if it was the other way around. But anyway, I've got some news that will cheer you up. Have you heard of Lumen?"

"The business club in Auckland?" It opened a few months ago. Kingi mentioned it on a Zoom call while I was in Europe. I vaguely remember him seeming annoyed, but he never explained why. "I haven't been there," I add. "I don't know anything about it."

"I met its owner at a conference a few days ago. Her name's Genevieve Beaumont—her dad's some rich French dude, and her mum's Māori. She did a talk on how she wants to empower women by supporting local female artists, especially Māori women. The club's tagline is 'Illuminating Women, Igniting Change.' But I think she called it Lumen in direct competition to Midnight. You know, light and dark?"

"Oh... So that's why Kingi was annoyed."

Helen laughs. "Yeah, they were all a bit put out by it. They know they're male-heavy here, and Lumen will appeal to businesswomen in the community. Anyway, I spoke to Genevieve after the conference, and she told me they're holding an Empowerment Auction."

"A what?"

"Women are being invited to this high-profile art and culture auction. She's holding a meeting about it tomorrow. She asked me to mention it to you."

I blink. "To me?"

"She specifically mentioned you. She said she has one of your pieces in her house and she loves your style. So… will you come?"

I'm immensely flattered that this executive has heard of me and has personally asked Helen to invite me. "Of course, I'd love to."

"It's at three p.m. at Lumen itself. I'd go but I have a doctor's appointment, and I'm no artist anyway. It sounds interesting, though. You'll have to tell me all about it afterward."

"Of course I will." The feather of hope inside me lifts once again, and this time it stays buoyant.

"It'll serve them right here if you end up working for Lumen," Helen says. "They've overlooked women for far too long."

Privately, I think that Helen has an agenda, and she's not being fair to the Midnight Circle. Six out of eight members of the Auckland branch are guys, but four of them were friends before they formed the circle, and the other two male members are Orson and Kingi's fathers, so it's not as if they chose men over women purposefully.

I'm not sure, I might be being unfair, but I wonder whether Helen asked to be in the Circle and they turned her down? I love her dearly, but she doesn't have the business background, expertise, or qualifications that the others have.

But of course she's a friend so I'd never say that. Instead I murmur, "I'm sure you're right."

"Of course I'm right," she says. "With someone like my father at the helm, women are never going to get a look in."

I follow her gaze to where Spencer Cavendish is sitting at a table on the other side of the pool. He's on his own, reading something on his phone.

Spencer is the father of both Helen and Orson, another friend of mine. Spencer was eighteen when he had Orson, so he's only forty-six now, hardly old, but still sixteen years older than me. He's tall and slim and obviously keeps fit, and when he was younger his dark hair bore silver flashes at both temples, the same as his son's, but Spencer's hair is threaded with gray now, so the flashes are less obvious. He's clean-shaven and handsome, an exceptionally good-looking guy, kinda like a young George Clooney. Part of his attraction is his looks, and the rest is his manner—his confidence and self-assurance. He's a self-made man who's worked hard to get where he is, and to him, any guy who hasn't done the same isn't worth his time or attention.

He's hot as fuck, and I've wanted him for years, but never been brave enough to tell him.

As I watch, a man stops by his table and says something to him. Spencer looks up from his phone and gives a short, cool nod. The man smiles uncertainly, then moves on. Spencer watches him go, a little amused, I think, at the guy's awkwardness.

His gaze scans the poolside—and then, to my alarm, he looks straight at me, catching me watching him. He doesn't smile, but he doesn't look away, either. My heart jolts as if it's been shocked with a defibrillator. Half of me wants to drop my gaze with embarrassment. But somehow I find the courage to keep my gaze on him, and we study each other across the pool. I let my lips curve up, just a little, and see his do the same.

Then I look back at Helen.

"A lone wolf," I comment, my pulse racing.

Helen gives a short laugh. "You know they call him The Wolf of Waiheke in the city?"

"Seriously?" I glance back at him, but he's returned his gaze to his phone.

"Yeah. He has the reputation of being ruthless and cutthroat. If he ever turned up dead with a knife in his back, the queue of suspects would stretch around the block."

Her casual insult shocks me, but I don't react. I've never hated anyone in my life, and I certainly can't imagine hating Spencer Cavendish. Sure, his confidence borders on arrogance, but he's always been nice to me.

He and my father have been business associates for many years. As a curvy teenager with brown skin and wavy, somewhat unruly muddy-brown hair, I was envious of his beautiful, elegant wife, Eleanor. She was tall, slim to the point of skinny, with pale skin and blonde hair that she tended to wear pinned up, although one day I saw her with it down, and I was jealous of the curtain of golden hair that cascaded down her back like Rapunzel.

They would come to the house for dinner parties, and Mum would let me sneak into the room until it was my bedtime, as long as I was quiet. I'd bring my sketchbook and sit to one side, drawing the guests while I listened to their conversation, most of which went over my head. I'd draw them all, but the majority of my sketches were of Spencer. I think about the one I found a few days ago, and try not to blush.

Eleanor died about six years ago now, of breast cancer. I half expected to hear of some blonde bimbo snapping Spencer up soon after—after all he must have half of Auckland sniffing around him—but as far as I know he's still single.

Helen yawns. "I need to go home. Are you coming?"

"I'll finish off my champagne first."

"All right. Let me know how tomorrow goes."

"Will do."

She stands and bends so we can kiss each other's cheeks, and then she smiles and walks away.

I turn my glass in my fingers. The party is winding down. Orson has left with his new girl, Scarlett, whom I met tonight, and others are starting to head off. Kingi has gone into the club with a group of friends; no doubt they'll be delving into the expensive whiskeys by now. A few people remain, talking and laughing as they finish off their drinks.

I let my gaze drift across to Spencer again.

He's still alone, still looking at his phone. He'll probably head to his suite soon. It looks as if he'll be going on his own.

Most of the guys at the party were wearing tees and swim shorts, but Spencer is wearing cream chinos and a long-sleeved white shirt with the sleeves turned up a few times, with a plain dark-blue tie. Because of the way he's sitting, leaning forward, his elbows on his knees, the cotton sleeves are stretched tightly across his impressive biceps.

The champagne has made me bold, and before I can think better of it, I rise with my glass and walk casually around the pool to his table.

He doesn't look up until I stop before him. He studies my feet, which are bare because I took my sandals off hours ago, and then his gaze slides slowly up my legs, over the short summer dress I'm wearing over my bikini, and up to my face.

"Hello," I say, trying not to shiver at his slow appraisal. I gesture at the chair next to him. "Can I join you?"

"Sure." His deep voice is a little husky, and it gives me goosebumps. He pulls the chair out for me, then leans back. I lower myself into it, placing my glass on the table.

My heart hammers, but outwardly I remain calm. Although music emanates from the club, the atmosphere around the pool is peaceful. Members of staff are sweeping up discarded serviettes and streamers, and collecting plates and glasses. Others are cleaning the barbecue and wiping down the tables.

"It was a nice party," I say.

He turns off his phone and places it on the table, hooks an arm over the back of the chair, and picks up his glass with the other hand. He has bright blue eyes, and more goosebumps pop out on my skin as he gives me his full attention. "Yeah," he says. "Kingi had a good time, I think."

"And is continuing to do so. I'm sure I can hear him singing." Sure enough, my brother's voice is audible over the top of everyone else's, belting out the wrong words to the Bee Gees' *How Deep is Your Love*. "And you come to me, on a submarine," Kingi sings, and Spencer and I laugh.

Spencer sips his drink. "How about you?" he asks. "Did you enjoy yourself?"

I shrug, leaning an elbow on the table and my chin on my hand. "Yeah, it was okay. Good to catch up with everyone again."

"You've been gone a long time."

"Six months," I concede. "I came back for a couple of weeks over Christmas, but you weren't around."

"I was in Australia."

"Oh? For what purpose?"

"Business."

I give him a mischievous smile. "You didn't indulge in any pleasure while you were there?"

His lips curve up, but he doesn't answer.

We sit there for a while, not talking. I look around the pool, my artist's eye taking in the subdued colors, the angles and poses of the staff and guests, imagining how I'd frame them in a painting. The silence doesn't feel awkward. I like that.

When I eventually look back at him, it's to find his steady gaze still resting on me. He doesn't look embarrassed at being caught watching me. I can't imagine that this guy is ever embarrassed about anything. He owns all his actions and words.

"Tell me about your *moko kauae*," he says softly.

My left hand rises, and I rest my fingers on the tattoo on my chin. Many Māori women choose to wear these. It flows symmetrically from the bottom lip to the chin, the patterns branching downward like roots and rippling outward like water. Culturally, it's a sacred mark of *whakapapa* or lineage, mana or personal power, and identity.

"Do you like it?" I ask shyly. As soon as the words are out, I scold myself for asking them. What does it matter whether he likes it or not? I didn't get it to please anyone except myself.

But he says, "It's elegant and beautiful. Like you." And I can't help but warm all the way through. I blush, and he smiles.

"I had it done here, just after Christmas," I admit. "Even though I enjoyed traveling, I felt lost—not physically, but spiritually."

"Because of your breakup?" he asks.

My eyebrows lift at his astuteness, and I nod. "You heard about that?"

"Rangi told me."

I give a short laugh. "I bet he did. My father never liked Connor."

"Nobody's ever good enough for a man's daughter."

I shrug. "Yeah, I know, but he *really* didn't like Connor."

"Because he was older? What was he, thirty-three? Thirty-four?"

"Thirty-five. That was partly it. But Dad thought he was too manipulative."

"Was he?"

I look into my champagne glass. My spine stiffens as I think about my ex, and I fill with shame at the thought of how I let him dictate what I wore, what I ate, even who my friends were.

"You don't have to answer," Spencer says.

Ah shit, what does it matter now? Slowly, I exhale and feel my body relax. "Yeah, it stings, but he was right. I didn't realize how much he dominated me until… I got pregnant."

His eyes widen. "Oh."

"I was switching birth control methods and thought I was protected, but obviously I wasn't. He said we weren't ready and it was too early, but I was heading toward thirty, and we had our own apartment. He wanted me to have an abortion, but I didn't see why we couldn't have it. We argued a lot. He pressured me heavily. And then, ironically, I had a miscarriage, so there was no decision to make."

His expression softens. "Ah, I'm sorry."

"Nobody knows," I warn him, wondering why it's all spilling out now. "I haven't even told my parents."

"I won't tell anyone."

I sigh. "Just a few months later, he cheated on me, and I walked out. I realized I didn't know who I was anymore." I'm half talking to myself, and I give him an embarrassed glance. "Sorry, that sounds very New Age."

But his gaze is gentle. "I understand."

"He didn't like my friends and family, or even this part of the country, so I hadn't been home for a long time. I wanted to reconnect with where I come from, and prove to myself that there was life after my breakup, and that I still have purpose and status as a woman on my own."

He tips his head to the side. "Of course you do. You're young and beautiful, and you're a successful artist, with your whole life ahead of you."

I meet his eyes and let my lips curve in a smile. "Are you flirting with me, Spencer?"

His eyes sparkle in the gleam of the solar fairy lights strung overhead. "Doesn't sound like something I'd do."

"Naughty boy."

"Now who's flirting?" He has such a relaxed, easy manner. Such charm. My gaze slides to his mouth, to his firm, narrow lips. What would he kiss like? And how would he be in bed? Would he be gentle with a woman, caress her and tease her to the edge of pleasure, then make love to her tenderly? Or would he be feral and demanding, taking what he wanted and driving us both to a passionate climax?

"Marama…" He scolds.

"What?"

"You know what."

"I'm just sitting here, finishing off my champagne."

But we both know there's something else going on. My pulse is racing, and there's magic in the air. I want him, and I'm pretty sure he wants me, too.

What will the rest of the night bring?

Chapter Two

Spencer

The beautiful girl sitting across the table from me gives a mischievous smile, and my pulse quickens.

It's been impossible to drag my gaze from her tonight. She's wearing a short summer dress in a burnt-orange color that complements her brown skin, and even though she's not tall, her legs seem to go on forever, especially as she's been barefoot all evening. Earlier, when she joined some of the others in the pool, she stripped off her dress by the poolside to reveal wonderful curves that were barely hidden by a bright blue bikini, giving me an instant hard-on, which meant I had to spend the next half an hour sitting with my back to the pool so I couldn't see her wet skin. Her brown hair shines in the fairy lights, looking like glossy melted chocolate where it curls over one shoulder. Her eyes imprison a wealth of emotions and secrets in their amber depths.

She's gorgeous.

She's also sixteen years my junior and the daughter of my business partner. Some relationships are doomed even before they start.

"You should go to bed," I tell her. "It's late."

She just laughs. "I'm not fourteen anymore." Her gaze turns sultry. "I'm a woman now. Or haven't you noticed?"

"Yes, I've noticed." How could I not? She was the most beautiful girl at the club tonight.

Her gaze drops to my mouth, and she moistens her lips with the tip of her tongue. She's thinking about kissing me. My heart bangs on my ribs as I picture leaning forward, sliding a hand to the back of her head, and crushing my lips to hers. I should put a stop to this now.

"You're in your twenties," I state firmly. "You're far too young for me."

"I'm twenty-nine," she scoffs. "I'm thirty next month. Thirty!"

"Even so. You'll always be the little girl who cried when she dropped her teddy bear in the pool. Do you remember that?"

Although I'd known her father at high school, he was older than me, and it wasn't until my last year at university that we connected through a friend. I told him about the financial business I was in the process of setting up and, maybe impressed with my ambition and drive, he invited me to his house on Waiheke Island for a summer barbecue. I was already married by then with a baby the same age as his son. Our wives got on well and were happy to sit by the poolside and talk motherhood, keeping one eye on Marama splashing about in the shallows, while Rangi flipped burgers and discussed business. When she dropped her bear, I was the one who jumped in and fished it out for her. She'd looked up at me with these big amber eyes that were glassy with tears as she'd mumbled, "Thank you."

"I remember," she says softly. "You kissed its nose before you gave it back to me. You said, 'All better.'"

"Did I?" I act nonchalant, but the moment is vivid in my mind.

She runs a finger around the top of her champagne glass. "I've got something to admit to you."

"Oh?"

Her look turns impish. "Do you remember when I used to sketch the guests at Mum's parties?"

"I do." Huia Davis used to let her daughter sit in the corner of the room with her sketchbook until dinner was served.

She sucks her bottom lip. Then she says, "The other day I found a box in Dad's attic full of my old art books. I was flicking through them. They're nearly all of you."

"Really?"

"Yeah."

I'm secretly flattered, but I just drawl, "I'm not surprised. I know I'm irresistible."

She giggles. "In one of them was a drawing I did when I was sixteen. You were standing by the window, looking out at the garden as you talked to Dad. I sketched you quickly and then completed it later when I went upstairs. I... um... made a small alteration."

"Oh?"

Her eyes dance. "I sketched you naked."

This time both of my eyebrows shoot up. I'm sure it's common for sixteen-year-olds to dream about older men, but I'm shocked that I was the subject of her fantasies. She's been attracted to me since she was a teen?

Uh-oh.

I decide to make a joke of it. "Do you mean you were naked while you were sketching, or that you drew me without clothes?"

That makes her laugh. "I still can't believe I did it. Blame my teenage hormones."

"Naughty girl," I admonish, lips curving up in spite of myself. "How did you know what a naked man looked like?"

"My friend didn't have parental controls on her internet."

"Well, I hope you made me look impressive."

"Wouldn't you like to know?"

"If you did, for Christ's sake don't exhibit it—the female population of Auckland would sue you for false advertising."

She giggles again. "Are you being honest or self-deprecating?"

"Wouldn't you like to know?"

Her eyes flare. "Maybe."

Ahhh… steady, Spencer. Stop flirting.

She sips her champagne. "The female population of Auckland? Been making the most of being single, have we?"

I give a short laugh. "That *would* be telling."

She smiles. "Is there anyone special?"

I meet her eyes. "No."

"Why not? You've been alone for… what? Six years now?"

I nod slowly.

"It's a long time," she says.

"It is."

She surveys me curiously. I think she's itching to ask if I've had girlfriends in that time, but instead, when she eventually speaks, it's to say, "Do you miss Eleanor terribly?"

The question surprises me. Nobody has asked me so openly before. I hesitate, not sure how to answer. I don't want to appear callous and unfeeling. I realize with surprise that I don't want Marama to think badly of me.

"I'm sorry," she says hastily. "I shouldn't have asked that. Of course you miss her. It was a stupid thing to say."

"No, it's fine." I turn my glass in my fingers. It's late, I'm tired, and for some reason Marama's big, gentle eyes make me want to confess. "Do you want an honest answer?"

She nods.

"The truth is that my feelings toward my late wife are mixed, and thinking about her makes me uncomfortable."

A frown flickers on her brow, but I don't think it's a disapproving one; she's just curious. "Uncomfortable?"

Her eyes are a beautiful amber. It makes me think about Eleanor's, which were light green, cold, and hard, like a stone that lies beneath a forest river. "Our relationship was… complicated. She treated it more like a business transaction. She wasn't an easy woman to love."

She looks surprised, but I'm not sure whether it's because of what I said or the fact that I was so open.

"I shouldn't have said that," I add, feeling guilty.

"It's okay. I'm glad you did, after I poured out all that about Connor. Was she always like that?"

I nod slowly, my eyes growing distant. "She was stunning when she was young. English-rose complexion, that beautiful blonde hair. Always smiling. I felt like a planet orbiting around the sun. But when I got to know her, I realized she was more like a comet, blazing her own trail, and made mostly of ice."

"Ooh." Marama gives a little mock shiver. "Why did you marry her then?"

"Because she got pregnant."

Her eyebrows shoot up. "That was careless of you," she teases.

"She told me she was on the pill." Even after all these years, I'm embarrassed to admit I fell for it.

But Marama doesn't laugh or mock me; instead her brows draw together, and she says, "Oh my God, that's awful. She got pregnant on purpose?"

"Yeah. She'd decided I was a good prospect and wanted to snare me, and she knew I'd do the right thing."

"Not every man would have. Most men would have said no way were they going to commit themselves to a woman who got pregnant on purpose."

"I'm not most men."

"No," she says softly, "I can see that." She leans her head on a hand. She's obviously tired, but I think that, like me, she's enjoying this conversation and doesn't want to go home. "How did you cope with the resentment?" she asks curiously. "There must have been some, surely?"

I breathe in, then let it out slowly in a half-sigh. "Yes. At times. But we were compatible in a lot of ways. She was a good hostess and companion socially. She was supportive of my career and didn't mind me spending long hours at work. Lots of people think I'm cold and hard. It could be argued that we were well matched."

Her lips slowly curve up. "I don't think you're cold."

"Well, thank you. But I'm under no illusions what people think of me."

"The Wolf of Waiheke?"

I chuckle.

"I think you rather like that nickname," she teases.

"It's better than the Wanker of Waiheke. Or the Asshole of Auckland. I'm sure I've been called both of those in the past."

We both laugh.

"I think it's all for show," she says. "I think you're a pussy cat beneath the tiger image."

"*Rawr.*"

She giggles, then swallows the last mouthful of champagne in her glass. I'm close to finishing my drink, and I was about to retire for the night, but suddenly I don't want the evening to end.

"Do you want one more?" I ask, gesturing at her glass.

She looks surprised. "Oh!" She glances at the poolside bar. "I think they've closed for the night." Les, the bartender, is wiping down the bar.

"They won't mind serving us." I hold up a hand and attract Les's attention, and he comes over. "Can we have the same again?" I ask.

"Sure." He smiles and goes off to get them.

"I forgot you own the place," Marama says.

"Not just me," I correct. "There are eight of us in the Midnight Circle."

"Wasn't the land yours, though? I seem to remember Orson saying."

"Yes, that's true. I inherited it when my father died. Huxley had approached us to ask whether we would be interested in joining a consortium with the idea of setting up a resort, and I put forward the idea of basing it here." Oliver Huxley runs a business club in the city, and he liked the idea of setting up another exclusive club with the intention of donating the proceeds to various charities. The rich businessmen and women who are part of the Midnight Circle were all keen to use some of their wealth to help others.

"It was a great idea," Marama says. "And very altruistic."

"We use it for money laundering."

"Well I know that's a lie. There's no way my father would be involved in anything remotely dishonest. The man has morals straight out of the Old Testament."

"Thou shalt not launder funds through a business that sells tequila and plays loud rock music?"

She laughs. "Something like that."

Les comes back with our drinks and places them before us, then, without asking, moves one of the heaters closer to us, which brings a welcome warmth to the late March evening. I thank him, and he smiles before returning to wiping down the bar.

The final group of friends sitting around the pool gets up and heads for the nightclub, leaving Marama and me on our own, with only a few staff members quietly cleaning up. Above us, the moon is a thin crescent. Marama has a Māori tattoo on her arm that includes the phases of the moon, presumably reflecting the meaning of her name.

I think how much she's changed since the last time I saw her, about eighteen months ago. She was still dating Connor then. Rangi, her father, had admitted to me that he disliked the man intensely, stating that he was a manipulative bastard. Marama had seemed her usual sunny self, although I had found it strange at the time that her partner hadn't come with her to visit her family.

Now, she seems sadder and quieter, more serious. She's average height, attractively curvy. Her *moko kauae* adds to her beauty, drawing attention to her full mouth, the dimples in her cheeks, and her light-brown, flawless skin. Even though she's obviously not been a child for a long time, for me it feels like a symbol of her entering womanhood.

She glances at my glass. "What are you drinking, vodka?"

"No. Just Sprite."

Her eyebrows rise. "Seriously?"

"I'm teetotal."

"Oh, why?"

I just smile.

"You're incredibly handsome," she says, surprising me. She's so open, as if she has no internal filter and says exactly what's on her mind. "I love your silver hair."

"Why do you like older men?" I ask, genuinely interested.

She shrugs. "Guys my age seem immature and childish."

"I wouldn't call Kingi and Orson childish."

"Are you serious? Can you hear Kingi singing?"

Sure enough, his deep voice is currently bellowing *Under Pressure* by Queen and David Bowie, once again singing the wrong words. I try not to laugh, and fail.

"You'd never make a fool of yourself like that," she says. "I like that you're in control."

My heart gives an unusual bang on my ribs at her mention of control. Her eyes glitter, suggesting her words hold a deeper, maybe sexual connotation.

She holds my gaze, and gradually our lips curve up.

"I'm sure another of your father's commandments would be 'Thou shalt not lead older men into temptation,'" I point out, determined to use humor to disarm the increasing sexual tension.

"Am I tempting you?" she murmurs seductively.

I don't answer, but I'm unable to tear my gaze from hers.

"I admire you," she says.

"Why?" I'm surprised, even baffled. Women are often attracted to my money, but Marama comes from a wealthy family, so it's not that. I don't think I'm bad looking, and I keep myself fit, but I'm hardly a stud, and I don't understand why I'm drawing her eye.

"The fact that you're a self-made man," she says. "I know you had issues with your birth parents, and were raised by a foster family. That you don't come from money. You've worked hard to get where you are. I think that's admirable."

I don't reply, but her words touch me. It's true; practically everything I have, I've made myself, with the guidance and support of my foster parents.

"You had Orson so young," she says, "and it makes you feel as if you're a different generation from the young guys who are on their way up, but I think you forget you're only forty-six, not sixty-six."

"That may be true," I concede.

She has a mouthful of champagne, and I imagine the bubbles dancing on her tongue, sliding down inside her.

"There are still sixteen years between us," I point out. "I'm old enough to be your father."

"Well, technically, maybe."

"That doesn't bother you?"

She shakes her head. She leans forward, both arms on the table. Her dress has a low neck, and it gapes forward a little. It takes all my willpower not to eye-dip her, but I'm aware of her beautiful breasts on the verge of escaping the bright-blue bikini triangles. Is she doing it on purpose?

"You're stunning," I murmur, unable to keep my words to myself.

Her expression lights up. Did she really not know that I found her attractive?

"Thank you," she says graciously.

"You were the most beautiful woman here tonight."

She likes that. Color appears on her cheekbones, and she gives a bashful smile.

I lean forward too, and now we're only six inches apart. I could kiss her, if I wanted to. I don't. But I could.

"Thank you for buying a piece of my work," she says softly. I admitted earlier this evening that I have a piece of her stained-glass artwork hanging in my home. Last year, I had a late business meeting on the outskirts of Auckland, close to a small art gallery. After the meeting, I saw that the gallery was open late for a special exhibition, and, curious more than anything, I wandered in with the intention of passing five or ten minutes before I went home. I was genuinely impressed by the stained-glass pieces that were displayed with lamps behind them, so they cast dazzling jeweled light across the room. I decided to buy one called Parson-Bird which features the tui bird with the white feathers at its throat that give it the nickname, its plumage a beautiful blend of blue, purple, and green. I find any natural talent fascinating, and this piece stayed with me. It wasn't until I got home and saw the name on the back that I realized the artist was Marama.

"I thought it was amazing," I tell her. "You have incredible talent. You could take this country by storm if you put your mind to it."

Her eyes widen. "Oh! Well, thank you."

"Amazing to think of what must be going on inside your head. I love your brain."

"Oh, it's my brain you find attractive?"

"Of course."

"Not my boobs?"

I give a short laugh. "I knew you leaned forward on purpose."

Her mischievous smile tells me I was right. She glances down, then back up at me, her eyes holding an open invitation.

Slowly, I let my gaze slide down her neck, over her collarbone, and then down the smooth skin exposed by the low neckline to the swell of her breasts. We're right under the fairy lights, and the top of her breasts are illuminated, and glow a rich creamy brown. I can't see her nipples, but I imagine them medium-brown, swollen in the warmth from the heater. They'd tighten, though, if I covered them with my mouth and sucked.

When I lift my gaze back again, her pulse is beating fast in her throat.

"That was the sexiest look anyone's ever given me." Her voice is husky with desire. "It was as if you were trailing a feather down me."

"I'd like to do that."

"Would you tie me up first?"

Ohhh… I did not expect this when I came to the party tonight. My cock twitches, and I'm glad it's invisible beneath the table.

I tip my head to the side. "Would you like that?"

She moistens her lips with the tip of her tongue, then gives a small nod. "Would you like to tie me up, Spencer? So I'm at your mercy, and you can do whatever you want to me?"

Her eyes are sultry, the pupils huge in the semi-darkness.

I now have an erection, and it's impossible not to think about stripping her naked, kissing her until she opens to me, and then sliding inside her.

She lifts a hand and touches the flash of white at my left temple. Then she slides her hand into my hair. Her nails run lightly across my scalp, and I close my eyes. Her fingers as they stroke me are tender, loving even.

I've never had a woman touch me like it before, and it makes me shiver.

"I'd like to paint you," she whispers, "a wolf with silver hair."

My lips part, and I'm close to moaning with ecstasy. If she moved her other hand under the table, slid down my zipper, and stroked my cock, I know I could come in less than a minute.

Argh. Exercise some self-control, man.

With some effort, I force my eyes open and lean back in my chair. Her fingers slide out of my hair, and she lowers her hand.

"I understand we're going to exhibit some of your work," I say, trying to lighten the mood and turn it away from sex. "Maybe you can add it to the collection."

She studies her champagne glass, then has a large mouthful. "Not really enough room in the Morepork." Before I can comment on the touch of sarcasm in her voice, she says, "I had some good news tonight, though. I've been invited to the business club, Lumen, tomorrow." Her expression is pleased, eager. "Apparently the owner wants to empower women by supporting local female artists, especially Māori women. I'm looking forward to that."

It's as if she's thrown a bucket of cold water over me. I stare at her, while my heart stamps its feet in my chest.

"I see," I say stiffly. "Well, good luck with that."

Her smile fades slowly. "What's the matter?"

"Nothing. Just don't believe everything Genevieve Beaumont tells you."

"You know her?"

"Unfortunately, yes."

She waits for me to elaborate. When I remain silent, she gives a short, humorless laugh. "Maybe Helen was right."

"About what?"

"About guys at Midnight not wanting women to do well."

I frown impatiently. "That's bullshit. Don't get caught up in my daughter's conspiracy theories."

"I thought you'd be pleased for me." She's genuinely hurt.

I push away my own misgivings. "I am glad that someone recognizes your excellent ability. Just keep in mind that everyone has their own agenda." I finish off my drink. "I should go now."

She stares at me, mouth open. "Seriously?"

"I have an early meeting tomorrow. I need some sleep."

"But…" She blinks, clearly confused. "I thought… after what just happened…"

"You're a very attractive girl," I say firmly, "but—"

"Don't call me a girl. I'm not fifteen."

"A very attractive woman," I correct, "but nothing was ever going to happen. You're too young for me. You're barely older than Helen."

"I'm four years older!"

"Even so, it's not enough. You're my business partner's daughter. Kingi's sister. And I have my position to think about."

That makes her laugh. "This isn't Regency England."

"Maybe not, but my business thrives on honesty and respect. A scandal would be damaging to my company, and I have more to think about than my own reputation—I have employees whose livelihoods rely on the success of my business."

"Jesus, Spencer, one night with me isn't going to bring down the empire."

I reach out and pick up the coil of hair lying over her shoulder. Before she can react, I wrap it around my hand, bringing her closer to me.

"Don't roll your eyes at me," I tell her. "It makes me want to put you over my knee."

Her eyes widen, and she inhales.

"And it wouldn't be one night." I fight with myself not to kiss her. It takes every ounce of willpower I have—and I have a *lot* of willpower. "If we had sex… if I tasted you… I would want you again. And again. And again."

Her breathing quickens, her breasts rising and falling rapidly.

"My lust would consume you," I say, my voice hoarse with desire. "It would consume us and ruin us both. So it ends here." I tug her hair, just a little. "You say you're not a child, so stop acting like one. Stop teasing me, stop taunting this wolf, because he'll eat you alive."

She stares at me, speechless, for ten seconds while I look into her eyes.

Then I let go of her hair and get to my feet. Without another glance in her direction, I stride off, heading for my suite.

I glance up at the moon, who's eyeing me with a baleful glare, and I scowl at her.

Then I go inside, and put this evening out of my mind.

Chapter Three

Marama

The huge sign above the building reads 'Lumen Business Club'. It's right in the heart of Auckland—prime real estate in the CBD, surrounded by law firms, accountants, insurance brokers, and coffee shops where people in suits can grab their morning cappuccinos before they head to the office.

I hesitate on the pavement, trying to pluck up the courage to go in. Unlike my brother and father, I've never been comfortable in places like this. I don't mind the Midnight Club because it's family-owned and run, and I know a lot of the people who frequent it. But I do feel intimidated when surrounded by successful, driven people. I have no expertise in business or finance. I'm not left brain at all. I'm entirely creative, and everything I do is based on instinct and gut feeling, which has gotten me into trouble more than once. So coming to a club like this which is going to be full of confident, successful women makes me more than a little nervous.

Unbidden, Spencer's compliment springs into my mind. *You have incredible talent. You could take this country by storm if you put your mind to it.*

I scowl. As nice as his words were, I can hardly rely on him to boost my confidence.

Every time I think about last night, I feel a stab of hurt, embarrassment, and shame deep inside. It doesn't matter that he twisted it into 'I want you so much that we can't risk it.' I don't believe him. He turned me down easily, and it really stings.

I push him out of my mind. Lumen isn't far from Huxley's Business Club, which is run by the same guy who heads the Midnight Circle. I've been to his club, and while women are very much welcomed there, its deep red and purple tones have a somewhat traditional feel. The Midnight Club has a midnight-blue and silver theme that, again, while not specifically masculine, somehow makes one think of businessmen like Spencer Cavendish with his silver hair. Or maybe that's just me.

Anyway, as soon as I walk into Lumen, I'm struck by the feminine color palette. The large foyer has light green walls, lavender-and-white pillars, and light-gray furnishings picked out with pastel-colors—soft blues and yellows, with the occasional splash of scarlet jumping out to claim you, like red lipstick on a demure woman. Pretty lamps cast soft light on the numerous pieces of art displayed on the walls. I stop to glance at some of them—they're all done by female artists, and they're all suggestive of the strength and power of women, such as one small collection featuring nudes of older women clearly unashamed of their aging bodies. They're pricey, so the artists obviously aren't afraid to charge a decent price for their work, and presumably they assume that customers are going to have money to burn.

The reception desk is staffed by two women—one Māori, one Japanese—in lavender pantsuits with white blouses and pastel-colored scarves. The place is busy with clients, and everywhere I look I can see smartly dressed businesswomen, walking to and from meeting rooms with briefcases or standing talking with takeaway coffee cups, all of them with carefully coiffured hair, long painted nails, and spotless makeup. There are a couple of men, so they're obviously allowed in here, but they're definitely outnumbered by the women. Do they feel intimidated or threatened by all this positive female energy? I do, a bit, and I'm a girl.

I look around, searching for a sign for the meeting at three p.m., and wondering whether I should check in at reception. I'm just about to head over there when I see a woman walking toward me with a big smile on her face.

She's tall, almost too thin, and elegant in a fawn pantsuit with a champagne-colored silk blouse. Her blonde hair is twisted up in a chignon, and she has heavy but expertly applied makeup. She's also wearing stiletto heels that are about four inches high.

"Marama," she says, holding out her hand. "I'm so glad you could come. I'm Genevieve Beaumont." Her voice has a touch of a French accent. If Helen hadn't told me that Genevieve's mother was Māori, I wouldn't have guessed, but Māori identity is based on genealogy and cultural connections, not the color of your skin.

Surprised to be both recognized and greeted by the owner of the club, I try not to feel self-conscious in my long black skirt and orange top. Clearly, I need to get myself a pantsuit.

"Pleased to meet you." I shake her hand. "It was very kind of you to invite me."

"I couldn't have a gathering of up-and-coming local female artists and not include you." She gestures for me to follow her across the foyer. "I've heard a lot about you, Marama Davis."

"Oh, really?"

"I did some investigation after I bought this." She turns a corner and stops by a long narrow window. My jaw drops. One of my stained-glass artworks hangs there. It's called Whānau—pronounced 'Far-no'—which means both family and to give birth, in the literal sense of childbirth, but also refers to the birth of a new idea. It depicts Papatūānuku, the earth mother, sitting cross-legged, pregnant and serene, surrounded by flowers and plants. Her round belly contains the beautiful blue-and-green world we live on.

"Goodness," I say, stunned by how amazing it looks with the bright sunshine behind it casting fragments of color all the way down the corridor, as if someone has thrown a handful of emeralds, sapphires, and rubies on the floor.

"It's stunning," Genevieve says. "Everyone comments on it. I love how you depict *atua wāhine* in such a strong and confident way." She's referring to the fact that this series I did features female goddesses. "I haven't been to the Midnight Club," she says, "but I presume they have pieces like this all over the site? It must be stunning."

My face warms. "Not really. They have agreed to exhibit my latest collection of landscapes for a few weeks though."

Her eyebrows rise. "Oh. Well, an artist of your caliber will still benefit from a display in the lobby I suppose."

"Ah, it won't be in the lobby. It's in one of the meeting rooms."

Genevieve's light-blue eyes fix me with a steely stare, and suddenly I'm convinced she was very much aware of Kingi's offer and my resulting disappointment.

Spencer's words spring into my mind: *Just keep in mind that everyone has their own agenda.*

I blink and frown. That's not what's happening here, I'm sure. I feel embarrassed and cross with myself for not challenging Kingi when he told me. I'm so grateful for any snippet of encouragement thrown my way. It must be nice to be confident enough not just to feel that you deserve attention and praise but to demand it.

I wait for her to criticize me for not standing up for myself, but she just says, "I see. Well, it's so good of you to come. Is it your first visit to Lumen?"

"Yes. It's very impressive. I love the color scheme."

She looks around, her pride evident. "I wanted women to feel not just comfortable here but empowered and inspired. Men are welcome, of course, but I'm not ashamed to say we give preference to women, including trans women. You know Victoria Brown?"

I nod at the mention of the transgender woman who is Oliver Huxley's good friend. "I've met her a couple of times."

"She comes here a lot." She leans forward conspiratorially and murmurs, "Between you and me, she feels more comfortable here, although she'd never admit that to Huxley, of course."

I'm surprised Victoria would express favoritism like that when Huxley is her business partner. There's no chance to ask for clarification, though, because Genevieve smiles and says, "Come on. I think everyone else is here, so we're ready to start."

I follow her along the corridor. We pass several meeting rooms with names like *'Whakamanawa'*, which means to encourage or inspire, *'Pūkenga'*, which means skills or expertise, and *'Mana Wahine'*, which refers to the prestige and strength of women. She stops at a doorway bearing a sign that says *'Maramatanga'*. It means enlightenment or insight, but I don't miss that the word also includes my name. Did she choose this room on purpose because I was coming? Surely not? It must be a coincidence.

Like the lobby, the meeting room is full of light and furnished with pastel colors—light-blue walls, cream blinds, light-gray chairs, and the odd splash of a more vibrant blue or red. More artwork hangs on the walls—clearly Genevieve is serious about promoting female artists. I feel a surge of pleasure and inspiration, and also a flutter of nerves at the sight of about thirty other women in the process of taking their seats as an attractive woman with a razor-sharp dark bob calls for attention.

Genevieve gestures for me to take a chair, and I slide quietly into one as she walks forward and takes the podium. A projector displays a presentation on the screen behind her, professionally produced,

MIDNIGHT SECRET

moving smoothly through the slides as she presses the remote in her hand.

"Good afternoon," she says, her voice ringing across the room. "Thank you all for coming today. I've approached each of you because your outstanding creativity has personally impressed me. I want Lumen to be a beacon of feminine strength and independence in New Zealand. I want to uplift women, and show them that the world belongs to them. Not to their fathers. Not to their lovers. And not to the men who think that money makes them gods."

I shift in my chair. I know she's referring to men like Orson, Kingi, my father, and Spencer of course. She's right that they're all rich, successful men whose confidence borders on arrogance. I'm hardly poor, though, so it seems a bit hypocritical to criticize them for having money. And the whole point of the Midnight Club is to donate the proceeds to worthwhile causes, so it's not as if they're all cruel, greedy guys who don't give a fig for other people.

But I can't deny that her philosophy is inspiring. As much as I don't want to put men down, it's difficult at times to ignore the feeling I am sometimes overlooked because I'm a woman, and a Māori one at that.

Genevieve is still talking about Lumen, explaining about how membership of the club provides access to its facilities, which include meeting rooms, offices, a top restaurant and bar, a gym, and what she describes as a 'coffee house'—a place to meet other women during the day to network and build business relationships.

Should I join the club? I haven't yet decided where I'm going to settle down. Connor and I shared an apartment in Wellington, but I moved out of that when I discovered he'd been cheating on me. I stayed in my father's house—the family home—over on Waiheke Island until I went to Europe, and I'm thinking of traveling again in a month or so, so I don't know how much use I'd get out of the club. I don't consider myself a businesswoman per se. But maybe I should. I want to sell my work, after all, don't I? I like the idea of supporting Genevieve and other women, so I might still sign up.

"I invited you here today for a specific purpose," Genevieve says. "Lumen is going to be holding an Empowerment Auction."

My eyebrows rise, and similarly, the other women glance at each other, curious and puzzled.

Genevieve smiles. "I can see you're all wondering what I'm talking about. Well, this is going to be a high-profile art and culture auction where influential female artists will offer an experience centered on their passions. The auction is for the privilege of their time and talent, not for the artists themselves—that's important to note."

A buzz of excitement runs around the room, and it's impossible to stop a similar sense of anticipation rising inside me.

"The money raised will support women-led artistic projects," Genevieve continues. "We have lots of ideas here at Lumen, including some we've already started." The presentation shows a series of slides with women in the process of exercising their creativity. "These include a sustainable fashion label that merges traditional textiles with contemporary design; a grassroots, mobile film-making workshop that travels to rural communities and teaches *wahine* Māori how to script, shoot, and edit stories; and the production of a community quilt, stitched by women, and including personal stories that represent sisterhood, land, and legacy. Men have always been the curators of our success… until now. It's time for us to be the architects of our own adventures."

She's a force of nature; there's no doubt about it. She practically glows with enthusiasm, and her energy makes me feel as if I can take over the world, too.

"I'm hoping that each artist will design a unique experience," she continues. "I'm happy to talk over ideas, but I'm thinking of things like the following." She flicks up a new slide illustrating each option. "For the artists among you: an afternoon painting lesson in your studio. For writers: an evening book club experience held at a local vineyard, where you talk about your writing process alongside a wine-tasting session. For musicians: a personal performance given at a curated dinner party, or a visit to your recording studio. Hopefully you get the idea. Crucially, it's important to note that you would retain full control. We would make it clear that the artist can decline any winning bidder, and that she sets the terms of the experience."

My mind is already working furiously. What could I offer? I suppose someone might be interested in a painting lesson. But that wouldn't appeal to anyone without artistic talent. What would a stranger be interested in bidding for? A piece of artwork commissioned by them, tailored to their business or their hobbies?

Or how about a portrait of them? A private studio session where they would get to sit for a portrait? I could make it a real experience; I have a small studio in the family home that would make them feel as if they're visiting my sacred workspace. Mmm… that might work.

"I'm thinking of holding the Empowerment Auction in just under two weeks, on Saturday April the Fifth," Genevieve states. "It's not too long to wait, and gives us the perfect amount of time to build a buzz. The local press has promised to cover the auction with plenty of fanfare, and I'm sure that women across the city will be pleased and excited to help us spread the word."

She gestures at the woman with the dark bob standing next to her. "This is my assistant, Carly. She's holding a pack with all the details I've just related, plus an application form. Feel free to take one, and to contact her if you'd like to book a meeting with us to discuss anything further. All applications need to be in by midnight this Wednesday, the 26th please. I know that only gives you three days, but it will give us time to produce the program which is going to be published on Kōrero this Saturday." It's the biggest news website in Auckland. "We'll also begin circulating and promoting the program in the local community. I'm hoping all of you will feel inspired to take part, and I value each and every one of you."

As she speaks, she looks directly at me and smiles. I warm through at being in her spotlight. I'm incredibly flattered to think she's noticed me. Although my piece of stained-glass artwork wasn't hanging in the lobby, it is being displayed in a prominent place where women walk past it daily, and that's without me being related to her. I'm heartened that she feels my work is worthy of attention.

"Now," she says, "I'm sure you must all have questions, so please, speak up if there's anything you'd like to ask."

A smattering of questions follow, and then she ends the meeting. Everyone starts talking and moving forward to take a pack, and I do the same. It's very professionally produced, and I study the application form, then return to my seat, take out a pen, and start filling it in.

A shadow falls over me a few minutes later, and I look up to see Genevieve standing there, smiling.

"I'm impressed," she says, gesturing at the form on my lap, which is half filled out. "And so excited!" She lowers onto a chair beside me. "What are you thinking of offering?"

I describe my idea of a private studio session, where I would paint a portrait of them, with a background inspired by their job or something else important in their life.

"I love it," she says, "I'm tempted to put in a bid myself!"

"How many people are you expecting to attend the auction?" I ask curiously.

"I'm hoping for a few hundred. We'll hold it here in our function room. I have a few friends in the press who are going to give the auction lots of attention, and I think the fact that we're pushing it as a high-class charity auction to help women will really get people interested. Not just other women, but men who believe that being seen encouraging women is good PR for their businesses."

I can't tell if she's being sarcastic or just telling it like it is. I'm sure she's right. Orson has said openly that his plan to give local iwi or tribes better access to the Waiora healing pool is good PR for the Midnight Club, so I know the guys aren't blind to ways to improve public relations. If they feel they're under scrutiny for not representing women better, helping to promote the auction is one way they can make themselves look as if gender equality is important to them.

"Helen has asked me to call her after this meeting," I reply. "If you like, I'll ask her to mention the auction to the Midnight Club. I know strictly speaking they're your competitor, but I'm sure they'll help to promote it for that reason." I wonder whether Spencer would want that? And how he knows Genevieve? Is it just through business?

"That would be great," she says enthusiastically. She hesitates, then glances across the room. "Look, I know you want to finish your form, but I'd like to introduce you to someone."

"Oh... okay." I slip the form back into the folder, rise, and follow her across to a striking Māori woman who's reading through some of the promotional material in the pack while she sips her coffee. She's probably in her fifties, with gray in her curly brown hair. She also has a *moko kauae* on her chin.

"Hariata," Genevieve says, "I'd like to introduce you to Marama Davis, a local artist. She created the stained-glass artwork that hangs in the corridor."

"Oh, the one of Papatūānuku?" she asks. When I nod, she says, "I loved it. It was so beautiful and imaginative."

I blush. "Thank you."

Genevieve says, "Marama, this is Hariata Pere. She's the managing director of Te Whaihanga Toi Foundation." It's a prestigious and respected organization, and I know it well. It funds and mentors projects by Pacific artists, and it offers numerous grants and residencies.

"It's so nice to meet you," I say, shaking Hariata's hand.

"Marama has just finished a collection of landscapes," Genevieve says.

"I've been traveling across Europe," I explain. "They're mainly watercolors."

"Very different from stained glass," Hariata says. "Do you enjoy working in other mediums?"

"I do, and it was interesting to visit famous galleries and see some well-known artworks." I pause, wondering whether to admit the thought that has been at the back of my mind over the past few days. "I was thinking of traveling again… but I have to admit that I'm feeling tempted at the moment to create a series that weaves together *pūrākau wahine*." It means ancestral stories told from a woman's perspective. "And to illustrate *atua wāhine*." I refer to female spiritual beings.

"Oh?" Hariata's ears prick up. "Tell us more."

I'm not going to get a better opportunity than this, and I decide to open up, which I rarely do. "I don't just mean goddesses like Hine-nui-te-pō," who is the goddess of death and transformation, "or Hineteiwaiwa," the goddess of creativity, weaving, and childbirth. "I mean our *kuia*," our elder women, "and our *tīpuna*," our ancestors, "and the way their mana still shapes us. Maybe it could involve doing portraits of important women in our community, like yourselves," I gesture at the two of them, "portrayed as modern-day *atua wāhine*."

"That sounds amazing," Genevieve says. "In what medium?"

"Probably acrylics for the richness of the colors."

"I'm very interested," Hariata says. She checks her watch. "I have to go now, but I'll be at the auction, and maybe we can talk more about it then?"

"Yes, of course. Thank you." I watch her walk away, then smile at Genevieve. "Thank you so much for introducing us."

"I'm glad I could help. That's what Lumen is about—women helping other women." She touches my arm. "Don't forget to finish your application!"

I return to my seat and fill the rest in, my heart racing with excitement. I'm so glad I came here today and met both Genevieve and Hariata. Genevieve is right—it's important for women to help other women.

SERENITY WOODS

Briefly, I think about Spencer, and how when I told him I was coming here, he said *Just don't believe everything she tells you.* I think he was being very unfair to her. Is it possible he's jealous because she represents the future? Hmm, I wonder whether it's more personal than that. Was he interested in her, and she rebuffed him? That might explain why he seemed so resentful.

I think about the way he dismissed me so easily, hurting my feelings and embarrassing me. I've never made it so clear to a man that I'm interested in him, and I won't be doing it again anytime soon.

I don't need a man to complete me. Talking to me as if I was a child. I don't need a man at all. For now I'm going to concentrate on my art, and forget all about how he promised he'd eat me alive.

My eyes glaze over. Then, crossly, I sign the bottom of the form and stuff my pen back in my bag. I'm not going to give him another thought.

Chapter Four

Spencer

I was not happy when my daughter announced she was pregnant at the age of twenty-two. Not because I disapproved of her choice—she was an adult, and while she wasn't married then, she was in love, and her body is her own, so I would never have been anything but supportive. But I was pissed off at the thought of being a grandfather at forty-three.

I wasn't a good father. I was absent too much, too tied up in my own life, and as a result I don't know how to communicate with my three-year-old grandson, who for some bizarre reason thinks I'm the best thing since sliced bread.

Saturday afternoon finds me wandering around Helen's lawn, holding Callum's hand in my left while I press my phone to my ear with my right as I talk to my PA.

"Move the Richardson meeting to three on Monday," I tell her. "And then I should have enough time for lunch with Stellar Associates."

"You want me to book the Italian as usual?"

"Please. There will probably be four of us." I look down as Callum tugs on my hand. We're almost back at the deck, where the rest of my family is sitting and chatting. He points up at the sky and says, "Duck."

"I'd better go," I tell my PA. "See you Monday."

"Have a great weekend," she says.

"You too, and thanks for organizing that."

I end the call and look down at my grandson. "Sky," I correct him. "Not duck."

"Duck," he insists. He promptly sits onto the grass and flops onto his back. "Lie down," he says impatiently.

I glance at the people on the deck and see my daughter studying us with a watchful eye. When Callum first came up to me and said he wanted to go for a walk around the garden, she said, "Granddad won't want to do that, darling," which stung a little, and was the main reason I agreed to go on a tour of the flowerbeds with him. So I resign myself to the fact that I'm going to get grass stains on my cream chinos, lower onto the lawn beside him, and lie back.

"Duck," he repeats, pointing up at the sky. And it's then that I see it—a blob of cumulus with a smaller piece that looks like a beak.

"Wow." I laugh. "Clever boy, yes it does look like a duck. How do ducks go?"

"Quack, quack, hiccup," he says, and giggles. He's currently fascinated by hiccups since the family Labrador had them and he realized animals can get them too.

I chuckle. "What color is the sky?"

He rolls his eyes at me as if he's fifteen and has been asked to do the dishes. "Blue, Granddad."

"Are you being cheeky?"

"Yes," he says, and pokes his tongue out.

"In that case..." I roll onto my side and tickle him until he subsides into peals of laughter.

"Stop it, you two," Helen says crossly. She glares at me. "You'll make him bring up his lunch."

"Bleugh," I say to him, pretending to vomit.

He laughs and echoes me, "Bleugh!" to his mother's horror.

Her husband, Michael, sitting next to her, snorts. "I should be videoing this. Nobody will believe me when I say that Spencer Cavendish was looking at clouds and getting grass all over his back."

I sit up and glance over my shoulder to see my lambswool gray sweater covered in strands of mown grass. "It's the new biophilic fashion. I'm bringing nature into the office."

"I think it's wonderful," Scarlett—Orson's new girl—says, surprising me with her outspokenness. "You're a lovely granddad."

She's barely said a word since she arrived here with him today. I'm not surprised. Is there anything worse than going to a friendly barbecue with your new partner's family? Michael's parents are also here, as are his two brothers, Vince—who's here with his wife—and Charles, who's gay and has brought his partner, Leo. Michael's father, Richard, is clearly uneasy with his son's sexuality and has ignored his boyfriend

MIDNIGHT SECRET

all afternoon. I've held my tongue, not feeling it's my place to interfere, but I'm starting to get annoyed by his obvious rudeness, and I'm sure it's not making Scarlett feel any more comfortable.

"Thank you," I say to her, adding a smile, touched that she was brave enough to speak up for me. We had a rocky start, as she's the daughter of Blake Stone, a guy I considered my enemy for thirty years. But Blake is dead now, and Orson has fallen in love with her, and I'm learning to try and put the past behind me. I watch as Orson picks up her hand and kisses it, clearly pleased that she's making an effort to get on with me. His puppy, Bearcub, jumps up at him, jealous of him showing affection to anyone else, and Scarlett laughs and picks the pup up, and they both fuss over him. Things are improving between Orson and me, due in no small measure to Scarlett's presence.

"Oh, I've got something to tell you all," Helen says. She glances at me—there's a touch of defiant mischief in her eyes. She slides a hand into the pocket of her maternity jeans and extracts a folded piece of paper. "Have you heard about the Empowerment Auction taking place next weekend?"

"Yeah," Vince, a lawyer, says. "The local press is having a field day with it. It's all over the city, everywhere you look."

I haven't heard of it. I've been in Dunedin the past few days, and before that I was in Wellington, so I'm a bit out of the loop. "What's it about?" I ask.

"It's an art and culture auction," Orson states. "You can bid on experiences offered by female artists. It's run by Lumen." His gaze meets mine. We've discussed previously how the new club is targeting female businesswomen and trying to draw them away from Midnight. I frown, remembering Marama's mention of a meeting at the club last week. It wasn't connected to this, surely?

"You should go," Helen instructs us. "It's an impressive lineup. Lots of really talented women offering unique experiences."

Richard gives his characteristic derisive snort. "The last thing I want is to sit and listen to some female poet waxing lyrical about her menstrual cycle."

Michael laughs as he looks at the piece of paper that Helen passes him. "I don't mind bidding on this: 'Sit for a portrait in the sacred workspace of this brilliant local artist.'" He smirks. "She's hot. I'll inspect her sacred workspace any day."

I glare at him, disgusted that he'd make the comment at all, let alone in front of his wife and the other women here. I'm pleased when Orson takes the paper from him and says, "Grow up, Mike." He scans the paper. Then his eyebrows rise. "Oh." He shows Scarlett.

To my surprise, after she's read it, she glances at me, then reaches down from her seat on the deck and lets the paper flutter onto the grass.

I pick it up and scan it while the others continue their discussion. It's a program, double sided, professionally printed and elegantly designed, and it lists a summary of the items being offered in the auction. It's an interesting idea, and I can see why the press have picked up on it. I can't see why Orson exclaimed or why Scarlett thought I'd be interested…

And then I turn it over, and my gaze falls on the item at the top, which is the one that Michael mentioned. The photo of the artist is small, but it's definitely Marama Davis's exquisite face. The text reads, "'The Face I See'—sit for a portrait in the sacred workspace of this brilliant local artist."

Fury billows inside me. I get to my feet and approach the deck. "This was your doing," I snap at Helen, tossing the paper onto the table on the deck. "Meddling in other people's affairs."

Her eyebrows rise. "You mean trying to help other women become more successful? Well, lock me up right now for that crime." She holds her wrists out to me, her eyes challenging me to disagree.

I'm happy to oblige. "Don't disguise this as some kind of altruistic act. If you wanted to help Marama, you wouldn't have introduced her to that woman."

Her lips curve up. "Something tells me someone is jealous."

"It's nothing to do with me," I snap. I gesture angrily at the program. "She's better than this. All those women are. I don't care how Genevieve Beaumont labels it. These women are selling themselves, and being told they're heroic for doing it."

Her smile falters, but she lifts her chin defiantly. "You're just angry because you know it's going to be successful."

"Oh, I have no doubt it's going to draw a lot of attention." I lower my voice so Callum can't hear me where he's sitting in a sandpit, shoveling sand into a bucket. "You're shit stirring," I tell Helen. The gleam in her eyes tells me I'm right, and that sends a pulse of frustration through me. "Is this about the board position again?"

Helen applied to be part of the Midnight Circle when it was formed. We'd already decided we'd limit ourselves to eight members, and the seventh position had just been filled when she announced her interest in joining. She was up against two other women for the eighth position—Joanna Waddington, who is the CEO of a nationwide real-estate chain, and Genevieve Beaumont herself. Genevieve is wealthy and accomplished, but shot herself in the foot during the selection process, which I try not to think about. Joanna, however, brought incredible business acumen, vast experience, and her own fortune, and all eight of us voted for her. Even though Helen is my daughter and Orson's sister, she's not the businesswoman she thinks she is, and although I love her, I know she only wanted the position because of the prestige she thinks it offers, and not because she genuinely wanted to help people. No doubt Genevieve has told her that she was also passed over, and the two of them have decided to make my life a misery.

"No," she says, but her face flushes.

"If you decide to pass over your only daughter, you've got to expect some kind of reaction from her," Michael says.

"She wasn't 'passed over'," Orson states sharply. "The person who got the position was better qualified."

"I don't want to talk about it," Helen says. "That's not what this is. Marama is a talented artist, and Lumen is including her in a prominent event. You should be happy for her."

"Some of the items look really interesting," Leo says brightly. "I was thinking of going. One woman is offering violin lessons, and I've always wanted to—"

"I can't imagine any man wanting to step inside that club," Richard says, cutting Leo off mid-sentence, as if he hadn't spoken. "You'll have to leave your testicles at the door. Or not have a pair to begin with." He gives a pointed, amused glance to both Charles and Leo, and Michael and Vince laugh.

I look at Charles, who's glaring at his father, but is too timid to challenge him, and at Leo, whose face has flushed from embarrassment.

"This might not be my house," I say to Leo, "but I'd like to apologize for how you've been treated here today."

Leo blinks and Charles mouths, "Thank you." Richard inhales, outraged, but I ignore him.

SERENITY WOODS

I pick up my car keys from the table. "Thank you for inviting me," I say to my daughter, "but I think it's best if I return to the office."

She heaves a big sigh. "Dad…"

I nod at Orson, who just gives a lopsided smile, and I lift Scarlett's hand and kiss her fingers. I go over to my grandson, bend, and kiss his head. Then I take the path around the house and head for my Bentley.

I sit behind the wheel, trying to regulate my breathing. Helen and Michael live on the other side of Waiheke Island from Midnight. I was planning to spend the evening in my house in Herne Bay, which means crossing to the mainland on the ferry.

But I know from experience that if I go home now, I'm just going to stew all evening. I'm furious that Genevieve has got her claws into Marama, and just as angry that Marama hasn't seen through her, and has instead been blinded by Genevieve's promise of glory.

I start the engine, head along the drive out of their property, and then take the road to Rangi Davis's house.

Rangi owns a large property on a decent section of land on the north side of Waiheke. Marama has been staying there since she returned from her travels across Europe. I hope she's home. Rangi will probably be there, too. I wonder if she's told him about the auction? I can't imagine him being best pleased either, despite the fact that he doesn't know Genevieve the way I do.

I glower continually for the fifteen minutes it takes me to get to their property. By the time I take the turnoff for the house, my stomach is like a bag of snakes, and I can taste acid in my mouth. My doctor has warned me that if I don't handle my stress better, I'm going to end up with a stomach ulcer, and at the moment I believe him.

The drive curves around gently rolling farmland, crests a hill, and then descends toward Rangi's property on the coast. The front of the house faces the drive, but the back has a magnificent view over the Pacific, and sprawls on one level across several wings. My tires scrunch on the gravel as I pull up.

To my annoyance, Marama's parents, Rangi and Huia, are just exiting the front door, heading for his car that's sitting on the drive. They both look over and pause in front of their car as I pull up. I turn off the engine and get out, wishing I'd been five minutes later.

Rangi is taller than me, well over six feet, with broad shoulders like Kingi. He used to wear his dark hair long like his son, but now it's cropped short and almost entirely gray. His ancestors were among the first to settle in this area many hundreds of years ago, and his *iwi*—his tribe—is regarded as the *tangata whenua*, the people of the land. His family led the region's dairy industry for generations and grew wealthy from it, but it was Rangi's sharp financial and business acumen that quadrupled that fortune. Within his *iwi*, he holds the status of a *rangatira*—a leader whose mana stems not only from *whakapapa*, or genealogy, but also from decades of service to his *whānau* or family and the wider community.

Huia is an older version of her daughter, beautiful, exotic, and with the same smooth light-brown skin—she's just curvier, with fine lines at the edges of her eyes and gray in her hair.

"Kia ora, Spencer," she says, coming over to kiss my cheek.

"Kia ora. You look extra beautiful today."

She rolls her eyes, but smiles. "You're such a smooth talker, but thank you."

"Kia ora," Rangi says. "Sorry, we were just on our way out. Do you need something?"

"No. I was actually hoping to catch Marama. Is she in?"

"She's painting on the deck," Huia says.

"Everything all right?" Rangi asks. He looks surprised that I want to see his daughter, but not shocked. I push away a twinge of guilt. It's perfectly acceptable that I've called in. It's not as if I'm here for romantic reasons.

I'm not sure if she's told him about the auction, though, so, I say, "I just want to talk about her exhibition at Midnight, ask her how many paintings she's thinking of showing and how she wants them displayed, you know, that kind of thing..." I stop, aware I'm waffling.

I never waffle, and Rangi's lips quirk up, but he doesn't comment. Instead, he says, "Well, go ahead, you can go around the side. We're off to a party."

"Have fun."

He hates parties, and he gives me a wry look before heading for the car.

I walk away, frowning at my verbal diarrhea, and take the path leading around the house. A gardener is in the process of pruning the rose bushes there. He's in his sixties, dressed in coveralls and wearing a cap. He raises a hand as I pass and says, "Afternoon, Mr. Cavendish."

"Joe... how long have we known each other? Twenty years? For Christ's sake, call me Spencer."

"Yes sir." He smiles.

"I'm just looking for Marama. I understand she's on the deck?"

"Yes, sir. She's painting."

"Thank you." I leave him to his work and continue walking around the house.

The living room and bedrooms all have sliding doors onto the back deck that stretches the whole length of the property, facing the sea. At one end the deck extends around a large hot tub that's partially sunk in the ground. The rest of the deck bears several tables and chairs, and various potted plants.

Marama is sitting about halfway along, at one of the tables. I stop and look at the scene. She's leaning back in a chair with her feet propped on another one, and a sketchpad is resting on her lap. On the table is a small palette of paints, a jar of water, and a mug with a tab on a string that suggests it's some kind of fruit tea.

She's wearing cutdown jeans and a warm orange T-shirt that complements her light-brown skin. It drapes gently over her generous breasts. Her feet are bare. Man, she's gorgeous.

She's pinned her hair up in a scruffy bun, but tendrils tumble around her face, and as I watch she tucks one behind her ear.

I climb the deck and walk up to her. "Afternoon."

Her head snaps around and her eyes widen as she sees me. She lowers her feet to the floor and sits up hurriedly.

"What are you doing here?" she asks. My smile fades at the tone of her voice. She's not pleased to see me. "Dad's out."

"I came to see you."

She stares at her sketchbook. "I don't have anything to say to you."

"Then you can just listen. I've seen the program for the Empowerment Auction."

Her gaze lifts to mine, and we study each other for a moment.

"Oh?" she says eventually.

"You can't do it," I announce flatly.

Her eyebrows slowly lift. "I beg your pardon?"

"Putting yourself up for sale? Don't you realize how demeaning that is? You've heard of Thomas Hardy?"

She flushes. "This isn't *The Mayor of Casterbridge,* and I'm not being sold by my husband. It's not the artists who are up for sale. People would be bidding for the privilege of our time and talent."

"Don't parrot Genevieve Beaumont at me," I snap. "You need to open your eyes. This whole thing is performative and degrading."

"It's going to raise money for women-led artistic endeavors," she says, and it's as if I can see Genevieve's mouth moving.

"Do you really think that rich and powerful businesswomen are going to be the ones bidding on this auction? No, it'll be men who are going to try to outbid each other to spend time with you. If you don't see how that cheapens you, well, I don't know what to say."

Slowly, she washes her brush, then puts down her sketchpad and gets to her feet. "You know why I went to Lumen? Because Kingi told me that the Midnight Circle had agreed to exhibit my work—in the Morepork room! It's not on the way to anywhere, Spencer. I'd rather it be displayed in the bathrooms—at least it would get more eyes on it there."

She has a point about the Morepork room, but I frown. "Did Kingi tell you that we want another exhibition later in the year in the lobby?"

She blinks. "No."

"We can't do it in April, that's all."

"Yeah, because you're exhibiting Jason Ridgeway. A guy who's five years younger than I am and nowhere near as well known. But of course he's a white man, so it's not surprising he was chosen."

I glare at her. Now she sounds like Helen. "Ridgeway won the Northland Fine Arts Competition last year. It's nothing to do with his gender or the color of his skin."

"Oh, really."

"No. We agreed to showcase his work before you came back from Europe. So grow up and stop throwing a childish tantrum when you don't have all the facts."

Her amber eyes flare with fury. "That's the second time you've accused me of acting like a child. I'm thirty next month, and I'd appreciate it if you stopped talking down to me."

I don't say anything. She's right, but I'm not in the mood to apologize.

She puts her hands on her hips and lifts her chin. She looks absolutely amazing, and despite being mad at her, I wish I could pull her into my arms and kiss her senseless.

"The fact is," she says, "Lumen has offered me a rare opportunity for exposure, and I'm going to grab it with both hands."

"Don't limit yourself to your gender and race," I tell her with feeling. "You're bigger than that."

"I don't know what you mean! You have no idea how hard it can be to get visibility when you're both a woman and Māori!"

"It's true, I don't. I'm a privileged white male, I know. But I wasn't born rich. I've had to fight for what I've achieved every step of the way." How can I make her understand? "Lumen isn't the beacon of truth and honesty that it seems. Genevieve wants to raise herself by stepping on men and crushing them under her four-inch stiletto heels. Is that what you want, too? Do you feel the need to punish half of society just because we have one Y chromosome?"

"I don't agree. I don't think it is about crushing men. It's about lifting women. You make Genevieve sound selfish and cruel, but she's open and accepting of all sorts of people. She told me that Victoria Brown prefers going there because she feels more accepted than she does at Huxley's."

I give a short, humorless laugh. "That's pure fiction. I'm pretty sure Victoria can't stand Genevieve. Ask her yourself."

"I will."

"Good."

We glare at each other. My stomach knots. This isn't going well, and I'm beginning to realize how foolish I was to try to convince her she's making a mistake. "Genevieve Beaumont is not what you think," I say carefully.

She gives me an impatient look. "So you keep implying. Do you want to tell me what you mean by that? What happened between you two? Did you make a move on her, and she rejected you? Is that why you're being vindictive—is it because she humiliated you?"

I stiffen. "No."

She lifts her chin. "I think she did. I think she turned you down, and it infuriated you. And you know what else? I don't think you're angry with me because you think the auction is demeaning. I think the idea of anyone bidding to be alone with me infuriates you. I think you're jealous."

A silence falls between us.

I can't deny it, because she's right. And I'm furious with myself for it.

She's standing there, eyes blazing, the wind tugging her hair, her nipples poking through her T-shirt like buttons, and I want her more than I think I've ever wanted a woman in my life. I want to push her up against the window, take her face in my hands, and kiss her senseless.

But I can't have her. Rangi would kill me. Kingi would skin me alive. Orson would never speak to me again. The Midnight Circle would throw me out. My business colleagues would mock the cool, calm, and collected Spencer Cavendish for giving in to his emotions, and I'd lose all respect in the community.

And I couldn't keep her anyway, because she's young, and she'll want a family, and she needs someone her own age who can love her the way she deserves. And I'm not capable of that emotion.

"You can think what you like," I tell her, making my voice hard. "But if you go through with the auction, you'll realize it's not what you think, and you'll regret it." I step down from the deck, then turn briefly. "Oh, and by the way, you washed your paintbrush in your tea. I just thought I'd point that out." Leaving her cursing, I stride away, back to my car.

Chapter Five

Marama

"What the hell am I doing?"

I'm standing in one of the meeting rooms adjacent to the function room where the auction is about to start taking place. The room is packed with the women taking part in the auction, and a slew of others helping with makeup, wardrobe, and the organization of the evening.

Helen, looking gorgeous in a designer maternity top and trousers, grins. "You're raising money for a good cause. Now for God's sake, finish off your champagne. You're trembling so much they'll think there's an earthquake." She's helping out tonight, fetching drinks for everyone behind scenes and running errands for Genevieve and her assistant, Carly.

I peer through a crack in the door at the hall. It's my first glimpse of it, as the artists all ate together here, because Genevieve wanted to keep us separate from the guests to prolong the suspense.

The stage at the front bears a podium with a microphone, and there's a row of seats behind it, which is where we'll all be sitting in a few minutes. The hall is filled with round tables decked out in white cloths that bear the remnants of the sumptuous meal. A bar to one side keeps the guests stocked with champagne, wine, and spirits.

Pieces of artwork, framed poems, and other artistic pieces by the participants are displayed around the hall in the hope of encouraging the bids. I can see one of my best acrylic paintings halfway along—of *Te Rerenga Wairua*, 'the leaping place of spirits', also known as Cape Reinga, where Māori believe a person's spirit departs for the ancestral homeland, Hawaiki, when they die. Spotlights bring out the vivid colors, and I've seen lots of people stop on their way past to have a look.

The mood is lively, and the auction hasn't even started yet. Genevieve has done her best to promote it as a high-class event you can't afford to miss, and tickets sold out within twenty-four hours. I saw the advert—the cost was two hundred and fifty dollars for a general ticket with a seated dinner and entertainment, three to five thousand for a premium table with better views, quality wine pairing, and a gift bag, and ten thousand for a sponsor table, which includes recognition in the program and a private meet-and-greet with the artists.

The place is filled with celebrities—actors, sports people, and politicians, as well as the top players in the business arena in the city. "Every chair is filled," I whisper.

"Yeah. You won't find another seat tonight unless you want to drop twenty grand," Helen says.

"Jesus. I had no idea it was going to be quite this prominent."

"Maybe you'll start believing in yourself now."

"I doubt it. I feel as if someone's listed me by mistake."

She just laughs and says, "You want to put this on?"

I turn away from the door and let her lift the purple satin sash over my head. It lays across me diagonally, resting on my hip, and bears the wording 'Empowerment Artist.' "It's pretty," I reply, "but it makes me feel a bit like I'm in a Miss World contest."

"Wait until you put your tiara on."

"What?" I stare at her, startled.

She snorts. "I'm kidding. You're so gullible. They have to make you stand out, especially afterward, when you get to mingle."

Some people have paid extra to meet personally with the artists. I'm nervous, but excited too at the opportunities that might be available here tonight.

"Now come on," she says, "they're about to call you to go on stage."

The other women are making their way toward the door and forming a line, and I join them, taking my place at number fourteen out of the fifteen artists, which is where Genevieve placed me on the program. Helen said the artists are in ascending order of importance, but I can't imagine that's the case. I'm hardly the second biggest artist here—I know several of the others and they're much more prestigious than I am.

I wish I was nearer the beginning. It's going to be agony having to wait until nearly the end. What if the other artists have huge bids put on them and nobody wants me? Realistically I'm sure that won't happen, but there's always a secret fear that might be the case.

"You look amazing," Helen reassures me. "That dress really suits you."

I've made a special effort on my appearance tonight. While I was traveling, I lived in jeans and sweaters, and the dress code around Auckland and in the Northland tends to be super casual in the summer, with everyone in shorts and tees, so it's been a while since I dressed up. But tonight I'm wearing a long black evening dress, off the shoulder and with a split in the skirt all the way up to my hip. Black high-heeled strappy sandals complete the look, and with help of one of the hairdressers here, I've pinned up my hair with an elaborately carved bone comb, leaving a single curl hanging on one side of my face. Winged eyeliner and dark red lipstick contrast well against my light-brown skin.

I stare at myself in one of the mirrors placed around the room, hardly recognizing the sophisticated and exotic creature looking back at me. I'm annoyed with myself for wondering how much someone would be willing to bid for me. With Spencer's voice in my head insinuating this situation mirrors the Hardy novel, I want to scream at myself, *They're not bidding for you!* They're bidding for my work, of course. It's not a reflection on me, or my self-worth, or my beauty, or my personality, or anything but the experience I'm offering.

But I'm only human, and I'm ashamed that deep down I know I'll be pleased if I receive a decent bid.

"Go and have fun!" Helen says.

I nod, hearing Genevieve's voice calling for quiet on the stage. She starts giving her introductory speech, explaining the idea behind the auction, and the charity art programs that everyone's money is going to be funding.

Then she asks everyone to give a round of applause for the artists, and I follow the others out of the meeting room and up the stairs onto the stage. It's all decorated in white and gold, with the words 'Empowerment Auction' emblazoned across the top. It's beautifully done, and all our chairs have golden ribbons tied around them, while the faces of the fifteen artists are projected onto the screen at the back, along with examples of our art or pictures of where we work.

MIDNIGHT SECRET

I continue to tremble as I take my seat and look out across the large room. Oh my God, there are so many people. It's a black-tie event, and the men are all in tuxedos, while the women are in sparkling long gowns. It's like the Oscars or Emmys. Most people are drinking champagne, and the menu consisted of multiple courses with luxury dishes containing premium local ingredients, like South Island Crayfish Tail with Citrus Beurre Blanc, and Line-Caught Hapuku with Champagne Velouté & Paua Ravioli.

There are plenty of women here, but there are also clusters of businessmen on their own, most of them older, red-faced, and clearly on the way to being drunk. I'm surprised, and for the first time I get a tingle of unease as I think about Spencer's warning again. I dismissed his words at the time, thinking he was just jealous, but maybe he was right. Are these guests really altruistic donors keen to help women artists? Or are they merely greedy old men hoping for private time with one of us?

Earlier this evening, I took a few minutes to check the guest list. I pretended to myself that I was looking to see if there was anyone I knew on it, but deep down I knew I was only looking for one name. Part of me had wondered all week whether Spencer would come to the house again to try to convince me not to take part, but he didn't. I wondered then if he would turn up to bid on me. But his name wasn't on the list, so clearly he's decided to steer clear and leave me to the wolves. Correction—the other wolves. I'm glad he isn't here. But it doesn't stop me being nervous about who is going to win the bid.

Shivering a little, I watch the first artist come forward to speak briefly into the microphone as she introduces herself and her art. She's much younger than me, a violin player lauded as a prodigy, and she's offering a private performance at a dinner party held at the winning bidder's home. It's a rare opportunity to see a skilled musician play close up, but as I watch as a couple of older guys lean toward each other, exchange a sentence, then laugh, I'm convinced they're not discussing whether she's going to play Brahms or Tchaikovsky.

Genevieve has made it clear that we artists can decline any winning bidder if we're uncomfortable, but I wonder whether any of us would have the courage to do that, knowing that the money is going to charitable causes. I look at Genevieve, half-expecting to see her frowning, but she's flushed and excited, apparently thrilled with how the evening is going. Again, I'm surprised. I would have thought she'd have made sure that more female guests attended, and somehow excluded the older, rich white guys. But I guess it's impossible to do that when the majority of people who run the businesses here in the city are of that demographic. They're going to be the ones raising the bids, so I guess it makes sense to take their money.

The young woman finishes talking, and Genevieve starts the bidding at five thousand dollars. Guests have all been given paddles with numbers, and across the room bidders lift them in turn, and the price slowly rises.

The violin player has toured Europe with several top orchestras and has soloed with the Auckland Philharmonia, so it doesn't surprise me that the bid reaches forty-five thousand dollars before Genevieve declares, "Sold to number one hundred and sixty-seven!"

Sold, like a prize cow at a market fair.

I shift uneasily, watching as the violinist takes her seat. I mustn't think like that. I'm helping to raise significant money for worthwhile causes. I have to think of all the women in rural communities who these programs will help.

Slowly, Genevieve works through the artists. Each woman gives a brief talk about her art and the experience she's offering, and then Genevieve begins the bidding.

I watch the process, growing increasingly stiff with resentment and outrage as the evening progresses and Spencer's warning plays out. The older women struggle to reach twenty thousand for their bids, while all the younger women easily pass forty thousand. One—a particularly beautiful, young, blonde poet—even gets to seventy-five thousand before Genevieve declares her sold. How fucking predictable.

Nobody else seems particularly bothered by this. Everyone appears to be having a great time, and most of the women look thrilled to think they're fetching a decent price. I think it's Spencer's fault—if he hadn't planted the idea in my head, I'm sure I would have been having a fantastic evening.

All too soon, Genevieve reaches artist thirteen, and then it's time for my turn. The mood is excited, even raucous, with people calling out, cheering, and whistling. I stand as she announces my name and approach the podium. I've written a short speech on a card, and I read it out, explaining to the audience that I'm offering a private portrait session in my studio on Waiheke Island. They already know this of course as it's written in the glossy programs sitting on their tables, but

I tell them a little about my studio and my process, and then describe why the title is 'The Face I See'. "You come to be seen, as I choose to see you," I tell them. It was Genevieve's idea—she thought it would make the bidders curious as to what my interpretation of their portrait would look like, and it naturally puts the power in my hands.

I stand to the side as Genevieve begins the bidding, starting at ten thousand dollars. Across the room, people begin lifting their paddles.

Genevieve increases the bids in five-thousand-dollar increments, and the price rises swiftly past thirty thousand, then past forty.

I stand there, hands linked in front of me, watching the bidding war take place. I force a smile on my face, but inside, my heart is thundering. I run my gaze along the tables at the front, which is where many of the final bids have landed. Most of the sponsor tables feature older, rich businessmen with florid faces, laughing and nudging each other as they outbid one another. Nausea rises inside me at the thought of one of them winning the bid. It doesn't mean anything, I tell myself furiously. It's just for a studio session—it's not for a date!

So why does it feel so cheap and… yes, Spencer was right… degrading?

My gaze skims across the guests—and then it slams to a stop. For a moment, I think I've conjured him up by thinking about him. Sitting at a table to one side of the hall, leaning back in his chair, one arm hooked over the back, is Spencer Cavendish.

He definitely wasn't on the guest list. He must have snuck in at the last minute. God knows how much his ticket cost him. Like everyone else, he's in a tuxedo, a three piece, as his jacket is unbuttoned and the waistcoat beneath is visible. He's wearing a wing-tip white shirt and a black bow tie, which complements his dark hair that's threaded with silver, and those distinctive flashes at his temples.

My heart bangs as our gazes lock. Almost immediately, though, I realize he's not bidding. His paddle sits discarded to one side, and as I watch he lifts a glass to his lips and takes a sip. He looks relaxed, almost bored. He's not here for me.

I tear my gaze away and look back at Genevieve. The bids have been slowly climbing, and she's just reached fifty thousand.

"Come on, ladies and gentlemen," she teases, "aren't you intrigued to see what this beautiful young woman will make of you in her studio? What vision will she have of you? Imagine what it will be like to hang an amazing, raw portrait of yourself in your home! Do I hear fifty-five thousand?"

Grinning, a man at a sponsor table raises his paddle, and she gestures toward him. "Fifty-five, thank you! Do I hear sixty?"

To my astonishment, the price continues to climb. It's all men bidding now. Sixty, seventy, eighty thousand. It's passed the maximum reached so far, and Genevieve's face is bright with excitement.

"Do I hear eighty-five?" she asks.

The man who bid eighty meets my eyes. He's in his eighties, by the look of him, overweight, and slightly balding, and even from here I can see his top lip is shiny with sweat. I try not to despair. This is a professional auction! I don't even have to be alone with him. I'll ask Helen or Mum or someone else to sit in the studio with me. It's not like I have to kiss the man! I scan the room, half-hoping someone else will continue the bidding, half-hoping it finishes here and I can slink back to my seat.

"Going," Genevieve declares, "going..."

"Half a million dollars," a deep voice calls out from the side of the room. "And I'll double it if you end the bidding now."

There's an audible gasp across the room. My eyes widen and my jaw drops. I already know who the voice belonged to. Spencer looks lazily amused, and lifts his paddle to show Genevieve his number.

I look at her. For a brief moment, her eyes flare with something, but the emotion is gone before I can pin it down, and then she smiles and says, "Goodness, well, what can I say to that? The bidding is over—sold, for a million dollars, to number two hundred and thirty."

The room erupts in a cheer. At most of the tables, people bend their heads to whisper to one another, no doubt wondering what on earth prompted Spencer Cavendish to place such an outrageous bid on a relatively unknown artist. I turn and make my way back to my seat, face burning. The other women smile, but I can see one or two envious looks. Genevieve gives me an amused, curious glance before turning her attention to the final artist.

When I'm seated, I finally look back at Spencer's table. Half of me expects to see him looking the other way with bored indifference; the other half is sure he'll be staring at me with his wolfish gaze.

To my surprise, his seat is empty. I scan the room, but he's vanished, presumably out of the side entrance, heading toward the lobby.

I sit there in a haze, my head spinning, as the bid rises to sixty-five thousand before Genevieve calls it a day. She gives a closing speech, promising that the artists will be available to those at the sponsor tables for a private meet and greet in the adjacent room in a short while. Then she ends the auction, thanking everyone for their attendance and for raising such a generous amount of money for worthwhile female-led programs.

We file off the stage into the meeting room. Helen is there, waiting, and she laughs as I walk up to her.

"What was that about?" she asks, amused.

"I have no idea." I'm flushed and confused. I don't know what to think, and all of a sudden I have to speak to Spencer. If he hasn't left the building, which is possible. "Can you tell Genevieve I'll be back in a minute?"

"You're supposed to wait... The press wants photographs..."

But I'm already walking away, toward the door that leads to the corridor down to the lobby, my heart racing.

Chapter Six

Spencer

I was planning to head home, but I got caught by the CEO of Ridgeway Investments, and I'm still standing there, unable to escape his long monologue about a new property development in the CBD, when Genevieve enters the lobby through a doorway across the other side.

Shit. Time to make a hasty exit.

"Why don't you get your secretary to call mine," I advise the guy in front of me. "I think this merits further discussion."

"Yes, of course, will do." He's been hoping to team up with Cavendish Enterprises for ages, and he looks pleased to have finally convinced me to meet with him. "I'd also like to talk to you about the Rutland complex. Rumor has it that it's up for grabs, and I think it has great potential for—"

"Absolutely." I glance at Genevieve—she's heading straight for me. "Got to go." I turn away, knowing I'm being rude, but I'd rather do that than suffer the consequences.

Leaving the guy standing there, still talking, I stride off. I'm halfway across the floor when she calls out, "Spencer!"

Her voice rings across the floor, and everyone in the lobby turns to look. I slow, then stop, cursing. Exiting now would give the many members of the press who are here fuel for their fire, and I have no intention of doing that.

I turn slowly as she closes the distance between us, and I survey her with distaste. On the surface, she's beautiful: tall and slender, with elegantly coiffed blonde hair and fine features. I can't put my finger on why I don't find her attractive. She's confident, even outspoken, but I happen to like women who are sure of themselves. She's witty and clever, and she's clearly an exceptionally talented businesswoman.

Then she glances to her left at a plus-size woman who's wearing a dress that's several sizes too small for her, and when she looks back at me, her eyes are full of amusement, and I realize why I don't like her. She's spiteful, cruel, and cold, and she reminds me too much of my wife.

Also, she usually has exquisite taste in clothes, but the shimmering gold gown she's wearing tonight looks like the inside of a chocolate bar wrapper.

"Well, well, well," she coos, resting a hand on my chest. "Spencer Cavendish bidding one million dollars for a woman. Never thought I'd see the day." Over to one side, I see someone lift their phone to take a picture. Fuck my life.

"The bid wasn't for Marama," I say icily.

"Really." She pats my jacket, smoothing the lapel as if it has a crease in it, which it doesn't. "You were quite clearly staking your claim, my darling. The whole of the city will be talking about it tomorrow."

"I'm sure you'll make sure of that," I snap.

She smiles. "I can see the headline now." She swipes her hand in front of her. "Wolf of Waiheke bids mysteriously exorbitant amount for unknown artist."

"What do you want?" I ask tiredly. It's been a long day, and I want to go home, get myself a coffee, and do my best to forget the woman with the *moko kauae* who has been haunting my dreams since the party at the Midnight Club.

"Just to give you this." Genevieve hands me a sheet of paper. It states that I won bid number fourteen tonight, and has Lumen's bank account details for me to deposit the funds.

I fold it and slide it into my inside pocket. She could have had Carly deliver that, or even a waiter. That's not why she caught up with me.

She looks up at me. "So… You do have a weakness. But it's not money, or pride, as I thought. It's Marama Davis. Your secret obsession?"

I stiffen. "Her father is my business partner. I didn't want him to hear about this ridiculous charade, so I took her off the market."

Her face flushes. "How dare you call it that. This evening has been immensely successful in raising the profile of up-and-coming women artists."

"There were other ways to do that than sell their talent to the highest bidder. You demeaned them. Had them perform and strut across the stage. And somehow convinced them they were empowering themselves." I feel nauseous at the thought of seeing Marama up there, looking nervously across the crowd, wondering which blubberous fool was going to win the bid.

Genevieve's eyes flare, and at the same time they turn a tad glassy. I feel a brief spike of guilt at my cruelty. She has raised a good deal of money for these women, and gained publicity and prestige for their work.

My guilt disappears though as I think about the Midnight Club. Ever since she opened Lumen, she's bad-mouthed Midnight, slating it as a men's-only club, which is ridiculous, and accusing all its members of being misogynistic. We've even considered taking legal action over it, but so far have held back, because lawyers are expensive, and Genevieve would have a field day promoting the image of men doing their best to bring down women, and dark overpowering light, and lord knows what else. But I will consider it if she doesn't stop being a major pain in my ass.

I'd rather have peace, though, and I make my voice gentle and say, "Just put the money to good use and it will have been worth it."

She moves closer to me. In her high heels she's almost on a level with me. She looks into my eyes and says, in a quiet but furious tone, "Fuck you, Spencer."

I don't react. I hold her gaze, knowing my disdain for her is evident.

"Genevieve!" Behind her, someone calls her name. She glances over her shoulder. Then, without another word to me, she pins a smile on her face and walks off to talk to a group of her guests.

My stomach churns. I want to get out of here. I turn toward the exit, then stop, surprised to see Marama standing there, clearly waiting for me.

I walk up to her slowly, hands in the pockets of my trousers. She looks amazing tonight. The slit in her skirt reveals an expanse of smooth light-brown thigh. Her black high-heeled sandals are incredibly sexy, and she's painted her toenails an erotic cherry-red. She's wearing false eyelashes that make her look sultry, like a movie star, but her *moko kauae* labels her as something more serious, a spiritual artist, Hina Marama—the goddess of the moon—made real. Genevieve is wearing gold but is cold as ice; Marama embodies the moon but has a heart of fire. She looks exotic and stunning, and I want to pull her toward me and crush my lips to hers.

I don't. But I want to.

The lobby is busy with people coming and going from the hall and staff dashing around frantically delivering orders and keeping the guests happy. We stand in the middle of them, as if we're in the eye of the storm.

For a moment, she doesn't say anything, and we study each other silently. Then, eventually, she says, "Why?"

"It was a worthwhile cause," I reply. "The world needs more women's art programs."

I thought she'd be either flustered or angry, but she just seems nonplussed. "I don't understand. You made it very clear you're not interested in me, and you don't want anything to do with me. And then you go and bid a ridiculous amount to have me."

The sentence makes me bristle. It *was* a ridiculous amount, and it's going to be all over the Internet tomorrow. "Not to have you," I snap. "I did this as a favor to your father, so he didn't have to worry about you being bought by some red-faced, lecherous octogenarian."

"You're a dog in the manger," she says. "You're angry because you want me, but your principles won't allow you to have me, and so you don't want anyone else to have me either."

I clench my jaw, furious that she's right. "Not at all. I did it to keep you safe."

She glares at me. "I don't need saving, Spencer. I'm perfectly capable of looking after myself. I'm not a child."

"That much is obvious," I say tartly, unable to stop myself glancing at the top of her gown. The low bodice barely hides her nipples and reveals an enticing swell of her light-brown breasts above the black velvet. It's too revealing, too sensual. The men at the auction tonight would have been unable to tear their gazes away.

Her eyebrows rise. "Did you just eye-dip me?"

I glare at her. "You have no idea of the wolves circling tonight."

"Including one from Waiheke."

I give her a sarcastic look. "I'm not the one you need to be worried about."

"'Stop taunting this wolf, because he'll eat you alive?' I thought you were the only one I had to be worried about."

"I wouldn't take advantage of you the way those other men would."

She lifts her chin. "I'm glad to hear it. Because I don't know what you thought you'd bought for a million dollars, but it doesn't include a night in my bed. Not after the way you treated me."

Her eyes flash, and I realize then that she's no longer the young girl I once knew. She's not even the hurt, broken young woman who fled the country after her boyfriend cheated on her. Her solo travels abroad have given her composure and a belief in herself that means her self-worth no longer rests on what other people think of her. She's every inch a stunning, powerful woman in her prime, confident in her abilities and her sexuality. She's magnificent, and I want her so much it hurts.

Our gazes lock. Her lips part, and I wonder whether she can see my desire in my eyes.

Then she tears her gaze away. "You have, however, won a commission for a portrait," she says. "As I choose to see you."

"It's okay. I won't be requiring that."

"I have to present a finished piece for the Empowerment Exhibition. You have to sit." She speaks with calm certainty, brooking no argument.

I'm not used to being told what to do, and my first instinct is to refuse and walk away. Nobody dictates what I do in my life anymore. I'm completely my own man.

But deep down, I'm intrigued. I want to know how she sees me, and how she's going to choose to portray that with her art.

"All right," I say, with some reluctance.

She rolls her eyes. "Well don't sound so thrilled about it."

My lips curve up. "When would suit you?"

"I can fit around your schedule. Part of the prize is to come to my studio and experience my sacred space."

It's inevitable that the statement evokes an intimate image in my mind. I open my mouth to reply, momentarily lose the power of speech, meet her eyes, and then we both just laugh. It breaks the tension, and we relax and let out long breaths.

"My parents are going away on Tuesday," she says. "Dad's speaking at a conference in Christchurch. Mum's going with him, and they're spending a few days down there. It means it'll be nice and quiet at home."

I'd much prefer it if Rangi wasn't there. In fact I'm hoping he doesn't get to hear about my bid at all. "I can move a few things around to free up the afternoon," I say. "How does two p.m. sound?"

"Perfect. I'll see you then."

I'm unable to suppress the thrill that rises inside me at the thought of spending more time in her company. But this is just professional. I have to keep it firmly in my mind. I made the decision at Midnight to make it clear that nothing would happen between us, and that hasn't changed.

"Goodnight," I say.

"Night." She hesitates. "And… thank you." Her words are sincere. Maybe she saw the type of men who were bidding on her, and she is genuinely relieved that I won.

I meet her eyes again. "You're welcome." Then I turn and walk away.

*

Marama

I watch Spencer go, my heart banging away. I don't know what it is about him, but when he looks at me I feel as if everyone else in the room fades away, and it's just the two of us, caught up in our own world.

I'm still angry with him for rejecting me. But equally, I can't help but be flattered by the amount he bid for me tonight. His insistence that he did it for my father doesn't ring true at all. When I said, 'You're angry because you want me… so you don't want anyone else to have me either,' his eyes flared, and I knew then that I was right. He does want me; it's just that he's convinced himself he's too old for me, and that it would be wrong because he knows my father.

He's probably right. Doesn't stop me wanting him, though.

I turn back to the lobby, and spot Genevieve standing not far from the door, talking to Hariata Pere, the Managing Director of Te Whaihanga Toi Foundation. I saw Genevieve's exchange with Spencer. His contempt for her, and her dislike of him, was palpable. It's clear that something happened between them in the past. Maybe I'll ask him about it when he's sitting for me. Something happens between a sitter and the artist during the painting of a portrait. An intimacy forms that's impossible to ignore.

Thank God he won the auction, and the bald, florid octogenarian didn't.

I decide to head for the meeting room, but as I go to pass her, Genevieve glances my way and beckons me over.

"Hello again," I say to Hariata as I approach.

"Hello," Hariata says, looking at me with renewed interest. "Well, well, well, this is a turn up for the books. Spencer Cavendish bidding one million dollars for a female artist?"

I'm guessing that's going to be the headline everywhere for the next week or two. "I'm a little embarrassed to say I think he did it out of a misguided sense of loyalty to my father," I admit.

But Hariata shakes her head. "I saw the look on his face just now," she says softly. "He has feelings for you."

Her voice is gentle, but I can feel Genevieve's hard gaze on me, and I shift from foot to foot, a little uncomfortable. "I think you're mistaken," I say. "He's been very clear that our age difference and the fact that my father is his business associate make me out of bounds." As I say it, and their eyebrows rise, I realize I'm admitting that Spencer and I have had a conversation about a possible relationship. I flush and lift my chin. "Anyway, I'm not interested. I can do better than Spencer Cavendish."

Genevieve smiles. "Definitely. But… it has given us an idea."

"Oh?"

Hariata nods. "Te Whaihanga Toi Foundation would like to offer you a commission for a solo exhibition of a series of paintings."

My pulse races. "Really?"

"Yes. To be displayed here." She gestures at the area to the side of the lobby at Lumen's gallery, where a large group of guests is gathered, viewing the art on show. It's prime real estate, the perfect opportunity to get noticed.

"When we spoke before," Hariata goes on, "you mentioned being interested in doing portraits of important women in our community, and portraying them as modern-day *atua wāhine*." Female goddesses.

"We'd like to build on that idea," Genevieve says. "We could call it Maramataka." She sweeps her hand in front of her as if showing me the word as a title. It's the name for the Māori lunar calendar, literally meaning 'the turning of the moon,' and of course it includes my name.

MIDNIGHT SECRET

"The moon is rising," Hariata says. "The sun has had his day. Men have had the galleries and the money long enough, don't you think?"

"Um… yes, I suppose they have."

"Your work deserves a platform," she continues. "It can be more than decorative. It can be revolutionary. It can be a statement of female ascendance."

"Women rising, claiming power, and outshining men." Genevieve's eyes are alight with zeal. "We want you to be bold and confrontational in your art. We'd like to see themes of female power and sexual agency. It can feature cyclical, feminine, and ancestral aspects."

"Yes," I say, excitement rising inside me as I think about the possibilities, "and things like renewal, growth, time, and spiritual rhythm."

Hariata nods. "The paintings should feature modern goddesses taming beasts and overturning male power."

"And the first one can be about Spencer Cavendish." Genevieve's eyes gleam. "A man who is all about the patriarchy and control over women."

"See if he'll model naked," Hariata teases. "I've heard he's an impressive man."

"Me too," Genevieve says with a grin.

Hariata leans forward conspiratorially. "I knew Eleanor quite well. Once, at a party, she'd had a few too many glasses of champagne, and she was being quite loud. He came over to tell her it was time to go and went off to get their coats. She was embarrassed and said, 'He probably wants to get me in bed. The guy's insatiable. All he thinks about is sex.'"

Genevieve laughs, but I shift uncomfortably. We complain when men objectify women this way. What makes it right for us to do it?

Genevieve's eyes flash. "I want you to find out and paint his weaknesses. Strip him of that smug confidence and expose the vulnerable man inside. Show us the Wolf of Waiheke, brought to his knees."

My excitement dims a little. Is this some kind of revenge ploy? As much as Spencer pissed me off when he turned me down, I don't want to be caught up in Genevieve's thirst for vengeance, or Hariata's obvious agenda.

Equally, this is one hell of an opportunity. To have an exhibit in the lobby of the most prestigious and up-and-coming female-oriented business club in the city, if not the country? Partially funded by Te Whaihanga Toi Foundation? I can only imagine the publicity and support I would receive. It's my opportunity to shine. How can I pass up on that?

Whatever Genevieve and Hariata's motives are, the paintings will be mine. I'm sure I can fulfil their criteria without being cruel or humiliating. I can still present women in the ascendence: Marama rising, shining down her light on the men below her.

Spencer can put that in his pipe and smoke it.

Chapter Seven

Spencer

On Sunday morning, when I wake and reach for my phone, I discover an email waiting from Oliver Huxley requesting my presence at a meeting of the Midnight Circle at midday.

I frown as I read it. That's unusual—we nearly always meet midweek, and hardly ever during the day; it's nearly always late evening, as our name implies.

With growing suspicion, I click on the Kōrero app. The word means a conversation or discussion, and it's New Zealand's most prominent news website. I scroll down to the local news section and, sure enough, right at the top is a large photo of me, taken at Lumen last night. It shows me leaning back in my chair, my gaze fixed on the stage, apparently captivated by something… or someone. I know perfectly well who it was.

Beneath it is the headline: Artist to Tame the Billionaire Wolf of Waiheke. It mirrors Genevieve's statement enough to convince me she's personally fed the details to one of the journalists.

Irritated, I click the link and skim the article's details, which state how I—one of the members of the prestigious Midnight Circle—bid the outrageous sum of one million dollars for a relatively unknown female artist. A photograph of Marama—also taken at the auction—is displayed next to mine. It's publicity for her, but not quite in the vein she was hoping for, I'm sure.

The article is phrased carefully to insinuate that my interest is personal rather than professional. A trashy clickbait piece that will no doubt entice those who enjoy spreading gossip through the business community.

I told myself I was doing it for her father, and for her—to save her from falling into the hands of some unscrupulous letch who believed he was bidding for a private date alone with her, with all that entailed. But I know I'm not being honest with myself. At that moment, I did it because I didn't want someone else to have her. I did it because I want her to be mine.

I toss my phone aside and cover my face with my hands. I'm such a fucking idiot. She's right—I'm a dog in the manger. I can't have her, but the thought of anyone else having her sends my blood thundering furiously through my veins.

And now it's all over the Internet, and the Midnight Circle is going to want to hear the gory details and demand I explain why I'm dragging their name through the mud. Although we don't advertise the fact that the Circle donates its proceeds to charities, we've worked hard to promote the Midnight Club as an exclusive and classy establishment, and to keep it free from gossip. This is exactly the type of publicity we don't need.

Well, there's no putting the toothpaste back in the tube. I just have to hope I can convince everyone that I did it for her and her family. Because I'm such an honorable guy.

Rolling my eyes, I head off to the gym.

When Eleanor died, I found myself rattling around in the enormous house she insisted we buy on Waiheke Island when she was pregnant with Orson. I lived there for over twenty years, but I never liked the place, and I don't think Orson and Helen were particularly fond of it either. When I found myself on my own, the kids having left before Eleanor passed, I spent six months looking around houses on the mainland, and eventually fell in love with a place in Herne Bay. The suburb is perfectly located—close to the Auckland Harbour Bridge that links the CBD with the North Shore, just five minutes from my office, with four beaches and half the best restaurants in the city.

Although nowhere near as big as the family mansion—only four bedrooms opposed to the mansion's nine—it has a large pool, and a beautiful north-facing view across the beach, so on the evenings I'm home, I'm able to watch the sunset paint Waitematā Harbour with oranges and purples until the stars pop out onto the midnight sky.

Eleanor was extremely sociable and loved to entertain, and I rarely had time to myself. But now I spend hours on the deck, reading, enjoying the fact that the only sounds I can hear are the waves tumbling across the beach.

MIDNIGHT SECRET

I installed the exercise equipment into a spare room shortly after moving in, and now I have my own gym, also facing the beach. I usually enjoy working out, but today I find little pleasure during the twenty minutes I spend running flat out on the treadmill, glowering instead every time I think about Genevieve Beaumont and the article in Kōrero. Trying to burn off my frustration, I put myself through a series of rigorous weight training exercises, pushing myself hard until my tee is soaked with sweat and my muscles are trembling with exertion.

Only then, as I head to the shower, do I see a message from Orson on my phone.

You know what the meeting is about? he asks.

I hesitate, wincing, then grit my teeth and reply, *Probably the article in Kōrero.*

It takes about thirty seconds—presumably the time needed to find and read the article— for him to come back with: *WTF?*

I don't reply.

Five minutes later, he messages again, *I'll be at the helipad at 11.30 if you want to join me.*

I message back, *See you then,* and I head to the shower with a growing sense of doom. It's just starting to sink in how stupid I've been. I should have made an anonymous telephone bid. But now not only do I have to contend with the reactions of the wider business community, I have to deal with my friends and family—and Marama's family.

I don't know whether I'm more concerned about Rangi or Kingi. Rangi is my business partner, and I respect our relationship and his advice and support.

But Kingi is protective of his sister. And he's a *lot* bigger than me.

I'm not really worried about him getting physical, and even if he did I can handle myself, but I do feel an unusual flicker of nervousness at the thought of both their reactions.

Half of me is tempted to cry off the meeting and say I'm busy or unwell. But I've never been one to shy away from my responsibilities, and I have to face what I'm sure will be the very loud and unpleasant music at some point, so I might as well get it over with.

As I headed into my forties, I knew that if I wanted to watch my weight and health I needed to eat well and exercise daily. I already had a personal trainer and dietician, and he suggested that intermittent fasting was a good method for men to keep their weight down. So for years I've only eaten between twelve and eight pm, and therefore I don't normally have breakfast. But it's Sunday, and I'm single and don't have to live by anyone else's rules anymore, so in a fit of rebelliousness I make myself a bacon and cheese sandwich and eat it on the deck while I catch up on my emails.

After that, feeling a little queasy and already regretting the sandwich, I change into a shirt, jacket, and trousers, and catch an Uber over to the helipad at Mechanics Bay.

Orson is already there, in the helicopter preparing for flight, and I cross the tarmac, open the door, and swing up into the seat next to him. He passes me a set of headphones, and I put them on and angle the mic in front of my mouth.

"Morning," he says.

"Morning."

He glances at me, but doesn't say anything further. Instead, he talks to the tower, requesting permission to fly, starts the rotor blades, and then the helicopter lifts and heads out across the harbor, heading east for Waiheke.

I look down at the Pacific Ocean, seeing the beautiful curve of a whale's fluke arc out of the water before it descends. It's a gorgeous day, the sunlight sparkling on the surface. But it's tough to enjoy it when I know what's coming.

Sure enough, we're only minutes out of the harbor when Orson says, "So…"

I study the fishing boats heading out for the day.

He blows out a breath. "Okay, what the fuck?"

I frown at him. My parents taught me that cursing was evidence of a weak character, and I've brought my kids up the same way, but Orson's language leaves a lot to be desired at times.

"Don't give me that look," he says. "If anything needed an expletive, it's that article. I'm not the one in trouble here."

I scowl at him, because he's right.

"What were you thinking?" he asks.

"I was trying to save Rangi's daughter from the pack of prowling wild dogs that were circling her."

"By bidding a million dollars?" he asks. "What was the bid before yours?"

"Eighty thousand."

He gives a short laugh. I glower.

"Well I guess that did the trick," he says. "What did Marama have to say about it?"

"She was… confused."

"Are you going to sit for the portrait?"

"I said I wouldn't, but I think I have to, because she has to submit a painting as part of the auction's exhibition."

"That'll be interesting. What style of portrait would you have done?"

"I don't think it's up to me. The idea of it being an Empowerment Auction was that the women are the ones in charge."

"Well, that's going to be interesting."

"Not sure that's the word I'd use to describe it."

He's silent for a moment. Then he says, "Can I ask you something?"

"Do I have a choice?"

"Not really. Are you… interested in her? In Marama?"

I open my mouth to reply. Close it again. Then say, "No, of course not."

"You might want to practice that before you get to Midnight," he advises.

"Thanks for the tip."

We don't talk again for the rest of the journey.

He lands the helicopter on Midnight's pad, hands the keys over to the staff who look after it, and we walk down the steps toward the main building.

I still find it strange when I think back five years to how this place looked before the club was built. My father had passed away just six months before, and although he left the house I grew up in to my mother, and he gave my younger brothers each a decent piece of land on the mainland, he bequeathed the vast area of his farmland in a prime location on Waiheke to me.

At the time, I thought I'd probably just sell it, but then Orson told me about Huxley's idea of forming a consortium of hand-picked wealthy businessmen and women, with the intention of developing a business club and resort, and donating the proceeds to charity. Orson said Huxley was looking for a site, and suggested the land I'd inherited.

My father—technically my stepfather, but I've called him my father since he adopted me when I was thirteen—was an incredibly altruistic man who took on me and my two brothers and made us into the successful businessmen we are, and for me it felt like a way I could honor him and give something back to the community. So I offered Huxley the land, and the construction of the Midnight Club began.

While anyone can stay here, we advertise it mainly as an exclusive resort that's especially suitable for business people. Our aim was to provide a luxury setting for companies to hold conferences and retreats, and so far we've had the biggest dairy, construction, and telecommunication companies come here, as well as the All Blacks rugby team. We offer a small amphitheater for lectures, several large function rooms, and many smaller meeting rooms with a big staff to wait hand and foot on the guests, offering them efficient business services, as well as first-class refreshments.

The Michelin Guide doesn't feature New Zealand, but we do have a Michelin chef working for us who produces the most amazing food that's won the restaurant a Kiwi Cuisine Good Food Award of Three Hats, which is the very highest that can be given, and of which we're incredibly proud. Our bars offer several hundred whiskeys and other spirits, and the nightclub is the very best, classy and well designed to provide nooks and private rooms for late-night business deals, as well as an entertainment outlet for those who need to let off some steam after a busy working day.

The buildings sit ringed by hills, nestled in a shallow dip that leads down to a private beach and the sparkling blue Pacific beyond. It's a superb site, created by an architect with expertise in biophilic design, which means it integrates nature-inspired elements like plants, water features, and colors to create a sense of connection to nature. The hotel rooms have open floor plans and large windows to make the most of the natural light, and the furniture is created from natural materials like wood and bamboo.

There are several large pools and hot tubs for guests, all laid out within carefully tended gardens full of palms and ferns. And the grounds, which include tennis courts and other sports facilities, are surrounded by locally sourced plants and trees that are starting to reach their full potential and make the place look as if it's sprung out of the natural bush. We even have a healing pool nearby, known as the Waiora, which belongs to Scarlett, Orson's girl, and the two of them are now developing the site and creating an area for guests to be able to partake of the healing waters and spend quiet time by the waterfall in a safe but spiritual setting. I want to take a walk down there at some point. It's a nice place for personal reflection and for thinking of those who have passed.

"You're quiet," Orson says as we cross the drive toward the building. "Are you worried about the meeting?"

"No," I reply, even though I am, a little. "I was thinking about your mother."

"Oh." He glances at me. We rarely talk about Eleanor.

He slows to a halt, so I stop too.

"I'm sure there must have been other women," Orson says, "but you never talk about them."

I don't reply. I know he had as difficult a relationship with Eleanor as I did, and his feelings for her are mixed. But she was still his mother, and I would feel awkward discussing my relationship with other women with him.

He looks away, at the ocean. Then he looks back at me. "I don't expect you to be a monk. Mum's been gone a long time, and I expected you to move on eventually. Maybe even marry again. But not Marama. Out of all people… She's not the one."

"I know."

"Do you?"

I stiffen. "I'm not going to be lectured about who I can and can't date by the guy who had no qualms getting involved with my enemy's daughter."

He frowns. "That's different. I didn't plan for that to happen."

"Nobody plans to fall in love."

"Do you love Marama?"

"Of course not. I hardly know the girl."

He tips his head to the side. "Are you *in* love with her?" It's a distinction I made to him when we talked about his feelings for Scarlett.

I hesitate. Then I say, "Absolutely not."

He gives a short nod, apparently mollified. "All right. Let's get this over with."

I follow him into the building, unable to still a flicker of unease deep inside me as I think about Marama's quiet, radiant beauty, and the warmth in her eyes as she looked up at me last night. But no, that's just lust, pure and simple. I want her—I don't deny that. My body lusts after hers. But my heart remains firmly separate.

We cross the lobby, order ourselves a takeaway coffee from the barista, then head for the offices, knowing that the Midnight Circle will be meeting in the main board room. Sure enough, as we approach the glass-walled room, I can see that the other six members are already there, seated around the table: Huxley and his wife Elizabeth, Mack Hart, Joanna, Kingi, and Rangi.

Orson pushes open the door and I follow him in. I glance around the room quickly as Orson walks around the table to sit on the other side. Elizabeth and Joanna say hello, then return their gazes to their phones. Mack and Huxley both say, "Morning," and there's a touch of amusement in both sets of eyes.

Kingi meets my gaze with a stony glare. No amusement there.

Rangi doesn't even look up. His gaze is fixed on the table, and he seems lost in thought.

I sit opposite Orson and sip my coffee.

"Sorry to call you all in," Huxley says. "But I assume you've all seen the article in Kōrero this morning, and I thought it merited a discussion."

"Is this about the latest episode of Shortland Street?" Orson asks. "Because I'm afraid I missed it."

I stare at him, surprised at his levity and oddly touched by his support.

Kingi glares at Huxley, who holds up a hand in an unspoken communication, as if they discussed this previously, and Huxley is indicating he'll take care of it.

"This isn't a laughing matter," Huxley states. "We've all worked hard to promote the Midnight Club as an exclusive high-class resort, and to make the Midnight Circle consortium a respected and trustworthy business. The last thing we need is gossip and scandal surrounding one of our members."

"Spencer," Joanna says, giving me a baffled, impatient look. "Seriously. What were you thinking?"

I lean back in my chair and rest an ankle on the opposite knee, holding my coffee cup. "I understand why you've chosen to go down the professional angle," I say to Huxley, and follow it with a glance around the room. "And I do apologize for any negative publicity I've brought to the Club or the Circle. That wasn't my intention. The last thing I would want to do is bring trouble for the Circle. But I didn't attend the auction as part of the Circle, and the article focuses more on me, so I'm confident it will impinge only on me personally."

"And Marama," Kingi says.

I study my coffee cup and don't reply.

Mack has ADHD, and he possesses a couple of fidget toys that he uses during meetings. He has one now, a tiny silver and black spinner, and he plays with it subconsciously as he says, "The Midnight Club franchise might have been Huxley's idea, but we're all aware of your generous donation of land for this resort, and of the fact that you brought a level of prestige and esteem to the Circle when you agreed to join. You're well respected in the business community. So I guess it's just that we're…" He tips his head to the side as he chooses his words. "…surprised by what happened last night."

I'm tired of tiptoeing around. Was what I did that bad that it deserves a dressing down from my peers? I lean forward, forearms on the table, and Rangi finally looks up and meets my eyes.

"When I first heard about the auction, I told Marama she shouldn't take part," I say. "We all know Genevieve Beaumont—she's smart, and she's ruthless, and she hates the Midnight Club because we didn't make her part of the Circle. She's already targeted Helen and convinced her to join her crusade. And now she wants to poach Marama too. She knows how to appeal to women's egos."

"That is true," Joanna says. "She's tried to get me to jump ship."

"And I know Victoria can't stand her either," Elizabeth adds. "You know how much she hates being used as a symbol of transgender issues."

"You weren't there," I tell Rangi earnestly. "Genevieve was parading these women across the stage like cattle at a market, and asking everyone to bid on them under the pretense of it being about empowering women. Do you think it was other women who won the bids?"

Rangi frowns, then looks away.

"No," I say, tapping on the table to emphasize my point, "the article didn't mention that, but every single winner was a man, most of them twenty or thirty years older than I am. And then it was Marama's turn, and she came on the stage looking young and beautiful, and all around me I could hear the whispers beginning." Fury billows through me. "I was not going to have that pack of snarling dogs bidding on your daughter like she was a prize heifer," I snap. "So I took her off the table. I did it on the spur of the moment, and I hope you would have done the same if it were the other way around, and it was Helen who was up there."

Silence falls. I glance around, relieved to see that they obviously believe me.

Even if I am lying.

I try not to wince. I was mostly telling the truth. The auction was degrading, and I did bid a million on the spur of the moment. But I have to admit that part of the reason for the outrageous amount was to impress Marama, and to stake my claim. Well, I'm not called the Wolf of Waiheke for nothing.

"On the bright side," Orson says cheerfully, "the million dollars will go toward women's art programs, so that's good PR for us."

"And Marama was a little under the radar before," Elizabeth says, "but it has put her in the spotlight. Okay maybe she'd prefer the focus to have been on her art, but I understand that it's landed her a commission from the Te Whaihanga Toi Foundation."

"Oh?" It's the first I've heard of it.

"Hariata Pere and Genevieve Beaumont have commissioned her to do a series of paintings for an exhibition to be displayed at Lumen," Elizabeth continues. "It's going to be called Maramataka."

"The lunar calendar?" Joanna clarifies, and Rangi and Kingi nod.

"The rising of the moon," Elizabeth says. "With themes of female power and sexual agency." She looks at me, and this time there's a touch of mischief in her eyes. "I believe your portrait is to be the first of the series."

Orson has just taken a mouthful of coffee, and he coughs and sprays some of it over the table. "Sorry," he says, mopping it up hastily with a serviette.

Kingi snorts, and Rangi's lips curve up. "Well if that doesn't show how karma works, I don't know what does," he says.

I roll my eyes. "Bring it on," I say. "I can handle it."

Huxley laughs. "All right." He gets to his feet. "Let's play it by ear and see how it goes. Thanks for coming, everyone."

The others also rise and start making their way out. I stay where I am, finishing off my coffee. "Thanks," I mouth to Orson as he passes.

He nods. "You want to come back on the heli?"

"Yeah, can you give me a couple of minutes?"

"Sure." He heads out.

MIDNIGHT SECRET

Kingi passes me and also nods, but doesn't say anything. Then there's only me and Rangi left, sitting at the table, as the door closes.

My old friend and business colleague looks at me. "You really did it for her, and for me?"

I nod. "You didn't see them. It was feral out there. I couldn't bear the thought of one of them having her."

He gets slowly to his feet and walks around the table, stopping when he reaches me.

Then he bends a little, so his mouth is near my ear—not that anyone can overhear us anyway.

"You touch her," he murmurs, "I'll break your fucking legs."

He waits a moment. I don't say anything and just study my coffee cup, outwardly calm, while inwardly my heart bangs on my ribs.

Eventually, he straightens. I half expect him to say something else, but he doesn't; he just walks past me, and heads out of the door.

Chapter Eight

Marama

As two p.m. approaches on Tuesday, I take a final glance around the room where Spencer and I will be spending the next few hours, my stomach full of butterflies. Mum and Dad turned this room into a studio for me when I was a teenager, and even though I've not lived at home for many years, they've kept this and my room the way they always were in case I visit, which I appreciate. Although I haven't worked here for a long time, as soon as I set up my first canvas and started to paint, I felt as if I'd never left.

I've spent all morning getting everything ready. The place is spotless, apart from the usual paraphernalia I need to work—the table full of disposable palettes, water pots, cleaning cloths, and of course the many tubes of paint.

I've set up the chair where I want Spencer to sit in the bay window with the garden behind him. It's nice and light, and it's also an attractive backdrop. I'm not using a canvas because I'm not planning on this work being the finished picture. Today I just want to do some sketches and try to capture his likeness ready for when I paint his proper portrait.

I've put a table nearby in case he wants a drink. I add a cushion to the chair, as I want him to be comfortable for a couple of hours and not fidget too much. Then I tell myself to stop fussing, and head out of the room.

I walk slowly through the house, enjoying the peace and quiet. Not that it's super noisy when my parents are home. Dad's usually either at his office in the CBD, at the Midnight Club, or working in his office here. But Mum often has friends around, usually belonging to one of the many societies of which she's a part. She holds regular gatherings in our dining room as the table can seat sixteen, and she has several members of staff on hand to supply the chatting women with drinks and food. But it always amazes me how noisy women can be. Continual talking and raucous laughter cut right through the house, and I end up putting on my noise-cancelling headphones when I want to work.

It's not an ideal arrangement, and I don't plan on staying here long term. But I'm still not a hundred percent sure what I want to do or where I'm going to live, and it didn't make sense to live out of a suitcase in a hotel. Anyway, it has been nice to see Mum and Dad a little, as Connor disliked all my family and refused to come up here to visit them.

I'm not going to think about him, though. My days of tears and regret over him are done.

I reach the living room just in time to see Spencer's blue Bentley Continental GT Speed pulling up on the drive. It's big, sleek, and dark, an unmistakable symbol of wealth and power. When Dad's home, his personal assistant, who doubles as his chauffeur, is usually here, and he'd normally approach Spencer and offer to garage the car or maybe clean it for him. But he's away, and this time Spencer locks his car and walks unimpeded up to the front door.

There are no staff at home at all today, as the housekeeper finishes at midday on Tuesdays, and any other people that Mum and Dad might require have been given a few days off on my insistence that I don't need anyone. Only Joe, the gardener, is here, and I can hear him on the sit-on lawnmower way off in the distance. So it's up to me to answer the door, and I open it as Spencer walks up.

My pulse immediately picks up speed. He's wearing a white shirt with a navy jacket, and oh my God, faded jeans. I've never seen him in jeans before. Wow, that's super sexy. Every inch of this man screams class and money. He certainly knows how to make the best of his wealth.

"Good afternoon," he says, his voice a deep purr, the same as the engine of his car.

"Afternoon." I move back to let him enter the house, and I receive a whiff of his cologne as he passes. It's classy and seductive, something woodsy, and expensive, no doubt. It clings to him like confidence. Like power.

Like sin.

My mouth has gone dry, and I swallow hard, closing the door behind him. I feel a little dizzy, as if I've had one glass of wine too many, although I haven't had any alcohol today.

"You managed to clear your schedule for the afternoon?" I ask. "Or do you have to go in a couple of hours?"

"No, all clear." He pushes his jacket off his shoulders and lets it slip down his back, catching it in a hand, then hangs it on the coat stand by the front door. Then he toes off his shoes and leaves them there, too. He turns back to face me, and I find myself breathless. His blue eyes are *bright as* today, vivid and clear. I think he might have just had a shower because the beautiful silver flashes of his hair are damp at the temples, and his jaw looks so smooth he must have shaved very recently. He's obviously changed out of his work suit, too. He's prepared himself for me. I feel oddly flattered.

"Come in the kitchen with me," I say, gesturing with my head, "and I'll get us a drink, and then we can head to the studio."

"You look stunning today," he says, following me through the living room to the kitchen.

I look down at myself in surprise. I always take care with my makeup, but my hair is up in a scruffy bun, and I'm wearing my favorite artist's gear—a pair of well-worn, tie-dyed dungarees in all the shades of a rainbow, over a white tee.

"I've hardly dressed up," I say wryly, going over to the coffee machine. "Want a latte?"

"Please. And it doesn't matter. The dungarees with the bare feet is an arresting combination."

I glance at my toes—I painted the nails a sparkly blue yesterday. "The color's not a step too far for you?"

"What do you mean?"

I turn the machine on and pop a capsule in while he leans a hip against the bench, folding his arms. I can't believe I'm alone with Spencer Cavendish. Feeling a surge of mischief, I say, "Older men are normally more traditional in their choices."

He lifts an eyebrow. That makes me giggle, and I go over to the fridge to retrieve the milk.

"I'm only forty-six," he says. "Not sixty-six."

"It was you who kept pointing out our age difference," I remind him, pouring the milk into a jug.

He doesn't reply, but his lips curve up, because he knows I'm right.

I'm conscious of him watching me as I make the coffee, steaming the milk and pouring it onto the espresso. I let him look, though, before finally turning off the machine and bringing his mug over to him.

He takes it. "Thank you."

"You're welcome."

We both sip them, our eyes meeting over the rim of the mugs. My pulse continues to race, and I still feel breathless. The air around us feels charged, I don't know why. Well, I know he's attracted to me. That much is obvious. But he's made it clear that he's mentally painted a red circle with a line through it over my head, and I can't imagine that Spencer Cavendish has ever given in to his desires. I'm sure he has iron willpower. He wouldn't have risen to the dizzy heights he has if he wasn't able to curb his appetites.

Briefly, I think about what those appetites might be, and my eyes glaze over. Spencer's lips curve up.

"Stop it," he scolds.

"What? I'm not doing anything."

"You know perfectly well what."

I poke my tongue out at him. "You want a cookie with your coffee?"

"No thank you."

I take a cookie out of the tin on purpose, even though I don't really want one. "Do you ever have any fun?" I ask tartly before crunching into it.

"Only between the hours of nine and ten p.m., and then only if all my reports are finished and my inbox has under ten emails."

I snort. "Wild man."

"You have no idea."

I don't know what he means by that, so I finish my cookie and remove the crumbs from my lip with my tongue, which earns me another wry look, and beckon with my head for him to follow me.

I lead the way through the house to my studio, open the door, and gesture for him to go in first. He walks in, and I follow him and close the door behind me.

I try to see the place through his eyes. It's quite girly, I suppose. The large room has off-white walls and kauri-wood floorboards. Several of my paintings on the walls add a splash of color. A sofa sits in the corner, covered with a colorful throw I bought in Italy and half a dozen mismatched cushions. It faces the floor-to-ceiling windows and the garden beyond—I use it for reading, and occasionally dozing off. Warm-white fairy lights run above the windows and around the walls, not for light, because it's a light-filled room, but because I like the magical quality they give.

"I painted a lot here as a teen," I say, "and it's been great to get back in here."

"Are you thinking of staying?"

"In the house?" I pull an eek face. "God, no. I don't want to live with my parents for the rest of my life."

He chuckles, walking around the room. "You'd like your own place, with a studio?"

"I'm thinking about it. A friend of mine in Wellington spent a long time turning her apartment into the perfect studio, and she lost it when the landlord decided to renovate the building into luxury offices. She was devastated. The light was perfect there, the neighbors were other creatives, and she thrived in that environment. She found it so hard to recreate it somewhere else. It's not just losing your house, you know. It's losing your shortcuts, your neighbors, the smell of the bakery in the morning. You don't just move people—you rip up the roots they've been growing for years. So I'm reluctant to make that commitment."

I'm babbling because I'm nervous. He nods but doesn't say anything, and I remember then that his business is property development, so he must be used to relocating tenants. Oops. Shut up, Marama.

Shelves full of books line part of one wall: books about art techniques and famous artists, nature books, because I love painting leaves and flowers and trees, and illustrated books about Māori mythology to give me inspiration, among many others. He browses the shelves, and the circular coffee table near the sofa that's covered with more books, magazines, and several sketchpads.

Then he walks over to the slanted desk where I do a lot of my drawing and bends to look at the sketches sitting there—stylized leaves and flowers that I'm trialing for the new series of paintings, some in pencil, some with watercolor as I practice different colors.

"These are good," he says. "You like painting natural objects." It's a statement not a question, and it reminds me that he went to my exhibition and actually bought a piece.

"A lot of my work blends fantasy and reality. Real-life people or objects depicted with fantasy elements, or mythological characters with accurate flora and fauna."

"A foot in both worlds?"

It's a nice way to put it, and I smile. "Maybe."

He stops to look up at one of my canvases on the wall. I sip my coffee, trying to quell the butterflies in my stomach.

Finally, he turns and wanders toward the chair that's waiting in the bay window. "For me?" he asks.

I nod. "Do you like the room?" I ask, somewhat shyly, half-expecting him to mock the girlish colors and fairy lights.

But to my surprise he says, "I do. There's a kind of spiritual atmosphere here, as if it's hallowed ground. Do you consider it *wāhi tapu*?" It's Māori for a sacred place.

I'm very touched that he understands. "I do. I prefer it if people don't come in here. The housekeeper dusts and vacuums, and my parents can come in, obviously, although they don't tend to interrupt me when I'm working. But I leave the door closed most of the time, and it has a 'Private' sign on it to discourage any of Mum's friends or anyone else visiting."

"Do you say a *karakia* before you paint?" It means prayer.

"I do, especially when I'm painting ancestors or powerful Māori themes. It sounds pretentious to say my work is spiritual, but I feel that creating art is a form of sacred storytelling and a way to honor my culture."

"I don't think that's pretentious. It must feel godly to be an artist. Bringing things into being that weren't there before."

It's exactly how I feel, and I warm through. "Right," I say as I sit on the stool by my easel, "take your clothes off and sit in the chair."

He stares at me.

"I'm kidding," I say with a laugh. "Don't look so scared."

He scowls. "I wasn't scared." He sits and leans back as if it's a throne that was personally made for him. Talk about owning everything you come into contact with. "Where do you want me to face?"

"Forward is fine. Find a point ahead of you and fix your gaze on it." I adjust my stool. I'm slightly to the right of him, with the easel at an angle, so I can see both him and the painting without moving my head. "I'm going to start with a pencil sketch, just to see if I can get a likeness."

"Okay."

"Do you paint at all?"

He chuckles. "No."

"Do you write?"

"No."

"Play an instrument?"

"The xylophone."

"Really?"

He laughs. "No."

I glare at him. "So what's your creative outlet?"

"I don't have one."

I purse my lips. "Kingi said he thought you were a robot, and I said I didn't believe that. I'm beginning to wonder."

He just sips his coffee, watching me over the rim of the cup.

"There's something you're not telling me," I say softly. "What don't you want to admit?"

He looks into his cup. Then he says, casually, as if he's talking about hedge funds, "I make doll's furniture."

My eyebrows rise. "Sorry—what?"

He shrugs. "From wood. Chairs. Tables. The occasional four-poster bed. I have a workshop in my house in Herne Bay. I spend most of my free time there, listening to music or podcasts while I work. It's an escape."

My jaw drops at this insight into his private world. The thought of the confident, somewhat aggressive Spencer Cavendish making tiny wooden objects that require finesse and care is unexpected and oddly intimate.

To hide my surprise that he confessed his secret passion, I turn to the sketchpad on the easel, pick up my pencil, and start to make light marks to get his features in proportion—eyes halfway down the oval of the face, the nose at the bottom of the middle third, and the mouth just above the halfway mark of the bottom third.

"When did you begin to make those?" I ask while I work.

"My father built dollhouses from scratch. They were things of beauty. Stained-glass windows, real parquet floors, sweeping staircases. I started making the furniture to go inside them when I was fourteen."

"Your father?" The head is five eyes wide, the space between the eyes roughly the width of one eye. "Is that your birth father, or your foster father?"

He looks surprised that I'm aware of his situation. "My foster father."

"How old were you when you were placed with him?"

"I'd just turned thirteen."

I start sketching the shape of his face. Men's skulls are different from women's—they have pronounced brow ridges, and the areas where the muscles attach are more defined. "Your two brothers were placed with you, is that right?"

"Yeah. My sisters went to another home." He sighs. "It worked out well in the end. The couple who took them were both doctors. Two of my three sisters ended up being doctors too and one is a nurse, and they all love their jobs. My foster father was a businessman, and my foster mother worked from home—she was a seamstress and altered clothes, and she also made tiny cushions and bedding and curtains for the dollhouses."

"Kingi said your father was the one who recognized your potential."

He smiles. "Yeah, he pushed us all very hard, but me especially. He saw something in me that I hadn't even recognized in myself. He paid for me to go to university, and invested a lot of time and money in me."

With the proportions marked, I begin work on the finer details, starting with his eyes. It means I'm able to spend time looking at them, which is enjoyable. "What do you think he saw in you?"

His expression turns quizzical. "I... don't know. He said my experiences had made me resilient and determined, which is probably true. He recognized that I had a talent with figures, and he pushed me to take mathematics and economics, and paid extra for a tutor to teach me about finance. And he was very open with his business, and let me go to work with him at weekends and shadow him, I'm not sure why."

"Probably because most teenage boys are smoking weed and drinking alcohol and knocking girls up."

"Well, one out of three ain't bad," he says, reminding me that he got Eleanor pregnant at eighteen.

I decide that this is going to be just a pencil drawing, and start adding shading for his brows. "So... tell me about Amiria."

The shutters come down, and his expression becomes carefully guarded.

Amiria was Scarlett's mother, and Kingi has told me the backstory there. Spencer and Scarlett's father, Blake Stone, went to school together and were firm friends, until Spencer started dating Amiria, and she went off with Blake. Kingi said there were other issues involved, with Blake also screwing Spencer over in a business deal, but he believes their thirty-year feud was mainly due to the fact that Blake stole the girl that Spencer truly loved.

"Was she the love of your life?" I ask.

He glares at me, and I'm sure he's going to tell me to mind my own business. But to my surprise he then sighs and says, "I thought she was, for a long time."

"Did you love her more than Eleanor?"

He tips his head to the side. "You like asking penetrating questions, don't you?"

"I'm interested in what makes you tick. And don't tip your head, please."

He straightens it slowly; I can see he doesn't like being told what to do.

"Why?" he asks.

"Why what?"

"Why are you interested?" His expression turns suspicious. "Are you supposed to report back to Genevieve?"

Part of the reason for my curiosity is due to Genevieve's request to "paint his weaknesses." To "strip him of that smug confidence and expose the vulnerable man inside." He turned me down in a way that made me feel an inch high, when I had opened up to him, as sure as if I'd physically pulled my ribs apart and exposed my heart. I hate him a little for that, and it's the main reason I agreed to do the commission—I want to put him in his place.

But that's not the only reason. So I say, "No." Well, it's not a complete lie. The painting is going to be a representation of what I find out. Not a report. "You fascinate me," I admit. "You ooze power, confidence, and wealth, and I want to peek behind the curtain and find out how you became the man you are."

His lips curve up. "And you're going to show that in the painting?"

"Maybe."

"Not sure I like that idea."

I shrug. "You bid for me. I was very clear that the portrait was The Face I See. How I choose to see you, not as you choose to be seen."

He doesn't reply, but I can see that makes him uncomfortable.

"Tell me about Genevieve," I say, starting to sketch his straight, almost Roman nose. "Did you two have a thing?"

I lift my gaze to his. His humor has faded. He really doesn't like her.

"No," he says.

That really surprises me. I was convinced they must have had a fling, and it was the fact that he didn't want more that has caused her bitterness.

"Seriously?" I say. "Are you sure?"

"I'm sure." Now he's amused.

"So… why do you both dislike each other so much?"

He shifts in the chair. "She wanted to join the Midnight Circle."

My eyebrows rise. "Oh… I didn't know that."

"Huxley personally approached six of us, and then spread the word that he was looking for an eighth member. Helen was one of the applicants, but she has no business experience to speak of."

Ah… that explains a lot. I'd wondered why his daughter was so bitter toward him, and why she'd gone over to Lumen.

"So Genevieve applied," I say. "Why was she not chosen?"

He doesn't reply. He observes me, clearly thinking about what to say.

I let him ponder and concentrate on the drawing. It's coming along well for an initial sketch. After this I might take some photos from various angles to use later in my main painting.

I've decided that I will do a standard-ish portrait for him, because the guy did pay a million dollars for it. But he will also be the subject of the first in the series I'm doing for the commission. And that one is going to be very different.

I glance back at him. He still looks thoughtful.

"You really didn't sleep with her?" I ask, puzzled.

He shakes his head. "I'm not sure I should say. She's kind of your employer now, right? I heard about the commission."

I start sketching strands of his hair. "I suppose. If I'm honest, I don't particularly like her personally. I admire what she's achieved. I do think it's harder to get on in business as a woman, and as a Māori woman especially. But I find her quite… snidey, I suppose."

His lips curve up again. "Yeah, that's a good description." He sighs, which I'm beginning to recognize as a sign that he's made up his mind. "She approached me," he says. "One evening, at Huxley's club, while Midnight was still being born, she came and introduced herself and sat at my table. She flirted with me all evening, outrageously so. Huxley was watching, and he quietly took me to one side and told me she'd applied for the final seat on the Circle. When she suggested we get a room together, I knew she was trying to influence me, and I told her she'd ruined her chances of getting the seat. I don't like people who use tactics like that to get what they want." His face shows his distaste that she'd sleep with him just to close the business deal.

"Hell hath no fury," I say. "I can understand that."

He gives me an impatient look. "It's very different from our interaction. She's almost the same age as me. She wasn't the daughter of my business partner. And I didn't want her."

My hand stops on the paper. My heart bangs. He didn't want her. But he does want me?

My gaze slides to him to discover him watching me. There's heat in his eyes now—yes, that was what he meant. Ohhh… fuck. Once again, the air feels charged, intimate, and emotional, and it's difficult to breathe.

This sexy, confident, determined guy wants me. I guess I should be relieved he's decided I'm out of bounds.

Not disappointed.

Chapter Nine

Spencer

Marama's amber eyes stare at me for a long moment, and then she drops her gaze back to the table at her side. She spends a moment rearranging her pencils, looking nonchalant, but I can see the pulse racing in her throat.

My lips curve up, just a little.

She looks amazing today. Her hair is pinned up in a very scruffy bun with crescent-moon-shaped clips, and tendrils tumble all around her face and neck. For a moment I didn't think she was wearing any makeup, but when I look closely I can see she is, but it's just in neutral tones, and expertly applied. Her rainbow-colored dungarees make her look flaky and a little wild, especially with the blue toenails. She's so unlike the women I'm used to being around, who are all cool, calm, and composed. But in this room, with her light-brown skin and *moko kauae*, she looks like Hina Marama in the flesh more than ever—a Māori goddess full of fire and life.

She makes my heart race—and it doesn't do that often these days.

She changes her pencil, then returns to sketching. "So you turned Genevieve down, and now she's out to get you?"

"Something like that."

She gives me a curious look. "Did she create Lumen because Midnight rejected her?"

"There's no way of telling, but I would assume so, wouldn't you? Lumen—the light confronting what she sees as Midnight's darkness. Approaching our women and luring them over."

She lifts an eyebrow. "We do have a mind of our own, you know. Maybe those who've gone over to her have done so because they feel she offers them better opportunities."

"I'm sure that's the case. But not every opportunity is what it seems."

She sketches quietly. Then she says, "You think the auction was just a way for her to exercise her agenda?"

"Yes."

"And my commission?"

I hesitate. Then I say, "It's not my place to say."

She snorts. "Spencer Cavendish, holding back on an opinion? I don't believe it."

I give her a wry look. "I can see how it's a great opportunity for you. And getting on the right side of Hariata Pere isn't going to do you any harm. Exhibiting at Lumen will mean your work will stand a chance of being noticed by many top businesswomen, and that can only be good for you."

"But…"

"I don't like to think of her using you, that's all."

"There's no way she could possibly be doing it because she truly believes in my talent?"

"Oh, I'm sure she does. But I don't think Genevieve Beaumont would do anything that didn't benefit her own business and personal beliefs in some way."

"Spencer… come on… the same could be said about you and any man in business."

I frown. "I don't believe that's true."

"I'm not talking about Midnight here, because I understand the charitable nature of that and I think it's commendable. But in your own business? You don't agree that every interaction you have, any deal you make, is purely to benefit you in some way?"

"No deal I make is done to fit an agenda. I'm not trying to raise men above women. I deal with women at the office all the time. I work purely to make money and to grow my business."

"Do you enjoy closing a deal?" she asks.

"Yes, of course."

"Do you like how it makes you feel?"

I don't reply.

"So it's not just about making money," she says, taking my silence as affirmation. "You do it because it makes you feel powerful. I saw you scowl when I called you the Wolf of Waiheke, but I think you love it."

I glare at her. She meets my eyes, then continues to sketch.

"I wonder whether losing Amiria, and then Eleanor becoming pregnant, made you feel out of control," she says. "And that's why you've cultivated this image of being dominant and assertive. If that's why you're so bossy." She glances at me. "Oh dear, have I touched a nerve?"

"People don't talk to me like this," I say, somewhat icily.

"Sorry," she says, not looking apologetic in the least.

My fingers tighten on the arms of the chair. "I didn't want this portrait in the first place. I don't know what I'm doing here."

She stops drawing then and lowers her hand. "I'm sorry if I made you uncomfortable," she says softly.

I glare at her, breathing hard.

"You fascinate me," she says. "I'm just trying to see the man behind the wolf."

I shift in the chair. I don't like the way she makes me feel unsettled and off balance. But if I don't like it, why is my heart racing, and why is my stomach full of butterflies?

I want her, but I can't have her. This relationship is forbidden—I shouldn't even be here, and I certainly shouldn't be having intimate conversations with her. But the atmosphere feels charged and intense. I'm close to having a hard on, and that's ridiculous, dangerous even.

"How many relationships have you had since Eleanor died?" she asks.

I don't know why she thinks she can ask me these questions. Nobody else talks to me like this. It's as if the world has tilted, and the tectonic plates are shifting. If I was standing, I'd be unsteady on my feet.

She looks at me.

"Zero," I say.

She stops drawing and her eyebrows rise. "You haven't had any relationships since then?"

"No."

"So what, mainly one-night stands?"

I shift awkwardly, uncomfortable with this line of conversation. "No."

"What do you mean?"

"I dislike the idea of one-night stands."

"But… I don't understand."

I huff a sigh. "I've only ever slept with one woman. Is that clear enough for you?"

She just stares at me, mouth open.

"It's not so shocking," I say irritably. "I met Eleanor at eighteen. She was my first girlfriend."

"What about Amiria?"

"We only dated for a few weeks. We never got that far. And I was a faithful husband."

"But why haven't you been with anyone since Eleanor died?"

I shrug. "Not met the right person."

"So you haven't had sex for six years? What about escorts?"

"I couldn't," I say distastefully.

"I would," she says ruefully. "If there were reputable ones for women. I did some googling a few months ago. There are agencies, but they mainly offer gay or bisexual guys, and they always look seedy. There's nothing… respectable." She rolls her eyes.

"What about Casanovas?"

"What?"

"In the CBD. I don't think they advertise as such, but I've heard they're high-class. Expensive. Discreet. Maybe you should check them out."

She glances at me. "Maybe I will."

I glower at the thought of her hiring a man to service her, and she giggles. Then her expression softens. "I can't believe the powerful, omnipotent Spencer has only been with one woman."

"Not all guys sleep around."

Her expression softens. "That's a fair comment, and I apologize if I insulted you."

I don't reply. If anything, I'm a tad embarrassed that I don't have a slew of affairs to brag about.

"You told me once that you wanted to put me over your knee," she continues, looking mischievous. "Are you dominant in the bedroom?"

My mouth goes dry. I should close this conversation down now. But her eyes glow like the sun, and I find myself saying, "I'm not into whips and chains, if that's what you're asking."

"Breath play?" she asks.

I glare again. "No."

"Collaring?"

"No."

"So Eleanor wasn't your sub as such?"

"God, no. My sexual experience has been quite vanilla," I admit. "Eleanor wasn't exactly... adventurous."

"But you like your women submissive?"

"I don't mind being challenged. Just don't expect to win."

The comment flips a switch. Our eyes lock, and the air between us becomes charged with electricity. Goosebumps rise on my skin, and my cock hardens until it strains at the seam of my trousers.

Something in my gaze makes her tongue tied. A slight flush stains her cheeks, and she moistens her lips with the tip of her tongue. She's all talk, until she realizes who's in charge.

I feel a flare of smug pleasure, quickly followed by the sting of regret. What the hell am I doing? I tear my gaze away. Marama wants me, I can tell, and she doesn't understand the nuances of what us having a relationship of any sort would bring, so she's not going to be the one to step back. I need to be the adult here, and take charge of the situation.

I look back at her. She's sketching again. Her cheeks are still flushed, and her smile has faded. She can feel that I'm rejecting her again, and it's hurt her feelings.

I rarely apologize, or feel the need to explain my actions, but I regret upsetting her. "I'm sorry," I say softly. "You have to understand why we can't get involved."

She doesn't reply. She moves closer to the easel and is quiet as she concentrates on part of the drawing. She's not working on a canvas, and she's only used pencils so far, no color. Occasionally she smudges with her fingers, so I assume this is just a sketch, and not a basis for a larger painting. I wonder what it looks like? I've seen her work, of course, but they've mainly been fantasy pieces with birds and foliage; I have no idea if she's any good at portraits.

We sit quietly for a while. She's at a slight angle to me, on my left, and earlier she asked me to face forward, but it's easy for me to glance at her while she sketches. She frowns slightly, but I don't know if it's from concentration or if she's thinking about me. I want it to be the latter. Dog in the manger, Spencer. If you're not going to take her, let her go.

After a while, she straightens and finishes off her coffee. As she puts the cup down, she says, "You said you're not interested in another relationship. Why is that?"

"I don't want the complication."

"You're never lonely?"

"I'm too busy to be lonely."

"Really?"

"I work long hours. When I am at home, I relish the opportunity to spend time in my workshop and listen to music, or sit on the deck and read to the sounds of the ocean."

"The lone wolf," she says. "Hmm." She picks up her pencil again. "What about at night? You don't get lonely in bed?"

"Eleanor and I had separate bedrooms from the time Orson was young. So no, not really."

Her eyebrows rise. "Why did you have separate bedrooms?"

"It was what she wanted. She liked to go to bed early, but I was never tired until after midnight. She hated being disturbed when she was asleep. And she liked her own space. She was very independent. It suited me well enough."

Marama's gaze settles on me. "Really?" She looks genuinely puzzled. "I have to say, I don't understand that. Part of being in a relationship is cuddling up at night and finding comfort in one another, don't you think?"

"I don't need someone else to complete me. I'm self-sufficient, and I prefer it that way."

"You've never had a relationship like that, have you?" she asks softly. "Loving and caring?"

"I'm not a child. I don't need mollycoddling. When I was married, it was my job to provide for my wife and family, to make sure they had somewhere to live, food on the table, to give the kids a good education, and ensure they had everything they wanted. Eleanor provided me with two children. She was a good hostess and did her wifely duty. I have no complaints."

She turns on her stool to face me, looking exasperated. "'Did her wifely duty'? Are you talking about having sex?"

"I… just meant generally."

"I bet she booked it in, right? Come to my room on Tuesdays and Saturdays at eight p.m. when the kids are in bed? You're glaring at me, so I presume that means I'm close to the mark."

I stiffen in the chair, resentful and angry that she's right. It was a point of contention throughout our marriage. I did my best to make sure that Eleanor enjoyed sex. But the truth was that I truly believe she could have lived without it. She had regular sex with me because she thought that being a good wife meant fulfilling certain roles, and making sure your husband was satisfied in bed was one of them. But she was not a passionate woman. I never felt wanted. Never needed.

And now I sound like a millennial, which pisses me off.

I can either get annoyed at Marama, or make a joke of it. I don't want to sour the mood, so I choose the latter. "It was Wednesdays and Sundays," I reply, "and ten p.m. so she could go to sleep afterward."

She laughs, because she was meant to. "I'm sorry," she says, "I'm honestly not mocking you. It's tough when your libidos don't match. Was she never into sex, not even in the beginning?"

"Maybe the first few years, although she suffered from endometriosis, and that made it uncomfortable for her. I tried to be considerate, but I think it was a big factor in why she just didn't enjoy it much. Maybe. I don't know. It could have been me." My lips twist.

"I'm sure it wasn't," she says softly. "I'm surprised you never had an affair."

I frown. "Of course not. I would never be unfaithful."

"Many men would, if they weren't getting what they needed at home."

Does that mean she blames herself for the fact that Connor cheated on her? I open my mouth to ask her, but before I can form the words, she says, "She was a very lucky woman."

"We were well matched."

She surveys me calmly. "You've said that before. I think that's what you tell yourself, because you don't like to think that you spent… what? Twenty-two years? With a woman who was emotionally distant, and who withheld affection. You've molded yourself into someone who likes clear rules, predictable responses, and who's in charge. I think playing at being dominant makes you feel emotionally shielded."

Astonished, I can only stare at her, as she tips her head to the side and continues, "But I don't think you're emotionally distant or cold. I don't feel that when you look at me. I feel heat, desire, and passion."

She leans forward a little, her eyes shining in the sunlight. "Can you imagine what it might be like to be with someone who is emotionally open, and sex positive? Who doesn't just want sex when it's appropriate and timely, but who thinks about you all the time, and wants you every minute of every day? And who wants to be with you because she likes you, and wants to spend time with you?"

My pulse races. Her words strike at my heart, because buried deep inside me is the thought that my wife didn't really like me at all.

I thought it was because I was unlikeable. I know my relationship with my children isn't great. My business associates deal with me because I get the job done, and I know how to make them money. But I don't have many close friends. Rangi and I have met up socially in the past because that's what you do when you're married—you attend dinner parties at each other's houses and talk business while your wives discuss which charities they're on the board for and discuss the antics of their nannies. Rangi and I understand each other and we work well together. But I haven't seen him much socially since Eleanor died. It's true that I've refused many invitations, but deep down I don't know that I've ever thought of him as a true friend, and we're certainly not close.

I tell myself I don't need friends. And I certainly don't need kindness, tenderness, or devotion. And yet Marama's words open up a crack in my steely heart and fill it with a deep longing I haven't felt since I was a child.

"You deserve love and affection," Marama murmurs, "just the same as everyone else."

"I don't need it." My voice sounds odd, hoarse with held-in emotion.

"I don't believe that," she says. "I think you want it, and need it, more than any man I've ever met." Then she straightens, picks up her pencil, and continues drawing.

I sit there, silently fuming, because it's as if she's shown me a beautiful gem hidden in the depths of a chest at the back of an attic. I'd forgotten this feeling, this unbelievable yearning. I had it all through my childhood, desperate for my parents to love me. By the time I met my foster parents, I'd grown an exoskeleton to protect myself. They loved me, and I loved them back, but I was never able to show it the way I wanted. I was too afraid of being hurt. That fear of rejection was only exacerbated when Amiria left me for Blake.

So in a way, Eleanor suited me perfectly. I understood why she got herself pregnant. In a strange way I admired her for it. She knew what she wanted and she wasn't afraid to do whatever she had to do to get it. I knew where I stood with her. She fitted nicely into my carefully constructed palace of control. She wasn't a great mother, in the traditional sense of the word—baking cakes and running three-legged races with the kids—but then I wasn't a great father either. The children were fed, clothed, sheltered, and cared for, and they received an excellent education, and although I'm sure Freud would find something to criticize about our parenting methods, I think both of us tried hard to the best of our abilities. And I learned to live in that structured world with her restricted, regulated love.

Now, though, listening to Marama's little speech, I feel a deep resentment at the thought that I've somehow missed out. It's too late now. I'm too withdrawn, too shielded, to ever love again.

"You're glaring at me," Marama says.

"Because you unsettle me."

"In what way?"

I shift, irritated, and the words burst out of me, "Because you make me want things I've buried so deep I forgot they were there."

Her eyes meet mine, and it's there again—that electricity, zapping through my system as if I'm Frankenstein's monster, and she's shocking me alive.

Dammit. This girl. She probes me and teases things out of me as if I'm a whelk in a shell.

"I'd rather not talk," I snap.

A smile touches the corners of her lips. "Whatever the customer wants. Would you like me to put some music on?"

"No, silence is fine."

She nods and continues to draw.

We don't talk for about ten minutes. She works studiously, sometimes leaning back and making long, free lines with her pencil, at other times leaning forward and taking time to fill in minute detail.

I sit in the peace and quiet, and watch her. She doesn't tell me off for not looking ahead, but allows me to observe her. I note the way the sunlight turns her dark-brown hair a coppery red. How it warms her light-brown skin, giving it a golden glow. I study her *moko kauae* and wonder what it would be like to kiss her mouth, then her chin, whether the power of it would make my lips tingle.

Growing sleepy in the warm room, I let my gaze slide down her curves beneath the dungarees—the swell of her breasts, the dip of her waist, the roundness of her hips, and all the way down her legs to her pretty feet with their sparkling blue nails. She looks young, healthy, and stunning, filled with life, a true spiritual being, an *atua wāhine* made real.

I don't even realize I've closed my eyes until a shadow falls across me. Something brushes across my lips like a feather. Opening my eyes, I see her moving back, smiling. My lips tingle, just as I anticipated. I think she kissed me. It was such a light touch that I'm not sure if I dreamed it.

"You dozed off," she says.

"No I didn't. I was meditating."

She laughs. "Anyone less likely to meditate I can't imagine. Come on, I've finished this one. Do you want to have a look?"

A little stiff where I've been sitting for a long time, I rise from the chair and follow her to the easel.

I don't know what I expected. I'd hoped that she'd catch my likeness in some way, at least. But I'm astonished to see myself staring back at me from the paper. It's a life-size portrait from the shoulders up, the planes and angles of my face formed from free, loose strokes, with just the eyes, nose and mouth defined.

"It's amazing. It's like looking in a mirror. Except I'm smiling." I'm looking at the viewer with quiet amusement, as if we're sharing a private joke.

"You smile more than you think," she says. "When you look at me, anyway."

She's standing right next to me, with our upper arms just a half inch away. I look down at her, and her eyes capture me, imprisoning me in their amber depths.

My gaze slides to her mouth. Her lips look soft, and I can imagine how they would feel pressed against mine. Would she open her mouth to me willingly? Allow me access, let me stroke her tongue with my own? Would she lift her arms around my neck, lean against me, slide her hands into my hair?

Can you imagine what it might be like to be with someone who is emotionally open, and sex positive? Who doesn't just want sex when it's appropriate and timely, but who thinks about you all the time, and wants you every minute of every day?

A deep ache fills me, my heart thuds, and my cock hardens. She obviously sees something of my desire in my eyes, because her eyes flare, and her lips part. I want her badly. It would be so easy to kiss her. To lose myself in her. To let myself believe it could lead to something more. I crave what she's offering—youth, beauty, sex, affection, maybe even love.

But it's only going to lead to heartache. I can't use her for one night and then discard her, and we can never be a couple because our friends and family would never condone it. Part of me thinks fuck them all, nobody has ever stopped me from having what I wanted. I once told Orson that our family motto was 'See, want, take,' and I believe it. But even if we ignored everyone else, it's unlikely it would ever work. She's going to want children, and I've had my family. And she's too young for me. When she's forty, I'll be fifty-six; when she's fifty, I'll be sixty-six, heading for seventy. Jesus.

We're like two binary stars, caught up in each other's orbit, but destined never to meet. And the sooner I come to terms with that, the better.

Chapter Ten

Marama

The moment that Spencer reasserts dominance over his desires is obvious; the shutters come down over his eyes, his expression hardens, and he tears his gaze away from mine.

He looks back at the painting. "So is that it?" he asks gruffly. "Are we done?"

It's best this way. And I'm not shocked. The man has closed billion-dollar deals without breaking a sweat. He obviously keeps a tight grip on his diet and exercise, which most middle-aged men struggle to accomplish. He's a force of nature, and he's not going to give in to his cravings just for me.

The depth of my disappointment does surprise me, though, and with it comes a touch of pity. While we were talking, I saw the hunger in his eyes when I spoke about being wanted and needed. He doesn't realize it, but for some reason, with me, his poker face is awful. I can feel his desire, for me and for the affection I spoke of. I don't think this guy has been loved or wanted for a long time—maybe never, and that makes me sad.

"You have somewhere you need to be?" I ask.

"No."

"Then no, we're not done. First, I'd like to take some photos, with your permission."

He frowns, but says, "Okay, if you must."

I pick up my phone and bring up the camera. "You don't like your photo being taken?"

"Not particularly."

"Why? You're a gorgeous guy." I take his arm and steer him back into the sunlight.

"Well, thank you. But I don't like looking at myself."

Puzzled, I don't reply, and spend some time getting him into the right position, so he's lit properly. Stepping back, I start taking photographs. If only I'd been able to do this when I was a girl! I take some front-on, both from a distance and zoomed in, causing him to look into the camera with an exasperated expression. Then I move to the side and capture him from various angles, not just his face, but his shoulders and arms, the angles of his body, the way he holds himself, his legs and feet. He was wearing Converses when he arrived, without socks, so now he's barefoot. His feet are tanned and attractive, the toenails neatly clipped. I don't have a foot fetish as such, but I feel a desire to kiss and caress them.

I move a little closer to him and spend some more time taking pictures close-up. His blue eyes are vivid and full of life, with long dark lashes. Laughter lines have creased the edges, even though he insists he doesn't smile much. I take a lot of photos of his hair, especially the silver flashes at the side. They're definitely going to feature in the painting.

"You're making me uncomfortable," he says after a while, when I'm close up, pointing the camera at his face.

"I'm sorry. I'm nearly done." I learn more about this man with every second that passes. This is making him feel passive. He doesn't like being examined. I think he feels vulnerable.

I take the last few photos and slide my phone into my pocket. I'm enjoying his presence in the studio, the masculine energy, and I like the way he looks at me. I know nothing will come of this, but I don't want him to go. Is that so terrible?

"How are you feeling?" I ask. "I'd like to start your portrait. But I understand if you'd rather get going. I can do it from the photos if I have to."

He hesitates. "I shouldn't." His eyes meet mine.

"Shouldn't?" I taunt. "Doesn't sound like a word in Spencer Cavendish's vocabulary."

He gives a wry smile. Then, to my surprise, he says, "Okay."

"You'll stay?"

He gives a reluctant nod.

My heart soars. "Want another coffee?"

"Yeah, okay."

"Come on then."

We return to the kitchen, and I start making the coffees. He spots a book on the kitchen counter—a big, coffee-table book by Dorling Kindersley called The Tree Book. "This yours?" he asks, leaning on the counter and pulling it toward him.

"Yeah." I wait for him to mock me for looking at trees.

Instead, though, he starts flicking through it and says, "Does it give you inspiration for your artwork?"

I nod, starting the espresso pouring. "This might sound weird, but when I paint, I like to get beneath what we can see. I took a course on the body, so I can understand bone structure and how muscles are attached to the bones. And I like reading about plants, trees, and leaves, and understanding what makes them grow."

"It's all part of your spiritual side," he says, studying a photo of an oak tree, with its accompanying diagram explaining its parts. "The artist Edgar Payne said, 'Art is the reproduction of what the senses perceive in nature through the veil of the soul.'"

"That's it exactly," I reply, pleased he understands and agrees.

"Will you be including much foliage in my portrait?"

"I'm not sure yet. Are you interested in the environment?"

"Very much so."

I steam the milk. "Are you religious?"

"No. If I was… I'd be pagan. Nature spirits and forest deities."

"That surprises me. You don't strike me as the type to dance naked in the moonlight."

"You have no idea what I get up to in the privacy of my own home."

I giggle and pour the milk over the espressos. "I'd like to see that."

He gives me a side glance. "I bet you would."

I grin at him and pass him his coffee. "Come on, back to the studio."

"You want me in the chair?" he asks as we return.

"Please. Are you comfortable enough?"

"Yes, I'm fine." He sits back in the chair. "If I nod off, though, I apologize if I snore."

I laugh and sit back at my easel. I have an idea, and I want to try to capture it in light pencil before I start painting.

Because the portrait will only be from the shoulders up, I let him move freely in the chair. He sits with one ankle resting on the other knee, and swaps sides occasionally, but mostly he seemed relaxed and comfortable.

I sketch for about an hour, while we chat about this and that. It surprises me how easy he is to talk to. He seems to have relaxed a bit, maybe now he thinks he's safe and I'm not going to make a move on him. He's surprisingly funny and knowledgeable about all sorts of things, and we talk about music, movies, and travel. He's been to Europe many times, and we compare our favorite cities, and talk about the art galleries we've visited. Even though he doesn't paint, he obviously loves art, and he asks me a lot of questions about how artists work.

When I finish sketching and all the proportions are laid out again, I give him five minutes to get up and walk around the room while I start drawing in some foliage around him. His mention of being interested in paganism and the Green Man has stirred something inside me.

Spencer wanders around, looking at some of the books, then, while I get my paints ready, unscrewing the tops and squeezing a little of the acrylic out, he says, "You mind if I take a look? Or would you rather I don't see it until the end?"

"No, I don't mind."

He comes to stand behind me. He's very close; I can feel his body heat near my back and shoulder, and I can smell his cologne. He studies the canvas, then reaches out and gestures at a line to the left. "Is that going to be a tree?"

I nod. "I'm going to paint you as Tāne Mahuta."

Tāne Mahuta is the god of the forest in Māori mythology. It's also the name given to the largest living kauri tree in New Zealand, which stands in the Northland's Waipoua Forest.

"Are you comparing me to a thousand-year-old tree?" Spencer asks.

I chuckle. "He's also called the Lord of the Forest. I thought you'd like that title."

"I do, as it happens."

"I'll fill the rest of the canvas with the tree and its leaves."

He surveys it, then nods. "I confess I'm relieved. I thought you might make me a devil or something."

"I did think about it." Guilt makes me shift uneasily on the stool as I think about the other painting that's forming in my mind. But I push it away. I'll worry about that later.

"Is that a bird in the background?" He leans forward to investigate the drawing, and at the same time rests a hand on my back.

I inhale, shocked at how I react so quickly to his touch. Goosebumps jump out on my skin, and hairs rise all over my body.

"Um… yes. Tāne Mahuta is the god of all the forest including the birds."

"Mmm." For a moment, he stays where he is, looking at the sketch of the bird, or pretending to anyway, because something tells me he's feeling the electricity sparking between us as much as I am. His hand doesn't move on my back, but I'm acutely conscious of the warmth of his skin, and the fact that this is the first time he's touched me.

Eventually, unable to stay still, I look up at him, and find my gaze level with his jaw. It looks smooth, not showing any five o'clock shadow yet, even though the day is wearing on. He smells so good… I want to lean forward and press my lips to his skin, then kiss down his neck to his Adam's apple and touch my tongue to the hollow at the base of his throat.

He turns his head a fraction, and looks into my eyes.

Oh wow. A jolt of electricity shoots through me like a touch of static, and my nipples tighten in my bra.

He doesn't look surprised or alarmed. Instead, there's a kind of lazy heat in his eyes as his gaze drops to my mouth.

I wait, and the seconds tick by without either of us moving.

"Are you going to kiss me or not?" I ask. I meant it to sound seductive, but it comes out as a breathless squeak.

He inhales, then huffs it out. "Not."

"Spencer…"

He straightens, walks back to his chair, and sits. Then, glaring at me, he adjusts the front of his trousers. Ohhh… he has an erection. Oh my.

We study each other across the few feet that separates us. My heart is racing. He looks a little sulky, as if his conscience is giving his libido a stern talking to. I can't help but feel smug that he's struggling.

"Don't smirk," he says.

I giggle, and his lips curve up.

"Tell me about your parents," I say, trying to distract myself, picking up my paintbrush and beginning to paint. "Peter and Joyce." I'm referring to his foster parents, and he gives me a smile at the fact that I've noticed that he obviously thinks of them as his parents.

I wondered whether he'd tell me he'd rather not discuss them, but to my surprise he begins to talk.

"Dad was very driven," he says. "His field was farming, not mathematics, but he had a sound business head on his shoulders, and he taught me that discipline and hard work are as important as talent."

"Did they have their own children?"

"No, they couldn't have kids. They tried a few cycles of IVF but couldn't get it to work, and in the end they decided they didn't want to keep putting themselves through that. So they started fostering. They fostered half a dozen kids for about six months each time until my brothers and I turned up."

"Did you get on with them immediately?"

"No. I was turning into a teenager, and resentful and angry at having to be looked after by someone else. But deep down, I was also relieved to not have to deal with my birth father anymore."

"Did you miss your birth mother?"

"Not really." He looks away and doesn't elaborate.

I sketch for a while, thinking. Then I say, "So what's Joyce like?"

That brings a smile to his lips. "Kind. Friendly. No-nonsense. She was very good with my brothers."

"You took longer to warm to her?"

"I just didn't know how to react to compassion. My birth mother was never kind, and she never hugged me. So I was distrusting and stiff and unyielding whenever Joyce came near me. But she was patient. She left me to Peter, who was more practical and didn't talk about feelings. We bonded by going out on the farm and spending time working on fixing fences together. Going for walks with the dogs. Creating furniture in his workshop."

"But you warmed to her eventually?"

"There… was an incident," he says.

I concentrate on blending the paints to get the right shade for his skin tone. "Oh?"

He's quiet for a moment. Then he continues, "My birth parents died in a car crash."

I pause and look over at him. Jesus. No wonder the poor guy is screwed up. "Oh, I am sorry," I say softly. "That must have given you very conflicting feelings."

"Yeah." He scratches at a mark on the arm of his chair. Then he sighs. "Peter and Joyce sat me and my brothers down to tell us. My birth father was an alcoholic. He'd gotten drunk, argued with my mother, and gone out to sit in the car. She came out and got in with him. He drove off—I don't know why, but just a few hundred yards from the house, he wrapped the car around a tree. He died instantly, and apparently she was DOA at the hospital."

"Aw, that's awful."

"My brothers were very upset. But I just went quiet. Peter took me for a walk, but I didn't really want to talk, and in the end we came back and he let me go to my room. Later, Joyce came in. I literally couldn't speak. I was so knotted up inside that I just lay there on the bed, looking up at the ceiling. She sat on the side of the bed and said it was okay to feel whatever I was feeling, whether that was grief or anger, or if I was just numb. And she put a hand on my arm." His eyes are distant. "It broke the dam. I looked at her and said I didn't feel angry. I felt relieved. And then she hugged me, and I…" He stops and looks down.

He was about to say he got upset, I think. He's breathing fast. I get the feeling he doesn't let himself relive the moment very often.

I paint for a bit and let him gather himself. Eventually I say, "How long was that after you moved in with them?"

"Eight months."

"What happened after that?"

"It was coming up to Christmas. And on Christmas Eve, the two of them sat us boys down and said they'd decided they wanted to adopt us. They said the courts were supposed to look for relatives from our biological family, but we didn't have any. Mum had a sister who lived in Australia. We'd never met her, and she had a family of her own, and she wasn't keen to take on three boys. And my father had two brothers—one had already died from cancer, and the other hated him and wanted nothing to do with us. So Peter and Joyce didn't think they'd have a problem adopting, if that was what we wanted."

"What did you say?"

He smiles then, an obviously pleasant memory. "We said yes. It took about six months for it to go through, but things started to improve for me almost immediately. Peter wanted us to take his surname, and I was more than happy with that."

"So he's where the name Cavendish comes from?"

"Yeah. Dad didn't expect me to take over the farming business—my middle brother was far more interested in that. But he said he knew I'd go far, and he wanted to help me achieve my potential. He was very good to me. He never pushed me to be touchy feely. He communicated his affection for me in other ways, and I never fully appreciated that until he'd gone."

So he's lost two fathers. That must have been incredibly hard for him. It helps me understand, too, his relationship with Orson and Helen. Orson has said that he's not super close to his father, but I wonder whether he's taken it into account that Spencer shows affection the only way he can: by being supportive and encouraging, rather than by hugging and kissing.

He shifts in the chair; I think he needs to stretch his legs again. I check my phone; it's nearly five thirty.

"I have some of the base colors on my canvas," I tell him, cleaning my brush, "but it's a long way from being finished. It'll probably take me a couple more hours until I'm happy with the first draft of the painting, and many more hours to finish it. I can do it from photos, but I'd be happier doing at least the first draft from life."

I turn to face him. Am I brave enough? Nothing conquered, nothing gained and all that.

I take a deep breath. "It's up to you," I say. "But would you like to stay for dinner? I could cook us something quick, steak and chips or something, and then I could do another couple of hours, try and get the basic painting done today while you're here."

He stares at me.

I scratch my nose. "Or not," I say lamely.

"I don't think it's a good idea," he says.

We study each other quietly in the afternoon sunshine.

"Are you busy?" I ask. "Do you have an appointment?"

"No."

"Another dinner date?"

"No."

"So you won't stay purely because I'm so irresistible?"

His lips curve up, just a little.

"You don't trust me?" I tip my head to the side, curious. "Or is it yourself you don't trust?"

"It's not that I don't trust myself. I've never lost control yet."

"Is that a challenge?"

He just gives a short laugh, then leans forward, his elbows on his knees. "You're stunning, Marama. By far the most beautiful woman I've seen in a long while, and maybe ever. Your youth and joie de vivre give you a radiance that shines from you, and the fact that you're not aware of it makes it even more enticing." His words are given easily, and with confidence; this man is incredibly sure of himself. "You really are an *atua wāhine*," he continues, "especially here, in your studio. You're a young, amazing goddess, and all I can think about is lifting you up in my arms, carrying you into your bedroom, stripping you naked, kissing down your body, and burying my tongue inside you."

I stare at him. Oh. My. God.

He looks amused at my shock as he leans back. "But you're out of bounds, and so it's not going to happen. I have the most willpower of any man I've ever met. I've spent years honing it. And as much as I want you, I'm not going to give in."

Chapter Eleven

Spencer

Marama is, quite clearly, speechless. I blink. What on earth came over me? I suppose I just need her to understand that it's not because I don't find her attractive. It is absolutely the opposite of that. It's almost agony being in her company and not being able to touch her. But if she thinks she can seduce me into bed with her, she can think again.

She turns to her paints and tidies them up, gathering her wits, I think. I watch her, my mischievous flare subsiding, to be replaced with a kind of resigned tiredness. I'd half-hoped she might tell me I'm being an idiot and that it doesn't matter what her father or anyone else thinks. Deep down, I suppose I hoped she would try to talk me into it. It's ridiculous, because I have no intention of giving in. But it would be nice to be wanted that much. To feel desired.

I've made my position clear several times now, though. I've spent years cultivating a persona that suggests I brook no arguments, and Marama—being a younger woman—is unlikely to be the first to stand up to me.

She finishes organizing her paints and wipes her hands on a cloth. I collect my coffee cup, and I'm about to get to my feet when she rises and comes over to stand in front of me.

My eyebrows rise as she bends forward and rests a hand on each arm of the chair. The bib of her dungarees and the top of her tee beneath it gape, and I have to fight not to look down her top, even though I think she wants me to.

"Right," she says, "this is what's going to happen. You're going to stay. I'm going to cook us dinner. And then I'm going to finish the first draft of the painting. After I finish the painting... we'll see what happens."

"Nothing is going to happen."

"We'll see," she repeats. In a low, husky tone, she says, "I know you want me."

I can't deny it because I've already told her I do, so I just lift an eyebrow.

She moistens her lips with the tip of her tongue, her gaze dropping to my mouth. Beneath the smell of pencils and paint is the aroma of her perfume, something deep and sensual, with amber and spice, making me think of exotic-sounding places like Samarkand and Marrakesh. I can imagine how smooth and silky her flawless, light-brown skin would feel beneath my fingers. How soft her lips would feel pressed against mine. How she would taste.

"I want you," she whispers.

My heart bangs against my ribs. Her open admission is an incredible turn-on. How simple my needs are. I crave to be wanted. To be desired.

"Kiss me," she says, her voice husky.

I tear my gaze from her mouth and lift it to hers. "No."

"You're going to," she says, with complete confidence.

I look her in the eyes. "I won't."

"You will."

My lips curve up. "I. Won't."

She lifts her eyebrows. "If you're so sure, then why won't you stay?"

I don't have an answer to that. She's right. If I'm so adamant that I can resist her, what's the problem with staying?

The truth is that I'm not sure. She's right—I do want her. Right now, I want her more than I've ever wanted anything in my whole life. I crave her. I want her young body pressed against mine; I want her under me, on top of me, dammit I don't care where she is, I just want to be inside her. And if I stay, it's going to be like slow torture, and I'm just making things hard for myself.

But if I leave, I'm admitting I can't resist her, and I've never backed down from a challenge.

And besides, I really fancy a steak.

"All right," I say. "Medium rare?"

She smiles. "Medium rare. I make an amazing blue cheese sauce." She straightens and holds out a hand. "Come on, old man, I'll help you up."

I snort, ignore her hand, and get up, and then we both laugh when my right knee cracks. "Ow," I say, following her out of the studio and down the hallway. "Don't mock the afflicted."

She giggles and leads the way into the kitchen. "Sit there," she instructs, pointing to the bar stools on the other side of the breakfast bar, "and you can entertain me while I cook."

"You want me to juggle?"

"I meant talk to me."

"I can do the blue cheese sauce if you like."

She looks at me in surprise. "You cook?"

"I do. Don't look so shocked." I go over to the fridge and look in it. "Come on then, let's get this show on the road."

Marama puts some chips in the air fryer, and while they're cooking she prepares two sirloin steaks, grinding some salt and pepper on them, and heating the pan until it's piping hot. I retrieve the ingredients for the sauce and start preparing them, making some beef stock, letting the cream stand for a bit, crumbling the blue cheese, and chopping some chives. I lean against the counter and we chat while she fries the steaks, and then when she's done she removes them and passes the pan to me. I pour the stock in and scrape up the bits from the pan, add the cream and blue cheese, and stir it until it's creamy.

Meanwhile, she puts a pack of frozen green beans, broccoli, and sugarsnap peas into the microwave and sets it heating. She pours me a Sprite, then she chooses a bottle of red wine from Rangi's wine stand and pours herself a glass. I look at the bottle with amusement—it's Babich's flagship red, a dark, rich blend of Cabernet Sauvignon, Malbec, and Merlot that's been aged for twenty-one years in French oak, and it's called The Patriarch.

"Very funny," I say when she smirks.

"You sure you don't want a glass? It's what you are, isn't it? The male head of your family and business?"

I shrug. "The word seems tied to toxic masculinity now."

She leans a hip on the counter and watches me stir the sauce. "What's your view on equality?"

"I believe women are equal to men. I just think they're better at ironing and doing the dishes."

She laughs. "I hope you don't say that to other women. They won't know you don't mean it."

"Give me some credit. I wouldn't say it to a stranger."

"So you don't consider me a stranger?"

"Of course not. I've known you since you were… what? Four?"

"Mm. Long time."

I stir the sauce slowly. "I'm sorry about Connor."

She sighs. "It was very hard at the time. Now, I'm kinda glad it didn't work out. When you're in something it's tough to see what's happening, isn't it? Like looking at a jigsaw puzzle too close up. It's only when you get some distance that you're able to see the whole picture."

"Yeah."

The air fryer beeps, announcing that the chips are done. She goes over and opens it, then tips the chunky chips onto two plates and adds the steak. I bring the pan over and top the steaks with the blue cheese sauce, she adds the hot veggies, and then we carry the lot outside to the smaller circular table on the deck.

We take our seats, and Marama holds up her wine glass to me. "To whatever tonight brings."

I give her a wry look and tap my glass to hers.

We cut into our steaks, which are plump and juicy and perfectly cooked, and chat about nothing as we crunch into the chips. We both enjoyed traveling, and we talk for a long time again about the places we've been and the people we've met.

My dinner finished, I stretch my legs out and rest my feet on the opposite chair, sipping my drink while Marama finishes her steak. It's quiet here, and it's now nearly six p.m. The clocks went back this weekend, and the sun has almost completely disappeared beneath the horizon. She's lit a citronella candle to keep any insects away, and it flickers in the evening breeze.

It's cooling down, and there's more than a touch of autumn in the air. Joe must have cleared the lawn today, but already a few brown leaves litter the surface. Clouds are darkening the sky even more; I think it might rain.

"Talk to me about sex," Marama says.

I look at her, eyebrows raised. She's finished her dinner and is now curled up in her chair, facing me, resting her head on a hand, her glass almost empty.

"No," I say, amused.

"Tell me what you like," she says, as if I haven't spoken. Her eyes glow in the dusky twilight.

I just tip my head and give her a sarcastic look.

"I know you like being in charge," she says. "I expect you prefer to direct the action." She sips her wine, then brushes a drop from her bottom lip. "Do you ever give up control?"

"No."

"Not even in bed?"

Unbidden, I remember a conversation I had with Genevieve on the night where she tried to seduce me. She'd had several drinks, and the conversation was enjoyable up to the point where she obviously decided it was time to make a move. She asked me if I'd ever fantasized about submitting to a woman, and started becoming quite aggressive in her sexual suggestions, naming several things she'd like to do to me that I found distasteful, if not alarming.

I feel a spike of dislike. "No. My pleasure is… not irrelevant, exactly, but secondary to the woman's. I enjoy giving sexual pleasure more than receiving. I have no interest in just lying there and letting the woman do all the work." She finishes off her wine, then studies the glass thoughtfully. Something occurs to me. "Have you dated anyone else since you broke up with Connor?"

She shakes her head.

That makes me frown. "So you haven't had sex for a year?"

"Nope." Her eyes dance. "Mr. Buzzington and I have formed a firm friendship."

Heat rises inside me. "Glad to hear you have help in that department."

She shrugs. "It's not the same as a man's warm tongue, but it does the job."

Our eyes meet. This is dangerous territory. No Man's Land lies between us—a minefield with barbed wire and No Entry signs plastered all over it.

But now all I can think about is Marama with her legs wide, head tipped back, moaning as she pleasures herself with her vibrator, and I have a hard-on that feels as if it might break through the stitching on my trousers.

Her lips curve up. "That turn you on, does it?"

"I'm a straight male. Of course it turns me on."

"I'm not surprised. I'm sure you have more than the regular amount of testosterone that most men have." I snort, and she giggles. "So come on then," she teases, "how often do you… you know? Indulge in a little DIY?" I roll my eyes, and she pokes my leg with her foot. "Don't tell me you don't do it," she says, "because I won't believe you."

"Of course I do it. If a man says he doesn't, he's lying."

Her eyes flare. The thought turns her on. "So how often?"

"As often as I need to. I'm not as young as I used to be."

"Once a week? Once a day?"

"A few times a week, I guess. More if I'm…"

"Horny?"

That makes me laugh. "I was going to say 'not tired,' but yeah, your word works too."

She smiles. Then she says, "I think you're an extremely sexy man."

"Well, thank you. I'm flattered that such a young, beautiful woman would say so."

"Aw, come on. Women must fall at your feet all the time."

"Not quite, no."

"Really?" She looks puzzled. "I thought they'd be throwing themselves at you."

"If they are, I haven't noticed. Most of the women I meet are married businesswomen. And I haven't been out much since Eleanor died."

"Why not?"

"Doesn't appeal to me. I have no interest in going to clubs. As you know, it feels awkward to go to dinner parties when you're single, and I hate small talk."

"Do you? You don't seem to mind talking to me."

"I don't consider this small talk. Small talk is talking to a stranger about the weather or what the latest celebrities are doing. It bores me. You don't, though. You're not a stranger."

"I'm glad you think so."

"You're very easy to talk to," I admit.

She smiles. "So are you. You only talk about things that matter. You only speak when you have something worth saying. A lot of people could do with learning that skill."

With some surprise, this relationship—such as it is—with Marama is different from any I've experienced before. We actually like one another.

"Why do you like me?" I ask, genuinely bemused. "I'm cold, hard, and standoffish. I'm bossy and unforgiving. I work too hard and I don't play enough. I don't see anything to like."

She tips her head to the side, her expression softening. "You're very hard on yourself. You have a great sense of humor. Yes, you work hard, and you don't suffer fools gladly. But in your line of work you have to be driven and tough. And anyway, I like a bossy man." She wrinkles her nose.

My gaze drops to her mouth. It would be so easy to lean across, pull her chair toward me, and crush my lips to hers. So, so easy. I want to do it so much it hurts. I want to lose myself in her beauty and her youth and her soft body. I want to be loved by someone who loves me back. I've never had that before, and I yearn for it.

I look away, across the garden. The sun has disappeared, and it's growing cool. "Are you going to be able to paint in this light?"

"There's this thing called electricity," she says. "You might have heard of it. It's pretty magical. You just press a button and it makes stuff light up!"

"Haha." I get to my feet and pick up my plate and glass, and she does the same. "I mean don't you need natural light?"

"No, I'm not precious about it. I can paint anywhere and in any conditions." She leads the way inside.

"Thank you for dinner," I say as we stack the dishwasher. "It was perfect."

"You're welcome. You want a coffee?"

"Yeah, okay."

So we make ourselves a coffee, then take them back into the studio.

Marama turns some lamps on, including a spotlight that shines on her canvas, and one to my left that illuminates me. With the fairy lights, the room glows like a grotto, a place full of mystery.

I sit back in my chair, Marama takes her place by her easel, and she begins to paint.

I'm nicely full, and the hot coffee grounds me with its earthy smell, providing me with a pleasant blend of being rooted in the real world that's touched by magic.

There's something magical about watching Marama work. Although she does talk while she's painting, I can see she's lost in the canvas, in the colors and the shapes she's producing with her brush. She works fast, using mostly long, free strokes—she told me she's concentrating on getting the first draft done tonight, the undercoat or base colors, and she'll work on the finer details later.

She glances at me from time to time, and her lips curve up when she sees me watching her. I don't look away though, not ashamed to be caught admiring her. She's so beautiful. I love a confident woman, and she looks completely at home here, with paint on her hands and her hair all messy, happy and content to be at her easel.

"You're supposed to be looking ahead." She stops to wash her brush.

"The view is much more interesting in this direction."

"My view would have been more interesting if you'd taken off your clothes."

"Well, so would mine, if we're being candid."

Her gaze trails down me lazily. "I'd love to sketch you naked." Her eyes return to mine. "I'll strip if you strip."

"Yeah, right," I scoff.

She puts down her paintbrush, then gets to her feet. She walks over to the windows, takes the curtain hanging on the right, and pulls it across the window, then does the same with the left one, so we're cut off from the outside world.

She returns to stand in front of her easel. Then she starts to unbutton the straps that hold up the bib of her dungarees.

My pulse rate immediately doubles. Holy shit, I didn't think she'd go through with it. "Marama…" I say in a warning tone.

She undoes one button. Then moves to the other one. She meets my gaze as she peels the bib down. Her expression is calm, with a touch of hope and maybe a smidgeon of fear that I won't respond.

I have a choice now. I should ask her what the hell she's doing, but that will make her feel foolish and embarrassed, and will bring this magical evening to an end. It's the right thing to do, the proper thing. So why does it feel so wrong?

Playing along doesn't guarantee that we'll end up in bed together. But it's the first step on a path I was adamant I wasn't going to set foot on. I'll be showing her that I'm not as strong as I thought I was. I'll be admitting I want her.

But I do want her. More than anything in the world. Fuck everyone else. See, want, take, right? Why shouldn't I?

Slowly, I get to my feet. Then I begin to unbutton my shirt.

Her whole face lights up with unbridled joy and excitement, warming me to the core.

I push the buttons of my shirt through the holes, while she undoes the buttons of her dungarees on her hips. I reach the bottom as she finishes, and, together, I let my shirt fall off my shoulders while she pushes her dungarees down and steps out of them.

She's wearing a tiny pair of cream lace panties. She's not overly tall, but her bare light-brown legs look long and incredibly smooth.

Her gaze roams across my shoulders and down over my chest. "I'm so glad you don't shave," she murmurs, looking at the scatter of brown hairs interspersed with lots of silver across my ribs. "You're in amazing shape."

"Thank you. You have amazing legs."

She meets my gaze. Then, lips twitching, she crosses her arms and takes hold of the hem of her T-shirt.

I lift my hands to my trousers, then stop. "Ahhh… I feel the need to apologize… but it's impossible not to react when a beautiful young woman is stripping in front of you."

Her gaze drops to my trousers, and her lips curve up. In one smooth move she lifts the tee up over her head and tosses it away. Now she's standing there in just her underwear—the lacy panties and a matching cream bra with demi cups that prop up her generous breasts as if preparing them for my gaze.

I look down at my trousers. Well, there's no point in being coy about it. I undo the button and slide the zipper over my erection, then let the trousers drop and step out of them. Hands on hips, I stand there in my tight black boxer briefs and let her ogle me.

Her eyes widen. "Oh my," she says. "The rumors were true."

"Rumors?" I know I'm not a small man, but I wasn't aware my size was a matter of gossip.

She just presses her lips togethers, eyes gleaming.

We study each other. Then, eyes filled with amusement, she lifts her hands behind her back and unclips her bra. Slowly, she draws the straps down each arm and lets it fall to the ground.

"Fuck." I brush my hand over my face. I lower my hand again, and we observe one another, trying not to laugh. Jesus, her breasts are amazing, high and round and with perfect medium-brown nipples.

I glance down at myself, then give her a rueful look. "Are you sure about this?"

"Get 'em off, Cavendish," she says. She hooks her fingers in her panties, pulls them down her legs, and steps out of them. Then she lifts her hands to her head and holds them there as she does a 360 degree turn for me.

I stifle a groan at the sight of her amazing butt, and the mound between her legs with its tiny, neat strip of hair. The rest of her is obviously going to be bare and silky smooth.

Fuuuuuuuuck.

She sits on her stool and picks up her paintbrush, then arches a brow at me.

I blow out a breath, lift the elastic of my underwear over my erection, push the boxer-briefs down and step out of them, then toss them away. As casually as I can, I sit back in my seat and face her, hands resting on the arms of the chair. It takes a lot of willpower not to cover myself up, but I fight the urge and instead sit back and let her drink her fill.

"Oh my God," she whispers. "Spencer! Wow."

"I guess that's a better reaction than 'is that it?'"

"Oh, you're as far from 'is that it' as it's possible to be. You're magnificent."

It's extremely shallow of me, but I glow at her compliment. What man doesn't like to be complimented on his family jewels?

She looks at the canvas, then lifts it off the easel and places it to one side. Quickly, she replaces it with a new, clean one. Picking up her pencil, she rakes me with her gaze, which makes my cock twitch. She notices, and she presses her lips together, her eyes dancing. Then she begins to sketch.

I sit there, aware that this is probably the most erotic thing I've ever experienced. Just the nature of posing like this, naked and exposed to her gaze, is more arousing than I would have expected, but being able to watch her as she works, to feast my gaze on her exquisite breasts, the curve of her waist, and the swell of her hips, is such a turn-on that my erection refuses to go down.

She sketches, but every time she looks at me her stare lasts for longer. Eventually, she moistens her lips with the tip of her tongue, and when I look down I see that the tip of my erection is glistening. I lift my gaze back to hers, and our eyes lock.

My heart bangs, and realization dawns on me. What the hell am I doing? This woman is extremely dangerous for me. And I don't just

MIDNIGHT SECRET

mean because of her age and the fact that she's Rangi's daughter. I mean because she's chaotic—she's emotional, artistic, and hard to predict. I react to her in a way I never have before, and I don't just mean my hard-on. I can feel my control slipping away, and that scares me.

I tear my gaze away, stand, and bend to pick up my clothes. "I should go."

She doesn't respond. I straighten and look at her. She's watching me, and as I look, she gets to her feet. "If you want to," she says calmly. "I'm not going to stop you."

Our earlier conversation jumps into my head.

Marama: Kiss me.

Me: No.

Marama: You're going to.

Me: I won't.

Marama: You will.

My confident denial seems incredibly stupid now.

She stands there, not a stitch on, all soft and alluring, her breasts begging to be touched, her lips begging to be kissed, and the urge to kiss her blooms in my mind like some gigantic Alice-in-Wonderland flower until it's all I can think about.

I won't.

You will.

I look at her mouth, despair engulfing me.

Fucking hell, man, you're naked, and she's naked, and she's so incredibly beautiful—what the hell did you think was going to happen?

Chapter Twelve

Marama

When I started unbuttoning my dungarees, it was a huge gamble. Ultimately, I told myself that it didn't matter if he didn't join in; I'd stop at the dungarees and paint him in my T-shirt and knickers. I'd get a kick out of him watching me, and I know him well enough to be sure he wouldn't embarrass me; he'd flirt and be kind and that would be that.

I was shocked when he stood and started unbuttoning his shirt, but thought maybe he'd stop and laugh; I certainly didn't think he'd continue. And I did *not* expect him to go all the way.

It was exquisite torture, sitting there and sketching him while he leaned back in his chair, so unashamed and sexy, his magnificent erection showing no signs of going down any time soon. And then he picked up his clothes, and I was convinced he'd come to his senses.

But he doesn't move. His gaze slides down me like the brush of a feather, making my nipples tighten and an ache grow between my legs, then returns back up, lingering on my breasts before returning to my mouth. For a long, long moment, I wait while he fights with himself, his conscience and his lust locked in a phenomenal battle, his chest heaving with his deep breaths as his brow creases with a frown.

Please, please, please, please, please, please... I beg silently, my breaths coming rapidly too. But I stay where I am. I need him to make the final move. I want him to cave.

I see the moment he makes up his mind. His frown disappears. He straightens a little, as if he was imprisoned in a small cage, and now he's been released and can stand and breathe. He drops his clothes, just tosses them away as if he's discarding his worries and fears.

Then, keeping his gaze fixed on my mouth, he strides toward me, takes my face in his hands, and kisses me. Fuck—zero to sixty in less than three seconds, even faster than his Bentley, which is saying something.

Ohhh… Spencer Cavendish kisses like a god. Part of me is surprised, considering his admission that he's only slept with one woman. Now he's made up his mind, he's obviously decided to give in to his desire one hundred percent, and oh shit, I'm at the receiving end of it. Heat sweeps over me, firing up all my nerve endings, and my heart pounds.

He takes big, hungry kisses, then, to my surprise, presses his lips tenderly to the *moko* on my chin, a gesture that makes tears spring into my eyes. But there's no time to think about it, because he returns to my mouth and brushes my bottom lip with his tongue. Obediently, I open my mouth, and he sweeps his tongue inside, while he sinks his hands into my hair. He tilts his head to the side, changing the angle of the kiss, and then proceeds to absolutely devour me, claiming my mouth, demanding, not asking, taking what he wants from me, as if I have no say in it.

I moan, dizzy with passion, excited and thrilled. In response, he groans and lowers his arms around me, sliding them down my back to rest on my butt and pull me against him. My hands were resting on his chest, but I lift my arms up around his neck. His hard cock presses against my belly, and his fingers tighten on my butt.

My head spins. I've never been kissed like this, not with such overwhelming desire, not as if we're the last people on earth and the world's about to end. He slides his hands up to rest on my breasts, and I arch my back to push them into his palms, tipping my head back when he teases the nipples with his fingers. Ahhh… that feels amazing… and the sensation only intensifies when he kisses down my neck, then fastens a mouth over a nipple and sucks.

I can't believe we're here, in my studio, doing this; it's all my fantasies, all my desires rolled into one. He straightens and kisses my mouth again, pushing me back a little, and I feel the edge of my table pressing against the back of my thighs. I lean across and switch off the bright lamp, which removes the harsh light from the room and casts us in the soft glow of the smaller lamps and fairy lights.

Then, without a second thought, I turn and sweep everything aside. Tubes of paint, brushes, sponges, everything skitters aside, half of it tumbling to the floor, but I don't care.

With a growl of approval, he lifts me so my butt is resting on the edge of the table, and then he kisses up my jaw. "I'm going to taste you now," he murmurs in my ear, his hot breath fanning across it and making me shiver.

"Oh..."

He kisses down my throat, big, hungry, wet kisses, as if he can't get enough of me, his mouth moving over my collarbone, then down to my breasts. I fall onto my elbows, my head tipping back and my loose strands of hair coiling on the table. I wrap my legs around him as he covers a nipple with his mouth and sucks. Ooooh, that feels amazing. He sucks once, a little harder the second time, then even harder the third, until I shudder and cry out. Chuckling, he swaps to the other, doing the same, and I give a long groan. This man is going to drive me crazy.

He teases my nipples with his mouth and fingers until my breaths are coming in gasps, and then he kisses down over my belly and drops to his knees before me. Placing a hand on each knee, he slides them wide apart, exposing me to his hot gaze. I lift my head and watch him devour me with his eyes, feasting his gaze on my moist, swollen flesh as he raises a hand and draws a finger down through my folds. He glances up at me, his blue eyes full of heat and desire, and I'm undone; I'm completely his at that point, turning to molten caramel inside.

Then he leans forward and slides his tongue inside me.

"Ahhh fuck!" It's been so long since a man has done this for me, and pleasure ripples through me from the tips of my hair to my toes. Argh, there's nothing like having a warm tongue sliding through you, a hot mouth sucking on your clit with just the right pressure... He adds a finger, caressing my clit while he kisses my inner thighs, then licks and sucks, giving appreciative groans while he does so. Finally, he turns his hand palm up, slides two fingers inside me, and proceeds to stroke them slowly in and out while he returns to teasing my clit with his tongue.

I was never going to last long—I've been keyed up all evening, and I haven't had sex for over a year, and I've always wanted Spencer, and I'm so excited that this magical, dreamy evening has ended this way. And so it's only a few minutes before I feel the delicious rising wave of an orgasm deep inside.

Sighing, I slide my hand into his beautiful hair, trying to relax into it, and he rubs the outside of my thigh with his free hand in such a tender way that it finishes me. I come on his tongue, clenching around his fingers, and he holds me while the pulses claim me, until eventually I fall back on the table, gasping, completely his at that point.

He kisses my clit gently, my thighs, my mound, and then up my belly as he gets to his feet. Eyes closed, I wait for him to kiss my mouth, but his weight lifts, and when I open my eyes he's gone.

Disappointment spikes, and I sit up hurriedly, panicking that, for whatever reason, he's decided he can't go all the way. Sure enough, he's picking up his trousers… but then I see him take out his wallet and extract something, and I realize with relief and excitement that he's just retrieving a condom. He tosses the wallet away and comes back to me with a wry smile, saying "Wasn't sure if I still had one in there." He gives me a curious look. "What?"

I slide my arms around his waist and rest my cheek on his chest, brushing the silver hairs there with my fingers. "I thought you were leaving."

He wraps his arms around me, and rests his lips on my hair. "We've crossed the line. No point in agonizing about it now." Sliding a hand beneath my chin, he lifts it so I'm looking up at him. "You're so fucking beautiful," he murmurs.

My eyes flare. Spencer Cavendish swearing, now that's a first. He's usually such a gentleman.

He kisses me, and I taste myself on his lips as he slides his tongue into my mouth. Mmm, that's hot, and I give a long, low moan at his luscious kiss. He takes his time, teasing my lips with his teeth and tongue, his hands finding their way to my breasts and beginning to arouse me again.

My body's burning, and I'm aching as if I haven't come at all. I open my legs and pull him toward me, and he chuckles and says, "Slowly."

"I need you. I want you inside me. Please."

His smile fades, and his eyes darken with dark pleasure. "You want me, baby?"

"More than anything in the world." I lower my hand to his magnificent erection, close my fingers around it, and stroke it. He swells in my hand, groaning, and kisses me the way I'm starting to love—sliding a hand to the back of my head to hold me in place before plunging his tongue into my mouth.

It's not long before he removes the wrapper from his condom, and then he rolls it on and guides the tip down to my entrance. My heart races.

He stops there and looks me in the eyes. "You're sure?"

I nod enthusiastically, and he gives a short laugh. Still, he waits, and for a moment I half expect him to say he can't go through with it and withdraw.

But he doesn't. He looks down with lazy, desire-filled eyes, brushes his thumb through my folds, and teases my clit a few times. My heart thuds with anticipation as he presses the tip of his erection into me, then eases inside.

He takes it slow, sliding in an inch, then easing back, gradually coating himself with my moisture before moving forward again, until he's fully sheathed. I tighten my internal muscles and we both groan at the sensation of him being all the way up, right to the top, stretching and filling me to the brim.

"You feel amazing," he says, his voice little more than a growl, and starts to move.

"Aaahhh…" I wrap my legs around his waist, tilting my pelvis up, then slide back onto my elbows. He leans forward to kiss me, and I moan at the change of angle—he's driving down into me, and fuck that feels amazing.

Clearly, he's trying to take it slow, but I don't want him to be calm and in control. I want to drive him crazy with desire. I want him to lose it with me.

I lower myself onto my back and lift my arms above my head, and he groans, covering my breasts with his hands before dropping his head to suck my nipples. I feel so abandoned like this; I stretch out, moaning his name.

It turns out to be a mistake, because my palette is still sitting at the edge of the table, and I plunge my hand straight into it. Lifting my hand, I discover my fingers and palm covered with a variety of acrylic paint.

I sigh and rub my fingers together, oddly turned on by the slippery feel and the bright colors. He lifts his head and sees it, but before he can react, I brush my fingers over his face, smearing the colors across his skin.

"Argh," he says, and to my surprise he laughs.

Feeling a surge of mischief, I scoop the paint into a mound on my finger, then write something in the middle of his chest. He glances at it upside down, then looks at me. It's just one word. Mine.

He gives long, slow thrusts, almost withdrawing before sliding back inside, but as he looks down at the word on his chest, he begins to move faster. I think maybe he secretly likes it. The thought that someone wants him enough to claim him. Who doesn't want to be wanted, especially if you were married to a cold fish for over twenty years?

The wine has mixed with the adrenaline that's pumping through me, and I feel almost dizzy with lust. "I've branded you," I announce. "Made you mine. Do you understand?"

He doesn't say anything, but he frowns.

"Say it," I demand. "You're mine."

He slows, then stops moving. His eyes bore into mine. I wait for him to tell me not to say things like that.

But to my shock, he says, huskily, "I'm yours."

He doesn't mean it. We're only playing. But it lights me up like a Christmas tree. "Say it again," I tell him, laying a hand over the word on his chest.

He begins moving again. "I'm yours, Marama. All yours." He slides a hand into my hair, which has come loose from the elastic, and pulls it back so he can kiss my throat. "I don't give a fuck what anyone else says," he growls into my ear, "I'm making you mine, and I don't want any other man touching you."

Ohhh... yes he knows how to play the game. He's starting to lose it. This is what I wanted, what I needed. He leans a hand either side of me and thrusts hard enough to make the table rattle.

"Yeah, fuck me like that," I instruct him with delight.

Our gazes lock, and his blue eyes blaze. "You like this?" he whispers. "You like me fucking you hard?"

"Mmm... I love it..."

"What do you want, baby?"

"I want you to fuck me into next week."

"Like this?" He thrusts harder.

"Aaahhh... yeah..." I groan. "That feels amazing. Mmm..." The sound of his hips meeting the back of my thighs fills the air, and it's so erotic that it makes me moan. I haven't had sex like this for an eternity. "Ohhh... don't stop..."

"I won't. You're so fucking beautiful." He strokes over my breasts, and I can feel my orgasm hovering in the wings. "Spencer…" I whisper.

He kisses me fiercely. I can feel the tension starting to build inside as, with each thrust of his hips, he grinds against me.

I groan. "I'm going to come…"

"Ah, yeah…" He kisses back to my mouth, still thrusting. "Baby…"

I let my knees fall wide apart and abandon myself to him and to the climax that wants to claim me. It begins deep inside, a gradual tightening, delicious and warm, and then spreads out through me, ooh… a strong one… so erotic and satisfying… a series of intense clenches that make me cry out loud because they feel so amazing.

He rides me through it, watching my face and murmuring, "Ahhh… you're so beautiful…" while I gasp.

And then, as my body finally releases me and brings me back to consciousness, I push up onto my elbows and look up at him through hazy eyes. He continues to move, smiling a little, looking at my mouth before he bends and kisses me. His hips move faster, harder, and I tighten my legs around him, encouraging him. It doesn't take long before he stiffens, his fingers curling into fists on the table, his muscles hardening, and he closes his eyes with a fierce frown as he comes inside me, which is *ohhh* so beautiful that it makes me want to cry.

"Yeah…" I whisper, opening my mouth as he kisses me, and our tongue tangle as his hips jerk with each pulse, until eventually his body releases him, and he lets out a long, heartfelt groan.

I let my head drop back, and he rests his forehead on my shoulder, his lips grazing my throat. "Mmmm," I murmur. "That was soooo good."

He lifts his head, and we look at each other for a long moment.

Gradually, the sexual haze that had claimed me subsides, and the full realization of what we've done settles over me.

He lost control. I drove him to the edge and pushed him over. And he might not be very happy about that. He was so adamant that he wouldn't do it. What if he hates me now it's done?

"Don't regret it," I whisper, tears pricking my eyes. He's still inside me. Oh God, please don't let him get angry before it's even over.

He blinks a few times. Then, to my relief, his lips curve up. "I don't," he says gently.

He looks down, holds the condom, and withdraws. Grabs a tissue from the box on the floor and disposes of it. Then comes back to me and holds out a hand. Sniffing, I slide mine into it, and he pulls me to my feet.

Then he wraps his arms around me and holds me tightly.

I bury my face in his neck, my arms curled up close to me, comforted by his embrace. On his chest, I open my hand, covering the word there. Mine.

"Thank you," he murmurs, kissing the top of my head. "You made me feel… wanted. That's a first." He moves back, looks down at us, and chuckles. "What a mess." We're both covered in paint.

"We should wash this off," I advise. "It's not harmful, but it might irritate the skin if it's there too long."

"Best we shower together," he says. "To save water."

That makes me laugh. "Yeah. Come on."

We pick up our clothes, and I take him through to my bedroom, and then into my bathroom. I turn the shower on and take a moment to clip up my hair, and then when the water's hot, we step into the cubicle and close the door.

Ooh, he's bigger than he seems at first glance; he seems to fill the cubicle both physically and with his sheer presence. Spencer Cavendish, naked in my shower. Wow.

I pick up the shower gel and pour a decent amount into my hand, then begin to wash him. He stands there patiently, taking the brunt of the water, his hands on my hips, watching me as I clean him.

I scrub off the paint on his shoulders and neck, then move to his chest. My hand hovers over the word that is still visible on his skin. Glancing up at him, I'm surprised to see him smiling, and affection in his eyes.

He told me, *You made me feel… wanted. That's a first.*

I want to tell him he's mine. But instinct tells me he's not ready for that. He played along, but even though he says he doesn't regret it, I think he's assuming this is a one-off.

We'll have to see what we can do about that.

I scrub the word off his chest. But I've branded him, and it's going to remain there, long after the paint has gone.

Chapter Thirteen

Spencer

Marama's hands glide over my skin as she washes the paint off, and then she offers me the shower gel. I pour some onto my palm and proceed to do the same to her, removing the splodges of color.

She watches me while I do it, her gaze steady. I keep my expression calm, even though inside my heart is racing.

Fuck, what have I done? All I can think of is Rangi's warning, *You touch her... I'll break your fucking legs.* I'm not physically scared. I'm confident I could take Rangi in a fight. But the thought that I'm considering taking him on is scaring me.

I've gone mad. I think I've actually gone insane. I could have any woman I wanted, pretty much. I know that sounds arrogant, but it's nothing to do with my looks or personality—it's no surprise that most people are attracted to vast wealth and confidence. So why have I just fucked my business partner's daughter on the table? I didn't even have the decency to take her to bed.

But even as the thought enters my head, I frown. That's not how it was, and I refuse to use that terminology. I didn't get carried away. I wasn't led by my dick. I knew perfectly well what I was doing. And the truth was that her warmth and desire, and her declaration of *I need you... I want you inside me...* totally unraveled me.

Mine, she wrote on my chest. I can still feel it, and I glance down, wondering if my skin is reacting to the paint, but it's not red. I think it's just the memory of the possessiveness of it, and the way she demanded that I tell her I was hers.

She slides her arms around my waist again and cuddles up to me, and I wrap my arms around her, and we stand there beneath the stream of hot water, just enjoying being close.

"Will you stay?" she whispers.

I kiss the top of her head. "I have to make sure my car's gone by the time Joe and the others arrive in the morning."

"I understand. But just for a while."

"Of course."

She moves back and gives me a shy smile, then turns off the shower. We go out, and when she picks up one of the big fluffy towels, I take it from her and proceed to dry her, taking my time to mop up the drips from her damp skin. She does the same to me, and then she takes my hand and leads me into the bedroom.

It's decorated like any spare room, in neutral shades of green and lavender, so I imagine that Huia had it repainted after Marama left home, but it still bears the remnants of her girlhood—a bright purple jewelry box on the chest of drawers; a painting on the wall of a Māori goddess that was probably done in her younger days; her poi—which are balls made from flax attached to cords that are swung to create patterns during traditional dances; and, on the shelves, a variety of school trophies. I glance at them, but Marama obviously doesn't think about the connotations of displaying her youth, and she takes me over to the bed.

She pulls the duvet back, and we climb onto the mattress and bring the duvet back over us. I lie back on the pillows, and she cuddles up to me.

"Thank you," she says. "I didn't expect this."

She thought I'd get dressed and say I have to leave. I probably should have. I should bring an end to this and walk away as fast as I can.

But Marama is soft, and she smells amazing, and I want to wring every last drop of pleasure out of this encounter before I move on.

So I turn to face her and wrap my arms tightly around her, until our legs are tangled and we're pressed together from our chests all the way to our thighs. She lifts her face to look up at me, and I kiss her slowly, leisurely, just enjoying the softness of her lips.

"Thank you," she whispers, during a brief respite in the kissing.

I kiss her nose. "For what?"

"For not turning me down."

I kiss her eyebrows. "I was powerless to resist."

"I would think there aren't many men who would say no when a woman sits naked before them and offers herself to them on a plate."

I kiss back down her nose. "That wasn't the reason."

"What do you mean?"

I taste her lips again. "You're beautiful. Stunning. I love your vivaciousness. Your spirit. But if I'm honest, it was the way you wanted me that made me cave."

She lifts up on an elbow so she can look at me. "Really?" She draws a finger across my forehead. "She really did a number on you, didn't she?"

"You mean Genevieve?"

"No. Your wife."

I don't say anything, but she's right of course. I still feel disloyal saying anything against Eleanor. She bore me two children, and she was a good life partner in many ways. But I'm only just beginning to realize what an effect her emotional coldness had on me.

She lays her head on my shoulder again, and we lie there in the semi-darkness, our hands moving slowly across each other's bodies, gently stroking.

I brush my fingers down her back and kiss the top of her head. "This can't happen again. You know that, right?"

She trails her fingers through my chest hair, and doesn't reply.

"Marama," I scold.

"I could come to your house," she says. "Nobody would know."

"I'd know. We couldn't risk it."

She turns her head and rests her chin on my chest, looking up at me with mischief in her eyes. "Don't you think it would be fun?"

My lips curve up. "I'm sure it would be amazing. But we can't."

"I could stay over. Then you could play with me all night."

Fuck. I'm getting hard again. Once, I could explain as getting carried away; a second time I'd have no such excuse.

"Stop it," I scold, pushing her away and sitting up. "It's not going to happen."

"You want to tell your cock that? I don't think it got the memo."

I throw her a glare, rise and pick up my underwear and trousers, and go into the bathroom. I grit my teeth and pace up and down until my erection has gone, then pull on my boxer-briefs and trousers.

When I come back out, she's pulled on her knickers and T-shirt, and she's sitting cross-legged on the bed.

"I have to go," I tell her, pulling on my shirt.

"I know." She rises onto her knees, shuffles forward, and beckons to me. I hesitate, then stand at the edge of the bed, and she does up my buttons.

"I'm sorry," I murmur.

She gets to the bottom of the shirt and brushes a crease away. "I understand. I enjoyed it, that's all." She lifts her gaze to mine. "And I want you again."

I suppress a shiver. "Don't."

"I can't help it." She studies my mouth. "There's so much we didn't get to do."

I close my eyes. "Marama…"

"I want you in other positions." She strokes down over my chest, brushing my nipples, and moistens her lips with the tip of her tongue. "I want to taste you."

Jesus. I pick up my wallet and walk out of the room.

She catches up with me as I reach the front door. "Aren't you going to say goodbye?"

I stop and turn to her. She stands there, looking young and hot in just her tee and knickers, her hair rumpled, her cheeks flushed. Her eyes are filled with hot desire, and I have no doubt that if I kiss her now, she'll be able to persuade me to start all over again, even though I came only twenty minutes ago.

"I have to go," I tell her.

"Aw." She looks so disappointed.

I can't help myself. I walk up to her, cup her face with my hands, and look into her eyes. "You're like a siren," I say huskily. "You drive me crazy."

"I love the way you look at me," she says. "The way you make me feel."

I kiss her, just a press of my lips to hers. She sighs, her breath whispering across my skin.

"Please," she whispers.

It would be so easy to kiss her senseless. To take her back into the bedroom and make love to her all night.

"I can't," I say, lowering my hands.

"I know. Your relationship with my father is important."

I meet her eyes, which spark with resentment. She means 'more important than me.'

It's true that Joe starts early in the morning, and if he sees my car here, covered in morning dew, he's going to know what happened. He's loyal to the family, and he might tell Rangi, and that would be the end of our friendship and business partnership. But that's not the only reason why I have to leave.

"Have you thought about your own reputation?" I ask.

Her expression turns wry. "My reputation? This isn't the nineteenth century."

"No. But even though you're not a member of the Midnight Circle, you're Rangi's daughter. The Circle wouldn't approve of us, and rumors spread quickly."

"I don't care what anyone else thinks."

"Would you care if you were accused of sleeping your way into exhibitions or money? What would Genevieve say if she knew you were sleeping with the man she wanted you to ruin?"

She drops her gaze, and her cheeks flush. She didn't realize that I'd guessed Genevieve's ulterior motives.

I slide a hand beneath her chin and lift it so I can look into her eyes again. "I don't care what Genevieve does to me," I say harshly, "but I do care about your reputation. She could tarnish your name as an artist and a Māori woman of integrity. This…" and I brush my thumb across her *moko kauae*, "is more than decoration. I understand that. And some people may claim you're not honoring it by sleeping with me. You need to think about that."

She blinks; that hadn't entered her head.

"I'm thinking about you," I tell her roughly.

She lifts her chin. "I can look after myself."

That makes my lips curve up. "I know that."

I brush my thumb over her bottom lip. Then I drop my hands, pick up my keys, shove my feet in my shoes, and leave the house.

It's dark out. I stride across to my car, get in, and start the engine. Glancing over at the house, I see Marama leaning against the door post, arms folded, forehead creased in a thoughtful frown. We study each other for a moment, before my lips curve up, just a fraction. Hers match, again, just a fraction.

Then I put the car into Drive and head off along the driveway, back to my suite at the Midnight Club.

*

Wednesday is the Midnight Circle's regular meeting day, unless someone calls for a meeting, the way Huxley did on Sunday. I hole up in my office at the resort for the morning, moody and irritable. I didn't sleep well. I lay awake for hours, going over the events of the night before, filled with a yearning I hadn't expected.

I miss her. But I know I mustn't contact her. And I hate not being able to do what I want.

"What?" I bark at Orson when he walks into my office around eleven.

His eyebrows rise and he holds up his hands as if to ward me off. "Steady, tiger. Just wondered if you had the report from Mackenzie's."

I grit my teeth, get to my feet, find the file at the bottom of a pile of folders I haven't gotten around to looking at because I can't concentrate, and pass it to him. I should apologize for snapping, but if I admit I was wrong, I'll have to explain why I'm in a mood.

He takes it, then pauses and his gaze skims my face. "You okay?"

"I'm fine," I reply tersely.

"You look tired."

"I didn't sleep well."

"You stayed the night here?" He knows I sleep better at my house in Herne Bay.

"Yes."

He studies me. Then he asks, "How's Marama?"

I glare at him. "What?"

"I know you went to see her yesterday."

"I sat for my portrait, yes. What's that got to do with anything?"

"Just wondered. Rangi's away, right?"

"I believe so."

"Was she okay?"

"She was fine. She took some photos and did a few sketches, then made us dinner."

Shit, why did I tell him that? Fuck me. Talk about a guilty conscience.

He meets my gaze. I hold it for a second, then put my hands on my hips and look down at the papers on my desk.

He clears his throat. "Are you coming to the meeting later?"

I give a short nod without looking up.

"All right. See you there." He hesitates as if he's about to say something more, but I sit down and open my laptop. Taking the hint, he backs away, then leaves the room.

Fuck. I massage my forehead with a hand. Get a grip, Spencer.

My phone lies on the desk to my right, and I reach out and slowly draw it toward me. I stare at the blank screen, then flick up the screen and turn it on. I bring up Snapchat and scroll down my list of contacts. She's there, her avatar looking surprisingly like her, with light-brown skin and dark hair up in a scruffy bun.

It would be so easy to start a message. Hey, good morning, just wanted to say thanks for last night and hope you're feeling okay today… or something else equally as cheesy. But that will suggest I want her to message back. And no doubt she'll ask a question, and it will be impolite not to return, and then we'll be having a conversation, and it's going to be impossible for me to stop. Better not to start it, right?

Only not messaging her seems rude, after what happened last night.

I sigh. While I understand that depression exists, I believe it's for other people, those with no willpower. Whenever I've felt low, I've countered it with exercise and action, and it's always made me feel better. Now, though, I feel a mist of listlessness settle over me. It's my choice to be alone. But is it what I really want? Or do I choose it because it's the easy, safe option? Because if you don't open your heart to anyone, there's no fear of getting hurt?

I look out of the window, thinking how wonderful it was last night to be wanted, and to feel loved and cared for, even in such a short space of time. The sex was great, but it was afterward, when we were lying in bed in each other's arms, that I felt truly at peace for the first time in… well, maybe ever. Eleanor just didn't seem to need me the way I needed her. When we had sex, I was always keen to provide aftercare, and offered cuddles and showers and massages, but she preferred to get up and return to her own room, and in the end I grew used to her rolling over and disappearing. So to be able to take Marama into the shower and wash each other lovingly, then to have her in my arms and kiss and caress each other, felt more precious than gold.

In the past, I've only been able to be romantic by giving gifts, or maybe acts of service. They were Eleanor's love languages, and she would much rather receive a new diamond necklace or have me do some jobs for her than receive hugs and kisses. I told myself that my

MIDNIGHT SECRET

love languages were the same, and tried to understand that when she gave gifts, that was her way of saying she loved me. But now I know I was lying to myself, because last night made it clear that physical touch and words of affection are much more important to me.

I stare at Marama's avatar, then turn off my phone and push it away. It may be true that I do need love and affection more than I thought I did. But there are plenty of women with whom I can find that. The daughter of my business partner and a young family friend is not one of them.

Bringing up my emails, I resolve to put her out of my mind once and for all.

*

The Midnight Circle does sometimes meet around Midnight, if we've all been exceptionally busy, or several of us are doing deals in the club, but today appears to have been a light day, and it's only seven p.m. when Huxley sends a message asking if everyone's available to meet earlier.

I enter the boardroom and take a seat at the table. Orson and Kingi are already here, and so is Joanna. Just a few seconds later, Huxley and Elizabeth come in with Mack, who closes the door behind him when he realizes he's the last.

"Thanks for coming early, everyone," Huxley says, taking a seat. "It'll be nice to arrive home before nine p.m. for once."

"You're getting old," Mack says.

"You wait until the baby's born," he replies. "Waking up in the night is going to make even you tired."

My eyebrows rise. "Baby? Something you haven't told us, Mack?"

He gives Huxley a wry glance, then smiles at the rest of us. "We hadn't announced it yet because she's only ten weeks, but yeah, Sidnie's pregnant."

"Oh… congratulations…" There's a general cheer and clinking of glasses.

"It'll be your turn next," Mack points out to Orson and Kingi.

"I'm working on it," Orson says.

Kingi just snorts and says, "Got a few more wild oats to sow yet."

I smile, but it makes my thoughts turn to Marama once again. She's in her prime, the perfect age for childbearing. She needs someone her own age who'll give her plenty of babies. It's yet another reason I have to keep my distance from her.

"So, I wanted to talk about Kahukura," Huxley says, referring to the commune on the land adjacent to the Midnight Club, and which is owned by Orson's girl, Scarlett. "We've finalized the charity donations, but I thought I'd raise the idea of offering a regular donation along the lines of the one we offer to the SPCA."

The others continue to talk about it, sharing their opinions. I keep quiet. It still goes against the grain for me to agree to help my old enemy's business, but I will accept whatever the rest of them decide. I'm determined to try to move on, for Orson's sake.

In the pocket of my suit trousers, my phone vibrates.

I take it and rest it on my thigh, under the table, and flick the screen up to open it. It's a Snapchat message from Marama. *Hello*, it says, *forgive me for messaging. I wasn't going to—I know you want what happened to be a one-off. But I missed you, and I wanted to say thanks. I had a great time.* She finishes with a smiley face with hearts.

I purse my lips. Well, it'll be rude not to reply.

Me: *Hey you. No worries. I appreciate the message. I had a great time, too.*

I add a heart emoji and send it, then wonder whether I should have included the heart. Oh well, too late now. She comes back almost immediately.

Marama: *I'm so glad. Where are you now, in Herne Bay?*

Me: *No, at Midnight*

Marama: *In your room?*

Me: *I'm actually in a meeting*

Marama: *Oh shit, sorry, lol*

Me: *It's okay. They're all talking. Nobody takes any notice of me*

Marama: *I can't believe that. You always dominate any room you're in*

Me: *Well that's very nice of you to say*

Marama: *It's true. I don't have eyes for anyone but you when you're around*

I read her words a few times, oddly touched. I don't know what it is about this girl, but she knows exactly how to slip through the chinks in my armor.

Thoughtfully, I pause. I shouldn't reply. I should tell her I'm busy and have to stop messaging.

I don't though.

Me: *I seem to remember your gaze glued to me last night like a laser while I posed*

Marama: *That might have something to do with you sitting there with your magnificent cock out*

I laugh, then look up as everyone glances over. "Sorry," I mumble, scratching my cheek. "Funny video on Facebook."

Huxley gives me an amused look, then continues talking. I glance at Orson, who's frowning, then drop my gaze back to my phone.

Me: *You just made me laugh in my meeting*

Marama: *Hahahaha what did they say?*

Me: *Orson's glaring at me. He asked me this morning how you were. He knew I was going over to see you*

Marama: *Well, fuck him. It's none of his business*

With a surge of rebelliousness, I agree with her. *True.*

Marama: *So when are you coming over again?*

Me: *I can't, you know that*

Marama: *I need to work on your portrait*

Me: *You said you could do the next step without me*

Marama: *I could. But I'd rather do it from life*

Me: *Naked?*

Marama: *Well, if you're offering…*

Me: *I'm not, to be clear*

Marama: *Spoilsport. I enjoyed our personal painting session*

I think of the way she smeared paint over me, and how much fun it was to wash it off.

Me: *Me too*

Marama: *Can you still feel what I wrote on your chest?*

Unbidden, my hand rises to rest over where she wrote the word *Mine.*

Me: *Did you brand me?*

Marama: *I did <devil emoji>*

I rub there, sure I can feel it burning my skin.

Marama: *Dad's not back until Monday*

I sigh. *Yeah, I know*

Marama: *What are you doing Friday evening? I'd like you to sit for me again*

My fingers hover over the keyboard. I shouldn't. I mustn't. I can't.

Marama: *I'll make dinner. My best meatballs and pasta*

I close my eyes briefly. The longing I feel is so strong that it makes me physically ache.

When I open my eyes, she's sent another message.

Marama: *I'll give Joe the day off on Saturday. You can stay the night then*

Ahhh… I thought I was stronger. I hadn't realized I was so weak where she's concerned.

Marama: *I'll serve dinner wearing nothing but an apron*

I stifle a laugh. Ah, to hell with it. YOLO, right?

Me: *Okay. I'll see you around six*

Marama: *I look forward to it. Oh, don't expect to get much sleep. I'm going to make the most of you while you're here*

She finishes with the devil emoji again. I give the message a heart, turn my phone off, and lift my gaze.

Everyone's looking at me.

"Your vote?" Huxley asks, amused.

I clear my throat. "Sorry, yes, fine by me."

"That Facebook video must be amazing," Joanna teases.

I just smile and pocket my phone. Across the table, I see Kingi dip his head to whisper something to Orson, who just shrugs, although his gaze meets mine before he looks away. Was Kingi asking who I was talking to? If he was, Orson obviously didn't offer an opinion. He's covering for me. I'm not used to that, and it's disconcerting, especially when I think about who I've been talking to.

Feeling like a schoolboy, I wait impatiently for the meeting to end, then head out of the door before Orson or anyone else can quiz me. It's one good thing about being a grown up. You don't have to answer to anyone. You can make your own choices—as long as you're prepared to live with the consequences.

MIDNIGHT SECRET

Chapter Fourteen

Marama

Friday

I spend the morning working. First, I assess Spencer's portrait in the early sunlight that streams into the studio. It's good; I'm pleased with the proportions and the initial base colors, and it's a good likeness. I've managed to capture the intensity of his gaze, and a shiver runs down my back as he seems to look right out of the painting at me. Later, when he's sitting for me, I'll start on the finer details, but for now I put it to one side.

Next, I prop the other sketch I did last night on the easel. I chuckle as I stand back and observe it. He's sitting in the chair, legs wide apart, completely naked. I only managed to get the basic pose down before he got to his feet, intending to leave, so you can't really tell it's him, unless you'd seen in real life the magnificent cock that juts out of the figure. Wow. Mmm. The man is truly marvelous.

I could stand and stare at it all day, but I take it down and put it to one side. I'll have to hide that somewhere! Now, I want to take some time to think about the first piece I'm doing for the Maramataka exhibition. Genevieve has texted to say she'd like to do a Zoom call at one p.m. to discuss it, and it would be great if I had something to show her, however basic it was.

First, I go through my blank canvases. The portrait I'm doing for Spencer is eighteen by twenty-four inches, so a decent size, but I want to go even bigger for the Maramataka painting. I pick up one that's thirty by forty inches and place it on the easel, turning it so it's portrait. I feel excited by the size of it. I want the space to be free with my brush, and to be able to create a suitable scene around the figures I intend to portray.

I make myself a coffee and some toast and bring it back to the studio. I wave to Joe as he passes outside the window carrying a bag of compost for the vegetable patch, and he nods and smiles back. He's more than happy to take tomorrow off as paid leave, and although I saw a glimmer of curiosity in his eyes, he didn't ask why.

I've already done some preliminary sketches, working on a composition that's pleasing to my eye. So I'm ready to start, and I choose a piece of charcoal and begin marking a light grid, then drawing the outlines of the major shapes.

For the first hour, I'm easily distracted, checking my phone, looking out the window, daydreaming, and sketching and re-sketching. But gradually I enter what I call 'the zone'—a magical, spiritual realm that most creative people will recognize. The real world fades away, and I become one with the canvas, descending into a focused plane of existence where all that exists are me, the canvas, and the charcoal in my hand. This happens to me frequently when I paint, and I've learned to go with the flow and enjoy it when it happens.

It's with some surprise when I finally check my phone and realize it's 12:45. I put down my charcoal and wash my hands, then come back to the canvas and observe the drawing. It's good. Getting the basic shapes of figures and animals is one of the most important things; there's nothing worse when you stand back and realize you haven't got the proportions right, and you have to start all over again.

To the left stands the *atua wāhine*—Hina Marama, the Māori goddess of female power and the moon. It's a self portrait, partly anyway, modeled on me, her body visible through a starlight-filled dress, her long hair lifting in the breeze and studded with stars that are going to form the night sky.

A wolf stands before her, large and powerful. Her hand rests on its shoulder, and its head is raised as it howls at her—at the huge full moon in the sky above them. I can already see the colors of the night sky—deep blues, purples, and greens; I'm going to draw on pictures from the Hubble telescope of far-off galaxies, and use silver and gold paint and glitter. I'm excited to start. I can't wait.

I make myself another coffee, then set up my laptop for Genevieve's call.

"Good afternoon," she says when I answer. She smiles. "How's my favorite artist?"

"If you mean me, I'm very well thank you."

She chuckles. "Of course I mean you. How are you doing? Did Spencer turn up on Wednesday?"

I nod, hoping I'm not blushing. "I made good progress on his portrait."

"That's good to hear. You have two weeks, of course, but it's always good to get stuck in."

"Oh, I'll definitely have it finished by then. I'll do some more this afternoon."

"Is he sitting for you again?"

"No," I reply, surprising myself with the lie, "I'll do the rest from memory." Why did I say that? There's nothing wrong with admitting that he's going to sit for me again.

But I realize I don't want her to know he's coming over. I don't want anyone to know. What Spencer and I have is nobody else's business. I don't want her mocking me, or trying to turn it to her advantage somehow. And anyway, I wouldn't be surprised if he changed his mind and didn't turn up, and I don't want to make a fool of myself.

"I made a start on the commission for Maramataka," I tell her, wanting to change the subject. "Would you like to see it?"

"Oh, please!"

I turn the laptop so it faces the canvas on the easel and let her look at it.

"Ohhh…" She says it softly. "That's beautiful."

Relief fills me. "I'm so glad you like it. I've already planned the colors, and I was thinking I might even add some collage—pieces of net, beads, and sequins for stars and planets."

"I'd love that. It would give it a kind of 3D effect, right?"

"A little, yes."

She nods. "What about the poses, are they final?"

I study them. "Pretty much. Why, do you have other ideas?"

"I'm not sure about the wolf…"

"He's howling at the moon," I point out.

"I understand. I'd prefer to see him looking at the ground. Maybe even sitting, head bowed. She's taming him, right? He's at her feet, subdued, subjugated."

I look at the picture, feeling a twinge of unease. That wasn't how I saw it.

"Female power and sexual agency," Genevieve reminds me. "Women subduing men, remember? That's what Hariata requested: powerful goddesses taming beasts and overturning male power."

I nod slowly. Te Whaihanga Toi Foundation is putting up the money. And it's Genevieve's gallery. When you're given a commission, you paint what's requested. It's been the same all the way through history; even artists like Michelangelo and Monet struggled with patrons and establishments, and I'm hardly in their league. I'm just an up-and-coming artist trying to get seen, and I have no leverage to argue against their requests. If I start getting precious about my work, they're likely to tell me they'll find another artist to back.

"Of course," I say, "that's a great idea. I'll make some changes."

"Excellent." Genevieve beams. "Well, I'll leave you to it. I'm so excited about this, Marama. I think we work well together. Good things are going to come from this, I can feel it."

I'm not quite sure what she means by that, but she sounds happy, so I nod and smile, and she ends the call.

I stand there, looking at the canvas. Hmm.

Thoughtfully, I go into the kitchen and start preparing dinner. I make the dessert and place it in the fridge. Then I start a basic tomato sauce by browning garlic, a chopped onion, a bay leaf, and red pepper flakes in olive oil, then adding tomato passata, or pureed strained tomatoes.

While that's simmering, I make the meatballs. I combine minced beef, pork, and veal, then whizz up some fresh breadcrumbs and let them soak in some full-cream milk for five minutes. I grate some sharp, salty pecorino Romano cheese and crush a garlic clove, and add that with some egg yolks, seasoning, and fresh parsley to the soaking bread, mashing it to make a coarse paste. Finally I add the minced meat, mix it all together with my hands, then form it into meatballs. It's an Italian recipe I picked up on my travels.

I brown them in hot olive oil, then place them in the crockpot. Finally I pour the sauce over the meatballs, turn on the crockpot, and leave it to cook while I tidy and clean the kitchen.

After making myself a sandwich, I fetch a water bottle from the fridge and return to the studio.

Taking a bite out of the sandwich, I study the canvas, thinking about what Genevieve said.

Putting the sandwich aside, I pick up a kneaded eraser, then lightly rub out some of the wolf. I don't need to erase it all—I'll be painting over most of it anyway. I consider the composition thoughtfully. Then I go over to the laptop and search for a picture. I find one of a real wolf, seated, looking down, head bowed. That's perfect. I pick up the charcoal and study the canvas. Then I begin to sketch again.

It takes me an hour, but eventually I get the proportions right and the wolf in the right place. I step back and take the whole picture in, stretching my back. I think Genevieve and Hariata will be pleased with the pose. I've made the wolf large, but the goddess's hand looks as if it's keeping him in place, pressing his head down. Spencer the wolf, subdued by a woman—exactly what they wanted.

Quelling the uncomfortable feeling in my stomach at what I'm doing, I wash my hands, then take the canvas, turn it around, and place it behind some of my other works in progress. I don't want Spencer spotting this one yet.

Eventually, of course, it's inevitable that he'll see it. I wince at the thought. There won't be anything specifically to say it's him, but of course the implication is going to be obvious. Oh well, I'll worry about that when it happens. He knows I've been given the commission, and I'm sure he'll have guessed what it entails.

Placing his portrait back on the easel, I study it with a smile. He won't be here for a few hours yet. I would still rather work on the finer details with him in front of me, but the base colors need some more work. So I put on some music, squirt some paint onto a palette, and start painting.

After a couple of hours, I have the foundation how I want it. I clean the palette and brushes, then head to my bedroom, feeling the first flutter of nerves in my belly.

I take a shower and wash my hair, then use the hairdryer until it's almost dry and roll it up in bendy rollers. My hair is naturally wavy, but these give it a lift and a prettier curl. Leaving my hair to dry, I do my make up carefully in neutral shades that complement my skin, then spend some time choosing what to wear.

I joked about serving dinner just in an apron and I'm prepared to do that if the mood is right, but I know that in many ways it's sexier to wear an outfit that needs removing than to appear naked at the start. Normally at home I'd wear jeans or yoga pants or shorts, but I don't want to wear trousers today.

I'll never be able to compete with the elegant Eleanor, nor with the driven businesswomen he mixes with every day. Equally I don't want to go slutty. I'm an artist, and I think he quite likes my boho look as it's different from what he's used to.

So I choose a light-blue dress that comes to just above the knee with short sleeves and a deep V neckline, with terracotta-colored embroidery that seems perfect for an autumn afternoon. I leave my legs bare. When my hair's dry, I take out the rollers and run my fingers through it so it tumbles around my shoulders, then add a flower clip to the side.

By now, it's getting close to six, so I return to the kitchen and put the oven on for the garlic bread and lay the table, choosing to stay inside tonight, as it's started to rain lightly. I give the meatballs a stir and put on some rigatoni pasta. Then, once it's bubbling nicely, I go over and sit on the seat in the bay window, overlooking the drive.

It's raining more heavily now, pattering on the gravel. There's no sign of Spencer's Bentley. I pull up my legs, wrap my arms around my knees, and rest my temple on the window. Suddenly, it occurs to me that he might not come. I know he has reservations about seeing me, and he's had a whole day for his brain to come up with reasons this is a bad idea. Surely he'd have texted me by now, though? He wouldn't just not turn up? No, he's far too polite for that. I pick up my phone, but no messages are waiting.

It's only just gone six. He might still turn up.

At ten past, I'm still waiting. I turn off the pasta and drain it, add it to the crockpot, stir it in, then turn the crockpot off. I'm just putting the garlic bread on an oven tray when my phone buzzes.

My heart sinks as I pick it up, convinced he's going to say he's not coming. My jaw drops, though, as I realize the message isn't from him. It's from my ex, Connor.

I stare at it, shocked. I haven't heard from Connor since I walked out of our apartment over a year ago, after I found out he'd been cheating on me. He didn't try to defend himself. He didn't run after me. And he didn't try to convince me to stay. So why on earth is he texting me now?

I open the message, and my eyes widen. It says *I'm outside. Can I come in?*

I text back, *Outside where?*

Your parents' house, he says.

I stride back to the bay window. Sure enough, a car is sitting on the drive, its lights illuminating the rain. I recognize it—it's his father's Ford.

Fuck.

My heart bangs as I tug the curtains shut. *What do you want?* I text back, my hands shaking.

Just to talk. I'm walking toward the door.

No, I text hurriedly, *I'm not letting you in.*

But at that moment he rings the doorbell, and I jump.

I walk through to the hallway, seeing his figure through the glass door. Oh fuck. Now what do I do? My spine stiffens with resentment. This is my house, and I don't have to do anything. I don't have to let him in.

Equally I want him to go in case Spencer does decide to turn up. So I summon all my courage and open the door.

Connor stands there, hands jammed in his pockets, shivering slightly as the rain sluices across him. He's a good-looking guy, tall with dark-blond hair, but he looks older and more tired than the last time I saw him.

"Hey, Mama." He sings it the way he always used to—it's the opening line of a Kanye West song. "Can I come in?"

I glare at him. "No. Go away."

"Marama, come on, please, it's fucking cold out here. Let me in. I just want to talk."

"No, I'm expecting someone."

His eyebrows rise. "Who?"

It annoys me that he assumed I'd still be single, as if I'd never find anyone else. "None of your business."

A fresh sheet of rain cuts across him, and he shivers. "This is ridiculous, I can't talk to you like this. I'm going to come in."

"No…" I go to close the door, but to my alarm he puts a foot out to stop it and pushes past me. He's bigger than me and he takes me by surprise, so I have no chance to stop him. My heart races as I suddenly realize I'm completely alone here. "I want you to leave," I state loudly.

"I just want to talk." He shakes his head, sending droplets flying. He's always been like this. Doing exactly what he wants with no regard for me.

"What about?" I push the door a little closed to stop the rain coming in, but make sure to leave it open so he knows I'm not capitulating. I don't think he'd do me any harm, but I keep my phone in my hand anyway, ready to dial for help if I need it. "I can't imagine what you think you have to say to me. I haven't heard from you for over a year."

He frowns. "I know. I didn't think there was any point in contacting you. You'd made up your mind that it was over."

"I don't know how you manage to make it sound as if it's my fault it ended."

He has the grace to look ashamed at that. "That wasn't my intention. I know what I did was wrong. And I needed to say I'm sorry."

I give him a baffled look. "Why now, after all this time?"

He runs a hand through his wet hair, then slides his hands back into his jeans pockets and hunches his shoulders. "My therapist said I should see you and apologize, face to face."

That surprises me. He was always very dismissive of counseling, and he'd be the last person I'd expect to go. "Why are you seeing a therapist?"

He shrugs. "My depression has been super bad since you left."

Something shifts inside me as he says that. His depression played a huge part in our lives when we were together. For a narcissist like Connor, it was the absolute worst condition he could have. When he was bad, he became incredibly self-centered, able to concentrate on nothing but himself. I was heartbroken when we broke up, but as time went by, I began to realize how his moods overshadowed my life, as if his depression was a monolith that blocked out the sun.

I no longer have to deal with that, and it's only now that I understand what a relief it's been to be free. I wasn't sure I was over him, but I've healed without realizing it.

"I'm sorry to hear that," I tell him, meaning it. "But I'm glad you're having therapy. Is it helping?"

"A bit."

"So… are you going to, then?"

He frowns. "Going to what?"

"Apologize, Connor. For cheating on me."

He runs his tongue over his teeth. Then he says, "I am sorry."

My throat tightens. I've longed for his apology, but now he's delivered it, even though it's possible he means it, it hasn't brought the consolation I'd expected. "Why did you do it?" I whisper. "Why did you cheat on me? I thought we were happy."

"Who knows why these things happen?"

I glare at him. "Well that's a fucking childish statement."

He blows out a breath. "I'm sorry."

"Stop saying you're sorry when you don't mean it."

"I do mean it."

My hands clench into fists. "This is pointless. I don't even care if you do mean it. The fact is that your cheating isn't the only reason I left. I was pregnant, and you wanted me to get rid of it."

Impatience flitters across his face. "Why are you bringing this up again? You had a miscarriage—there was no decision to make."

"That's not the point."

"What is the point?"

I grit my teeth. "Why are you here, exactly?" My spidey senses are tingling. A cheating ex doesn't travel in the rain just for closure. "What's really going on?"

"Nothing!" He wipes his face. "Can I have a towel?"

I blow out an angry breath. "Stay here." I march off and retrieve a towel from the bathroom, then come back out. To my annoyance, he's gone into the living room. "I told you to say put."

He reaches out and takes the towel from me without comment and wipes his face.

It strikes me then that it's Friday, not the weekend. It would take him an hour to fly to Auckland, and at least another forty minutes or so to get here on the ferry. He can't have worked until five. "Have you been at work today?" I ask.

He looks sullen. "I've been laid off."

"Oh..." He's a lecturer in art history. I'd heard that the university was cutting back; I guess art history was one of the first subjects to take a hit. "I'm sorry to hear that."

He rubs his hair, then clears his throat. "I saw that article in Kōrero about the auction you took part in at Lumen. I was really proud of you—you're doing so well."

I don't reply. When I was with him, he was quick to tell me that artists rarely sold enough pieces to make a living. I can only imagine it rankles that I'm starting to be successful.

"And I heard you're going to have an exhibition at Lumen," he continues. "That's really impressive."

"What do you want, Connor?"

"I don't want anything," he says defensively. Then he shrugs. "But I was planning to write to the owner, and I thought maybe you'd be able to put in a good word for me, you know, for old time's sake…"

Fury billows through me. "How dare you come to me now that I'm doing well, and ask for my help after you cheated on me."

"I said I was sorry," he says indignantly.

"You think a half-hearted apology makes up for what you did?"

"Oh, get off your high horse," he snaps. "Not everyone has Daddy ready to bail them out if they get in trouble. Most of us have to do what we can to get ahead."

"I can't believe you." Exasperated and almost tearful with fury, I gesture at the door. "I want you to leave."

For the first time, a touch of panic lights his eyes. "No, come on," he says, trying to backtrack, "I'm sorry. I'm at my wits' end, that's all, and it's scaring me a bit. The economic situation is absolutely dire, and art history isn't exactly at the top of anyone's list. I just need a bit of help, and then I promise I'll leave you alone."

"You didn't come here to apologize at all," I snap. "You came here because you saw that article, you realized my star is rising, and you decided to hang onto my coattails. Well, I'm not interested in helping you after what you did."

"Don't be so spiteful. Come on, for old time's sake…"

"Stop saying that. I don't owe you anything. I want you to leave, now."

He moves toward me and grasps my wrist. I step back, alarmed at the flare of bitterness and anger in his eyes, but he refuses to let go, and I exclaim as his grip tightens.

I'll never know what might have happened next, though, because behind me someone snaps, "Take your hands off her," and relief floods me as I turn and see Spencer standing there, eyes blazing.

MIDNIGHT SECRET

Chapter Fifteen

Spencer

Fury sears through me at the sight of Marama struggling against the hold of this strange guy in her own house. He stares at me, but doesn't release her, so I stride up to him and push him hard on the chest with both hands. He stumbles back and releases her, clearly shocked at the physical contact, but I don't let him take a breath; I push him again, and again, until he backs up against the wall. Then I lean my forearm against his throat, pinning him there.

"Fuck," he says, and tries to fight me off, but I'm taller, bigger, and stronger than he is, and I hold him there easily, privately thanking my personal trainer for pushing me to continue weight training and boxing as part of my exercise routine.

Eventually, he stops struggling. He sends a pleading glance to Marama and says, "Mama, tell him to get off me."

"No, I don't think I will," she says, her voice hard. "I think it's exactly what you deserve."

It sinks in then—this is no intruder who's burst into the house to rob it. He's a good-looking guy, in his mid-thirties, and his endearment suggests he knows her well—this must be Connor. I skim my gaze over him with disdain. This is the guy who Rangi said treated her like shit, who had some kind of hold over her and who manipulated her and tried to pressure her into having an abortion. I already disliked him even before I discovered him in the house.

His gaze comes back to me, and he frowns, and then his eyes widen. "This is the guy you've been waiting for?" He blinks, scanning me and obviously noticing my designer jacket, my expensive watch, my classy cologne, and the superior demeanor I've spent a lifetime creating. His expression darkens, and with a sneer he says to her, "Didn't realize you were dating grandads now."

I punch him then, for Marama, for Rangi, and because the irritating little fucker deserves it. He yells and claps his hands over his face.

"You've broken my dose!" he yells as blood seeps through his fingers.

"Don't be a pussy," I snap. "You'll live."

"You should go," Marama says. "Keep the towel."

He presses it to his nose. With a last glare at the two of us, he storms off, banging the door shut behind him. Marama walks to the window and peers through the curtains. I hear the Ford's engine start, and then it recedes into the distance, the tires scrunching on the gravel.

"He's gone," she says with relief, turning back to me. "Oh, thank God."

Then she bursts into tears, bringing her hands up to cover her face.

I can only imagine how scared she must have been. I'm guessing he either pushed his way in or she only intended to talk to him in the hall, and she'd obviously asked him to leave when he grabbed her arm.

"Hey…" I walk up to her and pull her into my arms. "He's gone. It's okay, baby, you're safe now."

She curls her arms up in front of her and buries her face in my neck, and we stand there like that for a minute or two, until her sobs subside. I stroke her back, just relieved I got there in time.

She looks beautiful today, fresh and gorgeous in her dress, with her hair loose around her shoulders. I lift a hand to touch it, only then realizing my knuckles are covered in Connor's blood. I flex my fingers and my hand throbs—damn, that's going to sting for a while.

Marama turns her head, sees me looking at it, and follows my gaze, then steps back with an exclamation. "Spencer…" She wipes her face. "Aw, look at you."

"It's not my blood." My voice holds a touch of smugness, and she gives me a wry look.

"Come on," she says, "let's get you cleaned up."

She takes me into the kitchen, and uses soap and water to cleanse the blood. I'm more than capable of cleaning myself, but I'm happy to let her do it. Her touch is gentle, and I observe the tenderness on her face as she rubs her thumbs over my skin and rinses it beneath the tap. Eleanor wouldn't have done this. She would have told me I was being ridiculous for fighting and insisted I sort it out myself.

It's kinda nice to be pampered.

When the skin is clean, Marama dries it with a few pieces of kitchen towel, then lifts my hand to her face and presses it to her cheek. "It'll be tender for a while," she says softly.

"It was worth it." I cup her other cheek with my free hand. "Are you okay?"

She nods. "I'm glad you arrived when you did, though. I wasn't sure if you were coming."

"I was delayed at the office." It's a half truth. I did have a meeting, but the reason I was late was because I was pacing my office for fifteen minutes, repeatedly telling myself I shouldn't see her again.

Clearly, it didn't work. All the way here I was cursing myself for being weak, but now I feel a surge of relief that I did come. Marama is an emotionally strong, independent woman, and I would never say that she needed saving, but what might have happened if I hadn't turned up?

She turns her head and kisses my palm, and the mound at the base of my thumb. Then she presses her lips against my wrist and touches her tongue to the sensitive skin there.

My pulse picks up speed, and my cock hardens in my trousers. Jeez, that was quick. Damn, this girl knows exactly how to get me going.

I don't move, caught up in her spell as she kisses back across my palm, then down my clean index finger. She kisses all the way to the tip, then closes her mouth over it, lifting her gaze to mine as she sucks. Her eyes are hot, and full of desire and longing.

Fuck.

Carefully, I extract my finger from her mouth, cup her face in my hands, and crush my lips to hers.

Aaahhh... her lips are so soft, and she tastes sweet as I stroke my tongue inside her mouth. She moves the sides of my jacket over my shoulders, and I lower my arms to let the jacket fall to the floor before returning my hands to her face. I'm wearing a shirt over the top of my chinos, and she rests her hands on my chest, then moves them down, lifts the hem of the shirt, and slides them beneath the fabric onto my belly. The touch of her fingers on my skin sends hairs rising all over my body, and I tingle as she strokes up around my ribs to my back, slipping her hands right up beneath the shirt to my shoulder blades, which for some reason feels secret and wicked and forbidden and sexy.

I groan, tipping my head to the side and deepening the kiss, and she sighs in response, lifting up on tiptoes and pressing against me. She's so soft all over, and my hands leave her face and travel over her hair and down her back, following the dip of her waist and the flare of her hips, and over the swell of her bottom. I clench my fingers there, pulling her tightly to me so she can feel my erection, and we both sigh.

She moves back and looks up at me, moistening her lips with the tip of her tongue, then takes my hand and leads me out of the kitchen. I assume she's going to take me into the bedroom, but instead she leads me into the living room and over to the plush cream leather suite. She moves me back until my legs meet the sofa, and then pushes me until I sit, following which she hitches up the skirt of her dress and climbs on top of me.

Sitting astride me, she takes my face in her hands and kisses me again.

I feel a twinge of guilt at the thought that I'm sitting on Rangi's sofa, kissing his daughter… but then I stroke up the outside of her thighs to her hips and realize she's not wearing any underwear, and every single thought flees my head, as my pheromones and hormones and nerve endings take over my ability to think and speak.

I grasp her butt and sink my fingers into the soft muscles there, and she moans against my lips and rocks her hips. Argh, she's pressing against my erection, arousing herself on it, and that's so fucking erotic that the last dregs of my resistance fade away.

Things turn heated then—not that they were exactly cool in the first place. I lift a hand and slide it into her hair, tightening my fingers on it to make sure she doesn't pull away as I kiss her exactly the way I want—fiercely, taking my pleasure from her, demanding she yield. She doesn't fight me; she just moans again, her tongue tangling with mine, and shivering as my fingers skate over her skin.

Crossing her arms, she lowers her hands to the hem of her dress, draws it up her body, and tosses it aside. Jesus, she's not wearing any underwear at all, and now she's completely naked astride me.

She's teaching me so much about myself; I thought I was strong and determined, and I thought I had incredible willpower, but with her it all dissipates like morning mist, to be replaced by this raw, feral hunger. I can't resist her. I want her more than I've ever wanted anything in my life, and that's saying something, as my drive in business is second to none.

I draw my hands up her back, lightly, because I like making her shiver, then bring them around to her breasts. They fit perfectly in my palms like two small cushions, the light-brown nipples soft and relaxed until I take them between my thumbs and forefingers and tug them. She gasps, and I growl as I feel the nipples tighten immediately to firm buds. I like having this power over her, being in charge of her desire. At this moment, she belongs to me—not Connor, not any other man. She's mine.

Thinking of the word she imprinted on my chest, I tear my mouth from hers, place hungry, wet kisses down her neck until I reach her breasts, and then I lift one so I can close my mouth over the nipple. She slides her hands into my hair, her nails grazing my scalp, and I suck, which in turn makes her arch her back and cry out.

I hadn't planned what I'd do when I got here; I wasn't even sure if my guilty conscience would get the better of me and we wouldn't make it this far. I'd assumed that if anything did happen that this time I'd take her to the bedroom and indulge in at least a little foreplay.

But it feels as if we're self-combusting, our passion like a flame that leaps into a fire between us. Our kisses become frantic, hungry, and demanding, hers as well as mine. I'm hard as a rock and so turned on I'm almost throbbing, and I'm not surprised when I slide a hand down between us, inserting my thumb into her folds to explore, and discover her already swollen and slippery with moisture.

"Condom?" she whispers.

"We should slow down," I scold, circling my thumb over her clit.

She bites her bottom lip and moans, then says, "Why?"

"Uh… I don't know, I can't think straight."

She giggles and I laugh, extract my wallet, and take out a condom. "Let me do it," she murmurs. She undoes my belt, unbuttons my trousers, carefully slides the zipper over my straining erection, then pushes down my boxers to release it.

"Spencer," she says in such an admiring tone that my cock swells even more in appreciation. "You're so magnificent."

"And you're a goddess. To look at, and in spirit." I lift her hand and kiss her inner wrist where he was grasping it. It still shows the imprint of his fingers. She's going to have a bruise there. I feel an uncharacteristic surge of rage. "He hurt you."

She glances at her wrist. Then she says, "Forget him. He's nothing." She tears off the packaging, places the condom on the tip of my erection, and rolls it slowly down. "You're everything," she says, lifting up and guiding me inside her. Then, keeping her gaze fixed on mine, she impales herself on me, our breaths mingling with our joint sighs.

"Fuck," she says loudly. She moves back and lowers again, and a third time, coating me with her moisture each time, until finally our bodies are flush, and I'm buried deep inside her. Tipping back her head, she groans. "I can feel you all the way up. Ohhh… that feels so good…"

I stroke down her body, enjoying the view, and turned on by the way she's so unashamed of showing her pleasure. She's so open, so warm, and I love the way she wanted me so much that she pushed me onto the sofa and decided to have me there and then.

I'm not stupid—I know part of it is the shock of Connor turning up, and a desperate need to retake control, but I'm more than happy to be the recipient of that.

She lowers her mouth back to mine and kisses me as she begins to move. I rest my hands on her hips, letting her go at her own pace, just enjoying being inside her. Ahhh, her skin is so smooth and soft. I trail my fingers lightly up her ribs and around her back while she kisses me, and she shivers, her nipples tightening even more.

"That feels amazing," she whispers. "Don't stop."

"I won't."

"Never stop touching me, Spencer."

I'm inclined to accede to her demand, but she delves her tongue into my mouth, silencing my retort. Her hands slide into my hair, and she kisses me deeply, claiming my mouth, her hips keeping up their relentless rocking. I'm not going to last long like this. The sensation of being wanted, being taken with such passion, is overwhelming me.

I skim my hands around her ribs to cup her breasts again and play with her nipples, and she arches her back so I can suck them, then tease them while they're wet, which makes her groan.

Her hips move faster, and it's not long before she says, "Oh, mmm… oh God…"

"Are you going to come for me, baby?"

"Yeah…" She kisses me, her forehead creasing in a frown, driving her hips forward and grinding against me, and it proves to be her undoing; she shivers, shudders, then cries out as her orgasm takes her.

I hold her, loving the sensation of her clenching around me, and drinking in her pleasure as she sighs against my mouth. "Ah, baby," I murmur, "you feel so good…"

Her body finally releases her, and she gasps and takes several deep breaths, while I kiss her cheek, her jaw, her neck, and around to her ear.

"You're so beautiful," I tell her, pressing my lips against her skin. "I love watching you come."

She moves back a little, brushing her thumbs against the silver on my temples. Then she starts moving again.

"You make me feel amazing, Spencer," she murmurs, placing light kisses on my mouth, my cheekbones, and across my eyebrows. "You know exactly how to turn me on. How to make me feel good."

My fingers tighten on her ass. I love feeling the muscles move as she thrusts.

"I love your silver hair," she whispers, kissing my temple, "and your smooth jaw, and your amazing mouth." She kisses it, then continues up to my eyelids. "And your blue eyes. And your strong body." She drops her hands to my shirt and undoes the buttons, then pushes both sides apart. Resting her hands on my chest, she brushes them over my skin and up to my shoulders. "You're in amazing shape, and you're so strong, I love how you just pushed him across the room. Do you know how much that turned me on?" She continues stroking me, up my neck, her thumbs brushing my throat, and then back down, feeling my collarbone, down my sternum, and teasing my nipples.

I don't know why this girl fires me up so much, but her admiration shines from her in both her touch and her words, and it unravels me, filling me with a warm glow that travels all the way through me.

I love the way she's riding me, thrusting her hips and driving me in and out of her. I lean my head on the back of the sofa, looking up at her, my heart racing as I feel my climax approaching at a rate of knots.

"I'm going to make you come," she says in a sassy voice, nipping my bottom lip. "I'm going to take you all the way, Spencer, my gorgeous silver fox, are you ready?"

"Yeah," I say hoarsely, more turned on by her declaration than I care to admit.

"Tell me how it feels," she demands. "Where does it start?"

"In the pit of my stomach," I murmur. "Aching and tightening."

"Mmm…" She kisses me, apparently turned on by that. "You feel a hormone rush?"

"Yeah… building up… the anticipation… excitement."

"Can you feel it in your balls?"

"Yeah, throbbing a bit, tightening up. Everything's getting… sensitive…" My eyes close, and I'm starting to lose the ability to speak.

"Tell me," she says. "Tell me when you reach the point of no return."

"Ahhh… close… It's coming…"

"You feel it rising from your balls, Spencer? Up through your cock?"

"Yeah…" My body stiffens, every muscle clenching, and then I exclaim as I come, ejaculating inside her. She says something, but at that point I'm just a ball of sensation, exploding into a world of ecstasy, relaxation, and pleasure.

I gasp, and she kisses me deeply, still moving, and the way her tight walls grip me as she thrusts keeps the pulses coming, drawing the orgasm out. It's powerful and intense, and when it finally finishes, my body trembles with the release.

"Good boy," she murmurs, cupping my face.

I give a short laugh, unable to contradict her, content to relax into the cushions and let her have her way with me.

She takes her time to kiss me, tasting me, delving her tongue into my mouth and letting it dance with mine, while my heartbeat slowly returns to normal, and my limbs gradually regain feeling.

Lifting her head, she surveys me with a smile. "Mmm. I think we need some dinner."

In response, my stomach rumbles, and we both laugh. She kisses me, then carefully rises. "Come on," she says softly, pulling on her dress. "Just ten minutes for the garlic bread and it'll be ready."

I dispose of the condom, stuff myself back in my boxers, and zip up my trousers, then follow her out to the kitchen.

"You okay?" she says, straightening after putting the tray of bread into the oven. She slides her arms around me. "You look a bit… other."

"I feel lightheaded. I think you drained me dry."

She giggles. "Was that a good orgasm?"

I put my arms around her. "The best. It went on forever."

"I'm glad. It's what you deserve after rescuing me." She kisses my chin.

"I didn't rescue you," I scold. "If I hadn't turned up, you'd have dealt with him. I have no doubt about that. You're a very capable woman."

Her eyebrows rise. "I think that's the nicest thing anyone's ever said to me."

"I mean it. You're confident and accomplished and talented."

"Three things you like in a woman," she says, smiling. She's thinking about Eleanor. And maybe about Genevieve as well.

"Yes." I kiss her nose. "But you're also open with it. Not afraid to share yourself. And you're a very sexual person. You want to have sex. You tease and respond and share your thoughts. I find that very attractive."

"You say such nice things," she whispers.

I open my mouth to say something, then look into her big brown eyes and feel a twinge of warning, deep inside, as if a bell has been rung and I can feel its ringing throughout my entire body.

Careful, Spencer. Careful.

"You deserve it," I say instead, and kiss her nose. "Now what's in the pot? It smells fantastic."

Chapter Sixteen

Marama

I serve up the meatballs and pasta, and by the time we've brought it to the table with a fresh green salad, the garlic bread is ready. Spencer pours me a glass of red wine and himself a Sprite, sits at the head of the table while I sit to his left, and we tuck into the meal.

The panic and fury I felt when Connor arrived is finally dissipating. His arrival made me feel mixed up and uneasy. They don't tell you that when you break up with someone, you don't stop having feelings for them. It's been over a year since I've seen him, but I still felt that tug in my solar plexus, that warmth you get when you're attracted to someone. But it was quickly overwritten by his casual disregard of the pregnancy, and then of course his final admission that he came to see if I'd get him a job.

Fucking cheek.

I'm so relieved Spencer turned up when he did. I don't think Connor would have pushed it further… but who knows what a man might do when he's desperate?

I bite into a piece of garlic bread, my gaze straying to the silver-haired man sitting beside me. He's normally so well turned out, but right now his hair is mussed, his shirt buttons are undone, and he looks relaxed and extremely sexy.

I think about the way he pushed Connor, then pinned him against the wall as if he weighed nothing, and a sizzle starts at the base of my spine and runs up my back. He's so commanding. His utter contempt for Connor was evident in his disdainful look that I know must have made Connor feel an inch high.

"Did Connor hurt your feelings?" I ask, scooping up a forkful of the pasta.

Spencer's eyebrows rise. "No, why?"

"He said 'Didn't realize you were dating grandads now.'"

His lips twist. "Well, I am a grandad, so technically he was right."

"Oh yeah."

He pushes a meatball around the plate, then looks up at me. "It's another reason we shouldn't be doing this."

"Because of your grandson?"

"No. Because you're going to want children, and I've had my family."

I shrug. "I'm not even sure I want kids anymore."

"I don't believe that."

"Not every woman wants children. I wasn't trying to get pregnant before, with Connor—it was an accident. I'm nearly thirty, and I'm only just breaking out in my career. I don't want to bring it screeching to a halt now."

"You can paint while you have kids," he teases.

I roll my eyes. "You know what I mean."

"I do… but you need to think carefully about it. Children are a wonderful gift, and you'd make an amazing mother."

The compliment surprises me. "I don't think so," I say with a laugh. "I'm not exactly the maternal type."

"Of course you are. You're warm, loving, and affectionate. What's that, if not maternal?"

I suppose he's comparing me to Eleanor. Helen has mentioned before that she wasn't the cuddly sort of mother. Both she and Orson have commented in the past that Spencer was a distant father, always working, and super strict at home.

"Do you regret not spending more time with your kids now?" I ask, crunching into some lettuce.

He gives me an amused look. "You really don't have a filter, do you?"

I shrug. "I'm not judgmental, only curious. If you don't want to answer, that's okay."

He leans back. "I don't mind talking about it. Regret is a pointless emotion. I can't turn back the clock, even if I wanted to. And I'm not sure I would. Work has always been my focus."

"Because of your upbringing?"

"I think so. No doubt my kids think they would have benefited from having spent more time with me, but I'm not sure that's the case."

"What do you mean?"

It's his turn to shrug. "I don't know that I have it in me to be that sort of father."

"I wish you wouldn't talk like that. You're not the ogre you portray yourself as."

"I know what people think of me."

"Yes, because you've carefully cultivated that image. I don't believe you're like that beneath the facade, though. I think it's something you've created to protect yourself. To stop yourself from being hurt."

He has a mouthful of Sprite. "You're very direct."

"Do you mean rude?"

He laughs and leans forward to continue his meal. "No. Nosy, maybe."

"I'll take that." I have a mouthful of pasta. "Tell me about your birth parents."

Immediately, the shutters come down. "Why do you want to know about them?"

"Because they're part of you, and I want to know everything about you. Don't scowl at me. Are you very like your birth father?"

"In looks, maybe a little. In every other way, definitely not."

He means he's determined not to be. He's modeled himself on his foster father and forged the rest of his personality to be as unlike his birth father as possible.

"Were your parents Catholic?"

"I'm guessing the six kids gave that away."

"It was kind of a hint. Are you religious?"

"No." He doesn't elaborate.

"Can you remember much about your childhood?"

"Yes."

I spear a meatball with my fork and wait.

He glares at me. Then he gives another sigh, and the tension leaves his body. "Every positive memory I have of being a kid is connected to being away from my parents. Sports days at school, going to camp, staying over at friends' houses. Life at home was hard. My mother was miserable literally all the time, physically and mentally exhausted from having so many children underfoot, and having no money to feed, clothe, or entertain them. I don't remember her ever having a kind word for me." He stabs a meatball with his fork. "And my father was permanently drunk." His expression is as hard as granite. He glances at me, then lowers his gaze. There's something he's not telling me.

Understanding dawns. "Is that why you don't drink alcohol? Because you're worried about being an alcoholic?" When he doesn't answer, I know I'm right. "So you've never had a drink?"

"Nope." He's obviously terrified of turning into his father.

I feel a prickle of insight. There's something he's not telling me. "Do you have a temper?" I ask, keeping my voice light.

"Not now."

"So you did?"

His spine is rigid, his face expressionless. He's resenting the hell out of this conversation. Equally, though, he hasn't changed the subject.

"What happened?" I ask softly.

He's quiet for a while, long enough that I start to think he's not going to reply. Then, eventually, he says, his voice low, "There was an incident one night."

I make sure to stay calm and relaxed. "Oh?"

"I came home late from a rugby game. He was yelling, throwing things. I knew what that meant."

"He was going to be violent?"

He nods. "I went straight up to my room. My siblings were all awake, cowering in their beds. I was terrified, but worried about my mother. I went back down to the kitchen. I could hear a horrible sound as I got close. It sounded as if he was smacking a piece of meat."

I press a hand to my mouth. "Oh no…"

"I peered around the door. He was punching her. There was blood everywhere. I didn't know what to do. I was about to run and get help… and then he turned around." He speaks faster now, as if the padlock has been undone and the words are spilling out. "The knife block sat on the table, and I took out the biggest knife."

My heart bangs so loudly I'm surprised he can't hear it. What is he going to admit to me?

But he just sighs and leans on the table. "I couldn't do it. I froze, and he lunged for me and knocked it out of my hand. And then he beat the hell out of me for it. Told me if I ever looked at him like that again, he'd kill me. And I believed him."

"Oh, Spencer…"

"Both Mum and I ended up in hospital. Shortly after that the authorities took us kids away."

"How awful for you."

He finally lifts his gaze to mine and gives a rueful smile. "I've never told anyone what I did. Not even Eleanor. I've spent my whole life trying to forget that moment. Not because I failed—but because I wanted to do it. I wanted him dead." His hands clench into fists.

I understand now. His urge to hurt his father was so strong that it frightened him. He thought it meant he'd inherited his father's anger. And he's spent his life attempting to contain it. Refusing to drink alcohol. No wonder the guy has such a thing about being in control.

He brushes his hand across his face. "I shouldn't have told you," he says roughly.

"No, I'm so glad you did."

"You'll think less of me."

I lean forward and put a hand on his. "Of course I won't. Your father was threatening your mother. And your siblings were terrified. You knew he could easily have turned his rage on them. So you tried to stop him. It was perfectly understandable. Commendable, even. It was extremely brave."

He frowns and blinks at me. "All these years I've been convinced that if I told anyone, they'd be horrified, maybe even call the police. How can you be so forgiving?"

Calmly, I sip my wine. "I don't know if you're aware, but a few years ago I worked for a publishing house. I used to do illustrations for government pamphlets. One I did was for a report on child abuse statistics in New Zealand. You know what the OECD is?"

"The Organization for Economic Co-operation and Development."

"Yes. It's a global policy forum, and it works with over a hundred countries. They say it works to build better policies for better lives. Amongst these countries, New Zealand has the highest rate of teen suicide, the sixth highest teen pregnancy rate, and the seventh highest rate of child homicide. In this country, a child dies every five weeks due to family violence. And we're thirty-fifth out of forty-one developed countries for child wellbeing outcomes."

"That's awful."

"It's shocking, and depressing. I'm not diminishing what you went through, just trying to say you're not alone. Childhood violence, abuse, and neglect are going to have a profound effect on you as an adult. I have no doubt that you suffer from CPTSD."

He looks startled at that. Then he says, "Well, everything these days is classed as traumatic. In the old days we just got on with it."

"That may be true, but it doesn't make what you suffered any less real. A single traumatic event can cause PTSD, but CPTSD—complex PTSD—stems from prolonged and repeated trauma. Have you ever been to counseling?"

He shoves his fork in his pasta. "No. Peter and Joyce wanted to send me, but I refused to go." No doubt he sees it as weak to seek help.

"Do you ever feel empty and worthless?"

"Doesn't everyone?"

"No, honey, that's the point I'm making. You've mentioned that you have difficulty forming and maintaining healthy relationships. That you have trust issues, and you isolate yourself socially. Didn't you ever think there may be reasons for that? It's not due to a weakness of character."

He doesn't reply, but I can see him thinking about it.

I understand more now about why he was an absent father. He struggles to show affection, to open up, and Eleanor's coldness would only have exacerbated that. Some men might have gone the opposite way, supplying the warmth and affection they lacked in their childhood. But Spencer must have thought it was safer to leave their upbringing to his wife and their nannies. He kept himself separate so he couldn't be a threat to them.

"I think you blame yourself for not being there more for your children," I say. "But you shouldn't. Despite your upbringing, or maybe because of it, you worked hard to provide for your wife and children. That's not a small thing."

"Maybe. But kids should have a father who's around to help them do their homework and to throw a ball with them. I think Dad was disappointed I wasn't more loving toward them."

He's obviously referring to his foster father. "I doubt he was disappointed," I say softly. "He knew what you'd been through, and he would understand why it was difficult for you to show affection."

He stabs his last meatball, clearly uncomfortable with the conversation, but I'm glad he's talking to me. It helps me see the real Spencer and understand him better.

I have the last mouthful of pasta, then push my plate away and lean back with my wine glass. "Do you think Orson and Scarlett will get married?"

He does the same, stretching out his legs. "Yeah, I think so. I've never seen him like this with a girl before."

"Are you okay with it? Her being Blake's daughter and all?"

"I'm trying to make peace with that. It was all a long time ago."

"You never told me about Amiria. You carefully sidestepped the question."

"Did I?" He smiles.

"I'm curious. What was it about her that you liked so much?"

He sighs and looks away, out at the darkening view. It's raining now, the droplets highlighted by the lamp that stands by the window. "I was eighteen," he says. "So young. She came into my life like a comet, blazing through my solar system. Now I realize it for what it was—my first crush—but I thought I loved her for many years."

"And that's why you hated Blake so much?"

"It was one reason. I thought we were friends, and when he took her away, it felt like a huge betrayal. You don't do that to people you love. I discovered we had very different views on a lot of things. He had no scruples at all. If he wanted something, he took it."

"I thought that was your motto? See, want, take?"

"I've joked about it," he says. "I don't believe it. I acknowledge that I've pushed people's limits, and I can be ruthless in business, but I'm not unscrupulous. I've never made a deal that wasn't completely above board." He's a little stiff, resentful that I might think that of him. What a puzzle this man is. Layered like an onion. No, more like a trifle. There's a sweetness to Spencer beneath his tough exterior. A softness he likes to hide.

"What are you smiling at?" he asks suspiciously.

"I was just thinking that you're more like Tiramisu than a casserole."

"What?"

"Never mind. Come on. Pour me another glass of wine, and I'll get dessert."

His lips curve up as I bring the Tiramisu over. It's in one big bowl, and I place it between us, move my chair closer to him, and pass him a spoon. "It's meant for sharing," I say, dipping into the creamy mascarpone mixture.

He leans on the table and takes a spoonful, and our eyes meet as we eat it. "Wow," he says, his eyes widening. "That's a helluva lot of rum in there."

"And coffee liqueur. You won't be able to drive home after you've eaten this." I'd forgotten that he doesn't drink alcohol.

"I see. You have ulterior motives."

"I do." I wait to see if he protests and declares he can't eat it.

He studies the dessert. Then he dips his spoon in. Lifting it, he looks at me and holds out his spoon. Pleasure flowing through me, I open my mouth.

He moves it to my nose and leaves a big blob of mascarpone mixture there. It's such an un-Spencer thing to do that I must look startled, and he laughs as he leans forward, closes his mouth over the bridge of my nose, and gently sucks the mixture off before pressing his lips to mine.

Mmm… a sweet, creamy kiss… my favorite. He takes his time, tasting me with his tongue, and by the time he moves back, my heart is racing and I know my face is flushed.

Smiling at each other, we eat the Tiramisu, both knowing it's more than a dessert. It's a symbol of the fact that he's decided to stay. We have all evening together, and then he'll go to bed with me, and I'll have him to myself all night. I'm so happy and excited I could burst.

Our conversation turns to lighter things—music, art, movies—and we chat away while we finish our dessert and drinks. After that, I clear the dinner things away while he makes us coffee, and then we take them into the studio.

As the rain continues to pour down outside, Spencer settles himself in the chair, I put some jazz music on, and then I pick up my brush and start to paint.

I work for maybe an hour and a half, starting to put the finer details to the base colors. Tonight I mainly work on his eyes, because I want to capture the beauty of the blue, as well as the expression they have when he looks at me. When I finally put down my brush, he rises and stretches, then comes over to look at the painting, his eyebrows rising as he sees himself looking out from the canvas.

"It's really good." He bends to get a better look at the brushstrokes.

"No need to sound so surprised."

He chuckles. "Do I really have gold flecks in my eyes?"

He's leaning close to me. I can smell his cologne and feel the heat from his skin. "Mmm, can't remember, let me look."

He straightens and looks at me, and my heart leaps. I move closer to him, looking up into his eyes. "Definitely," I murmur, my voice husky with desire, and then I lift onto my tiptoes and press my lips to his.

His arms snake around me, pulling me close, and I warm all the way through. I lift my arms around his neck, and we have a long, sensual kiss, while his hands travel up my back. They slide down my ribs and follow the curve of my waist before hooking up my dress and settling on my bare butt.

"It's been almost impossible for me to concentrate all evening knowing you're going commando under this dress." His hands skate over my skin, making my nipples tighten, and bringing goosebumps out all over.

"Mmm…" I shiver, and he groans.

"I can't resist you," he says hoarsely, pressing kisses to my face, my hair. "I know I shouldn't want you, but I can't keep away."

"I'm glad. I want you too." Once again, heat flares between us, and our kisses turn demanding, his lips crushing mine as he pulls me tightly against him. I love the way he reacts to me. I understand why being in charge is so important to him, but I love that I make him lose it.

I can't believe he's only been with one woman his whole life. That he hasn't been with anyone since Eleanor died. No wonder he says he can't resist me.

I tear my lips away from his and take his hand. Then I lead him out of the studio toward my bedroom.

The rain is hammering on the roof and windows. I flick on the small lamp on my bedside table. It fills the room with a cozy glow, and casts our shadows on the wall as I return to him and we start undressing one another.

"I want you," I whisper again as I push his shirt over his shoulders.

He lets it drop to the floor. "I want you too." He takes the hem of my dress in his hands, peels it up my body, and drops it onto the chair in front of the dressing table.

After unbuckling his belt, and letting him take out his wallet and toss it onto the bedside table, I undo the button of his trousers, then slide the zipper carefully down. He already has an erection. I love the way it strains toward me as if begging me to touch it.

He steps out of his trousers and flicks off his socks. I slide his boxers down his legs. And now my heart's racing because we're both naked, and I have him in my room, and he's mine to play with, all night.

I kiss down his chest, then his belly, and finally drop to my knees before him. I take his magnificent erection in my hand. Then I press my lips to it and kiss down the shaft.

"Ahhh…" He slides a hand into my hair and caresses it while I take my time exploring, kissing down to his balls and slipping a hand beneath him to caress them, then kissing back up and teasing the head and the slit at the top with my tongue. Finally, I close my mouth over the end and slide my lips down the shaft, and he groans and tightens his fingers in my hair.

I'm never going to be able to fit all of him in my mouth, and I'm no expert at deep throating, but I do my best, and his sighs and gasps suggest he's enjoying it. I was planning to try and take him all the way, but after a few minutes he says, "Marama," and puts his hands under my arms, and I let him lift me to my feet.

"Sorry," I say, "did I do something wrong?"

He just laughs and gives me a wry look. "No." He steers me to the bed and gestures for me to climb on.

I climb under the duvet and lie back on the pillows, and he slides in beside me and wraps his arms around me. Mmm… this is nice… he's warm, and he smells amazing, and there's something safe about being in his embrace like this.

"I wanted to make you feel good," I tell him.

He kisses me. "You do, baby girl. I just want to lead for a while."

"Oh. Sorry."

He chuckles and tips his head to the side. "It's nice to feel wanted," he whispers, his blue eyes burning into mine. "I like that." Then he kisses me, and every other thought flees my head.

Chapter Seventeen

Spencer

I'm determined to take my time.

It's not easy. Not only is Marama soft all over and plump and moist where it matters, but she's willing… more than willing, and that excites me more than anything. I've fantasized about this for years—about being with a woman who likes sex as much as I do. She's enthusiastic, her fingers skating over my skin, exploring while I touch her, keen to show me how much I'm turning her on. Her sighs and moans aren't loud and theatrical, but she is vocal, which I love. It fires me up to listen to her groan when I stroke her, or to hear her cry out when I suck her nipples.

I spend ages kissing her—her mouth, her neck, her throat, her breasts, the sensitive skin beneath her arms and the crook of her elbows, down her belly, and over her mound as I shift between her legs.

Slowly, I kiss down her thighs, then hook up her knees with my arms, widen them, and bury my tongue inside her. She squeals, then moans and arches her back, and I groan as I lick her, the amazing mix of sweet and salty, rich and heavenly.

"Ahhh…" She buries her hand in my hair, unashamedly dropping her thighs wide to give me better access, and fuck me if that isn't the sexiest thing ever. I slide two fingers inside her and explore that most secret part of her, finding her G-spot and massaging it. "Oh God," she says, tilting her hips up and moving them to match my fingers, making it clear that she likes it. So I continue while I tease her clit with my tongue, my own sighs and groans joining with hers as our bodies spiral with exquisite pleasure.

It's not long before her breathing changes and her breaths become gasps, but I don't stop, and she comes on my tongue and clenches around my fingers, crying out with every pulse.

"Oh fuck," she says when she can finally breath properly again. "Oh, that was so good."

I kiss her clit lightly, then press my lips up her belly as I move back over her. "I love making you come." I kiss each nipple, circling the tip of my tongue over them before sucking them into my mouth.

She moans and squirms beneath me. "Mercy," she whispers.

"No mercy," I murmur back, kissing up her throat to her lips. "We're both going to come again and again tonight, until you're a quivering wreck of a woman, exhausted and sticky and messy and covered in sweat and cum and any other fluids we can conjure up."

"Oh fuck."

I take out a condom and roll it on, then lean over her. "Yes, we're going to fuck, Marama. I'm going to fuck you, and then you can be on top and fuck me, and we're going to spend the whole night fucking."

She gives me a look that's full of longing and desire. "You're, like, the perfect guy."

"Maybe wait and see whether you still feel that way at the end, when you can't walk."

"Oh God."

I laugh and slide inside her, all the way up in one smooth thrust. We both groan, and then I lower down on top of her. "Too heavy?" I murmur, kissing her.

She shakes her head, wrapping her legs around my hips. "I like it."

I begin to move. "So do I. I like feeling your beautiful body. I like owning you and possessing you and making you mine. Because you are mine tonight."

"All yours."

"Mmm." I thrust slowly, almost pulling out each time before I sink back in. "You belong to me." I feel a little crazy. Maybe it's the alcohol from the Tiramisu making me a little dizzy, uncaring, my inhibitions and worries flying out of the window. There's nobody else here to judge. No one else to tell me what I should or shouldn't do. Here, in this room, it's just me and the beautiful goddess of the moon beneath me.

She's left the curtains open, and when I look at the window, I can see the two of us reflected in the glass. We look good together, her beautiful, smooth skin a light, cool brown against the warmer brown of my sun-touched body. Her gentle curves against my hard angles and defined muscles. I love the way she's wrapped around me, welcoming me inside her. How she moves with me, clearly enjoying the sensation of being penetrated and invaded.

I just love everything about this girl.

"Thought you were going to fuck me," she says mischievously.

I give her an amused look, not stopping the movement of my hips. "Am I missing something?"

"This doesn't feel like fucking." She lifts her arms up above her head, stretching out beneath me. "Are you making luuurv to me, Spencer?"

I kiss her, sucking her bottom lip and grazing my teeth on it. "Are you being cheeky to me?"

"Maybe. Watcha gonna do about it?"

I chuckle, lift up onto my hands, and give a sudden, hard thrust. She squeals, then moans, her face flushing. "It wasn't a complaint."

"Are you sure? You only have to ask, and I'll do my best to oblige."

I start thrusting hard, angling it so I'm grinding against her. I take each hand, one at a time, and interlink our fingers, then pin them above her head while I thrust. She looks up at me, helpless to do anything but take it, her eyes filled with sleepy ecstasy. Fuck, that's hot, and I have to fight to hold in my own desire, until her breathing grows erratic again, and her eyelids flutter shut as her orgasm sweeps over.

I ride her through it, hanging onto my sanity with my fingertips, then let my body do what it's been wanting to do for a while and thrust hard. She gasps and cries out, still clenching around me. I wait as long as I can, making her climax last as long as possible, enjoying her pleasure as much as my own.

She finally flops back and says, "Mmm… come over me, Spencer."

"You're sure?"

"Mmm, please…"

So I pull out, whip off the condom, and finish myself off with a few strokes. She watches, eyes alight, and then I frown, my eyes closing as I come over her, covering her body with each thick jet.

"Oooh." She trails a finger through it, then lifts it to her mouth and sucks it off.

I laugh and bend to kiss her, and she gives a "Mmmph!" of surprise, then delves her tongue into my mouth.

When I lift my head, she says, "That shocked me. Connor would never do that."

"Neither would Eleanor." We both give wry smiles.

She looks down at herself. "I should get a towel."

"Nope." I give myself another couple of strokes until I'm hard again, then roll on another condom and slide back inside her.

"Oh!" She slides her arms around me as I lower down onto her again. I lie on top, and now we're both wonderfully wet and sticky and sweaty. "Mmm," she murmurs, "you naughty boy."

I look at our reflections for a bit, watching myself moving inside her. Then I notice the light that marks the edge of the path and turn off the lamp on the bedside table. It's still raining, and the soft light from outside passes through the drops running down the glass and falls on us, covering us with rivulets of rain.

"Oh," she says, brushing a hand over my arms and chest, "that's beautiful."

"You're beautiful. You turn me on."

She looks down at where I'm thrusting inside her. "So I see."

"Tell me when you've had enough."

"Never," she whispers. "Never."

And thus begins the most erotic evening of my life. After a while I withdraw, roll her over, and take her from behind, and this time, under instructions, I come all over her ass, making both her back and her front wet and sticky.

We take a break and get ourselves a drink and a big bar of Whittaker's new Banana Caramel chocolate from the kitchen and take it back to bed. Then I get the great idea to leave a piece on each of her breasts, and after five minutes or so we discover it's partly melted, and I get the great job of sucking it off.

That leads to her climbing on top of me and riding me. By this point it's growing warmer in the room, and she lifts her hair up to cool her neck, looking stunning with the reflection of the rain running down her body.

We change position multiple times, and both come again and again. She matches me in stamina and desire, and just sheer pleasure of the other person's body. It turns out she's bought some massage oil for tonight. I insist on using it first, and give her a long, sensual massage before giving her a happy ending with my fingers. She then insists on returning the favor, and it's much, much later before we both stretch out on the bed, exhausted and sticky, just as I'd promised.

"Don't you ever say anything about getting old again," she berates me. "I can't believe how many times you've come tonight."

"Personal record," I mumble. "It's your fault."

"Oh my God, seriously Spencer, you were right, I'm completely wrecked. You're amazing."

My lips curve up. "You know how to make a man feel good."

She lifts up onto an elbow and looks at me, but doesn't say anything. I turn my head and meet her gaze, and we study each other for a long time.

I know what she's thinking, because I'm thinking the same.

Neither of us says anything, though, and eventually she suggests, "Perhaps we should have a quick shower."

"Yeah. And change the bed."

We both look at the messy sheets and laugh.

"Come on," she says.

We get up and shower together, and although it's still erotic to wash one another, there's also something tender and gentle in our touch. I've shared and done things with her tonight—emotionally and physically—that I've never shared or done with anyone else.

When we're clean and we've dried ourselves, we return to the bedroom and change the bottom sheet, then finally get into bed and draw the duvet up over ourselves. I turn her away from me and spoon up behind her, and she brings my hand up to her lips and kisses my fingers.

"Thank you," she whispers. "That was so amazing."

"Mmm."

"Are you asleep?"

"Mmm."

She chuckles.

Within a few minutes, her breathing evens out, and I know she's dozed off.

I lie awake a little longer, though. I shouldn't stay the night. For a start, Joe might decide he does want to work, or the housekeeper might turn up, or any other member of the staff, who decides to tell Rangi when he gets back.

But it's also not good for either of us emotionally. It's been a fantastic evening. But I'm kidding myself if I insist it's purely physical.

I'm sure other people can have amazing sex like that and remain emotionally distant, but I don't think either of us is like that.

I'm drawn to her free spirit, and her warmth. I can't get enough of her. I nuzzle her neck and kiss the skin beneath her ear, and she stirs and sighs. I don't want to wake her, so I don't do it again, but I want to. I want to touch her again, to arouse her, to make love to her repeatedly, until she can't think, feel, or remember anything except how it feels to be with me.

Inside, my stomach flips with unease. But I'm too tired, and before I can do anything about it, I fall asleep.

*

"Are you sure you won't stay for breakfast? I make a mean bacon and egg sandwich." Marama smiles.

I glance over at her. She's still in bed, lying on her front, the duvet bunched beneath her. It stopped raining sometime in the night, and the early sun falls across her, coating her curves in gold. She looks as if she's been touched by King Midas.

My cock twitches at the same time as my stomach rumbles. It would be so easy to stay. But I continue to get dressed, doing up my trousers and then pulling on my shirt. "No, I'd better go. I don't want to be seen."

"There's nobody around," she protests.

I ignore her, though, unable to still the anxiousness that lies heavy in the pit of my stomach. What if Rangi comes back early? I can only imagine what he'd say if he walked in and saw me having breakfast with his daughter in my boxers.

"I've got a lot to do," I tell her, "I need to go."

Her smile fades, and I soften my voice as I go over to her and say, "But I wish I could." I bend over her and kiss her, a peck that turns into a smooch. She lifts her arms around my neck, and I laugh and extricate myself. "Stop it," I scold, picking up my wallet.

She sighs, gets up, and tugs on a bathrobe. I lead the way out, and we pause in the hallway so I can tug on my shoes.

"I had a great time," I tell her.

She closes the distance between us, slides her arms around my waist, and rests her cheek on my chest. Frowning a little, I put my arms around her.

"Can I see you again?" she asks.

For a moment, I don't answer. I rest my lips on the top of her head, inhaling the smell of strawberries from her shampoo.

She moves back and looks up at me. "Don't tell me you didn't enjoy last night," she says.

My lips twist.

"I could come to your house," she suggests.

I tuck a strand of her hair behind her ear. "I don't think that's a good idea."

We study each other quietly. I wait for her to argue or to get upset, but eventually she just lowers her arms and says, "All right."

I pick up my car keys and hesitate. I'm all twisted up inside. I desperately want to stay, but I've already been weak, and I can't afford to give in to my desires again.

I can't think what to say; 'thank you,' would be insulting, 'take care,' would be feeble, 'see you later,' is lame. So in the end, I don't say anything. I bend and give her one last, quick kiss, and then I open the door and go out into the sunshine.

I take the ferry back to the mainland and drive the short distance to my house in Herne Bay. I have a shower and change, then make a coffee and take it out on the deck.

I'm just checking my emails when I get a message from Marama. I pull it up, wondering if she's going to ask to see me again, and half-expecting her to argue her point of view.

Instead, the message says, *Painting looks good, don't you think?* And she's sent a photo of it.

My eyebrows rise as I study it. She's photographed it in the early morning sunlight, and the colors are vivid and leap off the canvas. I only looked at it briefly last night, and now I take some time to zoom in on the brushstrokes. It's really good—she's so talented. She's really captured my expression, which is less sardonic than it normally is, because I'm looking at her. She's also started filling in the greenery around me that's going to turn me into Tāne Mahuta. The God of the Forest. I have to admit, I don't mind being compared to a god.

I'll have to think seriously about where I'm going to hang it. It's almost a crime that not many people will get to see it, because few people come to the house. Maybe I should hang it in my office. But I reject that instantly for several reasons. People are going to question my expression and the intimacy of the portrait. And she painted it for me—in a way, I don't want anyone else to see it.

I message her back, *I love it - it's coming along so well*
Marama: *Yeah, I'm pleased with the foliage too*
Me: *I like the way the leaves blend into my hair*
Marama: *Me too and the light green color will blend well with your silver locks*
Me: *locks, lol*
Marama: *You'd look great with long hair like a rock star*
Me: *We'll never know*
Marama: *Playing power chords in front of a mini Stonehenge*
I laugh at her reference to Spinal Tap.
Me: *What are you up to today?*
Marama: *More painting! I'm happy <smiley emoji>*
Me: *Glad to hear it <heart>*

I wait, then when she doesn't reply, I put my phone down and look across the harbor. That'll probably be the last I'll hear from her today. It's for the best. At least it ended well.

I reach for my laptop, open it up, and begin making notes on a new development I'm planning in South Auckland.

Ten minutes later, my phone buzzes again. I open the message, my lips curving up. She's sent me a song and the accompanying message says, *What I'm listening to right now.*

I set it playing while I work, the smile still playing on my lips.

*

For the next few days, we message each other constantly.

I repeatedly tell myself I should curtail our connection. Sometimes I manage to go a whole hour without contacting her. But inevitably she sends me something that makes me smile—a joke, a song, a meme, or a photo of herself pulling a face—and I end up replying with a sarcastic comment that she then teases me about.

She doesn't ask to see me again, and for that I'm thankful.

Despite this, I know I'm a little distracted at work. I do my best to hide it, especially on the occasions Rangi is in the room. The first time I see him, at a meeting on Tuesday morning, I feel uncharacteristically nervous, convinced that someone saw me leaving the house on Saturday morning and has told him. But he seems normal, chats away about his time down south, and doesn't mention Marama at all, and with some relief I think I've gotten away with it.

It's therefore a surprise when, on Wednesday, I look up from where I'm working at my desk and see him standing in the doorway, leaning on the doorpost, his hands in his pockets. I don't have a meeting planned with him, and I wasn't expecting him to drop by. I lift my eyebrows, forcing myself to stay calm, even though my heart is banging away inside.

"Hey," I say. "What are you doing here?"

"Just passing," he says, pushing off the post. "Kaye said you were free," he adds, naming my PA.

"Yeah of course." I toss my pen onto the desk and lean back. "What can I do for you?"

He walks into the room and stops in front of my desk. "Have you seen the front page of Kōrero this morning?"

"No…"

He gestures at my laptop. "Maybe you should take a look."

My mouth goes dry as I pull up the website and scroll down. I pause as I see my photo. The headline reads 'Beauty Tames the Beast: Midnight Club Tycoon Poses for Rising Star's Boldest Work Yet'.

I scan the article quickly. It refers to her new Maramataka exhibition—the first time the title has been revealed officially, and talks about what Elizabeth mentioned the other day: themes of female power and sexual agency. 'The moon is rising, the sun has had his day,' the article says, as well as, 'the series of paintings will feature *atua wāhine*, modern, powerful goddesses taming beasts and overturning male power.'

"This has the Wicked Witch of the West and Cruella De Vil written all over it," I say. I'm never disrespectful to women, so my reference to Genevieve Beaumont and Hariata Pere makes his eyes widen, and he gives a short bark of a laugh.

"Tell me something I don't know." He tips his head to the side. "Have you been modeling for Marama?"

I wonder whether he's asked her already, and is double-checking our stories. Well there's no point in trying to second guess what she said. Honesty is always the best policy.

"Yeah," I reply, "I've sat for her a couple of times. I told you—she had to paint a portrait as a condition of entering the auction. I'm guessing she's also started work on the first piece for her exhibition."

"What form does it take?"

"I have no idea. I haven't seen it." I shift uneasily in my chair. Marama didn't mention the other painting. "Why don't you ask her?" I say defensively.

"I did. She refuses to show me."

I meet his eyes, and for a moment we just study each other.

"Beauty and the beast," he says eventually.

"Genevieve has a fucking cheek to call your daughter a beast," I joke. Rangi doesn't laugh. "She's shit stirring," I say crossly, starting to get irritated. "She wants to cause trouble, and she's obviously succeeding."

"The Circle won't like it."

"Well they can shove their disapproval where the sun doesn't shine. I haven't done anything wrong."

His eyebrows lift at my vehemence, and I think he's going to challenge me. But then he sighs and says, "Yeah, you're right. I mean, you wouldn't do anything to sabotage all our hard work, would you?" His eyes meet mine again briefly before he turns around and heads out of the door.

Fuck.

I rub my stomach as acid threatens to rise. I'm going to give myself a stomach ulcer at this rate.

"Want some Gaviscon?" Kaye asks from the doorway.

I scowl at her. "I've just drunk too much coffee on an empty stomach."

Her lips twitch. "I'll get you a sandwich." She goes off.

I turn my scowl to the laptop and glare at the article. Beauty Tames the Beast. My jaw clenches. Genevieve knew the headline would humiliate me. Well, this wolf isn't going to be brought to heel by anyone. Nobody controls Spencer Cavendish—not Rangi, not Marama, and certainly not Genevieve Beaumont.

I close down the article and bring up the report for the new development. People are chaotic and unpredictable. Business is the only thing that matters. As always, I'll lose myself in my work, and let everything else fade into the background.

Chapter Eighteen

Marama

I don't hear from Spencer all day Wednesday. He's a busy man, so I don't expect him to reply to every message immediately. But I'm sure there's another reason he's keeping his distance.

I saw the article in Kōrero, but something tells me that in itself wouldn't be enough to stop him from replying. I'm sure he'd know I had no hand in it, and I half-expected him to message me to ask about the other painting, so not to hear anything from him is odd.

However, my father has questioned me about it, and I have a sneaky feeling Spencer's silence has something to do with him.

The Midnight Circle meets on Wednesday nights, so I don't have a chance to speak to Dad again until Thursday morning. When he walks into the kitchen at seven, showered and suited up ready for the office, I'm already there, sitting at the pine table.

"Hello, you," he says, surprised. "What are you doing up?" He starts making himself a coffee.

"I wanted to catch you before you left."

"Oh?" He gestures at the coffee machine.

I shake my head. "No thank you. Dad, have you spoken to Spencer about my painting? The one I'm doing for the Maramataka Exhibition?"

He busies himself with pouring the espresso into his takeaway cup and going over to the fridge to retrieve the milk. "Uh… yeah, I might have mentioned it," he says, so casually that I know he's aware he's causing trouble. When I don't reply, he sets the milk steaming, then looks over at me. "Why?"

"What did you say?"

MIDNIGHT SECRET

He stiffens. He doesn't like being questioned any more than Spencer does. "I discussed the article in the Kōrero and how it will impinge on Midnight." His voice is heavy with disapproval.

Furious, I sit there fighting against the urge to yell at him. I want to tell him. To bring it all out in the open. I hate the fact that I have to keep my feelings for Spencer secret. That we're sneaking around as if we're doing something wrong. Why will it impinge on Midnight? Why is it anyone else's business?

But Spencer doesn't want me to tell anyone, and I know for a fact that if I blurt it out to my father, Spencer is going to be the one who bears the brunt of Dad's disapproval. It'll probably destroy their friendship and possibly their business relationship, too, and Spencer will never forgive me for that. No, he has to be the one to tell people. Not me. That is very clear to me.

As gracefully as I can, I get up, slide my chair under the table, and walk out of the room.

I'm standing in the studio, looking at the portrait of Spencer on the easel, when Dad knocks and comes in.

He stands next to me and looks at the portrait. It's about two-thirds done, with Spencer's face mostly complete. I'm working on the foliage now.

I shift from foot to foot, a little uncomfortable that he's looking at it. I don't like people seeing my unfinished work, but it's not just that. This portrait feels very personal. It holds the memories of my time with Spencer, like a photograph that captures a precise moment.

"It's very good," Dad says.

"Thank you."

"He doesn't look as cynical as he normally does."

I refrain from telling him it's because Spencer was looking at me while I painted.

"Where's the other one?" he asks.

I go cold, thinking he's referring to the sketch I did of Spencer naked. "What other one?"

"You know perfectly well what I mean."

Oh, he means the exhibition piece. He's seen the headline in Kōrero.

When he obviously realizes I'm not going to answer, he says, "Is he going to sit for you again?"

"I don't think so." I make sure to keep the sadness out of my voice and sound brisk and professional.

"Probably for the best," he says.

I don't reply. I stand there, rigid with resentment and fury at how everyone is determined to regulate my feelings.

But then he says, "Sometimes what we want and what's best for us aren't the same thing."

I glance at him—he's looking at the portrait. He's talking about Spencer, not me.

My anger slowly dissipates. Of course, I'm coming at this from one hundred percent emotion. Dad is looking at it from purely a business point of view. He's seen the headline, and he knows how the description of being tamed is going to humiliate Spencer. It's the last thing he needs in a world where he rules the roost by maintaining his reputation of being cutthroat and disciplined.

And I do understand the implications on Midnight and the Circle. They pride themselves on being beyond reproach. Their financial dealings have to be spotless—they're regularly audited, and transparent with their accounts. Any glimmer of scandal reflects badly on all of them.

I clear my throat. "I'm going to get to work."

"Yeah, okay." He leans forward and presses a kiss to my brow. "Have a great day, kiddo. It's good to have you here."

He walks away, leaving me alone, and I give a big sigh. I take the portrait down, pick up the large piece I'm doing for the exhibition, and place it on the easel, then stand back and study it. The wolf at my feet, cowed by my magnificence.

I feel torn. I showed Genevieve this painting on Tuesday, and she was thrilled at the new composition. She gave me a long speech, explaining the importance of platforming indigenous voices and women, and how my solo exhibition is going to get global attention. It's impossible not to be flattered by talk like that, and by the time we ended the call I was convinced I was doing the right thing.

I didn't know she was going to go to the press with that headline. So far, there's nothing about the painting that says explicitly that the wolf represents Spencer, but now she's implied it, everyone's going to think that's who it symbolizes.

Why should I worry? He doesn't want me anyway. Not enough to make whatever we have public. I have no doubt he's flattered that I like him, and that he's enjoyed our time together. But he's right—we could never be together openly. His business, and our friends and family, would never allow it. He's a strong man, but the disapproval and mockery would be too much for him.

I feel suddenly tired, even though it's only seven a.m. I feel as if I could go back to bed and sleep for several hours. There's nothing stopping me. I don't have any commitments today.

But I spent enough time with Connor, and observed his habits when he was depressed, to know it won't be good for me. So I go and shower, get dressed and do my hair, make myself another coffee, then return to the studio, ready to put in a day's work.

*

I spend the rest of the day painting. When I get going, I work fast, and by the end of the day I've finished the portrait. I leave it on the easel to dry—it's acrylic paint, so it'll be touch-dry in an hour or so, although it'll take a little longer to completely harden.

I haven't messaged Spencer, and he hasn't messaged me.

I don't hear from him on Thursday either.

Friday, I awake somewhat rejuvenated. It's my birthday, and Dad waits for me to get up before leaving for work so he and Mum can give me my present.

I unwrap it and reveal the small box. I open it—it contains a set of keys. They exchange a smile. "Go on," Mum says.

I walk to the window and part the curtains. Then, jaw dropping, I run to the front door and go outside.

Mum and Dad come with me, and they stand next to me as I stare at the Kombi van.

"It's fully electric and retrofitted," Dad says.

Stunned, I go up to it and open the side door. It's beautifully designed, making the most of every inch of space. The sofa obviously converts to a bed, and it's a proper campervan, with enough mod cons to enable me to live out of it. But the far end has been turned into a tiny studio, with an easel, a fold-down stool, and a cupboard that I discover already contains a set of paints, brushes, and palettes, all ready should inspiration strike.

"You said you were thinking about traveling again," Dad says. "This way you can go wherever you want and take your art with you."

Touched by their hopeful and excited expressions, I tell them I love it and give them both a big hug.

"I'll paint the outside," I tell them. "Make it into a 1970s hippie van."

Dad laughs. "Whatever you want, my love. I'm glad you like it."

"We'll leave you to explore it," Mum says, and the two of them go back inside.

I climb into the van and spend a while opening drawers and cupboards and discovering all its nooks and crannies. Then I pull down the stool and sit, taking a moment to look around.

I'm trying not to be cynical. The van would have taken a while to sort out and refit, so maybe I'm being overly suspicious. But I know Dad well enough to suspect that part of this is him 'encouraging' me to leave. Sending me away, so I'm out of Spencer's reach.

I run a finger over the pristine tubes of paint. I'm thirty now. Shouldn't I be able to make my own decisions about my life? About what I do, who I see?

Thoughtfully, I get out and lock up the van, and go back into the house.

*

I meet some friends for brunch, then call in and see Kingi mid-afternoon at his office in the city.

"What are you up to tonight?" he asks after giving me a bearhug that nearly breaks my spine in two.

"Not sure yet." I massage my back, then rub my neck. "Your beard is super itchy."

He just laughs and strokes the long, wiry strands like a thoughtful wizard. "I wish you'd let us throw you a party. You're not thirty every day."

"Thank God."

He smiles. "Feeling your age, sis?"

"Nah, not really. Just feeling a bit... constricted, maybe."

He lifts a brow. "In what way?"

I tell him about the van. "It's lovely," I insist. "But I can't shake the feeling that Dad's trying to send me away."

He leans back in his chair. "Is this about Spencer Cavendish?"

I scowl at him. "Don't you start."

"I can read, same as everyone else. That headline was pretty damning."

"It was a work of pure fiction."

"So you're not painting a picture of a woman taming a wolf?"

I blow out a breath. "Genevieve is insisting on it."

"She likes the idea of bringing him to his knees."

"Hell hath no fury…"

"Yeah, I thought that was the case. She tried to make a move on him to get the position at Midnight, right?"

"Yes."

"And he turned her down."

"Yeah."

"Ouch. I bet she doesn't get rejected much."

I tip my head at him. "Do you like her?"

He shrugs. "She's an attractive woman. Not my type, though."

"Too old?"

"Too aggressive. I like 'em pliable." He smirks.

"You wait," I tell him, "you're going to meet someone who's going to bring you to your knees."

"Fine by me. While I'm down there…" He makes the V sign with two fingers, places them either side of his mouth, and wiggles his tongue, implying he'd happily go down on the girl.

"Oh God, gross." I can't help but laugh, though, and he chuckles. "My cue to change the subject," I say wryly.

We chat for a while, just catching up, and then Orson comes in, and he gives me a hug as well. "No party?" he asks.

"Nah. Not my scene. I don't like being the center of attention."

"So what are you up to this evening?"

"Just meeting friends," I say vaguely, getting to my feet.

"Well, hope you have a great time."

They both give me a hug, and I promise to catch up soon and head out.

I return back home and spend a couple of hours painting. I often need quiet time after I've been with people.

Afterward, I shower and change, and spend some time putting on makeup and getting dressed. I sit there for a few minutes, fighting with myself. Then, I call Scarlett Stone.

"Hey you," she says. "Happy birthday!"

"Thank you!"

"Orson said you weren't having a party. What are you up to?"

"Well, I was wondering if you'd do me a favor…"

*

Later, I head out to my car. I have a beautiful Alfa Romeo Spider, and I put the top down and take the ferry to the mainland, enjoying the autumn evening. When I arrive, I head for Herne Bay. Scarlett has told me where Spencer lives, as she's been to his house with Orson. She also found out for me that he was at a meeting not far from his house in Herne Bay this afternoon, and he told his PA that after it finished at four, he was heading home early, rather than returning to the office or going over to Midnight.

I swore Scarlett to secrecy, although I have no doubt she'll tell Orson, who might well tell Kingi. But at this point, I don't care. My heart races as I enter the affluent suburb and negotiate the roads to Spencer's house.

For the first time, I feel a twinge of alarm that maybe he's not alone. It's possible he lied to me when he said Eleanor is the only woman he's been with. It's much more likely that a rich and powerful man like himself would take girlfriends, one-night stands, or escorts home with him.

But then I think about our first time—his pure delight in me, the groan when he came that seemed to last for years—and deep down I know he was telling the truth. The proud but honest Spencer Cavendish could never do anything but.

I turn onto his road and drive slowly along the beach, past the large houses overlooking the harbor, until I come to the one called Tarāpunga, which means red-billed gull in Māori, a bird seen often around Waitematā Harbour. The drive is empty, but his Bentley is probably in the garage, no doubt alongside his vintage Aston Martin DB5. He's had it for years and it's in pristine condition—a sleek, silver bullet of a car that looks like it's driven straight out of a James Bond movie and suits him perfectly.

After sliding the Alfa Romeo onto the drive behind the garage, I get out and walk up to the front door. Then I ring the doorbell.

There's no reply.

I ring it again. And then a third time. Finally, I hear footsteps inside, and then the door is wrenched open, and an irritated Spencer glares at me as he barks, "What?"

"Hello," I say, standing my ground.

His glare vanishes as he realizes it's me, and his jaw drops. "Marama?" he asks, puzzled, and he glances around, either making sure I'm alone, or perhaps trying to see where the candid cameras are.

He's wearing black track pants, a well-worn gray tee, and a cooking apron, and he's holding a pair of tongs like a weapon. He's also barefoot, and his hair looks uncharacteristically scruffy, as if it's been tousled by the wind. Oh my God, the guy's even more gorgeous when caught unawares.

"What are you doing here?" he asks.

"I wanted to see you, and you wouldn't return my messages."

I half-expected him to be angry, but his expression softens. "Come in," he says, moving back.

I walk past him and stand there, hands jammed in the pockets of my jeans. He closes the door behind me and turns, and we study each other for a long moment.

Then I go up to him, slide my arms around his waist, and rest my cheek on his shoulder. To my relief, he sticks the tongs in his apron pocket, lowers his arms around me, and rests his lips on my hair, and we stand there like that for about a minute, just breathing each other in.

"I've missed you," I say, turning my face so I can bury it in the place where his neck meets his shoulder. He smells amazing, of his cologne mixed with the sea and a touch of barbecue.

"I've missed you, too."

"Really?"

"Yeah."

I move back a little so I can look up at him. He's smiling.

"It's my birthday," I say without meaning to.

His eyebrows rise at that. "What?"

"I'm thirty. Officially over the hill."

He cups my face, his expression tender. "Then what are you doing here, you crazy girl? You should be out with your friends, partying."

"I didn't want to. I wanted to see you." I look past him and sniff. "What are you cooking? It smells amazing."

"Have you eaten?" he asks. I shake my head. He sighs, then smiles again. "Come on. I'll make you dinner."

He leads the way into the house. It's not a mansion, like I'd expected a billionaire would live in, but a house this size and in this location would not have been cheap. I hadn't realized at first, but it's built into the hill, so it's on several floors. On the ground floor I glimpse a home gym and the room I suspect he's converted to his workshop, but he leads me up the steps to the next floor. It opens out into a huge living space. A large kitchen takes up one side with a dining table just off it. The living room has a soft leather sofa and chairs, a stylish wooden coffee table, bookshelves against the back wall, and an enormous widescreen TV. Sliding doors open onto the deck that overlooks the ocean, and I can see heat rising from the barbecue out there.

For some reason—maybe because he works such long hours, and because he's now single—I'd expected his place to be businesslike and bland, all chrome and glass and featureless, but it's not. There are bits and pieces from his travels around the world. An antique Persian rug with rich reds and navy blues. A Japanese *tansu* chest, which is like a storage cabinet, practical but elegant, made from dark wood. A Papua New Guinean tribal mask, probably a replica, knowing his high ethical standards. A walking stick with the head of an elephant, possibly from India. Outside, a Moroccan lantern hangs ready to cast star-shaped shadows on the deck.

The walls are filled with photographs and paintings. The photos are all black and white images of bustling markets, quiet temples, rainforests—did he take them himself?

The paintings are all mine.

I stare at them. I knew he'd bought Parson-Bird. I didn't know he'd bought the others. They're from various exhibitions I've done over the past ten years and show a range of styles and subjects.

I glance at him. He meets my gaze evenly.

"These are all mine," I say unnecessarily.

"I like your style." He crosses the room to the open sliding doors and goes out onto the deck.

I stay, though, caught out by my presence in the room. He hasn't bought these overnight. This collection would have taken him a while to track down and purchase from various collectors who'd bought them while they were being exhibited.

And oh, of course, I forgot… I run quickly down the stairs and out to my car, then return carrying the item I brought with me.

He's waiting at the top of the stairs and looks relieved when I run back up. "I thought you'd changed your mind," he says.

"No, silly." I hold up the canvas, its back to him. "I finished your portrait."

"Oh!" He glances around and slides a hand under my arm to bring me toward the windows. The sun is sinking beneath the horizon and the light is fading, but there's enough to see by.

I move back, take a deep breath, and turn the canvas around.

Because I'm facing him, I'm able to see his expression, and my heart lifts as his face lights up and he smiles.

"You like it?" I say hopefully.

He glances at me, wonder in his eyes, then back at the portrait. "It's fantastic." He looks away, at the wall behind me, marches over to one of the black and white photos, and lifts it off. After taking the portrait from me, he hangs it in the empty space. He carefully straightens it. Then, together, we move back to admire it.

"The Lord of the Forest," I murmur. "Tāne Mahuta made real."

The trunk of the ancient kauri tree is visible in the background, and kauri leaves and other foliage curl around him. The various greens and browns of the forest contrast beautifully with the rich warm skin tones and the vivid blue of his eyes. I'm so pleased with his expression; I feel as if I've managed to capture a little of the sardonic look he normally sports, but also a tenderness that's not normally there.

"I love it," he says. "You are incredibly talented."

I blush. "I had a good sitter."

"I'm sure I was a terrible sitter, but you've managed to make me look good." He turns to me then, cups my face, and looks me in the eyes. "You're amazing." He brushes his thumbs across my warm cheeks. Then he lowers his lips to mine, and we exchange a long, gentle, wonderful kiss that fills me with joy.

He hasn't refrained from contacting me because he didn't want to see me. He was trying to do the Right Thing, guilted by my father and the rest of the Midnight Circle, convinced it was the best thing to do for both of us. But my paintings in his house, and the way he's kissing me, show me he has feelings for me. He wants me. And all the time that's the case, I know everything's going to be all right.

Chapter Nineteen

Spencer

When I lift my head, Marama's eyes are shining. She sniffs and jokes, "Are those tongs in your pocket or are you pleased to see me?"

I laugh and kiss her nose. "I'm sorry I didn't get you anything for your birthday. I didn't realize it was this month."

"That's okay. What's for dinner?"

I hesitate then. "Nothing suitable for a birthday celebration. Would you like to go out for dinner?"

"And be seen in public?" she teases. "God forbid."

"Good point. I could order something in. There's a nice Italian not far away that does a great Carbonara."

"What were you having?"

"Steak, again."

"With?"

"I bought a baguette on the way home. I was going to make a steak sandwich."

"Mmm." She nods with approval. "Is there enough for two?"

"Yes… Are you sure?"

"It sounds perfect."

Feeling a surge of happiness, I lead her into the kitchen and open the fridge to get the pack of steaks. "Would you like a glass of wine?" I gesture at the bottle in the door. "I keep some in case Orson and Scarlett call in."

"No, that's okay."

"It's your birthday," I point out. "Don't worry about me—you have one if you want one."

"I came in the Alfa."

I'd forgotten that. She'll be driving home… unless she stays the night.

MIDNIGHT SECRET

I hesitate, meeting her eyes, caught between duty and desire. She could be with her friends right now, going to a club, partying the night away. Meeting young men, flirting, dancing, maybe even having a one-night stand. But she's not. It's her thirtieth birthday and she's chosen to come here to be with me.

"Why does a beautiful girl like you want an old man like me?" My voice is hoarse with emotion as I slide a hand to cup her cheek.

"You're not old. And I'm not a girl. I'm thirty now. I'm a woman, and I don't have to answer to anyone. Neither do you, Spencer. We're consenting adults, and what we do in the privacy of our own homes is nothing to do with anyone else. It's the twenty-first century, and we live in New Zealand, where love isn't curated or condemned. We don't have arranged marriages. We're free to love whomever we choose."

"Love?" My neck prickles with warning.

She gives me a wry look. "It's just a word. Don't get your knickers in a twist."

She's right, but it doesn't make me feel any better. I have a major crush on this girl that doesn't appear to be going away anytime soon, but I can't shake the feeling that I'm close to making a fool of myself. Am I having a midlife crisis? It's often joked about—men in their forties who get fake tans, have hair implants, buy penis-extension Ferraris, and hook up with women half their age.

Okay, I don't have a fake tan, I still have my own hair, I've had my Aston Martin for many years, and Marama isn't half my age. But I know how others will see this. Do I really want to ruin my friendship and business partnership with Rangi over her? Is she really worth blowing up my life over? It's just sex. I'd be better off hiring an escort, or, even better, jerking off to porn. Marama is nothing special.

But they're all just meaningless words that flutter around my head like torn pieces of paper tossed into the wind. She is special. And if it was just sex, why do I have her artwork hanging around my house? Why does my heart leap every time she sends a message?

"It's all right," she says, obviously seeing some of my thoughts playing across my face. "I understand. I shouldn't have come." She drops her gaze and moves away from my hand.

I catch her arm, turn her back to face me, and move up close to her, pinning her against the breakfast bar. "You're not going anywhere," I tell her, my voice husky with emotion. Then I take her face in my hands and kiss her.

181

This time I pour all my feelings into the kiss. Marama gasps, her mouth opening, and I plunge my tongue inside and kiss her deeply. My hands slide into her hair, which is loose and hanging around her shoulders in waves, and I sigh at the feel of the silky locks sliding through my fingers.

"Mmm…" She murmurs against my mouth, tipping her head to the side, and her hands tighten to fists on my chest, clutching at the material of my T-shirt.

It would be so easy to kiss her senseless, to lift her onto the worktop, to go down on her and bring her to orgasm with my mouth, and then to slide into her and drive us both to another orgasm. But I don't want to rush it tonight. It's her birthday, and I want to make it special for her.

So I lift my hand and kiss her nose, and she sighs.

"Steak sandwich," I tell her, taking out my tongs. "Gotta keep our strength up."

She pouts at me sulkily. I loosen the tongs and click them together near her nipples, and she squeals, then laughs and pushes me away. "All right," she concedes. "Dinner… first?" She adds the word hopefully.

I know I might regret it later, but I say, "Yes. So pour yourself a glass of wine. You're staying the night."

Her face lights up, filling me with a warm glow at the thought that I've pleased her.

Yeah, Spencer, you're not in trouble at all.

I fry the steaks until they're medium-rare, and we slice them, insert them in sections of buttered baguette, and add lettuce and tomato, and eat them sitting on the deck while we talk and watch the sun go down.

When we finish eating, I ask her if she wants to go inside, but she shakes her head. The Moroccan lamp contains a citronella candle, and I light it to keep the insects away, then bring her a throw, as the temperature is starting to drop.

"Thank you." She tugs it around her shoulders, curling up in her chair. I sit back beside her and stretch out my legs, resting my feet on the opposite chair. "This is a great spot," she says, "and a beautiful house."

I offer the bottle of wine and top up her glass when she holds it out. "Yeah, I fell in love with it when I saw it. It's very peaceful."

"You fell in love?" she teases. "Doesn't sound like something Spencer Cavendish would do."

"I'm not the Tin Man. I do have a heart."

She smiles. "I know you do." She leans her head on a hand. "I think you have a huge heart. You're a very passionate man. But it's obviously important for you to maintain an austere and reserved front. To hide your feelings."

"Emotion has no place in business."

"Yeah, I understand that. What about in personal relationships?"

I don't reply.

Her eyes are gentle. "I think Eleanor scarred you deeply. Because she wouldn't respond to you, you had to learn to protect yourself, so you locked your heart away and put chains around it and a padlock on the front, and you refuse to let anyone near it now."

"If I do, it's not a conscious thing."

"But you acknowledge that it's important for you to be in control?"

"Always."

She falls quiet for a while. I wonder whether I've upset her in some way, but she doesn't look upset. She observes me thoughtfully, sipping her wine, her gaze meeting mine before sliding down me, soft as a feather, bringing me out in goosebumps.

When her eyes return to mine, they hold more than a little heat.

"About my birthday present," she says, leaning the glass against her cheek.

"Yes…"

"I know what I'd like."

"Oh?"

The light from the lamp dances in her eyes. "Have you ever wondered what it would be like to give up control in bed?"

"No," I say honestly.

"I have. And I'd like to be in charge. To direct the action." Her eyes gleam.

I don't say anything. She said she hasn't been with anyone since she broke up with Connor. I don't know what their sex life was like, but she has made a couple of references that suggest he was extremely dominant. He manipulated and controlled her, and would never have allowed her power in bed or out of it.

"I understand your need to claw back control over your life," I say slowly. "And also your desire to experiment sexually. But I don't know that I'm the guy to do that with."

"I don't want anyone else," she replies calmly. "I want you, Spencer. I want you to give yourself to me, one hundred percent."

We study each other quietly.

"Do you trust me?" she asks eventually.

I hesitate. "Yes…"

She just tips her to the side.

"Yes," I repeat softly. "I do."

"You know I wouldn't do anything to hurt you?"

"Yes."

"You know I just want to give you pleasure?"

I don't reply for a moment. My heart is racing.

All my experiences, everything I've been through, have brought me up to believe that control means safety.

But I realize with some surprise that maybe one reason I'm attracted to Marama is because she's unpredictable. I don't know what she's going to say or how she's going to act. She makes me laugh, and she fascinates me, because of that.

Eleanor wasn't kinky in the slightest, and her endometriosis meant that sex was often painful for her, and she didn't enjoy certain positions, especially anything from behind or that involved me going deep. She wasn't impulsive or voyeuristic; she didn't like watching porn or even talking about sex that much. Sex was mainly missionary, initiated by me.

This girl—this woman—is offering an experience I've never had before. A chance to relinquish responsibility and control and give myself completely over to her. To let her be in charge of my desire and my pleasure.

Still, I hesitate.

Marama's lips slowly curve up. "Don't tell me the thought doesn't turn you on." Her gaze slides down. I follow it and realize she's spotted the hard-on jutting through my soft track pants.

"I'm nervous," I tell her. "Not a robot."

She wrinkles her nose. "We'll have a safe word."

My eyebrows rise. "Will I need one?"

She shrugs. "If it'll make you feel better."

"What exactly are you planning to do to me?"

Her gaze slides over me lazily. "Tie you up. Explore every inch of your body with my mouth and fingers. To edge you. And take you to the brink of pleasure multiple times before I let you come."

I groan, slide down in my chair, and brush my hand over my face. She giggles and moves her chair closer to mine so she can trail a finger down my chest. "Does that turn you on?" she murmurs. "The thought of me being in charge?"

"No."

"Liar." She continues down to my erection and strokes it through the fabric. "I think it does. I think it'll be exciting for you to give up control for once. To make yourself vulnerable to someone else. To put your desire in my hands."

"Are you trying to give me a coronary?"

She smiles, but continues, "You think control is strength. But letting someone see you emotionally naked… that's brave."

"You're suggesting I stand unarmed in front of you. You don't know what you're asking. That's not who I am."

She continues to stroke my erection. "Are you sure about that?"

A long time ago, I tentatively suggested to Eleanor that we experiment. She didn't mind oral, but I proposed that maybe I could explore her body more with my fingers and tongue, and she could do the same to me. I can still recall the look of distaste that passed across her face. The way she said, somewhat icily, "Straight, decent men aren't interested in that kind of thing, Spencer. You're not a horny teenager, you're a grown man—exercise some self-control, for God's sake." I remember the way it made me feel—an inch high, and like a pervert. I never mentioned anything like it again, and our love life remained vanilla right until the end.

When other men have joked about their bedroom antics, I've just raised an eyebrow and said that I don't share salacious tales about my wife, but the truth was that I didn't have any stories to tell.

Now the thought of Marama introducing new and interesting things turns me on and terrifies me in equal measure. Does it make me a pervert that I'm excited by it? Make me weak to give her the power?

Her expression flickers, as if maybe she understands a little of what I've been through. She smiles, gets to her feet, and holds out a hand. "Come on, Spencer. Let me take you to heaven and back."

I take her hand and let her pull me to my feet, then follow her into the living room, blowing out the candle on the way. She closes the sliding door behind us and locks it, then picks up her purse, and together we walk across the living room to the stairs on the opposite side.

I glance at the portrait as I pass it. *You come to be seen, as I choose to see you.* This woman has snuck into the dusty attic where I keep all my fears locked up, and she's prying open the shutters and letting in the sunlight, exposing all the ghosts that lurk there.

My heart bangs on my ribs as I lead her up the stairs to the bedroom above. I don't know if I can do this. If I can give myself wholly to her. Once she's wheedled her way inside my heart, how will I ever get her out again?

I open the door to my bedroom and we go inside. It's the master bedroom, and it has a magnificent view over the ocean in daylight. It's dark now, and the sky and the sea are the color of an eggplant, rapidly darkening to black. The moon is a few days off full, casting everything in a silvery light.

The headboard rests against a false wall, chest-high, a few feet from the back wall, and the bed faces the view. Marama puts her purse on the bedside table, then turns to me and moves me so my back is against the wall. She glances to my left, her eyes lighting with surprise at the sight of one of her paintings next to us—one of my favorites, of a Māori goddess dancing naked in the moonlight, modeled on herself.

Her gaze comes back to me. She moves up close and lifts onto her tiptoes. Then she kisses me.

I let her, trying not to do what I'd normally do, and take charge. It's her birthday, and if I'm going to do this, I want to do it properly. I want her to enjoy it, and to experience the feeling of being fully in control for once. She deserves it after everything she's been through.

And, let's face it, it's hardly a chore for me.

She slides a hand to the back of my head as she kisses me, pressing up against me, and I rest my hands on her hips, not directing, but wanting to touch her.

When you're young, you have no idea how difficult it can be in a relationship when your libidos don't match, or you have different kinks or limits. As a guy we're conditioned to think sex is all physical, and that it's our responsibility to ensure our partner enjoys themselves in bed. I never realized that the biggest turn on is being desired and wanted. And now Marama is taking that a step further and showing me that some women actually enjoy sex, and want to give pleasure too.

I thought I wouldn't like it, but somehow it's completely different to the experience Genevieve promised. That felt spiteful and manipulative, the same way it must have felt for Marama with Connor—that the other person wants to control you, to punish you, almost. To make you small. This just feels... exciting.

Her fingers are sliding to the base of my tee, and they slip beneath it, then spread across my skin, her nails scraping over my ribs. I murmur my approval, and she does it again, skating her fingers up to my nipples, which she circles with the pads of her forefingers. When I shudder, she chuckles and nips my bottom lip with her teeth, then draws my tee up my body, over my head, and tosses it away. Next, she takes off my track pants, and then my boxer-briefs, so I'm standing in front of her, naked.

"Get on the bed," she whispers.

Heart hammering, I climb on and lay back.

She goes over to her purse and opens it. What's she taking out? A couple of long silk scarves.

Holy shit.

She comes over to the bed, stands beside it, and unbuttons her jeans, then tugs them off and lets them drop. Next, she takes off her black top. I inhale—she's wearing a gorgeous set of lingerie—a matching lacy bra and knickers. Leaving them on, she climbs onto the bed and moves up near my head.

Taking the silk scarf, she loops one end around my right wrist and ties it, just once. She lifts my arms above my head, threads the scarf through the slat at the top, and ties the other end around my left wrist, again, just once. I look up at the knots. One wriggle of my wrists or tug with my fingers and they'd easily come undone.

"It's symbolic," she tells me softly. "Do you trust me?"

I nod, because I think if I speak it'll come out as a squeak.

"I want you to give me control," she says. "And this shows me you're willing. You can stop any time, see? But I'm hoping you won't."

It does make me feel better to know she's not going to do a constrictor knot. I don't want her to do unmentionable things to me while I'm restrained.

Do I? My cock appears to think otherwise.

"I'm sure you know the safe word colors," she says. "Yellow means pause. Red means stop. Right?"

I nod. I'm aware of them, although I've never had to use them myself. "This should be the other way around," I say hoarsely. "I should be pleasuring you on your birthday."

"You are," she says. "This is what I want." I wait for her to say 'To see the mighty Spencer Cavendish brought to his knees,' or something else demeaning like that. But instead she murmurs, "I want you to share yourself with me. To open up to me. To trust me."

I swallow hard. "I do."

She climbs on the bed and crawls up to me. Then she lowers her head and touches her lips to mine. "Then relax, sweetheart. And just enjoy yourself."

Chapter Twenty

Marama

I pick up the other scarf and bring it up to his face. "I'm going to blindfold you," I tell him. "I want you to concentrate on your other senses. Okay?"

He's breathing fast. But he nods, so I tie the scarf around his head and tighten it until it rests lightly over his eyes.

Then I kiss him again, longer this time, teasing his lips with my teeth, delving my tongue into his mouth. Out of the corner of my eye I see him flex his hands in the ties. I think he's finding it difficult to lie there and do nothing.

But he stays still, and doesn't try to escape. He sighs, his breath whispering over my lips, and I can feel him trying to relax, while we continue to exchange sensual, deep kisses.

Stretching out beside him, still kissing him, I begin trailing my fingers over his body, light touches that bring goose bumps out on his skin.

Lifting my head, I look at his firm, strong body, enjoying exploring him. He's acting calm, although he's still breathing faster than usual. It's obvious that he feels vulnerable, lying with his hands tied, exposed to my gaze and touch.

This is obviously the first time he's ever done this with someone. I can't imagine Eleanor being interested in doing anything like this. He would never criticize her, because in his mind that's not what a gentleman does, but he's dropped enough hints to suggest his relationship with her was very vanilla. From what I've read on Reddit and other forums, few men are truly vanilla, unless maybe they're very religious; they usually enjoy experimenting, and it's the main reason many of them stray—when they meet someone more open and adventurous than their wife.

I can tell this is turning him on—that much is obvious. I think he loves feeling wanted and desired. But will he be able to fight his instincts to take charge? Will he give all of himself to me?

I kiss him for a long time, still stroking his body, eventually moving from his lips to press kisses over his face—his nose, forehead, and jaw, which is just starting to show a five o'clock shadow. I kiss around to his ears, which I nibble and lick. Then I begin kissing down his neck, stopping to touch my tongue to his Adam's apple and the hollow at the base of his throat. I love how different he is to me. How masculine and manly.

Mmm, I'm starting to get hot and bothered. Time to step up the action.

Sitting back, I unclip my bra and slide the straps down my arms, then lean over him so I can kiss his arms and hands. My breasts are now level with his head, and I move one of my nipples to his mouth and tease his lips with the soft tip. Obediently, he opens his mouth, and I feed him my nipple, moaning softly when he sucks it and flicks the end with his tongue. Heat building inside me, I swap to the other one, still kissing his arms and hands. He shivers as I touch my tongue to his palms and suck each of his fingers in turn.

When I move back and shift down the bed, he gives a heavy sigh of disappointment, but he still doesn't move. Hiding a smile, I kiss down his arms, enjoying the swell of his glorious biceps. When I reach his underarms, I nuzzle there and inhale.

He frowns and growls, "Don't do that."

I lift my head to look at him. "Who's in charge here?"

He sets his jaw, so I know he's glowering, and I stifle a laugh before moving to the other arm and doing the same. He smells of shower gel and anti-perspirant and healthy male, a mixture that is very erotic to me.

He blows out a breath and shifts a little on the bed, then groans as I kiss each of his nipples and swirl my tongue over them. I carry on down, pressing my lips to each rib, and eventually following the happy trail of hair that leads down to his groin. He doesn't have a six-pack exactly, but he's nicely toned and obviously takes care of his body.

Shifting down, I pause as I reach his erection and study it with interest. It swells under my gaze and glistens. My mouth watering, I bend my head and brush my tongue across the tip, licking up the moisture that's already gathered there.

After that brief tease, I move back and continue kissing the rest of him. His flat stomach. His hips. His firm thighs, and down each leg.

He groans, and I giggle. "What's the matter, Spencer?" I taunt, kissing down his shins to his feet. "Tell me you don't like what I'm doing to you."

He doesn't reply, and I know it's because if he said the words, it would be a lie.

I lift each leg and kiss each foot in turn, pressing my lips to his insteps. His feet are attractive; clean and soft with nice, neat nails, and I poke my tongue between his toes.

"Argh." He squirms on the bed and tries to move his feet away.

I chuckle. "Does it tickle?"

"No."

"Then what's the matter?"

His chest rises and falls quickly. "It makes me feel uncomfortable."

It's a strange word to pick. "Why?" I kiss his big toe. "You have nice feet."

His forehead creases above the blindfold. "I didn't realize you were so kinky."

"Kinky?" Now I'm the one who's baffled. "I'm just kissing your feet. That's not kinky."

"I think my view of what's normal in the bedroom is a lot less risqué than everyone else's. Everything except straight sex is kinky to me."

"Seriously?"

"Not every woman is as open as you," he says. "Some women don't even touch themselves."

He means Eleanor, of course. He's implying she didn't masturbate. I've read that there are people who don't do it, but I wasn't sure if it was true.

"Shit," I say, "how come she didn't explode?"

That makes him laugh. "You're amazing," he says.

"I'm just normal," I correct. "I'm hardly accomplished where sex is concerned." I've only had a handful of partners, and none of them were experts in the bedroom. Connor was a bit more experienced, but he was also very controlling, and would never let me take charge like this, and I was limited to what he'd let me do.

"You're sex positive," he replies, his voice husky. "That goes a long way."

I'm genuinely shocked that a man could get to his age and not be more sexually experienced. It says something about his loyalty that he stayed married to her.

Well, now I'm even more determined to blow his mind and show him that a man's pleasure is as important as a woman's. I kiss back up his thighs and move between them, then lower a hand between my legs and stroke myself. Mmm... I'm more than ready for him, swollen and wet. "I'm touching myself," I tell him, closing my eyes and enjoying the feeling of my finger circling over my clit.

"Oh," he says. "I'd like to watch you."

"Later." Opening my eyes, I lift my fingers up to his mouth. I brush them across his lips, then lean over him and kiss him, and our tongues tangle, both of us tasting me, and he gives a long, deep groan.

I do that a few times, and when I finally move back, he's rock hard.

I open the tube, squeeze some lube onto my fingers, and stroke his erection so it's completely coated and my fingers glide easily over his skin. He's long and thick, and I explore him with my fingers, from his balls up to the swollen head. "Mmm... you are such an impressive man."

"Ah... please..." He bites his bottom lip as the word tumbled out without his permission.

But I just smirk and say, "No mercy," echoing his instruction to me the last time we had sex.

He sighs. "Fair enough."

"You want me to stop, Spencer?"

He tilts his hips up a little, swelling in my hand as I continue to stroke him. "No," he whispers.

I feel a surge of pleasure. I haven't taken this power from him. He's choosing to give it to me. This is what I wanted.

I move between his legs. Then I start kissing him while I stroke him.

I kiss around him—his hips, thighs, and stomach, and the base of his cock, then press my lips all the way up his shaft to the head before brushing my tongue over the tip. He groans, so I do it again, then slide my lips down the shaft and take him deep in my mouth. The lube is lightly cherry flavored, and I murmur my approval as it mixes with the gorgeous taste of him.

"Ahhh," he says with a sigh, "that feels good..."

My mouth is full so I can't reply, but I continue to stroke and suck him, feeling him push his hips up to match my rhythm. Mmm, I don't think he's that far from coming.

I lift my head, and lower my hand.

He groans and flops back on the pillow.

"Don't worry," I tease. "I'm going to take you all the way. But I want to try something I've never done." I don't want to do it without his consent, because I know some men are averse to the idea, and somehow I have a feeling he's not experienced it before. "I've read that stimulating the prostate is supposed to feel really good for the guy," I say a little shyly. "Will you let me try? I haven't done it before. But I won't do it unless you want me to."

He goes still. I think I've shocked him. "Ah…" He looks uncertain.

"Do you trust me?" I ask again. "I just want to make you feel good."

He swallows. Then he nods.

Feeling a swell of excitement, desperate to give him pleasure, I reach for the lube and squeeze a generous amount onto my fingers. Kneeling between his legs, I push them wide until he's completely open to me, vulnerable and exposed.

He's breathing fast, and his body is tense. I smooth the lube all the way down with my right hand, then caress his balls for a while as I continue to stroke his cock with my left. Only then do I slide my hand further down and gently tease him there with a finger.

"Fuck," he says.

"Color?" I ask sweetly.

"Ahhh…" He groans. "Yellow."

I stop, and just stroke the area south of his balls, letting him get used to the sensation. I can feel how tense he is. But he's also still hard, and he hasn't loosened the ties. He likes it. He just needs time.

Returning my mouth to the tip of his erection, I lick and suck him again, still stroking him with one hand, while I explore with the other. Making sure I have plenty of lube on my finger, I stroke over the tight muscle for a while, not inserting, just brushing lightly.

Gradually, he relaxes, his tense muscles loosening, and hips begin to match my rhythm again. I continue to stroke him beneath his balls with a lube-covered finger, and then, slowly, I press it against the tight muscle beneath.

"Tell me if you want me to stop," I murmur, and I tease him gently.

This time, he just groans.

I do it again, pressing the tip of my finger against the muscle, very slowly and gently. "Just relax," I say. "Give yourself to me, baby. I'm going to make you come, and it's going to feel so good."

He sighs, and then I feel him consciously try to relax. Gathering up the lube, I tease him again with my finger, then slide it slowly inside.

He groans.

I remove it, then do it again, a little further this time. Slow and gentle, letting him get used to it.

"Fuck…" He gives a deep, heartfelt groan.

"Does it feel good, baby?"

"Ahhh… yeah…"

"You want me to stop, darling?"

"Mmm… no…"

Smiling, I continue, gathering lube, teasing, pressing, inserting. Gradually, I slide my finger a little further. I've read what to do, and when I'm up to the first knuckle, palm up, I press up until I find the small swelling. Then I massage it gently.

"Oh," he says breathlessly. "Oh fuck."

"Is that nice, my love?"

"Mmm… yeah…"

"Just relax and enjoy it, honey. I'm going to take you all the way now, okay?"

"Oh shit…"

Smiling, I cover the head of his cock with my mouth.

I can only imagine how it feels for him. My mouth licking and sucking. One hand stroking his cock firmly. And the other exploring him, teasing him in the most erotic way possible.

He's relaxed now he realizes I just want to give him pleasure. He's giving himself over to me, thighs wide, completely open, letting himself be vulnerable and defenseless because he trusts me. I feel almost tearful that he has such faith in me. This is going to be an emotional nuclear bomb for him, and he has no idea it's coming.

His breaths have turned into irregular gasps, and his body is slowly tensing again, but in a different way this time. His stomach turns taut, and his thighs tighten as he says, "Ahhh… I'm going to come…"

I think he's trying to warn me in case I want to move back, because this is the first time he's come in my mouth, but I just slide my lips down the shaft as I continue to stroke and massage him, and then he tenses and cries out, erupting into my mouth and filling it with his silky liquid. I take it all, swallowing it down, and only when he gasps and trembles do I lift my head and lick my lips.

"Fuck," he says, "oh fuck…" His chest heaves.

I kiss up his body and stretch out beside him. Then I remove his blindfold and look into his eyes. "Are you okay?"

He nods, but I can see his emotion near the surface, threatening to overwhelm him. "I think my soul actually left my body for a moment." His voice comes out as a squeak. That breaks the tension, and we both laugh.

I kiss him, pressing my lips to his a few times. Then I lift my head and say mischievously, "I thought I might go for a ride."

His eyes light up. "Oh God, yes, please." He looks up at his hands. "Can I untie them so I can touch you?"

I love that he's asking me. At this moment, it feels as if he belongs to me entirely, and it's a wonderful feeling. "If you want," I say, and he picks at the ties and releases his hands.

I lift up to climb on him, but to my surprise he stops me and says, "Go and wash your hands first."

I laugh, but he looks me in the eye and says, "I mean it," so I chuckle and go into the bathroom to wash them quickly before I come back and climb on the bed.

I hold my hands up. "Happy now?"

"I'm tempted to examine your nails," he says wryly, pulling the pillow lengthwise beneath his head to make himself comfortable. Then he smiles. "Come on. It's my turn."

Lifting up, I straddle him, and he rests his big hands on my thighs and helps to guide me onto his mouth. I steady myself onto the headboard behind him, and then I lower myself down.

We both groan, me because the sensation of his tongue sliding into me is just like heaven, and him no doubt because he's discovered how turned on I am. Ahhh… there really is nothing like doing this with a man, and with Spencer it feels extra special… it's like my birthday and Christmas and Valentine's Day and warmed caramel and melted chocolate and the bubbles of champagne all rolled into one… a blissful feeling of warmth and excitement right at my core.

He brushes one hand over the outside of my thigh—a caring gesture that warms me through—and swirls his tongue over my clit while he moves his other hand beneath me.

Ohhh.. fuck… I'm not going to last long like this.

Part of me wonders if he's going to edge me and make me wait because of what I did to him, but he doesn't. He strokes me and explores with his fingers, licking and sucking my clit, and I'm so turned on that it's only a few minutes before I feel my orgasm begin to build. I rock my hips, grinding against his tongue while my fingers clutching the headboard, then gasp out loud as my climax hits and my body pulses, clenching around his fingers. Oh my God it feels so amazing… that moment of pure pleasure that's like nothing else… and it must only be seven or eight seconds, but it feels as if it goes on forever.

When it finally stops, I lift off and collapse next to him, and we lie there for a while, staring up at the ceiling, as our breathing returns to normal.

"Mmm." I feel a surge of happiness and roll onto my stomach to look at him. "Do you have any ice cream?"

He laughs. "Absolutely." He kisses my nose. "I'll go and get it."

I lie there, basking in the post-orgasmic glow, until he returns with three different Duck Island tubs: Cookies and Cream, Peppermint Slice, and something called Blueberry Buttermilk Gooey Butter Cake. He pops off the tops and passes me a spoon, and we sit in bed and help ourselves, passing the tubs back and forth.

We keep the conversation light, discussing movies and TV series, and testing each other with quotes from our favorites. When we've had our fill of ice cream, he returns the tubs to the freezer, and we decide to take a bath together. He has a beautiful bathroom, with a large, deep bath, and we sink into the water, up to our chins in bubbles.

"Thank you for wanting to spend your birthday with me," he says.

"You're very welcome."

He picks up one of my feet and massages it. "I would have thought you had lots of better invitations."

"Better than tying up the most gorgeous guy in the city and giving him an amazing orgasm?" I wrinkle my nose at him, and he chuckles. "Oh, I didn't tell you what Dad's present was," I add.

"You mean the van?"

My eyebrows rise. "You know about that?"

"Yeah, I helped him choose it last month."

"Oh… I didn't realize. He didn't mention you." My stomach flips. They chose the van together last month… before the auction, and before the headline that announced to the world that he was being tamed.

"How's the other painting going?" he asks.

I clear my throat. "Not bad."

Our eyes meet. I know he suspects what Genevieve has asked me to paint.

I change the subject, talking about a new book I've been reading, and Spencer listens, smiles, and nods, but he doesn't say much. Soon after that, we get out of the bath and make our way back to bed.

I'm sure if I ask him if he wants me to go home, he'll say yes. So I don't ask. I bring the duvet up over us, and snuggle up close to him. He tucks one arm beneath his head, lowering the other around me, and we lie there in the darkness as our bodies slowly drift down to earth.

I wait for him to speak, but he doesn't say anything. His hand rests on my back, not moving. For a moment, I think maybe he's dozed off. But when I eventually lift my head to look up at him, I see that his eyes are open, twinkling in the moonlight as he stares over my head at the view.

I rest my hand on his chest, and my chin on my hand. "Are you all right?"

"Of course." But his words are clipped, his expression shuttered. He opened up to me, let himself be raw and unfiltered, and now, as I expected, the emotional fall-out is making him feel uneasy.

I'd hoped that it would make him realize he can be totally himself with me. But it's clear that even if that's the case, he doesn't like the feeling. Knowing his penchant for power, it could have made him feel weak.

Maybe he just needs to get used to it. Perhaps after he's thought about it for a while, he'll feel more comfortable with opening up to me emotionally, and start considering the idea of us being a couple.

Or maybe he'll retreat to control, and shut me out completely.

My heart races, but I try not to show my fear. I need to give him time, that's all.

Should I try and talk to him about it? I open my mouth to say something, but at that moment he says, fairly briskly, "Turn over."

I close my mouth and do as he bids, and he moves up close behind me, tucking his arm under my breasts.

We lie there in the darkness, not talking, looking out at the cold moon as she shines her cool silvery light down on the flat sea.

Chapter Twenty-One

Spencer

I'm torn.

My heart wants Marama. My body wants her, desperately, and it doesn't seem to matter how often it has her; five minutes later, it wants her again.

But I know the relationship is doomed. There are a hundred reasons why it would never work. I desperately need to exercise some self-restraint and tell her it's over. But it's impossible when I crave her so badly.

It's a while before we both drift off. I know she can sense my unease, and the urge to tell her she needs to get up and go home is so strong it feels like a river straining against a dam.

But I can't bring myself to say the words. I've slept on my own for twenty years, and it's so amazing to have her here, warm and soft in my arms. Just before I drift off I feel her kiss my hand where it's tucked under her chin, and that tender gesture is like a candle in the dark that makes all my fears recede into the shadows. Momentarily content, I let the sound of the ocean and Marama's breathing lull me to sleep.

I wake sometime in the night from a dream of being lost in the city. I was constantly turning down different streets and going around corners to discover I wasn't where I thought I'd be, and when I jerk awake, my heart is racing and for a moment I don't know where I am.

"Shhh." Marama strokes my face. "It was just a dream." She leans over me and presses her lips to mine.

Guilt and regret mix in my stomach, and I know I should push her away, but instead I pull her toward me, and she tumbles onto my chest with a laugh. Sliding a hand into her hair, I bring her head down to kiss her, and she gives a muffled exclamation, then sighs and returns it.

"I want you," I tell her hoarsely in between kisses, needing her presence to help me battle the demons that want to claim me.

"I'm all yours," she whispers back, opening her mouth to my searching tongue.

I kiss her while I stroke my hands down her back, wanting to commit her curves to memory, because I know this has an end date and soon she won't be mine to touch anymore.

The thought makes me mad. Why can't I have her? It's not like I wouldn't be good to her. I'd make sure she didn't want for anything, whether it was money or attention. I'd treat her like a queen. But the rest of the world would mock me and condemn me for it.

I wish I was like her, and I didn't care what people thought. But I do care. My status and my place in the business community matters to me. I'm not a free spirit. I envy her so deeply it's as if I truly have a wolf inside me, trying to claw its way out. I am a lone wolf. I was meant to be alone.

These thoughts whirl around in my head and my chest, but gradually they dissipate as desire takes over. Holding her tightly, I lift up and twist so she's beneath me, then take her hands and pin them above her head with one of mine. With the other I lift her breast to my mouth and suck her nipple hard, and she inhales sharply and arches her back with a moan.

I enjoyed her taking charge; I can't deny it. It was erotic and it turned me on. But this is better. Driving the action, having her at my mercy; it fires me up, sends heat searing through me. I let it consume both of us, and by the time I roll on a condom, we're both hot and sweaty and panting, clawing at each other's skin, desperate and hungry for one another.

"Ahhh…" She moans as I slide inside her, all the way in with one smooth thrust because she's so wet. "That feels so good…"

"Hold on baby, this is going to be fast," I tell her, and I begin to move, plunging down into her soft body with long, hard thrusts.

"Yeah," she says enthusiastically, wrapping her legs around me. "Fuck me, Spencer. Hard as you like."

Her encouragement, and the fact that she doesn't mind it a little rough, fires me up even more, and I let my body take over and do what it wants to, and pound her into next week. She cries out with every thrust, digging her nails into my back.

"Ah yes, ah yes," she exclaims, tightening around me, but there's no time for me to enjoy her orgasm because I'm coming too. My climax slams into me, and I roar as I come, thrusting us both to the edge of pleasure, so we tumble over together, clutching hold of each other all the way down.

Afterward, I ease out of her and dispose of the condom, then hold her tightly as she presses up close to me, our legs entwined.

"I didn't hurt you?" I murmur, stroking her hair.

"Mmm... no, you were magnificent."

I chuckle and kiss her hair. "You're amazing."

She presses her lips to my chest. "No, I'm just normal." She rests her lips there, then says, "I need to say something."

"Uh-oh," I joke.

She doesn't laugh. Instead she says, "I know you're frightened of falling for me because you've been starved for affection, but you have to know that Eleanor was unusual, and most women enjoy sex. There will be someone else out there who is more suitable for you who enjoys it."

I swallow hard at her mention of being unsuitable. "Marama..."

Her eyes shine with unshed tears in the moonlight. "I'm not saying I want you to meet someone else." She rubs her nose. "I hate her already."

"I don't want anyone else," I tell her gently.

"Of course you do." She curls up beside me. "You can't go through the rest of your life alone. You're too passionate and loving for that."

Passionate and loving. Two words I can't imagine anyone else ever saying about me.

She's right, of course. She's not alone; there are plenty of other women out there closer to my age who enjoy sex. And plenty of other guys who will be more than thrilled to have her as a partner, as a wife. We'll both be happy with other people, eventually.

I lie there in the darkness, passing my hands across her soft skin, and tell myself more lies as I watch the moon rising in the night sky.

*

The next morning, we breakfast out on the deck together, keeping the conversation light, and not discussing our future. Marama then announces it's time for her to go, and I see her to the door.

MIDNIGHT SECRET

"Are you going to the party at Midnight tonight?" she asks. Mack has formally announced that his wife, Sidnie, is pregnant with their first child, and everyone's gathering to celebrate.

I nod. "I guess I'll see you there."

We hesitate, facing each other across the doorstep. I think we both know this could be the last time we see each other privately.

Then she smiles. She reaches up to kiss me on the lips, and I quickly slide an arm around her and hold her there for a longer embrace.

When I finally release her, she sighs and flicks me another quick smile, then heads off to her Alfa Romeo. I wave and go back inside, although I stand just behind the closed door, waiting until I hear the car purring down the street.

*

I'm restless for the rest of the day. I try to work, and fail, and end up making a sandwich for lunch, taking it into my workshop, and starting a new project—a four-poster bed, complete with hand-turned bedposts and a carved headboard.

I listen to some true-crime podcasts while I work, and gradually relax as I lose myself in the creative pursuit. It's a pleasant afternoon, but it's brought to an end when a message arrives on the Midnight Circle's Slack chat. I bring it up and groan. Huxley has asked us to get to the club thirty minutes early for a brief meeting before the party starts. I check the time; I need to start getting ready.

Wondering what he wants to see us about, and irritated because I can't shake the feeling it's going to be something to do with me, I check the Kōrero website, but there are no new headlines and no photos of me. Scowling, I go off to have a shower and a shave, then change into a pair of light-brown chinos, a white shirt, and don a navy jacket before heading off in my Aston for Waiheke Island.

I arrive at the club, slot the Aston into the space out the front with my name on it, and head inside. It's six-thirty, and the Midnight Club is open and already half full, mostly with business people who are staying on site, meeting up with colleagues for deals over drinks, as visitors tend to arrive later.

"Hey," Mack says as he crosses the lobby, coffee in hand.

"Evening. Where's Sidnie?"

"Just getting ready for the party."

"When's she due?"

"Early October. I'm already terrified."

I chuckle as we head along the corridor to the main board room. "Yeah, it's a big change. But you'll make a great dad."

"Thank you. I appreciate that."

As he opens the door to the boardroom and we go in, it occurs to me that he and the other younger members of the Midnight Circle see me and Rangi as father figures. With some shock I realize that if Marama was to have children, they'd be younger than my first grandchild. Shit. That makes me feel old. And it's yet another reason I have to stay away from her.

I glance at my phone as I sit at the table. We've messaged each other on and off all day, and there's one sitting there now, sent ten minutes ago, short and sweet: *See you soon!* X

I frown and pocket the phone without replying.

The others are here, and Huxley says, "Hey guys, thanks for coming. Sorry to get you here early but something has come to my attention that I wanted to discuss."

I glance across the table at Rangi. He's looking at me, and he doesn't smile. Does he know what's coming?

"It's about Genevieve Beaumont," Huxley says. "Apparently she's planning to open a rival retreat on Waiheke Island, with celebrity investors and a 'feminist focus'." He puts air quotes around the term.

"For fuck's sake," Joanna says, exasperated.

"Yeah," Huxley replies with feeling.

"I don't understand," Kingi says, "what's she hoping to achieve with this? Midnight is established here and incredibly popular. She's going to struggle to get another Lumen up and running."

"I don't think its success is her main concern," Huxley comments. For the first time, he looks at me.

"What are you saying?" Joanna asks. "That she's doing this purely out of spite?"

Elizabeth nods. "You saw the headline?"

"About the painting and Spencer being tamed? Yeah."

"That was one hundred percent Genevieve behind that."

Joanna looks at me. She's a good person—hardworking and generous, but she hasn't got where she is by refusing to pull her punches. "A personal attack is one thing," she says. "But this is starting to have an impact on Midnight, and that means we have to do something."

I grit my teeth. "We should just ignore her. Giving her attention is playing into her hands—it's what she wants."

Joanna shakes her head. "She's not a toddler, Spencer. We can't just step over her while she has a tantrum. Another club on the island would have a real, physical knock-on effect for us."

"Unfortunately, I think she's right," Huxley says.

"I don't know that there's anything we can do about it," I say hotly.

"Maybe you should talk to her—" Orson begins.

I cut him off. "No. I'm not giving that woman a second of my time."

Huxley looks at Rangi. "What do you think?"

He studies the table quietly, thinking. Then he says, "My first priority has to be Marama. The exhibition at Lumen is a real opportunity for her. And honestly? Part of me understands Genevieve's angle, and her desire to bring men down a peg or two."

"That's easy for you to say." I glare at him. "It's not your name being splashed all over the Internet."

"No, because I have the sense not to bid a million dollars on a woman half my age."

Fury flares inside me. "I'm not sixty." I'm close to yelling. It's the first time I've shown emotion, and everyone's eyes widen.

"I was being metaphorical," Rangi says. He's half amused and half annoyed.

Huxley clears his throat. "Let's try to put aside our personal feelings and concentrate on the Circle. It's clear that another club here would be bad for us, especially one oriented toward women. Any publicity that Lumen gets now is going to reflect badly on us. Journalists love the light and dark analogy, and the male/female competition."

"Maybe we should take on more female board members," Mack suggests.

"You want to bring Genevieve on board?" Elizabeth snaps.

He gives her a sarcastic look. "No. I was thinking about Victoria."

"I asked her, remember?" Huxley says. "She wasn't interested. She's got enough on her plate."

"Neither Joanna nor I believe in tokenism," Elizabeth says. "If we decide to enlarge the board, we'll accept the best person for the job, no matter their gender, color, or sexual preferences.

"We do need to try to placate Genevieve somehow," Huxley states.

"No." I bang my hand on the table. "We don't move an inch for that woman. We don't talk to her, we don't issue press releases, we don't do anything that implies we've even noticed she exists. There's more at stake here than my personal pride."

"Like what?" Joanna asks.

"Like Marama's career," I reply heatedly. "She doesn't fully appreciate Genevieve's motivation behind the exhibition. But nevertheless it is an exceptional opportunity for her, and I don't want to be the one to take that away from her."

"I understand," Joanna says, "but your personal connection is adding fuel to the fire."

"There is no personal connection," I snap.

"I appreciate that this is a delicate issue. But Spencer, you bid a million dollars on her."

"For her father," I say irritably.

She looks from me to Rangi, then back at me. "I don't think any of us believes that." She looks at me over the top of her glasses. "Do you?"

I get to my feet. "I'm not going to listen to this. It's exactly what Genevieve wants—to drive a wedge between us."

"I don't think it's Genevieve who's doing that," Joanna says. "We've all noticed that you're distracted, Spencer. You're making mistakes you would never normally make. And you're acting oddly. In the past, if someone posted a headline like that one about you being tamed, you'd have ripped them a new one. You'd never have stood for someone threatening the Circle's legacy. But now your suggested action is to... what? Do nothing? To let this woman think she has you on a leash?" Her gaze turns curious. "Is this all because of Marama? Maybe she is taming you, after all?"

Rangi slams his hand down on the table, but before he has a chance to speak, I shove my chair under the table, then turn and walk out before I say something I regret.

I stride across the lobby and go outside. The sun has set, and the solar lights around the building are all on, giving it a warm, welcoming glow. I should head for the Club—everyone will be gathering there ready to celebrate Mack and Sidnie's good news. But I don't feel like celebrating. And I don't feel like being sociable.

Equally, I'm not ready to get in the Aston and head home while I'm still angry. So instead, I turn toward the main hotel and head for my suite.

Once I'm inside, I turn on a single lamp, then pace the floor, trying to calm down. I really should go to the party or it will only spread the rumor that I'm not myself. But the thing is… I *am* distracted. Joanna was absolutely right. I am making mistakes, and I'm acting out of character.

Marama might have been the catalyst for it, but she's not the cause. I think it's been coming for some while, building up inside me like steam in a kettle. It started with Eleanor's illness and death and continued with Blake's passing, turning forty, becoming a grandfather, and watching my son fall in love with a girl and realizing that I don't think I've ever been in love, or been loved in return, the way he currently is. Add to that a growing understanding that my job doesn't fulfil me the way it used to, and it's left me with a deep unease and dissatisfaction with life that won't go away.

Being with Marama triggered my current restlessness because it's made me aware of what life could have been like if things had been different. If my wife had been open and affectionate. If she'd wanted me the way I wanted her. Of course the endo wasn't her fault, and I understood why sex wasn't always as enjoyable for her, and blamed it for her lack of enthusiasm.

But I also read a great deal about it, and other women's experiences, and there were many who insisted that with a gentle, caring partner who had plenty of patience, they could still enjoy sex. I was prepared to be patient. I would have done anything to please her. But now that I've been intimate with Marama, I'm starting to realize the problem went much deeper than the physical.

I don't know what psychological problems caused Eleanor to be the way she was, and to be honest, I don't really care now. I stop pacing and stand by the window, tired and dispirited. I spent a lifetime with her, trying to make her love me. I think she did, in her own way. At least, I don't think she was unfaithful. I think she loved me as much as she was able. It just wasn't enough for me.

Now I've met someone warm and full of life who is affectionate and loving the way I've always wanted. And I'm not allowed to be with her because our relationship wouldn't fit what society sees as the norm.

I realize I'm deeply angry about it. I have a knot in my stomach, formed from resentment and guilt and frustration, and I don't know what to do about it, or how to get rid of it.

I need to ignore it and just keep on carrying on, as they say. But I'm not sure I can. I'm not a passive man. If there's a change to be made, I'm going to be the one to make it. I don't like just letting things happen to me. I don't think things can stay the same, though. But what can I do?

There's a knock at the door.

Frowning, I turn and stare at it. Has Rangi come to have it out? Or maybe it's Orson. I'm sure the Circle had a conversation when I left about placating Genevieve, and maybe they've sent him to put me straight and insist I go and see her. I'm not going to do that, and I don't want to argue with him about it.

But the knock sounds again. I'm not a coward, and I'm not going to pretend not to be in to avoid confrontation. So I huff a sigh, go over to the door, and wrench it open.

It's Marama.

"I saw you in the lobby," she says. "You looked angry. I was worried about you. Is everything okay?"

"This isn't a good time," I reply, relieved to see her, nevertheless.

She observes me calmly. "You want to talk to me about it?"

"No."

"I'm a good listener," she says as if I haven't spoken.

She ducks under my arm and goes into the room. Unless I physically propel her out, it looks as if she's here to stay.

"Did anyone see you come up here?" I ask her, closing the door behind her.

She frowns thoughtfully. "I don't think I was followed." Then her expression turns wry. She's teasing me. "You're my friend," she says, lifting her chin. "I'm allowed to come and make sure you're okay." Her expression turns kind then. "*Are* you okay? Kingi told me that Huxley had asked you all to come in earlier for a meeting. I'm guessing it was something to do with you?"

I shove my hands in my pockets. "There are rumors that Genevieve is opening another club on Waiheke as a direct rival to Midnight. Apparently it's going to have celebrity investors and a feminist focus."

She exhales and studies the carpet. Tonight she's wearing a long green skirt and a pretty white top. She's pinned up her hair with a clip but, as usual, long strands curl around her cheeks. Sparkly green eyeshadow matches the skirt. She's also wearing a dark-red lip gloss that makes her look older and more sophisticated. She's so fucking beautiful, it makes me ache.

Lifting her gaze to mine again, she says, "And they're blaming you for it?"

"It's revenge on her part, pure and simple. Toward me and the rest of the Circle. They know that, but they also accused me of being distracted and not challenging her."

"Why aren't you?" she asks. I hesitate, and her eyebrows rise. "Because of me?" she asks, surprised.

"The exhibition is an exceptional opportunity for you. It should have been us who offered it. I know that. And I'm not going to be the one to take it away from you."

Her expression softens. "That's very sweet of you. But I don't want you to get into trouble with the others because of me."

"I don't care about the others. I only care…" I pause, then think fuck it. "About you."

She moves closer to me and rests her hands on my chest. Her eyes glow in the lamplight. "You care about me?"

I tuck a strand of her hair behind her ear. "Of course I care about you. How could you even ask that?"

"I love you," she says.

My lips part, but no words come out. I can't bring myself to say it.

"It's okay," she says, "you don't have to say it back. I just wanted you to know." Then she lifts up and presses her lips to mine.

My arms automatically wrap around her, and I groan as I pull her against me. The frustration, resentment, and guilt tighten in my stomach, but now there's an added reaction: shock.

Because, although I don't have the courage to tell her, I know now. I do love her.

Chapter Twenty-Two

Marama

I didn't honestly come up here expecting sex, but I'm certainly not going to turn it down.

It's clear to me that Spencer is suffering. I didn't tell him, but when I bumped into Kingi, he'd just walked out of the meeting, and he said, "I don't know what you're doing to Spencer, but he's in trouble."

I'm ashamed that part of me felt a flare of pleasure that I'm affecting him as much as he's affecting me. But equally, I don't want him to suffer. This business with Genevieve is going to hit him hard. I still can't believe that he's refusing to confront her because he doesn't want to ruin my dealings with her. I'm incredibly touched by that.

I don't care about the others. I only care about you. His words prompted me to tell him I love him, not because I expected him to say it back, but because I needed him to know that he is loved.

He tilts his head to the side, slanting his lips across mine, and our tongues tangle, electricity sparking between us and making my nipples stand on end. He releases the clip holding up my hair, bringing it tumbling down around my shoulders. This man undoes me physically and metaphorically. I love his sure, skilled hands, his confidence, his no-nonsense attitude. I love that he can't keep away from me.

If this is so wrong, why does it feel so right?

He strips off my skirt and top, then groans as he sees my lacy white bra and matching knickers. "You're so beautiful," he says in hushed tones, his hands skating over my skin as if they can't get enough of me. "Marama…"

"Yes…"

"I want you…"

"I'm all yours." I undo my bra and toss it away, then take off my knickers.

He pushes me up against the window, chuckling when I gasp as my warm back meets the cold glass.

"Wicked man," I protest, tilting my head to the side so he can kiss my neck.

"I wasn't, until I met you." He gives my skin big hungry kisses, trailing his tongue down my throat and then closing his mouth over where my pulse is pounding. When I moan, he growls, "Yes, moan for me, baby," and takes my hands and pins them to the glass as he kisses my breasts.

I shiver, arching my back as he sucks on my nipples, my body going from zero to sixty in seconds. I ache for him, and when he kisses down my body and drops to his knees, I tip my head back on the glass and sigh as he slides his tongue into the heart of me.

I'm so turned on that it's only minutes before he kisses back up my body and gets to his feet. "You're so wet," he says huskily, taking out his wallet and extracting a condom.

"Charming." I take it from him and rip the packaging off.

"It was a compliment." He undoes his trousers and pushes down his boxers, and I roll the condom on.

"A compliment to be told how slutty I am."

He just laughs and lifts me up, wrapping my legs around his waist. "As long as you're only slutty for me, my darling."

I kiss his forehead as he directs the tip of his erection beneath me. "I'm glad your frown has vanished."

"You make me happy," he says simply, lowering me a little so he penetrates me. Then he lowers me a bit more, so he slides inside me, and I'm impaled on him, all the way up.

We both groan, our foreheads touching as we adjust to the sensation. Then he kisses me and starts to move, pushing me up against the glass as he thrusts.

Ahhh… it feels amazing, and I love pretending that there's nothing I can do about it—he's going to take me all the way whether I want him to or not. Ohhh… I adore that he hasn't even undressed, I love his white shirt that he hasn't bothered to undo, and the fact that I'm naked just makes it even more erotic.

"Fuck," he says against my lips, still thrusting hard, "ah Marama, you're so fucking hot."

I know he's wiped all my lip gloss off, and my mascara has probably smudged, and my hair is mussed, but I don't give a damn. I don't even care that there are probably people who are having an evening walk along the beach who can see us outlined by the lamp behind us. My whole being is focused and concentrated on my mouth and my nipples and between my legs, and as he thrusts against my clit, I feel the rise of my orgasm, as unstoppable as the rising moon.

"I'm going to come," I whisper urgently, and he gives a groan of appreciation, his thrusts turning faster and harder, and then my orgasm hits, and I clench around him, giving him everything, all my body and my heart and my soul as the exquisite pulses claim me.

"Yes," he hisses against my mouth, "you only come for me, baby."

I nip his bottom lip with my teeth, and he groans and then stiffens as his climax hits him. I kiss him while he comes, wanting to capture his sighs and make him mine in that moment.

It takes a while, but eventually he opens his eyes and looks into mine. He gives me a wry smile, and we both start laughing.

"I can't control myself when you're around," he scolds, lifting me off him and lowering me to the ground.

"Good." I tremble a little, my legs still wobbly.

"Careful," he says. He disposes of the condom, then comes back and gives me a hug. "You okay?" He kisses my hair.

I nod, nuzzling his neck. He smells so good.

We stand like that for a long while. My arms are curled in front of me, and he strokes my back. Mmm. I could stay here forever.

"Come on," he says gently. "You should get dressed." He bends and picks up my underwear and hands it to me. "Well, unless you want to go to the party like that."

My euphoria fades. "I don't want to go to the party. Can't we just hang out here?"

"Our absence will be noted," he points out, pocketing his wallet.

Slowly, I pull on my knickers and my bra, then my skirt and top. "Where's the bathroom?" I ask stiffly.

He gestures, and I pick up my purse and hairclip and go over to it. Once inside, I shut the door and lean on the sink, looking at my reflection.

God, I look a mess. My face flushes at the sight of my mussed hair and smudged lip gloss. I feel suddenly foolish and embarrassed. What did I expect? That he'd ask me to stay the night with him, knowing that our friends and family would easily work out what was going on?

He's not suddenly going to want to announce to the world that we're an item. He's made it quite clear that he wants to keep this a secret from everyone.

I think by asking for him to give up control with me, I did more harm than good. I wanted to establish trust and intimacy between us, but instead I think he saw it as a weakness.

He had no intention of having sex with me again. This was a spur-of-the-moment thing, and I'm being an idiot if I think anything else.

Quickly, I use a tissue to clean up any smudges and add some fresh gloss. Then I attempt to wrestle my hair back into the clip. It doesn't look as elegant as before, but it'll have to do. I straighten my clothing and give myself one last glare in the mirror. Then I head back out to the living room.

He's still standing by the window, looking out at the view in the darkness, although he's holding a bottle of water now.

Suddenly, I need a glass of wine.

"Maybe I should head over there first," I say, a touch tartly.

He just nods. "Probably a good idea."

I clench my jaw, silently fuming. I hate this. His refusal to acknowledge me. His insistence on adhering to his principles. I hate it and admire it at the same time. And that really pisses me off.

He comes over and gives me a last hug. "Thank you," he says.

What am I supposed to say to that? You're welcome?

I extricate myself from his arms and walk over to the door. "Don't worry, I won't talk to you at the party."

He frowns. "You can still—"

I don't listen to the end. I go out and close the door behind me.

*

I make sure to stay away from Spencer. The party is being held in one of the rooms adjoining the main club, but people are coming and going all the time, and moving between tables, so it's not noticeable that I don't go near the table in the corner where he's sitting with my mum and dad and a few others.

I congratulate Mack and Sidnie, and circulate a little, pinning a smile on my face and making sure that nobody could possibly criticize me in any way.

Then after an hour or so, I quietly tell Scarlett that I have a headache, which isn't a lie, and I slip away.

I stride out of the club in case he's following me, then realize sadly that he was never going to, and slow my step as I cross the gravel drive to one of the waiting taxis. It's starting to get cold at night now we're halfway through April, and I shiver, wishing I'd brought a jacket.

The taxi takes me home and pulls up next to the Kombi van. I've decided to paint the outside of it with big flowers so it looks like I'm off to Woodstock. I thought about calling it The '69 and was going to tell Spencer because I thought it was funny, but I forgot.

I should keep away from him now. It's what he wants, and prolonging any contact is only going to make it more difficult.

Tears prick my eyes, but I sniff and refuse to let them fall. I've cried enough over men in my life. I'm not going to do it anymore. I'll celebrate what I've had, and it's time to move on.

*

I stay at home for most of the next week, spending all my time in the studio, painting.

I know I'm only delaying the inevitable, and there are decisions to be made. I can't live with my parents forever. At some point I need to decide what I'm doing going forward, whether I'm going to travel, or relocate and find an apartment or house in another city.

And I will. But right now I need to work on the paintings for the Lumen exhibition. I spend a long time reading, researching myths and legends, and sketching ideas. Genevieve has suggested a total of six paintings, and a date for the exhibition of 21 June—the celebration of Matariki. It gives me a good two and a half months, which should be doable, and it also gives me space to breathe.

The house has extensive grounds and also a private beach, and I spend a lot of time walking. The sea has healing properties, and I wait for the quiet rattle of the waves on the pebbles to bring me the peace and serenity I crave.

But it doesn't. Maybe I'd be able to start healing if Spencer had completely abandoned me. Eventually my resentment would kick in and I'd probably end up like Genevieve, craving revenge and wanting to hurt him.

But even though we don't see each other physically, he still messages me constantly. Not in a needy way—just photos of his day, or little messages to say he's thinking of me, and I discover that I can't keep away. I crave the dopamine buzz of seeing something from him, and I think he feels the same. He isn't refusing to see me because he doesn't want to. He's trying to do what's best for both of us. How can I criticize him for that?

I know my parents are worried about me because I'm isolating myself. Dad checks on me every evening when he gets home, and Mum is constantly popping in to bring me a treat—a muffin or cookie or something else she's baked for one of her women's groups. But the truth is I'm happy on my own, listening to music, either walking or painting.

I'm therefore surprised and a little nervous when on Friday morning, Genevieve emails me and asks whether she can come and see my work in progress. "I have something I'd like to discuss with you," she adds at the end. I reply that of course, she's welcome to call in, because I can't very well tell her I'm not receiving callers or I'll sound like a character out of a Jane Austen novel.

I don't tell Spencer she's coming, though.

She arrives at two p.m., pulling up outside in a gunmetal-gray Range Rover, the perfect car for a woman who walks into boardrooms and takes no prisoners. She's wearing a light-gray pantsuit and black high-heeled stilettos that I'd never be able to walk in. Her hair looks as if she's just walked out of the stylists, and her makeup is immaculate.

I open the door, relieved that my parents are out. I don't think Dad likes her any more than Spencer does.

"Hello!" She gives me a bright smile. "Beautiful location."

"Yes." I move back to let her in and close the door behind her. "My grandfather built the house."

"It's amazing. Do you want me to take off my shoes?"

"No, please, don't worry about it." I cross my fingers, hoping her heels don't mark Mum's beautiful kauri-wood floorboards. "Can I get you a drink? Tea, coffee, soft drink?"

"No, I'm fine, thank you, I've just had lunch."

She's so thin, I can't imagine anything more than a lettuce leaf passing her lips. "This way, then."

I lead her into the studio and over to the window. I've leaned the six canvases against the glass, and we stop in front of them. I've sketched out all six paintings in charcoal, but I've only started painting the first—Spencer's one.

"Ohhh…" She walks slowly along them, bending to look at each. They feature a variety of goddesses, each with a large wild animal at their feet. The goddesses are only roughly sketched.

"I mentioned to you and Hariata about featuring modern-day *atua wāhine*—important women in our community—and thought maybe you'd like to give me a list of those you feel it would be good to feature. I could then visit them for some sketches."

"Good idea. I'll talk to Hariata." She stops by the first painting and slowly lowers down to her haunches to examine it. "This is spectacular," she says breathlessly. "You've done exactly what I'd hoped for. He looks completely cowed." She laughs.

I suck my bottom lip, shifting uncomfortably. That's not what I was going for. I'd hoped that it looked as if the wolf was bowing his head to her, acknowledging her presence, but I can see how it could be interpreted as if she's pushing him down.

She gets to her feet. "This is going to be a spectacular exhibition."

"Well, wait until they're finished," I say nervously.

"Marama, you need to be confident with your talent. Lift your chin and believe in yourself, girl."

"It doesn't come easily."

"It does to men, and we need to start not just following in their footsteps, but leading the way."

I nod, more than a little intimidated by this striking, assertive woman.

She smiles. "Can we sit for a moment?"

"Of course." Surprised, I lead her over to the chairs that surrounded the coffee table.

She perches on the edge of one and surveys me with a direct gaze. "I'd like to offer you a job," she says, eyes gleaming.

My jaw drops. "What?"

"I'd like you to be Lumen's *Tohunga o te Marama*."

It's an ambiguous term that I would interpret as 'expert of the moon' or 'expert of enlightenment'. But Genevieve then clarifies, "You would be our Curator of Light. An Artist-in-Residence with an Advisory Role."

I'm still not sure what it means, but it sounds interesting. "What would it involve?"

"You'd have a public profile. You'd lead talks or panels, and have a say in Lumen's artistic direction."

My heart rate increases. It's impossible not to feel excited by the offer. *Tohunga o te Marama*. Now I think about it, it's a very clever play on words, echoing my name and feeding into the Lumen branding at the same time.

"You'd be the face and symbol of all indigenous creative women in the city," Genevieve promises.

I'm not stupid; I know that my presence would be great PR for her company. My *moko kauae* would be a branding tool, announcing to everyone that Lumen is serious about promoting diversity, and my new exhibition will feed into her intention to elevate women and show them as being better than men.

I'm not particularly comfortable with being the figurehead for her modern version of feminism. That's not how my mother brought me up. I have lots of male friends who aren't dicks, and I don't feel the need to crush them to lift myself higher.

But—and it's a big but, and I cannot lie—I can't imagine being offered this kind of platform anywhere else, including at Midnight. It's incredibly tempting.

Would it be insulting to ask if I can have some time to think about it?

Luckily, Genevieve says, "You don't have to answer now. I know you're thinking about traveling and seeing more of the country. I will say that I'm sure we could combine that with your role. Your van could be the Lumen Bus! You could exhibit the works you do as you travel under the Lumen brand. Anyway, think about it and let me know, okay?"

"I will," I tell her, "thank you so much for considering me, though."

"You are a national *taonga*, Marama." It means treasure. "We'd be honored to have you. Anyway, I'd better get going. Lots to do before the weekend."

I see her to the door and wave as she returns to her Range Rover and heads back along the drive to the ferry. I close the door and walk slowly through to the kitchen, where I make myself a coffee. It's a long way to come to visit me. I wonder why she didn't ask me to come to her office?

It's impossible not to feel flattered by her personal visit, or the position she's suggesting.

Carrying my coffee, I return to the studio. I stand in front of the first painting. Should I tell Spencer about her offer?

I don't think I will just yet. There's no point until I've decided whether I'm going to take it. I need time to think about it.

I lift the painting and place it on the easel, looking at the way the woman—me—is pushing down the head of the wolf.

Thoughtfully, I pull up my stool and sit there looking at it while I drink my coffee.

Chapter Twenty-Three

Spencer

On Sunday morning, shortly after waking, I go for a run along Sentinel Beach Reserve. It's a hidden gem—a secluded haven in the middle of the busy city, and the early sun glitters on the surface of the harbor like diamonds.

I push myself hard, wanting to wear out my body and rid myself of some of the sexual tension I've been feeling over the past few days. Since Eleanor died, I've trained myself not to think about sex too much. It's not as if I met someone and made the conscious decision not to get involved. For a good couple of years I wasn't ready for someone new, and then after that I just got caught up in work and family, and the time was never right.

But now there's someone in my life, and there shouldn't be, and I want her and I can't have her, and it's tearing me apart. I think about her twenty-four-seven. Like, literally, all the time. I'm constantly fantasizing about what I'd do to her if I saw her again, and that gets me hard, and I spend hours trying to ignore my erection, growing exceedingly grumpy, until I get to the point where I get angry with myself and just want it to stop. Then I growl and go off to the bathroom to alleviate the ache, which is both a relief and makes me feel slightly ashamed. I'm a grown man, not a horny teenager. I should be able to control my lust. But I can't. And it's driving me mad.

So I run until I'm exhausted, then go back home and take a shower. But when the water cascades over me, it makes me think about the way Marama's breasts glistened beneath the stream, and how she washed off the word 'mine' from my chest—even though I can still feel it burned into my skin—and within minutes I'm hard again. So I take myself in hand and jerk off angrily, coming with an aggressive roar, then lean my forehead on the glass, my fingers curling into fists with my frustration.

Afterward, I take my laptop out onto the deck with a cup of coffee, sit at the table with my feet propped on the opposite chair, and pull up the Kōrero news site. My brain is in neutral; it's what I do every morning, checking out the international and local business news. I'm therefore completely unprepared when I scroll down to the city section and see another photo of myself.

I have no idea where it was taken, but I'm in one of my best business suits, and I'm glaring at the photographer, clearly unhappy at my picture being taken.

The headline reads: "Marama Davis is painting Spencer Cavendish as the beast—and she's breaking him."

What the fuck?

I read the article quickly. It takes me five seconds to guess it's been fed to the website by Genevieve. It talks about Marama's new exhibition, the pièce de résistance of which is to be called Whakakōpaka, which means to restrain, or forceful repression. It explains that the *atua wāhine* in this painting—Hina Marama, the goddess of female power and the moon, clearly representing Marama herself—is being portrayed as subjugating the wolf before her. The wolf, of course, being me.

It doesn't state that we're in a relationship, because they know I'd have them for libel. But it does heavily insinuate it.

It goes on: "Speculation is mounting that the Lumen CEO has quietly offered a prestigious new position—Curator of Light (*Tohunga o te Marama*)—to the Māori artist. Sources close to Lumen suggest the role would place Davis at the forefront of selecting and curating future exhibitions, with a focus on local talent, indigenous storytelling, and emerging female voices in contemporary art. While Lumen has not yet confirmed the appointment, the move would align with its recent push for greater cultural diversity and empowerment of *wāhine toa* (strong women) within the elite arts community. Davis, known for her deeply personal and symbolic work, has yet to comment."

I sit upright slowly, ice filtering through my veins. It's now clear to me what's happening. Genevieve is trying to poach Marama the same way she stole my daughter. She wants to punish, embarrass, and humiliate me, and at the same time make the Midnight Circle seem old-fashioned and out-of-date, despite us having both Māori and female members.

Feeling nauseous, I head inside to the bedroom. I change out of my track pants and tee, and into a pair of jeans and a casual navy shirt. Then I pick up my keys, go out to the Aston, and head for the ferry terminal.

It's mid-morning by the time I pull up outside Rangi's house. I get out of the car and head around the side, waving to Joe, who's removing some dead leaves from the nearby palms.

I discover the family sitting on the deck having brunch together— Rangi, Huia, Kingi, and Marama. My heart skips a beat as I round the corner and see them all sitting there, but it's too late to back out. Kingi sees me and says something, and they all look around, so I continue walking.

It's only as I approach the table that I spot Marama's red eyes, and Rangi and Kingi's resentful glares. Oh shit. They've been talking about the article.

"Good morning," I say. "I'm so sorry to interrupt. I should have rung first."

"Of course not." Huia lifts her chin. "Kingi, grab another chair will you? Join us for brunch, Spencer? There's plenty to go around."

I hold up a hand. "No, thank you."

"No, I'm sure he's far too busy." Rangi's voice is icy.

"Rangi," Huia scolds. "Manners. Remember what we talked about."

Rangi puts his serviette down with a bang, making them all jump as the cutlery rattles. "You don't think him being here will add fuel to the fire?" he asks his wife.

"I think you're determined to make something out of nothing," she snaps back. "He's your oldest friend. He wouldn't do something like that to you."

Ah, fuck. I curl up inside like a poked spider.

Kingi gets to his feet. "I think you should leave," he states, fixing me with a hard stare.

I glance at Marama. I need to talk to her, but if she shows any sign of not wanting to see me, I'll go.

She just looks tired, though. "Have you come to see me?" she asks.

"Yes please, if you have a minute."

"No," Rangi states, but Marama ignores him. Getting to her feet, she gestures with her head toward the bottom of the garden, and the steps leading down to the beach. "Come for a walk with me," she says.

I hesitate, torn between wanting to talk to her and not wanting to upset my old friend. Kingi is still standing, and he glances at his father like a mastiff waiting for his master to bark a command. Rangi meets my gaze, his expression a mixture of fury and hurt. But to my surprise, he doesn't say anything. Instead, he just looks down at the table, and slowly, Kingi sinks back into his chair.

Marama holds out a hand. "Come on."

Without thinking, I slip mine into hers and let her lead me across the lawn.

After a few steps, I withdraw my hand gently and slide my hands into the pockets of my jeans, and she does the same. She's wearing cut-downs and a bright pink tee, and she looks young, fresh, and beautiful.

"Thank you for agreeing to see me," I say as we approach the bottom end of the lawn. "I'm guessing you were all discussing the article?"

She nods, opening the gate, and we go through and begin walking down the steps to the private beach. It's breezy here, but not too cool.

"You need to understand that I didn't know she was going to publish that," Marama says quietly.

"You think Genevieve wrote it?"

She snorts and gives me an amused look.

"Yeah," I say, "I thought so too."

We get to the bottom of the steps and turn onto the sand. It's a small, crescent-shaped bay, with golden sand fringed with rocks and a grassy bank, the deep-blue Pacific Ocean sparkling in the sun. Marama slips off her sandals, her toes sinking into the sand. Without discussing it, we set off along the beach, Marama splashing in the shallows, following the curve of the bay toward the opposite end.

"Was the topic of the painting her idea too?" I ask.

She takes an elastic band from around her wrist and fastens her hair on top of her head in a loose bun. "It was my idea to paint a series of goddess pictures," she says. "Hers and Hariata's to show them taming men as wild beasts."

I'd suspected as much. In that sense, being as it was a commission, Marama wouldn't have had much choice.

"What about the position?" I ask. "Is that true?"

She nods. "She asked me on Friday. I didn't tell you because I needed time to think about it."

"*Tohunga o te Marama*? It sounds impressive."

She just gives me a wry look.

"There were lots of buzz words in that article," I point out.

"I know. You don't have to tell me."

"Are you going to take it?"

"I'm not sure yet."

"But it appeals to you?"

That earns me an impatient look. "Of course it appeals to me. I'm practically unknown. Where else do you think I'd get a position like that? Is Midnight going to offer me a job?"

Our eyes meet, and I feel a touch of shame. She's right—it's a hell of an opportunity for her. Can I really tell her she shouldn't take it?

But that's not the point here. "You're being manipulated," I tell her earnestly. She needs to understand what Genevieve is like. "She's framing it as a cushy, high-status position, which sounds great, but it's ambiguous and ephemeral. You might think it feels like artistic freedom, but it's not—it's curated rebellion. Your empowerment will become a trap. You might gain power, but you're losing creative control. Do you really want to paint pictures of women suppressing men?"

Her eyes flare. "Men have held all the power for far too long."

"Now you even sound like her. Your *moko kauae* has become a branding tool for her. She can market you without giving up control. It lets her play the long game and use you as a face and a symbol."

"Stop it," she snaps. "You're as bad as my father. You both just want to control me. I know what I'm doing."

So Rangi has obviously tried to talk her out of it, too. "Genevieve is going to market the exhibition and the job as a feminist rebuke to patriarchal power," I insist. "You can't deny it—she's already doing it. She has an agenda, and she's going to push it no matter what. Lumen doesn't stand for true balance. She wants control, not harmony. She's fueled by revenge, not progress."

She stops walking. "I don't need you or my father making the decision for me. I'm not blind. I know I'm being used and manipulated. But that doesn't mean I shouldn't take the job. It will still mean exposure for my work that I desperately need. The job may be ephemeral, but it's exciting and it'll get me out in the community, talking to artists and galleries."

"You don't mind crushing Midnight in the process?"

"Oh come on," she scoffs, "you're as much of a drama queen as Dad. It's not as if Midnight is going to go under if I take this role."

"So Rangi said the same thing?"

That makes her think. She looks away, across the gently rolling waves, to where the cornflower-blue sky meets the sea.

"I'm not trying to control you," I say sincerely. "I just don't want you to be manipulated. You are going to be a great artist. You don't need Lumen to do that. I'd be happy to help you get exposure for your work, if you want me to."

She swallows, then looks back at me. "Yeah, that doesn't sound patronizing at all."

I frown. "I have connections, and you don't. How is it patronizing?"

Now her eyes turn glassy. "I want to make it on my own." Her statement is heartfelt. "It's important to me."

"I understand… but there's nothing wrong with having a helping hand from friends and family. Most young people do at some point…"

"Oh for fuck's sake, stop talking to me as if I'm fifteen!"

Jesus, she looks magnificent standing there, her eyes blazing, radiant and beautiful, like a true goddess.

"I'm not a child," she says.

"I know."

"I need to make my own way… it's important to me that I can support myself."

"I understand. I know your dad has bought your cars and given you money all your life, and it feels important to be able to earn your own money so that—"

"No." She cuts me off mid-sentence. "It's not that." She hesitates. "I wasn't going to tell you yet."

"Tell me what?"

"I'm pregnant."

We stand there silently. A wave creeps up the sand, heading for my shoes, and I take a step back. She notices and frowns as if she thinks I'm moving away from her. I wasn't. Was I? I'm so shocked, I can't even process the information.

She swallows. "Say something."

"Is it mine?"

She meets my gaze, her eyes widening. "Seriously?"

Shit, I've insulted her. I can't get my brain to function. "We used condoms," I point out.

"They're not infallible. And your first one must have been at least six years old, right?"

It's true, but I still can't believe I've been that unlucky. Jesus. How can this have happened to me twice?

As soon as I think that, another thought enters my head. "Did you do this on purpose?"

"Did I tear a condom on purpose?"

I glare at her.

"No," she says, aghast. "Of course not. I'm not like Eleanor." She looks hurt. I think she was expecting—or maybe hoping—that I'd be secretly thrilled. Say 'I've been dreaming about this,' or something similar and sweep her up in my arms. Or at least give her a hug and tell her it doesn't matter, and everything will be right.

But it does matter. She might not have done it on purpose, but she's obviously going to want me to be involved. It's still a form of control.

I feel angry, and I know that's unfair, because she didn't ask for it either. If it truly was an accident, it would have been as much of a shock to her as it was to me. But it's impossible not to feel as if she planned it.

"Are you going to keep it?" I ask.

The breeze throws salt spray over us, and she shivers, wrapping her arms around herself. "I'm literally only two days late. I took a test because I'm usually pretty regular. I wasn't going to say anything because obviously there's a high risk of miscarriage. So it feels a bit early to be talking about that."

"Surely the earlier the better, right?"

She glares at me. "You're being incredibly insensitive."

Fuck. I'd forgotten about what happened with Connor. He wanted her to have an abortion. And of course, she miscarried, so that's why she mentioned that.

Guilt stabs me. I'm angry at myself for reacting the same way, but I can't help it. "Insensitive because I want to know what effect this is going to have on my life?" My heart is racing, and panic is rising inside me. "You have no idea what an impact this could have on me. What is your father going to say? Your brother? How do you think this will reflect on me in the business world? Knocking up a girl half my age?"

Her eyes blaze. "I'm not a girl! And I'm not half your age!"

"Marama, come on. You know what I'm saying. I'm a grandfather. Christ, the number of times I warned Orson not to get pregnant..." I close my eyes and massage the bridge of my nose, mortified at my stupidity.

I fight with my frustration, and do my best to wrestle it under control. When I finally open my eyes, she's watching me, her expression carefully blank. I know I've disappointed her, and that kills me, but there's nothing I can do about it. I can't brush this off. It feels catastrophic, and I can't change that.

We study each other while the cool breeze blows salt spray across us. I feel miserable and constricted, as if I'm a hostage who's been forced into a cell too small for me to stand upright. The door's open, but I can't bring myself to walk out of it and face the waiting crowd, because I'll have to admit it's all my own doing.

"You don't have to worry," she says eventually. Her tone is cold and hard. "I don't want anything from you. If I don't miscarry, I'll decide what to do, and I'll cope with the fallout alone."

I frown. "I would always support you financially..."

"I don't want your money." Her tone is icy. "You didn't have a say in this, and I would never force you to be involved. But equally, I won't be your dirty little secret. If you don't want to acknowledge this child, I won't tell anyone you're the father. Including the child. You won't exist, as far as it's concerned."

It's as if she's slipped a knife between my ribs and is turning it slowly. "Marama..."

But she turns and walks away, back toward the stairs.

I should run after her, catch her hand, and pull her into my arms. Tell her I'm sorry, that I didn't mean it, that I'm thrilled, that I'll marry her, and that I can't wait to hold the baby in my arms.

But I can't. I watch her running up the stairs, and then she disappears through the gate, without looking back.

I walk over to one of the large rocks, sink onto it, and lean forward, my head in my hands, staring at the sand. I feel numb. I've been such a fool. My heart aches. More than anything, I want to tell her that I'll stand by her, but I can't get past the effect it would have on my life. I've seen colleagues who've been in this position, who've had affairs and got caught, and their personal lives have been revealed to the world, as if their chests have been cracked and their ribs opened and their heart has been exposed for everyone to see. People think it's amusing to bring down powerful men—it makes them seem human and small. It doesn't matter that I consider I've climbed the executive ladder ethically and responsibly—I've cultivated a ruthless and brutal reputation, and it's going to come back and bite me in the ass. Even if Marama doesn't admit I'm the father, it will be a feeding frenzy because of the recent headlines. Genevieve is going to be like a Burmese python at a goat buffet.

My hands slide further into my hair, and I close my eyes. I feel perilously close to tears, which is unlike me. I can't believe I've fucked everything up so completely. I've spent a lifetime creating myself a solid reputation to protect myself, and it turns out it can be torn down like a paper screen.

And to top it all, I've lost the one thing that made life worth living. I wouldn't be surprised if she never spoke to me again after this.

It's another ten minutes before I feel able to walk back up the stairs, and then I only do so because it's starting to rain. I don't want to have to enter the grounds, but there's no other way out, so I go through the gate and cross the lawn. Luckily, the family have gone inside, and there's no sign of Marama.

I circle the house and stride out toward the Aston. Unfortunately, as I get close, the front door opens and Kingi comes out.

Part of me wants to run to the car, jump in, and drive away before he gets there, but I force myself to stop and turn to face him.

He marches up to me, six-foot-four of pure muscle and hair and fury, and before I can say anything, he draws back his arm and punches me, right in the face.

It explodes with pain. I stumble back, lose my balance, and fall onto my ass on the gravel. When I lift my hand to touch my lip, it comes away covered in blood.

All my fight has gone. I sit there miserably, wishing the ground would open and swallow me up, the rain soaking my shirt.

Kingi glares at me. "Mum convinced Dad that he was bigger than this and should keep out of it, but I don't have any such convictions. You've hurt my sister, and you're old enough to know better."

I wipe my mouth on my shirt sleeve. "I know."

"You fucking idiot," he says. "Of all the women in the city you could have picked. She's one in a million, Spencer. And you treat her like this?"

Has Marama told them she's pregnant? Or is he just angry that she's so obviously upset? It doesn't matter. His reaction is totally justified.

At any other time in my life, I would have subdued him with a mere glare and told him to mind his own fucking business. But I'm so ashamed that I just sit there, elbows on my knees, hands hanging, fighting to control my emotions.

Kingi doesn't say anything for a long moment. Then, eventually, he sighs and holds out his hand.

I stare at it mutely, then look up at him. To my embarrassment, there's pity on his face.

He flicks his fingers and says, a bit more gently, "Get up."

I take his hand and let him pull me to my feet.

"Wait there," he says. Then he turns and goes back to the house.

I hesitate, desperate to go, but force myself to wait as I try to staunch the flow of blood with my shirt sleeve.

A few minutes later, he comes back out with a wet cloth and hands it to me. He stands there, shielding me from the house while I wipe my face and hands.

"Put some pressure on it," he advises. So I press the cloth over my split lip for a bit until eventually the blood stops flowing.

He's holding something else, and he hands it to me—it's a T-shirt. I look down and realize my shirt is covered in blood. Without saying anything, I unbutton it and take it off, then accept the tee and pull it on. It's too big for me, but it's clean, and I appreciate the gesture.

I toss the blood-covered shirt into the Aston. Then turn back to him. "Thanks."

"You're a good guy," he says, puzzled. "Why did you do that? To her? To us?"

I check my lip. It has nearly stopped bleeding. "Because I love her."

His eyebrows shoot up. "What?"

I hold out the cloth. He shakes his head, so I toss that in the Aston as well.

"Have you told her?" he says.

"No."

"Why not?"

"Nobody is interested in my feelings, Kingi. Only in how it looks."

He studies my face. He has the same amber eyes as Marama. He's a good-looking guy beneath all the hair.

"She loves you too," he says simply.

"I know." I glance at the house. Is she watching? I sigh. It doesn't matter. "Thanks for the tee." I get into the car.

He leans on the door and bends to look at me. "You deserved to be hit."

I shiver as the breeze blows the light rain into the car. "You think I don't know that?"

"Not everyone wants to see you fail, Spencer."

I swallow and wince, tasting blood. "I think we both know that's not true."

He goes to say something, then moves back. I close the door, start the engine, and head off down the drive.

When I glance in my rear-view mirror, I see him watching me, oblivious to the rain, before he finally turns and goes back inside.

Chapter Twenty-Four

Marama

On Tuesday, the first thing I do when I get up is vomit into the toilet.

When I'm done, I rinse my mouth, then sit on the edge of the bath. The last time I was pregnant, I didn't have morning sickness. After it was over, I read that studies suggest that women who experience nausea and vomiting during the first trimester may have a lower chance of pregnancy loss, and I wondered whether my lack of it was a signal that something wasn't right. Does it mean that this time I'm less likely to miscarry?

I look down at my stomach. That's a good thing, right? A miscarriage is a horrible experience, and I don't want it to happen again. I start trembling. If I don't miscarry, and I do go through with it, it means I'm more likely to have a baby. A real, live, human being who will depend entirely on me, and me alone.

Emotion sweeps over me, and I burst into tears.

Connor didn't want me, and neither does Spencer. His reaction to the news didn't surprise me, but it devastated me, nevertheless. His reputation and other relationships mean more to him than I do. It's hard to swallow, and I feel crushed. I thought I was special to him. And maybe I am; I can't believe he felt nothing for me. But he didn't love me enough.

I cry solidly for a minute, until my throat is raw and I feel exhausted. Then I slowly dry my tears and splash cold water on my face. I look at my reflection in the mirror. I look awful; there are big dark shadows under my eyes, my hair is limp and lifeless, and my skin looks dull and blotchy. No wonder nobody wants me.

Oh man, talk about a self-pity party. I lift my chin, take a deep breath, and let it out slowly. I know it's not true, but even if it is, it's

MIDNIGHT SECRET

no excuse to feel sorry for myself. I'm worthy of love, and I don't need a man to complete me. Even though I don't agree with him, I do understand why he doesn't want a relationship, and I'm not going to get on my knees and beg him to have me.

It rankles that it wasn't my fault that I got pregnant, and yet I'm the one who's going to have to deal with the consequences. It's so easy for the guy to walk away. I can't do that. The only thing I can do is terminate the pregnancy, and then I'll have to carry that guilt for the rest of my life.

If I did have a termination, I would be free. I'd be able to travel the country in my van, beholden to no one, and I wouldn't have to think about anyone except myself and my art.

Then I cringe, conscious of sounding selfish and immature. You're thirty now, Marama. You've got to grow up some time.

Slowly, my hand creeps to my stomach and rests on it. I'm not religious as such. I enjoy reading about Māori gods and goddesses, but they're more like interesting myths and stories for me. However, after saying that, I've always thought of a child as a blessing, and it's impossible to shake that now. I've been given a gift. Do I really want to throw it away because it doesn't fit perfectly with my life?

Thoughtfully, I turn on the water and have a long, hot shower. Afterward, I dry my hair and swirl it up in a ponytail, then pull on a pair of jeans and a loose sweatshirt. I put on some concealer to hide the shadows under my eyes, and add some eyeshadow and mascara. There—at least I look a bit more presentable now. I need to concentrate on feeling good for myself, not for a man.

I think of Spencer, and my eyes sting. But I hold the tears in, grab my purse, and head out of the door.

I jump in the Alfa Romeo and head over to Kahukura—the commune close to Midnight, which is owned by Scarlett Stone, Orson's girl. I'm picking her up and we're going over to the city for lunch. She's spent most of her life in the commune, and she admitted to me the other day that although she loves it there, and she's relieved that Orson is happy to get a place on Waiheke so she can continue to run her therapy classes there, she wants to feel more comfortable in his world. I suggested I introduce her to a few of my friends from Emerge—a female-run Auckland arts group. It'll be nice for her to make some more friends, and good for me to take my mind off my current situation.

She's waiting when I arrive, and we head off to the ferry. It starts to rain as we board, which is a shame, but we buy a coffee and sit inside and watch the drops run down the windows as we chat. Scarlett's younger than I am, but her mother was Māori, and she's also an artist and includes art in the therapy sessions that she runs for abused women at the Kahukura shelter, so we have a lot in common.

I'm tempted to confide in her about being pregnant. I don't really have anyone else I'm comfortable talking to. I love my mum, but I don't know how she would react to my admission that Spencer is the father. He's a little younger than Dad, but they are business associates, and he's been to the house often with Eleanor, so I understand that it might be weird for her. I'm going to have to think about what I'll tell them if I decide to keep the baby. Maybe I should say I had a one-night stand in the city. It would be a little embarrassing to admit I got pregnant by an almost-stranger, but at least it would explain why the guy wasn't around.

So I can't really talk to Mum about it, and I've kind of drifted away from most of my friends. When I moved to Wellington, I left my school and uni friends behind, and most of them have moved on now, scattered to the four corners of the country. Most of the friends I made in Wellington were couples, and it's strange how many of them drift away when you're single.

I've got on really well with Scarlett since I met her. But she might tell Orson, who'll probably let it slip to Kingi because he can't keep a secret, and then the cat will be out of the bag and I'll never get it back in. It wasn't Spencer's choice to make a baby, and he doesn't deserve to be punished for it. I understand how it would impact his career. People aren't kind to men of his age who fall for younger women. I need to keep it to myself, which means no confessions to anyone.

So we chat about art and the commune, and it's close to midday when we arrive. I head the Alfa Romeo out to The Velvet Table—a small but classy cafe in Parnell, a suburb known for its galleries, boutiques, and charming streets, close to the Auckland Domain or park.

We go inside, and I spot the other four women already there, sitting at a table by the window.

"Oh dear," Scarlett murmurs.

I chuckle. "Don't be nervous. Come on."

I lead the way over, and the others look up and smile as we approach. "Morning!" I say, and introduce Scarlett, then each woman in turn. Lou is a potter; Anna runs a perfume business; Jane is a painter, working mostly in watercolors; and Iris is an older woman who makes the most beautiful wedding cakes.

We take a seat and give our orders for a light lunch and coffee.

"Awful weather," Iris says once the waiter has gone away with our order.

"And it's so cold for April," Jane adds, shivering, even though she's wearing a beautiful lambswool sweater.

"So, Scarlett," Lou says, "you run Kahukura! That must be so rewarding."

Scarlett nods. "Oh yes, very much so. I like being able to use my art to help others."

"That's so great to hear," Jane says. "Not every artist has such scruples."

Anna makes an odd movement, and Jane jerks, then stifles a laugh. Did Anna kick her under the table? Why so? I glance around the table, but none of them are looking at me. I shift in my chair. There's an odd atmosphere… or am I imagining it? I look at Scarlett, but she's busy talking about her therapy sessions, and she doesn't appear to have noticed.

The conversation moves on. Scarlett asks them about their current creative projects, and they spend a while describing what they're working on. I stay mostly quiet, feeling uneasy.

Our coffees arrive, then lunch, and we start eating while Iris talks about her latest order, making a whole cupcake station for a wedding. "Have you two set a date yet?" she asks Scarlett.

Scarlett blushes. "No… we haven't discussed marriage yet."

"He hasn't proposed?" Iris looks astounded.

"Not yet." Scarlett replies calmly, but I look at Iris with irritation. What a rude thing to say. They've only been dating for a month. Orson's crazy about her, and I'm sure he is going to propose, but at the moment they're just getting to know one another. Scarlett comes and stays with him at Midnight or in his apartment in the city, and he occasionally stays over at the Village. It's all very new for them. And rude to comment on it, especially considering that Scarlett has hardly been out of the commune, and I've told them she's hoping to make friends and acquaintances in the city.

"I must admit, we were all surprised when we heard who he was dating," Anna says. "His last girlfriend was… from a very different background, shall we say."

Scarlett's smile fades, and she fiddles with the serviette on her lap. Now I'm getting annoyed. Nobody likes to be reminded that their partner has had previous partners. And what the hell is Anna implying by 'from a different background?' I'm going to assume she's talking about Scarlett's upbringing. Please God, don't let her be referring to the fact that she's Māori.

"So," Lou says, "Marama, you need to tell us about the exhibition at Lumen. We've all read about it."

The four women exchange amused looks—I'm definitely not imagining it. I glance at Scarlett, who meets my eyes and frowns.

I scoop up a forkful of my chorizo hash. "Yes, I'm doing a series of paintings that are going to be displayed in Lumen."

"Such a cool break," Jane says. "It really helps to be Māori at times like that, right?"

Scarlett stops with her fork halfway to her mouth. I stiffen. "It's nothing to do with being Māori."

"Oh come on," Jane says in a teasing voice, "it's obvious that Lumen wants to up its diversity quota. Add to that the fact that you're painting a rich white guy in a demeaning position and it's a win-win for Beaumont."

"I still can't believe he bid a million dollars for you," Lou says. "That must have felt amazing."

I can't think what to say, and put down my fork.

"Bit hypocritical, though, painting that picture of him after he paid all that money for you," Jane says. "Was that Genevieve's idea, or yours?"

"It wasn't like that." But I'm embarrassed, because Jane is right. With everything that's happened, I'd forgotten that he bid all that money for me. And how have I repaid him? By agreeing to a commission that has humiliated him. By pressuring him into a relationship he didn't want that now threatens to embarrass him even more. He didn't ask for any of this. I mean obviously, he could have said no and turned me away. But I know I've pushed him and led him on, and suddenly I'm ashamed.

It's also impossible to shake the feeling that there's a grain of truth in the suggestion that me being Māori is connected to Genevieve's interest in me. It does feel tougher sometimes, being a woman and being Māori, and I was glad of the attention and the commission, but I don't like feeling manipulated.

"We're only jealous," Anna says. "I mean, you've landed a huge opportunity for your work and the gorgeous Spencer in one fell swoop." Her eyes gleam. "Come on, spill the beans… is he as generously endowed as the rumors say? And did he get what he paid for?" She giggles, and the others grin.

My face burns. They're implying that he paid for sex with me. Oh my God, he got it, too. Normally I'd make some witty retort, but I'm flustered, and I can't think what to say.

Scarlett clears her throat. "So tell me about Emerge. Marama told me the group helps aspiring artists?"

She draws the others' eyes back to her, and they start telling her about their plans for the initiative. I have a few more mouthfuls of the hash, but my stomach churns uneasily, and in the end I lay down my fork with the rest uneaten. I feel miserable and unhappy, and embarrassed that I brought Scarlett to meet these women, implying they were friends when they're clearly not.

Scarlett is listening to the others talk, but she glances at her phone and brings up a text, then rolls her eyes. "Ah, dammit." She huffs a sigh and gives me an apologetic glance. "I'm so sorry, my sister says they've had an incident at Kahukura and they need me back there urgently." She smiles at the others. "I'm sorry to have to cut this short, but it was great to meet you all."

"Of course," Jane says, and Lou adds, "It's a shame, but we understand."

Scarlett and I rise and say our goodbyes and go over to pay for our meals. Then we head outside and cross the road to my car.

"Did you really get a text?" I ask her as we open the doors.

She blows a raspberry. "No. But I didn't really want to stay after they were so rude to you." We get into the Alfa, and she clips in her seat belt. "Was I wrong to do that?" she asks, suddenly concerned. "I mean, I know they're your friends—I hope I didn't make things awkward. I just felt that they weren't being very nice to you, and you didn't deserve to be spoken to like that."

I swallow hard. Then, without warning, I put my face in my hands and burst into tears.

"Oh no!" She hurriedly unclips herself and moves forward to rub my arm. "Hey, it's okay."

I shake my head. "I'm sorry," I squeak, pressing my fingers to my lips. "I think I'm so upset because deep down I wonder if they were right."

"Oh bullshit. They shouldn't have upset you like that, it was totally uncalled for. You got that commission purely on your own merit."

"But Spencer…"

She gives me a pitying look. "Don't listen to them. He's a grown up and more than able to handle himself."

I look at her gentle eyes, thinking about how crushed he looked on the beach, how unlike his usual self. "I'm not sure that he is."

"What do you mean?"

"He didn't want to get involved with me." It's the first time I've admitted to anyone that we're having a… what? Fling? Affair?

She frowns. "I can't imagine Spencer being pushed into anything he didn't want to do."

"You might be surprised." I think of how I took off my clothes in the studio and wince. He's only human. What guy was going to turn down such an offer when it's handed to him on a plate?

"Look, I do have mixed feelings about him," she says carefully, "but it's clear to me that he's a good man deep down. I haven't asked you about what's been going on because I didn't want to pry. I mean, I've seen the headlines, but I figured you'd tell me when you were ready, and I didn't want you to feel awkward because I'm dating his son. But… do you want to talk about it? Is it just a fling or is it more than that?"

"He doesn't want more. But… I'm pregnant." Tears pour down my face.

Her eyebrows slowly rise, and her mouth opens. "Oh, sweetie," she says, and she puts her arms around me.

I cry for a while, unable to stop the floods of tears. When they finally slow, I move back and brush a hand tiredly over my face. "I'm sorry, I think it's the baby hormones," I joke weakly.

"Of course, it's not a problem at all. Have you told him?"

I nod. "He said he'll support me financially, but he doesn't want to be involved."

She exhales. It's every woman's worst nightmare, I guess.

"Well, fuck him," she says fiercely. "He doesn't deserve you."

I give a short laugh, dig out a tissue, and start drying my face.

"What are you going to do?" she asks. "Are you going to keep it?"

I wipe away the smudged mascara, then tuck the tissue back into my bag. "I'm not sure yet. I'm still thinking about it. I'm only a few days late."

"Well, if you do decide to visit the clinic and want someone to come with you, you know I'll do it."

"That means a lot, thank you." I take a shaky breath and blow it out slowly. "It's a horrible decision to have to make."

"I understand. We've had a few women at the refuge who've been in the same position. I mean, obviously, there's no abuse here, but it's still a difficult decision to make."

I study my hands in my lap. I feel ashamed as I think about the fact that there are women who've been forced into my position. Okay, so maybe it wasn't my choice, but Spencer hardly forced himself on me. It was just a mistake, or bad luck. Once again, I think about the fact that I've always thought of children as a blessing.

"Would it be terrible if I kept it?" I murmur.

Her expression softens. "Of course not."

"I'd have to hide the fact that he's the father. Say I had a one-night stand or something."

She nods. "I understand. I won't tell anyone, not even Orson, I swear."

"You're so sweet. So much more a friend than those women will ever be. I'm never going back there again."

"They were just jealous."

"Maybe, but women should come together to support each other, not to bring each other down." I start the engine. "Come on, let's get home. So much for introducing you to the city lifestyle! I think you're better off in the Village."

"Me too," she says fervently.

I drive us to the terminal, and we take the ferry back to Waiheke. I drop Scarlett off at Kahukura, exchanging hugs with her and promising to call, then drive slowly back to the house.

There are a few cars out the front, so I know Mum must be holding one of her groups. I go around the back and let myself in the sliding door that leads to the studio. I have a coffee machine in there, and I make myself one, then take it over to the window where I paint and put it on the table.

I look at the half-finished painting on the easel, the *atua wāhine* pushing down the wolf, pick up the canvas, and put it to one side. I go over to the blank canvases, choose one, and bring it back to the easel.

I stand back and study it, planning out a new scene in my head while I sip my coffee.

It's time I made my own decisions about my life, and stopped letting others control or manipulate me. It's time I stopped being a pawn in Genevieve's revenge. My art is my own. I have to be true to myself and paint from my heart. What's the point in doing this exhibition and getting exposure when I'm just doing someone else's bidding? My art has always been about exploring my truths and beliefs, not anyone else's.

Thoughtfully, I pick up a piece of charcoal and start sketching.

MIDNIGHT SECRET

Chapter Twenty-Five

Spencer

It's been a helluva week.

I haven't contacted Marama, and she hasn't contacted me. She's made it clear that if I refuse to go public with her, she doesn't want me involved with the baby, and so even though I've missed her terribly, now, more than ever, I need to keep my distance.

I think about her all the time, though. I'm sure the memory of her previous miscarriage must be weighing on her mind, and it pains me to think she's worried about it happening again. The pregnancy might be extremely inconvenient, and she might even be considering a termination, but that doesn't make a miscarriage any less of a tragedy.

After growling my way through meetings and biting the heads off most people in the office all week, I'm supposed to head a meeting about a new property development in the CBD on Friday lunchtime, but one of my colleagues tactfully suggests that I might be feeling under the weather and that he runs the meeting instead, and I can't concentrate anyway, so I reluctantly agree.

I have a heap of work to do, but I haven't been sleeping well, and I'm tired and dispirited. I feel claustrophobic and enclosed, even though my office has a great view across the harbor. I'm tired of high-rise buildings, steel and concrete and glass. I miss the biophilic nature of my suite at the Midnight Club, the view across the Pacific, the palms and ferns, and the fresh country air. I could go for a walk down to the Waiora and see how the work is coming along, maybe even have a swim. Anything has to be better than staying here and moping in my office. So I tell my PA I'll be out for the rest of the afternoon and take the Aston down to the ferry.

When I arrive on Waiheke, I drive the short distance to the club. It's not as sunny as I'd hoped, and in fact it starts spattering with rain as I pull up, putting paid to the idea of going for a walk, unless I want to get soaked. I guess I'll go to my suite until it lets up.

I get out of the Aston, and I'm about to run inside when my gaze falls on a Range Rover parked a short distance away. There are several in the car park, most of which are either black or gray, so it doesn't particularly stand out. But it's the number plate that draws my attention. It just says LUM3N. It's Genevieve's car.

I run my gaze along the line of VIP parking spaces. All the other members of the Circle are here. On a Friday afternoon?

I was about to cross the complex to the hotel, but, gritting my teeth, I go into the main block and march up to the receptionist.

"Is Genevieve Beaumont here?" I bark at her.

She blinks and stutters, "Y-yes sir. She's in a meeting in the boardroom."

"With whom?"

"Th-the other members of the Circle, sir."

I feel as if I've been punched in the stomach. Leaving the receptionist red-faced and flustered, I walk along the corridor, past the offices to the boardroom at the end. As I near, I can see them all through the glass wall, seated around the table. Huxley's at the head as usual, with the Circle on one side of the long table, and on the other, Genevieve and two other women.

Without stopping, I walk up to the glass door, push it open, and go in.

Genevieve is currently talking, but she stops as I enter, her eyes widening. When the others see her looking, they all turn to follow her gaze. Most of them wince or frown when they see me.

I stop at the bottom end of the table. "What's going on?" I demand.

Huxley leans forward on the table. "We're having a discussion, that's all."

"About what?"

"About the new club that Lumen is planning," Huxley says.

I look at Genevieve, who gives me a nasty smile.

I glance around the table, glaring at each of the members of the Circle in turn, ending with my son.

"It's just a preliminary discussion," Orson states carefully. "We're not making any decisions. We wanted to find out about the location, design, and launch timeline of the new club."

"Why wasn't I invited?" I demand.

"I was going to report back to you," he says. "I just didn't think you'd want to be here for this."

"You had no right to meet with a rival club without me," I state to them all. "If no other reason than that Midnight is built on my land."

Huxley has the grace to look regretful. "You're right," he says carefully. "And I apologize for how it looks. We just thought we'd get the lie of the land before we brought you in."

I understand—of course I do. They've obviously seen the headlines about Marama's painting, and they would probably have heard rumors about my deteriorating relationship with Rangi. They might even have heard about Kingi decking me last weekend, as it's impossible to keep things like that secret—someone would have witnessed it and enjoyed telling everyone else, or he might have told them himself.

But I'm angry from a professional standpoint, and hurt from a personal one. "You're letting the fox into the henhouse," I snap. "How dare you bring her here?" I turn my glare on Genevieve, and she lifts her chin. "You're just doing this to piss me off," I snap at her.

She gives a short laugh and glances around the table. "See what I mean?" she says. She looks back at me. "Talk about arrogant. Not everything is about you, Spencer. We have every right to open another club on Waiheke. It's the perfect location—close to the city but with the atmosphere for a more relaxed resort."

"You just want to poach our clientele," I point out.

"We're discussing a non-compete agreement," Huxley says cautiously.

"She'll never agree to that," I say incredulously.

"We don't have to," Genevieve replies. "We'll be going after different clientele. Lumen is the… ah… next generation of luxury, shall we say? You can have all the old white guys and we'll take the young, dynamic business people. There's a market for both." Her eyes dance as they meet mine, while the women sitting beside her both stifle their laughter. "We might even display Marama's exhibition in our new foyer," she adds. "I think your girlfriend would like that, wouldn't she?"

I'm not looking at Rangi, but I hear his sharp intake of breath, and in my peripheral vision I see the way Kingi stiffens and Orson covers his eyes.

I hold Genevieve's gaze, and her smile slowly fades.

"I never meant to hurt you personally, Genevieve," I say quietly. "And I'm sorry that what's taken place—or, rather, what didn't take place between us—has led to this. These are good people," and I gesture around the table. "They spend their money helping others less fortunate than themselves, and you're being vindictive and spiteful and selfish by threatening to siphon off the profits from Midnight for your own benefit. Only the charities that benefit from our generosity will suffer, not us, so think about that when you gleefully plot our demise."

Her jaw drops, and her face flushes. Obviously, she's not used to being spoken to like that.

Huxley clears his throat. "Clearly, tempers are running hot at the moment. Maybe, Genevieve, you and your colleagues could give us ten minutes to discuss the matter, and—"

"No need," I state. "I'll leave you to it, as I'm clearly not wanted here." I turn on my heel, go through the door, and head along the corridor.

I go outside, cross to the Aston, get in, and reverse out of the parking space. As I do, I see Orson come striding out, but I don't stop. I go down the drive, and before long I'm on the open road.

Blind with fury, I don't even think about where I'm going. I pass the turnoff for the ferry and just keep driving, my wipers do their best to keep the rain off the windscreen. I bang the steering wheel and curse out loud as I drive. I can't believe the Circle met with Genevieve without me, and it hurts even more that they met at Midnight. Rangi would have known I was due to be in a meeting, and he must have thought they'd be safer there. Fuck them. Fuck them all. Fucking Judases. Motherfucking arseholes, all of them.

But my fury gradually dissipates as I drive along the winding roads through the vineyards and olive groves, leaving me feeling oddly upset and alone. When I finally realize I'm on the road to my family's farmhouse, I don't know whether I'm surprised or not.

My brother and his family live in the farmhouse with my mother now, but he and his wife will be out working, and the kids will be at school. My mother used to work in the vineyard too, but now she's in her seventies my brother has talked her into taking life a little easier, and she's slowed down a bit.

The house sits on the far side of Waiheke, looking out to the Pacific. It's not as grandiose as Rangi's mansion, but it's not tiny either—an updated farmhouse, comfortable and sprawling. I pull up out the front, sit there for a minute, then get out and walk around to the side door that leads to the kitchen.

Sure enough, I discover her in there, cleaning up after finishing some baking. Joyce Cavendish is slender and wiry, her skin tanned and lined from years of working outside. She wears her gray hair in a simple long braid. She only ever buys clothes in earth tones, and sure enough today she's wearing brown slacks and an olive-green top; I don't think I've ever seen her in blues or pinks.

"Spencer!" Her face lights up as she sees me. "Honey! I didn't know you were coming." She knows I'm not normally a hugger, and so when she comes over to me, she goes to kiss my cheek, but I surprise her by pulling her into my arms. "Oh!" She stiffens, then slides her arms around me, and we exchange a big hug.

"I'm sorry I haven't seen you for a while," I say, my voice husky with emotion.

"That's okay, I know you're a busy boy." She moves back and looks up at me with concern, then cups my face with a hand, her eyes searching mine. I wait for her to ask what's wrong and why I'm there, but she just says, "Take a seat, and I'll make us a coffee. I've just taken some apple muffins out of the oven if you'd like one."

"I'd love one." I take off my jacket and hang it over the back of one of the chairs around the wooden table in the center of the kitchen, then sit.

The warm aroma of apples and cinnamon takes me straight back to the days where I would sit here with my father and brothers after we came home from school, talking about our day. After we sated our ravenous hunger with muffins and milk, we'd then have an hour or two before dinner, and I'd go off with Dad to the workshop and help him with his furniture. The memory is so strong it brings a lump to my throat.

Mum brings over our coffees, glances at me and obviously sees my emotion, but she doesn't comment. She brings the plate of muffins over and puts them on the table with a tub of Lurpak, which has always been my favorite butter, then sits next to me. I take a muffin, halve it, smear on thick dollops of butter, and take a bite. The warm taste of soft apples fills my mouth, and I sigh.

"So…" she says, leaning back and sipping her coffee. "Not that I'm not enjoying your company… but what are you doing here, sweetheart?"

I'm having trouble swallowing. I have a large mouthful of coffee, trying to wash down the muffin that's lodged in my throat. I don't know what to say. I've never been good at talking about my feelings. I didn't come here because I wanted to confide in her. I don't know why I'm here, really. "Not sure," I say. "I was at Midnight, and… then I found myself here."

I look around the room. This kitchen has an atmosphere I haven't really experienced since I left home as a teen. When my children were young, the house Eleanor and I shared never felt like this because both of us were always out, busy with our lives. As I think about Marama and her baby, though, I know her house will be like this, with kids' pictures stuck on the fridge, dogs' bowls in the corner, and the comforting aroma of baking wrapping around you when you walk in. The thought makes me ache.

"Is this about a woman?" Mum asks.

My eyebrows rise. "What makes you say that?"

She just smiles. "You wouldn't be here if you were wrangling with a business decision."

I lean back, take a deep breath, then let it out, long and slow. I meet her eyes, an exchange that tells her everything, then sigh again, looking away, out of the window.

"What's her name?" she asks softly.

I massage the bridge of my nose. "I can't tell you."

"Why? Do I know her?"

I don't answer. She knows all the Davis family, albeit not well, and suddenly I'm ashamed to admit what I've done.

"Okay," she says. "So I do know her. Is that the problem?"

"Not in and of itself."

"So…"

I put my cup down, lean my elbows on the table, and cover my face with my hands. Suddenly, the weight of it is too much to bear.

"She's pregnant," I say from behind my hands.

There's a long silence. I dip my head, sinking my hands into my hair, then sit up and lean back again with a sigh.

Mum is watching me, her gaze bright and direct. "I don't see why that's such a disaster."

"I'm forty-six, for a start. I have a grandchild."

She shrugs. "At least he'll have someone to play with."

I give a short laugh. "If only it were that easy."

"What's the issue? Is she married?"

"No."

She looks relieved. "Well, that's something. Look, Spencer, babies don't always come along when they're meant to, but, speaking as someone who can't have them, I have to say that I can't see them as anything but a gift."

I pick at the muffin, feeling thirteen again. She always knew how to make me feel ashamed of my behavior without raising her voice.

"Sweetheart," she says softly. "Talk to me. What is it? Do you want more and she doesn't, is that it?"

I shake my head, my throat tightening again. "I don't want to tell you," I say huskily. "I don't want you to think less of me."

"Less of you? What do you mean?"

I run a hand through my hair again. Then I think ahhh… what the fuck does it matter? It's all going to come out eventually. "It's Marama Davis."

She blinks. I can see her working through it, realizing who I mean, and then the implications of that. "Ohhh…" She nods slowly. "I saw the articles in Kōrero."

"Yeah."

"They were true? You bid a million dollars for her?"

"Yeah. I did it to take her off the market. I said it was because it was demeaning and I did it for Rangi, but that wasn't the reason. I didn't want some random guy winning the auction. I wanted her for myself."

"She's painted a portrait of you?"

"Yes, it's amazing, I have it in my house."

"And the one for Lumen? Taming the wolf?"

"I haven't seen it, but yes, she's implied that's what she's doing."

"Because Genevieve Beaumont asked her to?" At the time, I told her about Genevieve's bitterness when she couldn't get into the Midnight Circle.

"Yes. I think she's struggling with having to paint it that way, but obviously it's a commission, so she has to do what they want."

She nods slowly. "And you've fallen in love with one another?"

I lower my gaze to the plate. "I haven't said so in so many words."

"Has she?"

"Yes."

"Do you love her?"

I lift my gaze back to hers again. "Yes."

Her lips curve up. "So what's the problem again?"

"She's young, Mum…"

"She's not eighteen, love. What is she, twenty-eight, twenty-nine?"

"She's just turned thirty."

"There you go, then. There's nothing wrong with that."

I just give her a sarcastic look.

"There isn't," she says. "Age is just a number. What matters is that you love each other."

"I don't think her father would agree. I know how I'd feel if a guy in his forties knocked up Helen."

That makes her hesitate, and she gives a big sigh. "Yeah, I can see how it might look to Rangi. But you'll just have to persuade him otherwise."

I have a mouthful of coffee, wishing it could wash away the shame that feels so heavy, it's weighing me down.

As if she can see it, Mum says, "What's really the issue here, love? Is this to do with Eleanor?" When I look at her with surprise at her astuteness, she says, "Honey, I'm not blind. I knew what Eleanor was like. From the outside, she was a good wife and a good mother, but I saw her pull away from you enough times, and the look on your face when she did it. You've spent a lifetime trying to pretend you don't need love, locking yourself behind padlocked gates. What's the matter? Are you afraid that if you let her love you, you'll open yourself to being hurt?"

"Yes," I say, my voice husky. "And that I'll look like a fool."

"For being in love?"

"People don't look kindly on men in my position who profess to fall for younger women. They'll say it's a midlife crisis. That she appeals to my vanity."

"Is that what it is? You like having a younger woman on your arm?"

I think about Marama, how her smile warms me through, how she makes me feel. "No. It's not that at all. She makes me feel… complete." I give her a lopsided smile.

"Aw, your whole face just lit up, honey."

"Oh, stop it."

"It did. You obviously have feelings for this girl. Why are you so worried about what people think of you? Are you really going to let someone else's jealousy get in the way of your happiness?"

"There are things to think about, Mum. When she's fifty, I'll be heading toward seventy."

"That's true. But it still means hopefully you'd have a long and happy life together."

"I don't want to be an old father."

"Do you think of me as old?"

"Of course not."

"That's what I mean. Age is in the head, my love. You'll never be old in that way. Look, we don't choose whom we fall in love with. Cupid's arrows fly where they will. The only control we have is the choices we make afterward. Are you going to walk away from her, from your child, from love, because you're afraid of what others will think of you?"

"I think it might already be too late," I say softly. "I've hurt her badly."

"Did you say sorry?"

"She didn't really give me the chance."

"Hurt feelings can be mended by true love, Spencer. You just need to be honest and unafraid. Yes, if you open your heart, you stand the chance of being hurt. But love is about being naked—not just physically, but emotionally, and putting your heart into someone else's hands."

"I'm not used to being vulnerable," I mumble. "It sucks."

"It does. But there's also something wonderful about it, too, when the other person takes your heart and holds it so gently, as if it's something precious they never want to let go."

I squeeze her fingers. "I miss Dad." I don't let myself think of him much, and my throat tightens.

She swallows hard. "Me too, darling. He was a good man. I'd give anything to have him back with me. So if you stand even a small chance of happiness with this girl, I'd say go for it, and to hell with everyone else." She clears her throat. "Now, I'm about to put a leg of lamb in the oven for tonight. Why don't you stay for dinner? I'm sure your brother would love to see you."

"Okay," I say. For once, I feel the need to have my family around me. And then maybe tomorrow, I'll think seriously about where I go from here.

Chapter Twenty-Six

Marama

I park my Alfa in the car park next to Lumen, turn off the engine, and blow out a relieved breath. Friday at four p.m. means heavy traffic in the city, and for a while I thought I was going to be late, but I made it just in time.

I get out of the car and retrieve the painting that I slotted behind the front seats and that only just about fits. I've been painting solidly, hardly sleeping at all, and finished it last night. I used acrylics so it's mostly dry, although it'll take a few days to properly cure. I lift the sheet that's covering it, crossing my fingers that the paint hasn't smudged, but it's fine.

Leaving the sheet on because it's raining lightly, I lock the car, cross the car park, and head through Lumen's front doors. I go straight to the reception desk and announce that I'm here to see Genevieve Beaumont. They tell me to take a seat, but I've literally just rested my butt on the edge when I see her walk into the foyer.

"Marama." She comes over and holds out a hand, and I shake it. Her gaze goes immediately to the canvas resting beside me. "That's it?"

I nod. "Can we go to your office?"

"Yes, of course, come on."

She leads the way along the corridor and into a large office, closing the door behind me. A neat desk sits at an angle to one side of the room, fronted by two chairs. On the other side, a cream leather sofa and armchairs surround a glass coffee table. Several pieces of artwork hang on the walls. The color scheme and furnishings all look classy and of quality. This woman knows how to project success.

A month ago, I would have felt intimidated sitting here. I was desperate for her approval. I wanted to be like her. But I no longer feel that way. I already know this will be the last time I'll set foot in Lumen, and that gives me the confidence to believe in myself.

She gestures to the suite, and I sit on the sofa, leaning the canvas next to me.

"Can I get you a tea or coffee?" she asks. "Or a cold drink? Maybe even a glass of champagne to celebrate?" She smiles, gesturing at the canvas.

"I think you should see it before you offer me a drink," I tell her.

Her smile fades, and she lowers slowly onto one of the chairs. "Why so?"

I've prepared my speech, but my words falter as I look at her properly for the first time. Her skin—always pale—looks wan. She leans back in the armchair, lacking some of her usual composure. She looks tired and somewhat beaten.

"Are you okay?" I ask.

"Long day," she replies. "I had a meeting…" She looks away, out of the window toward the view of the inner courtyard beyond. She opens her mouth as if she's about to confide something. Then her gaze comes back to me, and she closes it again. "Never mind," she says. "So, you finished the piece?"

"Last night," I confirm. "And… it's not what we discussed, I'm afraid." I take a deep breath. "I decided that I couldn't paint what you and Hariata were asking."

Her face remains expressionless. "Couldn't, or wouldn't?"

"Both, actually. I do want to lift up women, but not at the cost of pushing down men. Yes, most of them are major pains in my ass, but I just don't feel that way about them. I… I know what this means. I understand that I've lost the commission. I want you to know that I'm disappointed because I really admire what you've done here, and the way you're empowering women, especially women of color. I wanted to be a part of that. But I can't do it at the expense of men because I don't see them as the enemy."

I have to fight not to rest my hand on my stomach as I think about Spencer and the child he's put inside me. My throat tightens, and I want to burst into tears, but I clench my jaw until the wave of emotion subsides.

I know she's seen it, because she frowns, but she doesn't say anything.

I clear my throat. "Anyway, I brought it to show you because I thought you deserved to see it. If you were to like it, even though it doesn't do what you asked, I would be very glad to gift it to Lumen, and you could hang it in the bathroom or something..." I joke, but she doesn't laugh. "But of course," I mumble, "I'm sure you won't, and I'll just take it with me..." Dammit, I wish I hadn't come now. I shouldn't have brought the painting. I should have just called her and told her I wasn't going to do the exhibition.

But it's too late now. I'm here, so I might as well get on with it.

I get to my feet, remove the cloth, and turn the canvas to face her.

She studies it silently, her eyebrows slowly rising. My mouth gradually goes dry as the seconds pass. She blinks a few times, and I can see her gaze passing over various parts of the painting before they return to the male figure on the right.

Eventually, her eyes lift to mine. "You're missing a great opportunity to make a statement," she says.

I shrug. "I feel as if I am. It's just that the statement is mine, not someone else's." I smile to soften it.

She stares at me. Then, to my surprise, she smiles back. "Good. That's what I wanted to see."

My jaw drops. "What?"

She rises to face me. "There's nothing more powerful than a woman asserting her own artistic voice and philosophy. Not by being defiant, but because she's grown in confidence and now believes in herself." She looks down at the painting, then drops to her haunches in front of it to look at it more closely. "We asked for a piece of art that empowered women. We wanted you to be bold and confrontational in your art, and to see themes of female power and sexual agency. And that's what you've produced. I love it, Marama." She rises again, bringing the canvas with her. "It's exciting and full of energy. It will have pride of place at the exhibition, and I'm sure it'll look amazing among the other pieces you're going to produce."

My heart lifts. "You still want me to do the exhibition?"

"I do." She rests the canvas on the sofa, leaning it against the back, and retreats to look at it again. "I have an idea," she says. "Tomorrow we're having an open day—we've sent hundreds of invitations to encourage women to come to Lumen and have a look around, and to network. I think we'll hang this in the foyer as a teaser for the

Maramataka exhibition that will be coming at Matariki. What do you think?"

I press my fingers to my mouth as emotion swells inside me. "Really?"

This time she gives a genuine smile. "Really." She looks back at the painting, tipping her head to the side. "Has he seen it?"

I shake my head.

"It is him, I take it?" she asks.

I just smile.

"Fair enough," she says softly. "Okay, leave it with me. I'll get Carly to hang it. Will you come for the unveiling tomorrow? Say, one p.m.?"

"Of course." Oh my God, I still have the commission? "Will Hariata agree?"

"Leave Hariata with me. She'll be fine. Neither of us minds being challenged if it leads to something better. We're big enough to understand that sometimes we make the wrong decisions." She looks away again, suggesting that she's thinking about something other than the painting, but then she smiles at me. "So you have more paintings to do! What about after that, have you thought about what comes next?"

Spencer, the baby, my art... my head spins. "Not really. The future is a scary place."

"It doesn't have to be. Are you religious?"

"No, not really."

"Me either, but my father always used to quote Matthew 6:34, 'Do not worry about tomorrow, for tomorrow will worry about itself. Each day has enough trouble of its own.' At the time I thought it was nonsense, but I can see the wisdom in it now."

Her words hold a whole heap of meaning; they suggest she had a father who used the Bible to keep her in line, and no doubt that formed her present low opinion of men. I wonder if her father is still alive, maybe over in France. Does she ever see him? I'm too shy to ask, but it does show me that people sometimes act the way they do because of holes in their past. It's not easy to understand who we would be if our experiences and memories hadn't shaped us.

"Thank you for coming to see me," Genevieve says. "I look forward to the unveiling tomorrow."

She leads me out of her office, and we part ways. I head across the foyer, then out of the doors and into the blustery day.

I can't believe what's just happened. I'd steeled myself for her to be angry, even furious, and at the very least to throw me out on my ear because I hadn't bent to her will. Instead, she was gracious and forgiving, and that's shocked me more than anything.

God, these baby hormones... I press my fingers to my lips. I feel emotional all the time, although I suppose that might be something to do with what's been happening with Spencer too.

I get in the Alfa and sit there, thinking about him. I haven't heard from him since I told him I was pregnant. It hurts... but then I was the one who told him that if he wouldn't acknowledge the child as his, I didn't want him in our lives, so I can't be surprised that he's kept away.

Might he change his mind and want to be a part of the baby's life? He was shocked and angry at being blindsided, so it's possible that might happen. But even as I think it, I know what it would lead to: scandal and shame, and I don't think he could live with that. I shouldn't expect him to, either.

I have lots of things to think about, including the five other pictures I have to paint for the exhibition, as well as the more obvious conundrum of whether to keep the baby. If I do, I can hardly travel around the country in my van; I'd need to decide where I'm going to settle, and things like where the kid would go to school. I'd probably be more likely to stay up here near my parents... which would in itself bring more problems, but would also mean I'd have Mum around to help, and it would be cool for them to have regular access to their first grandchild, especially as Kingi doesn't look like he's going to settle down anytime soon. But do I want to live up here? No doubt I'd see Spencer from time to time... and how would that play out?

Do not worry about tomorrow, for tomorrow will worry about itself. Each day has enough trouble of its own. Wise words indeed, Matthew.

I start the engine, back out of the parking space, and head out into the autumn afternoon, glad to see that the rain has stopped and the clouds are starting to lift.

Chapter Twenty-Seven

Spencer

"Have you heard?" Orson asks.

Still holding the phone to my ear, I open the sliding door onto the deck and go out, bringing my smoothie with me.

"Heard what?" I sip the blended mix of milk, oats, and bananas, looking out at the ocean. I've been for a run, and I'm feeling more positive than I have in a long while.

"About Marama," he says.

I stop with the glass halfway to my lips, and my heart bangs on my ribs. "What's happened?" Ah fuck. For a moment, I'm convinced he's about to say she's lost the baby. I'm surprised at the deep stab of pain I feel in my gut at the thought.

"Nothing, she's okay," he says, "I meant the unveiling. Did you see the headline?"

"No. Unveiling of what?"

"There's some kind of Open Day at Lumen today, and they've announced they're going to be unveiling Marama's first painting, as a teaser for her upcoming exhibition."

I look at my glass and swirl the last inch of smoothie around the bottom. "Oh, really?"

"Yeah. I... thought you should know, after everything that's been going on." He hesitates. "Dad, I wanted to apologize for what happened yesterday. You should absolutely have been invited to that meeting. I should have insisted. I did actually think you wouldn't want to be there, and that I'd scout it out and report back to you, but I appreciate how it looked. We honestly were just trying to get the lie of the land and find out what the new club would look like. We're just trying to find a way to stop it being a complete disaster."

I finish off the smoothie. "It won't be a disaster. In a way, she was right—Lumen does appeal to a different clientele. We don't target movie stars and models at Midnight. I think Elizabeth and Joanna would object to the 'old white guys' accusation, but we're a business club first and foremost, and I think there's room for both of us."

"Oh," Orson says.

My lips curve up. "Huxley's already called to apologize, and we had a long talk about it. I understand why I wasn't invited. I've… not been at the races lately, what with one thing and another. I'm sorry about that. I've let my personal life intrude on my business one, and that just makes everything more difficult."

"It's okay," he says softly. "Look, Scarlett and Marama went out for lunch midweek and had a long chat, so I kinda know what's going on."

That shocks me. "She told Scarlett about the baby?"

"About the what?"

There's a long silence.

"Fuck," I say eventually.

"Baby?" he says. "Marama's pregnant?"

"Ah… yeah…"

"And you're the father?"

I wince, put down the glass, and massage my brow. "Yeah."

He's silent again for a long time.

I lower onto a chair and lean forward, elbows on my knees, letting him process the news. I don't want to apologize, because that implies my relationship with Marama was a mistake, and it wasn't, and I'm not sorry about it. But equally, I know I must have hurt his feelings, and I do regret that.

"I apologize for the shock," I say eventually.

"The baby was a mistake?" he asks. When I don't reply, he says, "Sorry, that was rude."

"It was a fair question. We didn't mean for it to happen."

"Is she keeping it?"

"I don't know."

"How long have you known?"

"Less than a week."

"So you're not… together?"

"No. Not yet."

My relationship with my two children has never been amazing. Helen is her mother's daughter, and we've never been close. I've been thinking about her a lot, and I do intend to try harder with her, especially now she has Callum, although I suspect she's not going to be forgiving, and it'll take a while to mend all the bridges between us.

But Orson is my firstborn and my heir. It doesn't mean as much nowadays, but somehow it does still mean something. I wanted him to grow up physically and mentally strong, and I know I was too hard on him. I set my expectations high, and although he met them most of the time, that pressure had a detrimental effect on our relationship, which is often strained. I want to mend that. As with Helen, it's not going to happen overnight, especially if Marama keeps the baby. But this is my mess, and I'm the only one who can fix it.

I take a deep breath. "I don't know what's going to happen," I admit. "I didn't react well when she told me. All I could think about was the impact the scandal and shame would have on me, my friends, and my family. I'm hoping to correct that, but I'm not sure how she'll react; she has every right to tell me to go fuck myself. If she doesn't… it will become public knowledge, and that's obviously going to impact you. The thought of your father having a child at my age must be embarrassing. I am very sorry about that, and also for any distress it causes you."

"Dad…"

"Let me finish, son. I want you to know that I regret that we're not closer, and I'd like to rectify that. You've turned out to be a fine man, a good one, strong and honorable, and I'm incredibly proud of you. And I wish I'd been a better father to you and Helen." I stop, my voice husky.

"Jeez," he says, "I didn't expect this when I woke up this morning."

"Well, I like to keep you on your toes."

We both laugh.

"You were a good dad," he says firmly. "Yeah, okay, maybe we didn't throw a ball around in the garden much. Yes, you were tough on me. But it made me resilient, and it pushed me to work harder. I wouldn't be where I am now if you'd been different. I've always been proud to say you were my father, both at school and in business."

"Thank you." My voice catches, and I clear my throat. "That means a lot."

"Obviously," he continues, "I don't know how Marama will react to you either. But I want you to know that I don't care how old she is; only that she makes you happy, and that you're good to her, too, as I like her a lot. And as for the baby… I think you'll be a much more relaxed dad now, and he or she would be very lucky to have you. Don't worry about me. I'm fine with it. And I don't care what anyone else thinks or says. Words don't matter. It's actions that count."

"When did you get to be so smart," I tease.

"I was taught by this wise old sage…"

"Hey, less of the old."

We both laugh again.

"Anyway," he says, "Scarlett wants to go to the unveiling to support Marama, so I'm going with her. I just thought I'd let you know. I'll call you afterward, if you like, let you know what the painting looks like."

"No need," I say. "I'll be there."

There's a stunned silence. Then he says, "Wait, what?"

"I'll be there," I say calmly. "I want to see the painting."

"But… you've read about how she's painted you…"

"I know. And I'm sure I deserve it. I'll face the music. And if that doesn't convince her to have me, I don't know what will."

"Well, you're a braver man than I am, Gunga Din. Are you sure about this? Genevieve's going to have a field day."

"Again, I probably deserve it. I'll take what they throw at me, and hopefully emerge a better man for it."

"Or it'll completely crush you."

"Best to look on the bright side."

He gives a short laugh. "All right. I'll see you there." He pauses. "I admire you for going."

"It's either going to be the smartest thing I've ever done or the most stupid, and that's saying something."

He laughs again, and ends the call.

I put down the phone and look out at the ocean. Despite my cavalier attitude, and the fact that I don't get anxious very often, I'm nervous at the thought of going to Lumen and facing the music in front of everyone. But I wanted to make a grand gesture to Marama, and this might be just what I was looking for.

She hasn't lost the baby. Earlier this week I thought that might be the best outcome, as horrible as it would be for her. Now, though, I'm surprised at the relief I feel. Of course, she might still be planning to end the pregnancy, and I won't try to stop her if that's the case. But I don't want her to feel she has to do it because it's the only option for her. I want to give her a choice, and then she can make up her mind.

First though, there's something I need to find, and I only have a couple of hours to do it.

I get to my feet and head indoors to have a shower and get dressed. Might as well look my best for the big event.

*

At ten minutes to one, I get out of the Uber and approach Lumen's front doors. I'm wearing one of my best suits, a three-piece Italian cut, dark gray, with a pink-and-silver-striped tie and a pink pocket square. I've shaved and combed my hair, and used the cologne I know Marama likes.

Outside, posters declare the club is open to anyone and everyone today. Guests are welcome to look around the club, talk to staff, and to have a glass of wine and nibbles while they meet and chat to clients and other visitors. It's a smart move on Genevieve's part, as I'm sure there are many women especially who've wondered what goes on behind the closed doors, and it gives them a commitment-free opportunity to discover the facilities during a time when it looks busy and productive.

My mouth has gone dry and my palms are sweating, but I gather my courage and walk through the doors with my head high.

The foyer is packed with people, all talking and laughing while they munch on finger food, sip from champagne glasses, and exchange business cards or scan QR codes on each other's phones. There are more men here than I thought there'd be; I wonder whether that was planned on Genevieve's part? A woman-focused club is an interesting idea, but it doesn't make sense to me for her to limit membership, and maybe she's come to that realization too.

I can see members of staff in their distinct lavender-colored suits showing small groups of visitors around, while at the front on a temporary stage, Genevieve is talking to Marama, clearly about to address the room. To their left, a large canvas stands covered with a cloth.

I glance around and spot Orson and Scarlett not far away, talking to Helen and a couple of others. Orson sees me and gestures with his head for me to go over. I thread through the crowd, nodding at a couple of people I recognize.

"Dad!" Helen stares at me. "Holy shit. I didn't know you were coming."

"Hello." I smile at the group, seeing from their astonished expressions that they're obviously shocked that I'd be here to witness my own demise. I point at the savory ball in Orson's hand. "Any good?"

"Crab puff," he says. "Exceptional."

Scarlett tries not to laugh and lifts a glass of orange juice from a passing waiter. "Here." She passes it to me, her beautiful dark eyes full of amusement. "Hello."

"Thank you." I sip it, then turn with the others as there's a loud whistle of feedback.

"Ah… even the microphone is excited to hear me," Genevieve jokes, and the crowd laughs. "Welcome to Lumen," she says. "I'm so glad you could all make it for the Open Day today. Please, avail yourself of all the opportunities to look around, try out the facilities, and talk to the staff and current clients." She gestures at the sign above reception. "As you can see, here at Lumen we're focused on empowering women. Illuminating Women, Igniting Change is our policy statement. With that in mind, I'd like to introduce you to up-and-coming artist, Marama Davis."

She gestures at Marama, who moves forward to stand beside her. Wow, she looks amazing today. She's wearing a long cream boho-style dress, which suits her arty temperament, and her hair is half-pinned up but with attractive curls tumbling around her face and neck.

"Marama is currently creating a series of paintings for an exhibition that will open during Matariki. This is the first in the series, an exceptional piece that suggests themes of…"

Genevieve's voice trails off as her gaze falls on me.

I can see my presence here has thrown her. Heads start turning as she continues to stare, and murmurs rise as everyone sees whom she's looking at.

I wait calmly, my gaze fixed on Marama. She's seen me, and her jaw has dropped. I hold my breath—will her expression show anger or frustration at seeing me?

To my joy, though, as I watch, her whole face lights up, and relief spreads through me. At that moment, I know everything's going to be all right.

MIDNIGHT SECRET

Genevieve glances at Marama, then back at me. I wait for her to say something cutting or sarcastic. But to my surprise, her expression softens.

"Where was I?" she says. "Oh yes, Marama's paintings." She looks at Hariata Pere, who's in the crowd. Hariata nods, and Genevieve clears her throat. "I originally hoped that Marama's exhibition would show women rising, claiming power, and outshining men. I do still want Lumen to be primarily focused on helping women achieve their full potential, but I'm not ashamed to admit that Marama has produced something far more worthy. I'm going to let the artist herself read her personal statement."

Marama moves forward and takes the stand. "Good afternoon," she says. Her eyes meet mine, and then she looks across the crowd as she reads from a card. "The moon rises not to conquer the sun, but to bring light in a different way. She does not burn; she reflects. She watches. And when she takes the sky, the world is hushed. Power is not always loud. Beauty is not always soft. This painting explores the moments where we rise—not alone, but in rhythm. Not every ascent is a rebellion. Some are invitations to dance."

She lowers the card as everyone claps and gives an embarrassed laugh. "That sounds very pretentious, but it's my way of showing my belief in balance. The exhibition is going to be called Maramataka, or the turning of the moon, but this first painting is called Whakatau. It means to bring into balance or harmony, and it also means to make peace."

Her gaze meets mine briefly, and my heart thunders. I've seen the headlines, and I thought I knew what to expect—the Wolf of Waiheke, being brought to heel and tamed at her feet—but both her and Genevieve's words suggest something different.

She turns and nods at Genevieve, who, together with her assistant, removes the cover showing the painting.

The crowd gasps, and my eyebrows slowly rise.

On the left, a Māori goddess stands in a forest glade. Above her head, the letters of her name—Hina, the goddess of the moon—are woven between the leaves of the kauri trees. She stands in a shaft of moonlight, her light-brown skin touched with silver. Her long brown hair tumbles down her back, interlaced with moons that look just like the crescent moon clips Marama wore in her hair that day in the studio. She's wearing a cleverly painted almost-transparent gauzy dress so you can't quite tell if it's made from cloth or moonlight. The main thing that stands out to me about the figure, though, is that she's obviously pregnant, the dress clinging to her swelling figure.

Her hands are outstretched toward the hands of the figure opposite. It's a man, not a wolf, and the letters above his head in the trees spell his name, Tāne Mahuta, the god of the forest. His skin is like bark, and his hair and clothes are made from leaves and vines that curl around his body. Their fingers are just touching, and at the place where they meet, silver flowers bloom. The man stands in a shaft of sunlight, and he's bathed in golden light. His features are mostly occluded by the leaves, although his eyes are a startling blue that stand out in the color palette of rich greens and browns. It's the only sign that it might be me. But I know it is, because she's already painted me as this figure before. It's not humiliating at all. He looks powerful but dignified, the perfect match for her quiet, strong beauty.

The crowd erupts into a round of applause, but I continue to stand there, unmoving. I'm so touched, I can hardly breathe. I see Orson glance at me out of the corner of his eye, smiling, but I don't look at him.

I walk through the crowd, conscious of people turning to look at me as I pass, but I ignore them, keeping my gaze fixed on the stage and the woman who's now watching me, her eyebrows rising.

People part to let me through, and I approach the steps up to the stage, pause, then climb them. Genevieve moves back, and when I glance at her, her lips curve up, just a tiny bit. I give her a small smile back, then return my gaze to my girl.

"Hello," I say.

She gives a short laugh and looks at the crowd, then back at me and says bashfully, "Hello."

"I love the painting," I tell her. I know the microphone is probably picking up our conversation, but I don't care—in fact I'm glad everyone is witnessing this moment.

Her smile lights up her face. "I'm so glad."

"You're amazing," I tell her. "So incredibly talented."

She blushes. "Oh. Thank you."

"And I'm very much in love with you," I say.

The crowd gasps, and to one side I see Genevieve press her fingers to her lips, but I keep my gaze fixed on Marama. Her eyes have widened, and now they're shining with tears.

I gather my courage, slide one hand into my trouser pocket, and bring out the small velvet box. Slowly, I crack it open and turn it to show her the ring. It's not a traditional diamond solitaire. It's a large pink tourmaline surrounded by a white-gold band set with diamonds which wraps around the stone like a ribbon and makes it look as if the tourmaline is floating, and it looks like a rose. I also bought matching earrings, and the set cost several hundred thousand dollars.

I wanted something special to suit her artistic character and creativity, and when I rang a friend who owns a chain of jewelry stores, he knew exactly what I was looking for. Once I'd confirmed through photos that I liked it, he had it sent over. I'm not a hundred percent sure it's the right size, but I'll get it fitted perfectly... if this goes well.

Cheers are already starting to rise in the crowd, and they only increase as I lower to one knee.

"Marama," I say, "I love you, and I want to spend the rest of my life with you. Will you marry me?"

Her hand rises to cover her mouth. Her eyes shine.

And then she bursts into tears.

As one, everyone in the crowd goes, "Awwww..."

Ah, shit. Does that mean yes or no?

I get to my feet, give the crowd a wry smile, then put my arms around her. She covers her face with her hands and buries her face in my neck. Ahhh, she's totally lost it.

"All right, baby," I murmur, and I bend, slide my arm beneath her legs, and lift her into my arms. I walk carefully down the steps, then nod at Genevieve as she gestures behind her to an open door, and I carry Marama into the office behind the stage.

"Everyone out," I bark, and the members of staff who were working there hurriedly exchange glances, then head out, closing the door behind them.

"Hey, it's okay." I lower into a chair and cradle her on my lap. "Shh, everything's all right." I rub her back.

Gradually, her sobs die down. I rest my lips on the top of her head and kiss her hair, wondering what she's thinking. It was a huge gamble, proposing without knowing how she'd react, but I hoped she'd see that as me unzipping my fly and showing her I'm prepared to be vulnerable for her. Now I wonder whether she was upset because she didn't want to turn me down in front of all those people.

I don't regret it, though. I needed to show her how I felt.

SERENITY WOODS

Just don't let it be the end... I don't think I could bear that...

Chapter Twenty-Eight

Marama

At last, I feel as if I can breathe again. For a moment, my throat tightened so much my breaths wouldn't come, and I nearly fainted. I don't know if it was the shock of his proposal or the fact that everyone was watching... Don't some women faint during pregnancy, too? Maybe my blood pressure dropped...

My thoughts are spinning like clothes on a rotary washing line in a high breeze, and I'm having trouble pinning them down. Spencer proposed to me. He wants to marry me. Did I dream it? That beautiful ring, the hope in his eyes, his shocking words, *I love you, and I want to spend the rest of my life with you*? No, it really happened, and oh my God I burst into tears in front of all those people... And he picked me up and carried me somewhere. I was hardly aware what happened, I was so overcome with emotion.

Without moving my head, I look around the room. It's some kind of office, and luckily it's empty. I'm sitting curled up on his lap, and he's holding me tightly, kissing my hair and murmuring sweet nothings to me.

He looks amazing. He's so incredibly handsome. I spotted him immediately from right across the room. I couldn't believe he'd come to the unveiling. As far as he knew, the painting was going to show him being subjugated, tamed and brought to his knees by a woman.

Something occurs to me then, and I move back a little and look up at him.

"You didn't know I'd changed the painting?" I whisper.

He shakes his head.

"You were going to propose even though you thought I might have humiliated you?"

He nods. His eyes are kind.

My bottom lip trembles. "Can I see the ring?"

"Of course." He extracts the box from his trouser pocket, opens it, and hands it to me.

I study the ring. I'm guessing it's white gold. The pink stone is enormous, and there are so many diamonds…

"I've never seen anything like it," I admit.

"I wanted something different. Do you like it?"

"Of course, it's beautiful."

"I'm glad."

"Can I put it on?"

He blinks and looks suddenly uncertain. "You haven't given me an answer yet."

I stare at him. "Oh my God… Spencer, of course I'll marry you. Oh, I'm so sorry… I didn't give you an answer in front of everyone…"

"I don't care about that," he says, his voice hoarse. "I just thought maybe you didn't want to…"

"No, I do, I do!" I start crying again and throw my arms around his neck. "I love you, I love you…" I press kisses all over his face, over his eyes, his nose, his brows, his cheeks, his jaw…

Eventually he laughs, takes my face in his hands, and holds me still, then lowers his lips to mine, and we exchange a long, slow kiss that gradually calms the roaring emotions inside me.

When he lifts his head, he touches his lips to my tears, kissing them away. "Sweetheart," he murmurs. "I love you."

"Really?" I can't believe it.

"Really." He looks into my eyes. "And I want to say that I'll support you, whatever decision you make about the baby. I understand if you're not ready for a family. But I do want you to know that I spoke to Orson this morning, and I thought he'd rung to tell me you'd had a miscarriage, and I was gutted until he said that wasn't it. I realized then… if you want this baby, I'd like to be a part of his or her life. I'd like to be a father again, if you'll have me."

I rest a hand on my stomach. "I'd already decided I was going to have it."

His face lights up. "You're sure?"

"Yes. I knew it would be a piece of you I could keep and treasure."

He smiles. "You can have all of me if you want."

"I do want."

"You know only dogs can hear you right now?"

I smack his arm, and he laughs and pulls me into his arms. "I adore you," he murmurs, kissing me again. "And I don't care who knows it. I want to tell the world that you're going to be mine."

"Oh, Spencer…"

He takes his pocket square out and hands it to me, and I try to mop up the fresh tears. "Are you sure?" I say. "What about my father?"

"Well, I was thinking about how I'd feel if Helen fell in love with an older man. Maybe initially I'd be suspicious. But if she told me she loved him, and he asked her to marry him, I hope I'd be big enough to believe that you don't choose who you fall in love with, and all that matters is that you love one another."

"I do love you," I tell him sincerely.

"And I love you." He takes the pocket square from me and wipes carefully under my eyes. Then he pauses and frowns a little. "I know I'm not an easy man to live with. I've spent a lifetime cultivating a reputation of being emotionless and cold and ruthless in the boardroom, and sometimes it's tough to stop that filtering into my personal relationships. But I want to be better. A better husband, and a better father."

"I know you'll be amazing." I love his honesty. I can't believe that Spencer Cavendish, the lone wolf that everyone believed was cold and heartless, has stood up in front of a whole crowd of people, including his son and Genevieve, and told them all that he loves me and wants to marry me. It must have taken huge courage to do that.

He brushes his thumbs across my cheeks. "I thought your painting was amazing."

"I'm so glad you liked it."

"Are you going to take the job at Lumen?"

I shake my head. "I've decided to concentrate on my own art… and the baby."

He smiles, then tips his head. "But Genevieve still wants to go ahead with the exhibit?"

I smile. "She was surprisingly forgiving and understanding."

He looks thoughtful. "Hmm. I wonder if that had anything to do with yesterday?"

"Why, what happened yesterday?"

"There was a meeting at Midnight… I'll tell you about it later." He looks over as there's a knock on the door, and then it opens. It's Orson, with Scarlett right behind him.

"Sorry to interrupt," Orson says, "we just wanted to make sure she was all right." He smiles as I get to my feet.

"I'm fine," I say, "feeling a bit silly. I was overwhelmed."

"Aw, that's okay!" Scarlett grins.

"Are congratulations in order?" Orson asks cautiously.

I nod happily, trying not to cry, and Scarlett laughs and gives me a hug, while Orson and Spencer exchange a bearhug.

"I'm so excited for you!" Scarlett then turns to hug Spencer, and Orson grins and envelops me in his arms.

"You'll be my stepmum," he says mischievously.

"Oh God, don't start."

He laughs and releases me. "I'm thrilled for you both. It's great news. And… what about the baby?"

"Orson!" Scarlett glares at him, then says, "I didn't tell him, I swear."

"No, that was me," Spencer says apologetically.

I chuckle. "I'm keeping the baby," I tell them happily. "And we'll bring him or her up together."

That leads to more hugs. It's only when we break apart that I see Genevieve standing in the doorway, watching.

I walk up to her, surprised when she holds out her hands. "I'm guessing by the hugs that the answer was yes," she says, smiling.

I take her hands, and we exchange a kiss on the cheek. "Yes, I agreed to marry him," I whisper.

"I'm thrilled for you," she says. "He obviously loves you very much." She turns as Spencer walks up, and she does the same with him, reaching up to kiss his cheek. "She's a lucky girl," she says, smiling as she touches his arm.

He looks taken aback, but just says, "I'm the lucky one."

She nods and hesitates. Then she says, "I've decided not to open a new club on Waiheke."

He stares at her. "Oh! Why not?"

"I don't want to be associated with all those old white guys," she says. To my surprise, she gives a teasing smile, and I realize she's joking.

His lips curve up. "Yeah, God forbid you get too close to that toxic masculinity. You might get infected."

She gives a short laugh. Then she says, "Actually, I was hoping maybe you could set up another meeting for me with the Circle—with yourself present too, this time. I'd like to put forward the idea of a charity partnership. Not working as part of the Circle, but alongside it, to donate some of Lumen's funds to the charities you work with. Quietly, not for publicity. But I understand if you'd rather not."

"I think that's an amazing idea," Spencer says. "I'll set up the meeting and let you know."

She smiles at me. "Come on, people are asking to meet the artist."

"Oh God, how do I look?"

"Amazing," she says. "You're all glowy."

"Hold on," Spencer says, and he holds out the box containing the ring.

I take the ring out and slide it onto my fourth finger. It's a very tiny bit big, but it'll do just fine for today. I meet his eyes and smile. Then Genevieve takes my hand and leads me back out into the foyer.

I enjoy my fifteen minutes of fame, walking around the room, talking about my work, and accepting congratulations on my engagement as I show everyone the ring. But the best bit is when I glance over and see Spencer's gaze following me. His eyes never leave me. They're full of love. And I'm filled with an incredible warmth that I hope will never, ever go away.

SERENITY WOODS

Newsletter

If you'd like to be informed when my next book is available, you can sign up for my mailing list on my website, http://www.serenitywoodsromance.com

About the Author

USA Today bestselling author Serenity Woods writes sizzling New Zealand billionaire romances. A reader once called her the Queen of Happy Endings because her books have no cheating and no cliffhangers, just super-soppy HEAs!

She likes to describe her heroes as 'nice guys doing naughty things,' so if you like your men hot, rich, funny, and respectful out of the bedroom but wicked beneath the sheets, you've come to the right place!.

Website: http://www.serenitywoodsromance.com
Facebook: http://www.facebook.com/serenitywoodsromance

Printed in Dunstable, United Kingdom